Angel Classics

ARTHUR SCHNITZLER

English translation.

ARTHUR SCHNITZLER

Selected Short Fiction

Translated from the German
with an introduction and notes by
J. M. Q. DAVIES

ANGEL BOOKS
London

For my Parents
in fond remembrance of
our Vienna years

First published in 1999 by
Angel Books, 3 Kelross Road, London N5 2QS
1 3 5 7 9 10 8 6 4 2

British Library Cataloguing in Publication Data:
A Catalogue record for this book is available from the British Library

This book is printed on acid free paper conforming to the British Library
recommendations and to the full American standard

Funded by
THE
ARTS
COUNCIL
OF ENGLAND

Typeset in Great Britain by Ray Perry
Printed and bound by Redwood Books, Trowbridge, Wiltshire

Contents

Translator's Note

The text used for these translations was that of the two volumes *Die Erzählenden Schriften* in the Collected Edition of the Works of Arthur Schnitzler, *Gesammelte Werke*, published by S. Fischer Verlag, Frankfurt am Main, 1961, by kind permission of the publishers. A number of Schnitzler's stories were published posthumously; dates in the contents list of the present volume are putative dates of completed composition as given on pages 991-94 of the second volume of *Die Erzählenden Schriften*.

The work of Arthur Schnitzler is published by permission of the Arthur Schnitzler Estate and Eric Glass Ltd.

Introduction

It is difficult to dissociate Arthur Schnitzler (1862–1931) from the myth of carefree, decadent *fin-de-siècle* Vienna – the world of dashing officers, adulterous affairs, masked balls, gambling, duels and dinners at the Riedhof, of Brahms and Strauss and Lehár's operettas, of Sundays in the Prater and summers at the royal spa, Bad Ischl.[1] Indeed, with witty, satirical comedies like *Anatol* (1893), *La Ronde* (*Reigen*, 1900) and *Countess Mizzi* (1909), which though in some cases stormily received initially, have since become stage favourites, and the many variants of the *süsses Mädel*, or sweet young actress, milliner or seamstress that occur in his stories and novellas, he has played no small part in the perpetuation of that myth.[2] And the Young Vienna circle of innovative writers he belonged to that met regularly at the Café Griensteidl in the 1890s and included Hermann Bahr, Peter Altenberg, Hugo von Hofmannsthal, Felix Salten and Richard Beer-Hofmann, has achieved a legendary status rivalled only by the artists of the Secession who broke with the Academy under the leadership of Gustav Klimt.[3] Yet Schnitzler's stance as an observer of Viennese society is typically detached, with a slightly melancholy yet compassionate awareness of the fragility of life and love, the unpredictability of fate and the human carnival as ineluctably a dance of death. This perhaps reflects what he referred to as 'a certain coolness in my nature', as well as his consciousness of being in some measure an outsider: in his autobiography he repeatedly reverts with bitterness to the rising tide of anti-Semitism in Vienna from the 1880s on, and mayor Karl Lueger's willingness to exploit it for political advantage.[4] The coolness may also be related to his training as a doctor, a profession about which he felt ambivalent and a little squeamish from the start, and the ironic bitter-sweet tone of many of his works has distinct affinities with Chekhov.

Looking back on the late Habsburg era in *The World of Yesterday* (1944), Stefan Zweig saw it as in many ways a golden age of order and stability – hierarchical and rooted in the past yet deeply civilised, a confluence of centuries of European culture.[5] And for a while at least, the imperial ideal and spirit of enlightenment prevailed even as the old order was being undermined from within by Bohemian and Serbian nationalism, industrialisation and migration to the cities: Vienna's population quadrupled between 1860 and 1914, as the parks and stately edifices along the Ringstrasse replaced the glacis built against the Turks round the medieval Inner City, and the suburbs began to mushroom.[6] Joseph Roth, another contributor to the Habsburg myth in retrospective novels like *The Radetzky March* (1932) – recounting the elevation and decline of the peasant Trotta family after the young Lieutenant Joseph Trotta saves the Emperor in battle – was more critical of imperial despotism and patronage and the ramshackle bureaucratic and military structures that supported it.[7] Schnitzler writing a generation earlier is essentially the chronicler of the Danube Monarchy's metropolitan culture, and when outposts like Lemberg or Przemysl are alluded to it is as places it is a relief to get away from. Yet though the primary focus of his stories tends to be on the volatile, turbulent inner lives of his protagonists and he eschews the artistic pitfalls of direct political debate, he always deftly invokes the wider social context. A tired little flautist dies at his post but the Royal Presence in the house, at once remote and reassuring, bids the show go on. Lieutenant Gustl is driven to the point of suicide after failing to respond at once when a baker rebukes him at a concert, because this has rendered him *satisfaktionsunfähig* – incapable of demanding satisfaction according to the prevailing military code of honour.[8] The nocturnal adventures Fridolin's matrimonial restlessness impels him to pursue in *Dream Fantasia* (*Traumnovelle*, 1926), despite his fear of syphilis, lead him to an aristocratic secret society of masked and naked revellers given to sadomasochistic rituals. The cumulative effect is to tarnish but also to humanise the myth of Gay Vienna, putting one in mind of the ancient Mrs Swithin in Virginia Woolf's *Between the Acts* when she remarks: 'The Victorians . . . I don't believe ... there ever were such people. Only you and me and William dressed differently.'[9] Schnitzler shared the post-Darwinian existential outlook of many of his Victorian contemporaries, and his characters are often acutely aware that they live and die alone. If there is not the same radical sense of alienation in Schnitzler that we get in more symbolic works like Hofmannsthal's *Tale of the 672nd Night* (*Das Märchen der 672. Nacht, 1895*) and much of Kafka, it is partly because his protagonists are still anchored in a social context. [10]

Much has been written about the analogies between Schnitzler's introspective vision and that of Freud, whose professional interest in hypnosis he shared and whose work he kept up with and in some respects anticipated. Freud for his part admired what he regarded as Schnitzler's intuitive understanding of the human psyche, observing in correspondence that he had somehow evaded meeting him lest he encounter his own double.[11] The parallel is perhaps most evident in Schnitzler's interest in dreams, unconscious sexual impulses and other psychopathic states – Fräulein Else's fantasies and exhibitionism for instance, or in the mildly uncanny story *Flowers* (*Blumen*, 1894) the narrator's fixation on the floral mementos of the dead woman he has wronged. Indeed, love and death occur together almost like a leitmotif in Schnitzler's stories, and in his experiments with associative interior monologues he anticipated Joyce by decades.[12] In *The Wise Man's Wife* (*Die Frau des Weisen*, 1896), with its discreetly suggestive symbolism, the lovers' island outing takes them past first a lighthouse, then a church; and in *Dead Men Tell No Tales* (*Die Toten schweigen*, 1897) the heroine betrays herself by something very like a Freudian slip. But Schnitzler himself felt uneasy about Theodor Reik's early Freudian interpretations of his work, and today Oedipal readings of say Fräulein Else's loyalty to her Papa are apt to seem reductive.[13] Some of his stories do read a little like case histories, and these tend to be less successful, though *Andreas Thameyer's Farewell Letter* (*Andreas Thameyers letzter Brief*, 1900), with its fine balance of humour and compassion, is a notable exception.

Often, in fact, the psychological power and subtlety of Schnitzler's stories is at least as much the product of his sure sense of form as of his knowledge of the human heart – a sense derived from his experience in the theatre. Indeed, light-hearted sketches like *Success* (*Ein Erfolg*, 1900) where a street puppeteer is glimpsed in passing, or *An Eccentric* (*Exzentrik*, 1902), set in the new variety theatre Ronacher's, are essentially well-turned one-acters, hinging on wit-and-butt reversals, which one could easily imagine being performed. Frequently, as in *Dead Men Tell No Tales*, *Lieutenant Gustl* (1900) and *Fräulein Else* (1924), Schnitzler places his protagonists in what Mikhail Bakhtin thought of as threshold situations, which force them to reappraise their entire lives, and explores how they react.[14] *The Wise Man's Wife*, with its splendidly stage-managed suspense, is structured round Joycean epiphanies. Fräulein Else's suicide is made more plausible by the way, much as in Greek tragedy, the pressure on her is relentlessly increased: telegrams with escalating demands urge her to approach the ageing roué Herr von Dorsday to bail out her Papa who has embezzled to pay gambling debts; and after she has publicly disgraced herself and is lying only apparently unconscious on her bed, she is further assailed by her aunt's talk of confining her in an asylum and the mocking hostility of her rival, Cissy. In *The Grecian Dancer* (*Die griechische Tänzerin*, 1902), a beautifully evocative story capturing the atmosphere of affluent gatherings in country villas near Vienna and the bohemian night-life of Montmartre, Schnitzler achieves an additional psychological dimension by leaving us in doubt as to whether the first-person narrator is reliable or not. Was Mathilde's death precipitated by her sculptor husband's philandering with the lady from the Moulin Rouge who modelled for the Grecian statue in the garden, as the narrator is persuaded? Or is the narrator projecting his own unconscious jealousy and envy onto what had in fact been a happy trusting marriage, as she had all along maintained?[15] One is left with a genuine aporia.

Another appealing aspect of Schnitzler's fiction from a contemporary perspective is his understanding and sympathy for the plight of women from many walks of life. An amusing glimpse of the extent to which the Habsburg monarchy was a profoundly patriarchal culture is afforded by Franz Werfel's observation, supported by the photographic record, that 'the streets were peopled with numerous Franz Josephs. Everywhere in the government departments one saw familiar and unapproachable faces with white sideboards. Even the keepers at the majestic gates of the palace wore the same mask.'[16] In story after story Schnitzler shows himself aware of how the economic dependency of women and the unspoken double standard interfere with human happiness. As a paterfamilias would have had to get established, discrepancies in age and interest such as those between Emma and her professorial husband in *Dead Men Tell No Tales* cannot have been uncommon. And her refusal to elope with her latest clandestine and ill-fated lover Franz is as much for want of means as out of fondness for the child she has neglected. The tensions generated by the expectation that upper- and middle-class women remain chaste before and chattels within marriage are exemplified in Fräulein Else's hysteria and in her reflection that there was ultimately little difference between submitting to the voyeuristic Herr von Dorsday's conditions and selling herself in a marriage of convenience as her friends have done.

The real risks involved in philandering with married women of the upper classes are apparent in *The Duellist's Second (Der Sekundant,* 1927–31), a marvellously atmospheric threshold story of love and sudden death which again illustrates Schnitzler's ability to give the complex ironies of life dramatic shape. Duelling though illegal was condoned in the large imperial standing army to keep officers on their mettle, their elevated position in Habsburg society helping to preserve the status quo,[17] and reservists and duelling fraternities ensured that a duel remained a threatening possibility in civilian life until the dissolution of the Monarchy.[18] Offences against the code of honour were vetted by a special court, and officers who – like Gustl taking exception to the lawyer's remark that not everyone joins the army for patriotic reasons – challenged a civilian and killed him would normally receive a pardon from Franz Joseph.[19] In *The Duellist's Second* we catch a glimpse of how the code of honour while ostensibly protecting women actually imprisoned them, perpetuating hypocrisy, deception and the double standard in marital relations. The narrator recalls how as a twenty-three-year-old second he had been dispatched to report the fatal outcome of the adulterous Loiberger's duel to his neglected wife Agatha, and how before he could bring himself to break the news the two had found themselves in one another's arms. Of particular interest in this story, with its splendid situational irony, is the way Schnitzler reveals how absurdly hamstrung all the characters are by their shame culture's customs and social expectations. Loiberger's opponent Captain Urpadinsky has no choice but to issue a challenge, once anonymous letters disclose that his wife's affair is public knowledge. The pistol duel itself is a highly ritualised affair, which takes place in secret at dawn in a clearing outside a village near Bad Ischl, and the collapsing Loiberger and attendant doctor are compared to marionettes. When Agatha finally receives the news, her instinct is to conceal her complex emotions behind a mask of dutiful respectability. And years later when having remarried she encounters the narrator again socially, she avoids all acknowledgement of the tender hour they spent together under such macabre circumstances. The narrator's own enduring loyalty to the code of honour Schnitzler so deftly ironises is betrayed by his opening remark that at least in those days the threat of being called to account gave life a certain dignity.

Schnitzler was plagued by recurrent doubts about his standing as a writer, reaching the rather severe verdict in the jottings for his autobiography that 'I am aware . . . I am not an artist of the highest calibre.'[20] Always conscious of the brevity of life – as a child he once alarmed his parents with his nocturnal sobbing at the sudden realisation of his own mortality – he compressed a good deal into his sixty-nine years – as physician, playwright, philanderer, man of letters, amateur musician, political observer and compulsive diarist.[21] It is generally conceded that his most perfect achievements outside the theatre are in his shorter fiction, even a modest selection revealing the range and depth of his social and psychological awareness. Successful formulae are indeed repeated, but as deft and sometimes symphonic variations on a theme. In *The Prophecy* (*Die Weissagung,*

1904) for instance, the theatrical dénouement of *His Royal Highness is in the House* (*Der Fürst ist im Hause*, 1888) recurs in an outdoor country house setting, as the climax to a very *fin-de-siècle* and in some ways Hardyesque tale of the inexorability of fate. Some recurrent motifs reflect the same self-mythologising tendencies as the autobiography *My Youth in Vienna* (*Jugend in Wien*), and it is often hard to resist reading for glimpses of the man behind the many fictive masks. The *flâneur* or Don Juan type with whom Schnitzler identified, for instance, occurs in as many guises as the *süsses Mädel*, starting with Anatol – the pseudonym he used for his earliest poems and sketches – and culminating in the protagonist of the beautifully structured and only nominally historical *Casanova's Homecoming* (*Casanovas Heimfahrt*, 1918).[22]

But the relationship between Schnitzler's life and art is a complex and often temporally displaced one. The love triangle in *The Wise Man's Wife* of 1896 seems to draw in part on memories of his unconsummated relationship with Olga Waissnix, wife of the proprietor of the Thalhof Hotel at Reichenau outside Vienna, almost a decade earlier – though that gentleman, far from a model of forbearance, had been intensely jealous and suspicious.[23] *The Green Cravat* (*Die grüne Krawatte*), a parable about difference and intolerance written in 1901, recalls Schnitzler's and Beer-Hofmann's youthful penchant for flamboyant neckties,[24] while the Montmartre sequence in *The Grecian Dancer* of the following year echoes his all-night saunter with his relatives, Sandor and Mathilda Rosenberg, on his first visit to Paris in 1888.[25] Stories like *Flowers* and *The Prophecy* (*Die Weissagung*, 1904) reflect the depressive, nihilistic streak in Schnitzler's nature; and in the latter the Baron's dilettantish dabbling in the arts, the Chinese box of framing narratives used as a distancing device, and the cleverly reflexive ending are all biographically revealing, but obliquely so. *Dream Fantasia* which draws on Schnitzler's experience as a doctor and on the tensions in his marriage to Olga Gussmann, generated by her desire to pursue her own career as a singer, is perhaps something of a wish-fulfilment in that it ends on a note of domestic reconciliation, whereas the Schnitzlers had parted after eighteen years together in 1921.[26] In Herr von Dorsday we catch an insightful and in part self-conscious glimpse of male prowess in decline; and the gambling debts of Else's father seem to echo the difficulties of Schnitzler's uncle Edmund.[27] *Lieutenant Gustl*, which was drafted in an incredible six days and which so affronted the military establishment that Schnitzler lost his commission as a reserve army doctor, is a test case of his ability to create characters unlike himself.[28] As a study of the

psychopathology of a limited, obtuse and chauvinistic officer completely in thrall to the code of honour it is very convincing, and like
The Prophecy provides sobering insights into the inflated status and
entrenched anti-Semitism of the army in Habsburg society.[29] But
there is also perhaps some imaginative disjunction between the brag-
gart soldier in Gustl and his more sensitive, lyrical and sentimental
side, where Schnitzler's own sensibility seems to take over.

Yet ultimately Schnitzler is no more an artist of the egotistical sub-
lime than any other post-Romantic writer in the mimetic mode,
indeed he reproached both his parents and himself for being too self-
absorbed.[30] There is a wide variety of moods and voices in these stories, from the bleakly pessimistic to the gay and life-affirming, and
from all – though predominantly the upper – strata of society. And
even though a first-person narrative point of view is often adopted,
this is normally qualified by irony. Schnitzler's perspectivist, or in
Bakhtin's terms 'dialogic' tendency to make us aware that there is
always more than one side to every issue, enhanced no doubt by his
experience in the theatre, also comes out in the way stories on similar themes often seem antiphonally related.[31] Adultery is presented
from the female point of view in *Dead Men Tell No Tales*, but in *The
Wise Man's Wife* chiefly from the male – though here the currents of
thought and feeling within Friederike are also kept skilfully before us.
Vienna itself is largely taken for granted and seldom described in
filmic or Naturalistic detail, though as with Joyce's Dublin its land-
marks, streets and districts are often used as signposts. But one feels
the pulse of *fin-de-siècle* Vienna's cultural and spiritual life and the joys
and tribulations of its citizenry as in no other writer. Indeed, the
Impressionist sensitivity of Schnitzler's characters to the sights and
sounds surrounding them moment by evanescent moment –
Fräulein Else listening to snatches of the 'Valse Noble' and 'Recon-
naissance' from Schumann's *Carnival* for instance, one of many suggestive evocations of music in these stories – strikingly anticipates
what one finds in writers like Katherine Mansfield and Virginia
Woolf.

And yet his psychological acuity, his sympathy with women and
his hostility to bigotry and militarism – he wrote an early essay critical of patriotic fervour and was deeply perturbed by the Great War –
can beguile us into recreating him too much in our own image. He
presents the human predicament sceptically, in all the complexity
Friedrich Schlegel thought of as characteristic of Romantic irony.[32]
But though it is true that his attitude to the foibles of his characters is
never overtly didactic or judgemental, and he himself claimed that 'it

was little part of my nature . . . to display any moral indignation', even his more complex dialogic stories almost always have moral implications.[33] We may be left to draw our own conclusions when the protagonist of *The Wise Man's Wife* eschews the final assignation, or when the bully in Gustl reasserts itself after his reprieve by fate, but Schnitzler's intent in selecting these rather than other modes of closure is not in serious doubt. Perhaps it is precisely the degree of tension between code ethics and individual desire that most clearly distinguishes his art and era from our own.

Notes

1 See Arthur J. May, *Vienna in the Age of Franz Joseph* (Norman: Univ. of Oklahoma Press, 1966), pp. 68–87 and 102–20.

2 See Arthur Schnitzler, *My Youth in Vienna*, trans. Catherine Hutter (New York: Holt, Rinehart & Winston, 1972), pp. 92, 123, 237 , 247 and 273. This work includes a list of works by Schnitzler translated into English in Appendix II, pp. 283–86.

3 See Bruce Thompson, *Schnitzler's Vienna* (London: Routledge, 1990), pp. 15–31.

4 Schnitzler, p. 56; and pp. 6, 62, 77, 119–20, 128, 131, 177 and 229; and see Felix Czeike, ed., *Das Grosse Groner-Wien-Lexikon* (Vienna: Groner Verlag, 1974), pp. 220–21.

5 Stefan Zweig, *The World of Yesterday* (1944; 3rd ed. Sydney: Cassell, 1945), pp. 1– 19.

6 See S. A. M. Adshead, 'The Genesis of the Imperial Mind', in Mark Francis, ed. *The Viennese Enlightenment* (Beckenham: Croom Helm, 1985), pp. 28–31.

7 Joseph Roth, *The Radetzky March*, trans. Joachim Neugroschel (London: Penguin, 1995); and see Philip Manger, '*The Radetzky March*: Joseph Roth and the Habsburg Myth', in Francis, pp. 40–62.

8 See Thompson, pp. 138–39; and Kevin McAleer, *Dueling: The Cult of Honor in Fin-de-Siècle Germany* (Princeton: Princeton Univ. Press, 1994), pp. 3–4, 26, 35f., 106, 110.

9 Virginia Woolf, *Between the Acts* (1941; London: Granada, 1978), p. 127.

10 Hugo von Hofmannsthal, 'The Tale of the 672nd Night', trans. Frank G. Ryder in *German Literary Fairy Tales*, ed. Frank. G. Ryder and Robert M. Browning (New York: Continuum, 1983), pp. 282–97.

11 See P. F. S. Falkenberg, 'Arthur Schnitzler's literary diagnosis of the Viennese Mind,' in Francis, p. 131; Francis and Barry Stacey, 'Freud and the Enlightenment', in Francis, pp. 88–128; and Thompson, pp. 32–54. Schnitzler was sceptical of Freud's theory of the innate bisexuality of all human beings and thought the role attributed to homosexual drives overestimated – see Schnitzler, p.58.

12 See Richard H. Lawson, 'Thematic Reflections of the "Song of Love and Play of Death" in Schnitzler's Fiction,' in *Arthur Schnitzler and his Age: Intellectual and Artistic Currents*, ed. Petrus W. Tax and Lawson (Bonn: Bouvier Verlag Herbert Grundmann, 1984), pp. 70–89.

13 Thompson, pp. 46, 52 and 43; Lawson, p. 85.

14 See Mikhail Bakhtin, *Problems in Dostoyevsky's Poetics*, trans. Caryl Emerson (Minneapolis: Univ. of Minnesota Press, 1984), pp. 170–71; and Charles I. Schuster, 'Threshold Texts and Essayistic Voices', in J. M. Q. Davies, ed., *Bridging the Gap: Literary Theory in the Classroom* (W. Cornwall, CT: Locust Hill Press, 1994), pp. 85–95.

15 See Martin Swales, *Arthur Schnitzler: A Critical Study* (London: Oxford Univ. Press, 1971), pp. 81–86.

16 Quoted in Francis, p. 51. See Franz Hubmann, *K. u. K. Familienalbum: Die Welt von gestern in alten Photographien* (Vienna: Verlag Fritz Molden, 1971), p. 153; see pp. 66, 69, 184, 188, 200 and 202.

17 See McAleer, pp. 108–09.

18 See McAleer, p. 34.

19 Thompson, p.5; see McAleer, pp. 101–02.

20 Schnitzler, p. 4.

21 See Schnitzler, p. 48. Schnitzler recalls an episode in which his father, having read in his diary about his interest in the 'Greek goddesses' of the Kärntnerstrasse, sent him to look through medical books on syphilis, and mentions the reserve between them this breach of confidence contributed to (pp. 69–70). Later Schnitzler would closely guard his diary even from his wife Olga, partly because he recorded in it the fluctuations in their relationship – see Frederick J. Beharriell, 'Arthur Schnitzler's Diaries', *Modern Austrian Literature*, 19.3/4 (1986), p.6.

22 *Casanova's Homecoming*, trans. Eden and Cedar Paul in Schnitzler, *Plays and Stories*, ed. Egon Schwarz (New York: Continuum, 1982), pp. 155–247.

23 See Schnitzler, pp. 183f. Elements of the affair, such as Olga's taking a (not fatal) overdose of morphine, would also find their way into *Fräulein Else*. Olga was Schnitzler's superior in culture and sophistication at the time, and though their affair which he thought of as the 'adventure of his life' was effectively over by the end of 1886, the fact that they continued to correspond until her death a decade later is a measure of the extent to which he depended on her encouragement in his artistic aspirations. See Helmut Scheibel, *Arthur Schnitzler* (Hamburg: Rowohlt, 1976), pp. 40–41.

24 See Schnitzler, p. 116; and Renate Wagner, *Arthur Schnitzler: Eine Biographie* (Vienna: Verlag Fritz Molden, 1981), p. 49.

25 Schnitzler, p. 250.

26 Wagner, pp. 112, 146, 184, 203, 231, 287, 306, 313, 322–23.

27 Schnitzler, pp. 43, 46, 233 and 250.

28 When called before a military court of honour, Schnitzler refused to go on the grounds that it had no jurisdiction over a work of literature, waiving the right to appear in person to defend himself in language which mimicked the pompous army officialese. The affair was heatedly debated in the press. See Wagner, pp. 114–15 and 121–23, 127–28.

29 Katharine Arans, 'Schnitzler and Characterology: From Empire to Third Reich', *Modern Austrian Literature*, 19.3/4 (1986), pp. 97–127, links Schnitzler to a pre-Freudian Social Darwinist view of man as innately more or less gifted, which gave 'support [to] the continuation of class structure ... in opposition to the adherents of 'Red Vienna' and ... education of the worker.' And she suggests that 'the modern reader has taken Gustl more seriously as a psychological entity, while the turn of the century reader may have taken him with a grain of salt as a lower-class person with typical senseless pretensions ...' (pp. 116 and 122).

30 Schnitzler, pp. 35, 56, 109.
31 Bakhtin, pp. 18, 5–46.
32 See Friedrich Schlegel, *Dialogue on Poetry and Literary Aphorisms*, trans. Ernst Behler and Roman Struc (University Park: Pennsylvania State Univ. Press, 1968), pp. 38–39, 126 and 140–41.
33 Schnitzler, pp. 147–48.

His Royal Highness is in the House

Florian Wendelmayer sat at his place in the orchestra, flute to his lips, and looked attentively across at the conductor, who had just tapped the rostrum twice with his baton. The entire house had become hushed. The overture began. Florian Wendelmayer played his flute as he had done every day for the past seventeen years. He no longer looked at his music: they had played the same piece a hundred times before, and he knew it off by heart. He played his part utterly mechanically – indeed he didn't even listen. For the last seventeen years he had been sitting there, on the same chair, before the same music stand. Three colleagues had once sat and played beside him. One had died, two had taken up appointments at other theatres. Now a young man who also gave private lessons sat next to him. Florian had lost his own pupils; he reflected on this during the overture, and wondered whether to place an advertisement in the weekly paper again, and perhaps secure new pupils.

And now came a long rest for the flute, which was silent for forty-two bars, and Florian peered over the orchestra out into the splendid bright full house. Most of the audience he knew. The town was not large, and it was always the same people who came to the theatre. Now a slight stir ran through the house, and all eyes were turned towards the royal box, where the prince had just appeared beside his adjutant. The prince adjusted his chair, doing so very softly, almost inaudibly; he was always very considerate.

The forty-two bars were over, and the flutes started up again. The end of the overture approached. All the instruments joined in fortissimo. Finally three long chords, accompanied by a roll on the drums, and the curtain went up. It was a production of an old comedy, the first performance of which Florian had participated in ten years earlier. Most of the musicians made hurriedly for the open air. It was a warm spring evening, and they were accustomed to stroll up and down behind the theatre, or sit on the green painted bench which stood outside. They chatted and smoked cigarettes.

Florian however remained in his seat inside the theatre. What was the point in going outside? They only had a few minutes. It was all so unnecessary and tedious. He laid his flute on the music stand in front of him and looked up at the stage. Ah yes, the same old play! It seemed strange to him when people laughed. Again and again the same old jokes, and again and again people would clap, laugh and thoroughly enjoy themselves. Florian wished it were all over. Then he could go across to the tavern, drink his glass of beer, and then on home to bed. He was so weary he felt old.

How long, how many years he had now been sitting there; he could scarcely remember when it had ever been otherwise. And yet, what a different person he had been once. He had composed, songs and symphonies; his songs had even been sung occasionally at concerts, fifteen or twenty years earlier. Now melody did not exist for him. Little by little his love of music had expired. To him it was now all mere sound and fury – quite insufferable, all this fiddling and piping that so delighted people. Yet the flute-playing had to go on: it was his living. Oh, how devoted he had once been to his art! He had not been to university or studied anything. For hours on end he had wandered through the woods, melodies surging up within him, to which he only had to listen. He had not written much down. Such superabundant inspiration was impossible to capture. The murmuring of the breeze, the rustling of the trees, the crunch of his own footsteps, all had turned to music.

All this was long since over, and even the painful sense that it had vanished had receded. Now he just played his flute and did his duty, and his impecunious life flowed quietly on.

The whole house was laughing. Florian smiled too – smiled for the hundredth time at the same inane jokes. It was nearly the end of the act. The lower door to the orchestra pit opened and the musicians reappeared. They all stooped so as not to bump their heads on the lintel, except for the stocky double-bass player, who strode toward his place with head held high. The conductor too came in, seated himself on his raised stool and took up the baton, ready to give the signal for the music to begin as soon as the curtain fell.

The curtain descended amid lively applause. Already the orchestra had struck up, and mingled with the laughter and conversation in the auditorium. It was strangely noisy today, or so at least it seemed to Florian Wendelmayer. It was also hotter than usual, and when he had to sustain a fairly long note he felt a little dizzy. He began to play again: how odd, his hands were becoming so heavy. He played on. Again the dizziness came over him. The house grew darker . . . swayed . . . the lights went out. The flute fell from Florian's hands. What a noise. The house must be collapsing! Florian tried to stand up, to save himself – but he could no longer see anything. His feet felt heavy. He couldn't move them. And then he fell off his chair in front of the music stand, and the chair fell over backwards. The musicians turned round. Florian's neighbour leaped up in alarm. In the audience people noticed the disturbance and stood up in their seats. The prince in his box leaned over the balustrade, but the conductor waved his baton up and down and said quite audibly: 'Play on!' 'What is it, what is it?' people asked, and the manageress hastened from the stage out towards the orchestra door. They now knew what had happened. A flautist had been taken ill. The conductor continued to beat time but no one was playing any longer. All eyes were turned towards the door to the orchestra pit.

Two theatre attendants had appeared and were making their way between drummers and trombonists towards the spot where Florian Wendelmayer was lying. When they raised him, his eyes were half open, and his lower lip hung limply. They took him by the arms and, supporting him under the shoulders, gripped him round the waist and carried him out. From the auditorium it looked as if he were actually walking. 'What is it, what's up?' people whispered in the audience. 'It's nothing, no, no, really nothing, a musician has been taken ill, but he is back on his feet already.' And scarcely had the orchestra door closed than the conductor tapped the rostrum twice, and the music began again. The other flautist picked Florian's chair up and laid his colleague's flute on it. The audience, however, was not yet ready to settle down. The manageress was standing behind the orchestra door. 'Today of all days,' she exclaimed, 'today of all days, this disturbance had to happen, just when His Highness is attending. Could he not have gone out quietly of his own accord?'

The two men laid the flautist on the floor in the narrow passage leading to the street and stood quietly by. 'He's had a stroke,' said one of them. The manageress looked closely at the dying man. Thus far only murmurs from the audience had been heard. Now several gentlemen came out, asking questions and seeking information in evident concern. 'Oh, it's nothing,' the manageress asserted, 'I must ask people not to trouble themselves further, it's really nothing. He's already opening his eyes. Everything necessary is being seen to. Has the doctor been alerted?'

'Müller has gone to fetch him,' replied a stage hand.

Now people were coming in off the street as well. The manageress was in despair. 'Would people kindly not make a fuss, nothing at all has happened. Stand back, please, ladies and gentlemen. Wherever can the doctor be?'

Just then he arrived. People made way for him. 'But what's all this,' he said, 'you don't just lay a sick man on the floor, this is incredible. Bring a stretcher, quick.'

'Bring a stretcher,' the manageress repeated .

The doctor bent down and felt the flautist's pulse. It was very quiet in the room, and a faint murmur penetrated from the auditorium.

'A light, please,' said the doctor, 'I can't see a thing.'

A gentleman took the little oil lamp down from the wall. A dim light fell on Florian Wendelmayer's countenance, which the doctor studied carefully while continuing to take his pulse. 'The man is dead,' he exclaimed. While everyone was standing there in shock, a footman came in. 'His Highness is pleased to enquire,' he said, 'how the sick musician is.'

'Please convey respectful thanks to His Highness,' replied the manageress in a somewhat constricted voice, 'the musician is already feeling better.' The footman went out. And then she thanked everyone for their kind concern and requested them to clear the narrow passage, which was uncomfortable enough as it was. The gentlemen from the audience were visibly perturbed. It seemed so strange to have to go back into the theatre to watch a comic play, and in this they found yet another proof of how strange and contradictory a thing life was. Slowly they dispersed. The door to the street was wide open. People walking past who had noticed the commotion stopped outside it. The soft spring evening air blew in. The manageress turned to the bystanders from among the audience. 'No need for everyone to hear about this, wouldn't you agree?' she observed.

No, no, they would say nothing.

'Has he any family?' asked the doctor.

'No,' replied the manageress, 'it's Wendelmayer, remember.'

'Ah, of course, Wendelmayer,' said the doctor with a reassured expression, as if to say 'It's all right for Wendelmayers to die.' And he stood up and hung the oil lamp on the wall again. Two men had arrived; outside the bier was standing ready, and they lifted up the dead man and laid him out on it.

The theatre had quietened down. The music was playing before the beginning of the second act. The gentlemen who had seen the dead man were now composed and dignified, and when people asked them about the flautist's condition, they answered earnestly and reassuringly. The curtain was just going up when the door to the royal box opened and a footman was seen entering. The prince turned round to him. 'The musician is perfectly all right, Your Highness,' said the servant.

The prince looked down at the audience again, where a few faces had turned towards him. He thought he read a question there, and in response he nodded in a friendly way. With a reassuring smile he intimated to his loyal people that the flautist Florian Wendelmayer was feeling perfectly all right.

Flowers

I have just spent the whole afternoon wandering about the streets, where white snow is silently descending – and now I am at home again, the lamp is lit, my cigar smouldering and my books laid out before me, everything calculated to make me feel thoroughly at ease . . . But it is all to no avail, and my thoughts keep coming back to the same thing.

Hadn't she been long dead to me? . . . yes, dead, or rather, I thought to myself with the childish self-pity of a man betrayed, 'worse than dead . . .?' And now, ever since I have known that she is not 'worse than dead' but simply dead, just like so many others lying out there deep under the earth, for ever and ever, in springtime, when sweltering summer comes or when snow is falling as it is today . . . without any hope of their returning – ever since then I have come to realise that for me too she had not died a moment sooner than for other people. Pain? – No. It is really only the universal horror that grips all of us when someone who once belonged to us sinks into the grave and whose being we can still picture clearly – the light in their eye and the sound of their voice.

At the time it was certainly deeply distressing to discover her unfaithfulness . . . all those tumultuous feelings! . . . The anger and the sudden hatred and the revulsion at existence and – I can't deny it! – the wounded vanity; indeed it was only gradually that I became conscious of the pain. And then came the consoling thought that brought some relief: she too must be suffering. I still have all her dozens of tearful plaintive letters begging for forgiveness, and can read them again at any time. I can still see her in her dark English dress and little straw hat, as she stood on the street corner in the gathering dusk when I stepped out of the front door . . . gazing after me . . . And I still recall that final meeting when she stood before me, her large eyes wide with bewilderment in her round child-like face, which had grown so pale and care-worn . . . I did not take her hand when she departed – when she departed for the last time. And I watched her from the window as she walked to the corner of the street, and then disappeared – for ever. Now she can never return . . .

It was quite by chance that I heard about her death at all. It could have taken weeks or even months. I just happened one morning to run into her uncle, whom I had not seen for at least a year and who seldom stays in Vienna very long. I had spoken with him on only a few occasions previously. The first time was three years ago during an evening of skittles, which she too was attending with her mother. – Then the following summer, when I was in the Prater with a few friends at the 'Csarda'. Sitting at the next table with two or three gentlemen in convivial, almost jolly mood was the uncle, and he drank a toast to me. As he left the garden he stopped beside me and, as though it were a great secret, intimated that his niece was simply mad about me. And in my half-befuddled state I couldn't help finding it curiously amusing, and a little bizarre, that the old fellow should be imparting this to me here amid the sound of cymbals and soaring violins – to me who was well aware of it and on whose lips the fragrance of her last kiss still lingered . . . And now again this morning! I almost walked straight past him. More out of politeness than interest I asked after his niece . . . For I knew nothing of her circumstances; even her letters had long since ceased; all she sent regularly were flowers. Reminders of one of our happiest days, they arrived once a month with no note attached, silent humble flowers . . . And when I asked the old man about her, he was utterly amazed. 'Didn't you know the poor girl died a week ago?' I was deeply shocked. Then he went on to tell me more. How she had been languishing for some time, but had not been in bed more that a week . . . What had been the matter with her? . . . 'Some emotional disorder . . . anaemia . . . One can never pin those doctors down.'

For some time I stood rooted to the spot where the old man left me; I felt utterly exhausted, as though after some extreme exertion. And I now have the feeling that I must regard today as a watershed in my life. But why? – Why? What has occurred is something completely external. I no longer felt anything for her, indeed I scarcely thought of her at all. And writing all this down has done me good: I have grown calmer. I'm beginning to appreciate how comfortable my home is. – It's futile to torment myself by dwelling on things further . . . There is sure to be someone else who has greater reason to grieve today than I.

I have been out for a walk. A bright wintry day. The sky so clear, so cold, so vast . . . And I'm completely calm. The old man I ran into yesterday . . . I feel as though it happened weeks ago. – And when I think of her, I imagine her in curiously sharp and perfect outline; only one thing is missing: the rage that always used to accompany the memory of her. I don't have any real sense that she is no longer of this world, that she is lying in a coffin, that she has already been buried . . . I feel no pain. The world today seemed to me quieter. At some point I came to recognise that there is no such thing as happiness or anguish; – there are only grimaces expressing joy and sorrow; we laugh and cry and invite our souls along. I could sit down now and read serious books, and soon be immersed in their wisdom. Or I could stand in front of old paintings that used to leave me cold, and their dark beauty would now dawn on me . . . And when I think about loved ones who have died, I no longer feel the old constriction of the heart – Death has become a friend; he goes about among us and has no desire to harm us.

Snow, deep white snow on all the streets. Little Gretel came round and declared that we really ought to take an outing in a sleigh. And so we found ourselves out in the country, dashing along bright slippery roads to the jingling of bells, the pale grey sky above us, swiftly, swiftly on between the glistening white hills. And Gretel leaned against my shoulder, her eyes fixed contentedly on the long road ahead. We came to an inn that we knew well from summer when it had lain nestling amid greenery; now it looked so different, so lonely, so unconnected with the rest of the world that it was as though one were discovering it afresh. And the stove burning in the parlour was so hot that we had to pull the table right back, as little Gretel's left cheek and ear had become quite red. I couldn't help kissing her on her paler cheek. Then the ride back in the gathering dusk. Gretel snuggling close beside me, taking both my hands in hers. – Then she said: At last, today I've got you back again. Without brooding over everything, she had found the right words, and this made me very happy. Perhaps too, the dry winter air out in the country had liberated my senses again, because I felt freer and more light-hearted than I had done for weeks. –

Recently, as I lay half-asleep on the divan one afternoon, a strange notion came to me. I had a vision of myself as cold and utterly hard-hearted. As someone who could stand beside the grave into which a loved one has been lowered, without a tear, indeed without any capacity for feeling. As someone so hardened that not even the horror of a young person's death could placate him . . . Yes, that was it, implacable . . .

It's all over, over and done with. Life, pleasure and a little love have driven the whole silly business from my mind. I am going out into society a little more. I quite enjoy it; they are harmless people, and prattle on gaily about all sorts of things. Gretel too is a dear tender-hearted creature; and she is at her most beautiful standing beside me like this in the bay window, with the afternoon sunlight shining on her blond hair.

Something rather strange happened today . . . It is the day on which every month she used to send me flowers . . . And the flowers arrived again today . . . as though nothing had changed. They arrived by post first thing this morning in a long narrow white box. It was very early and I was still half-asleep. It was not until I was actually opening the box that I fully came to my senses. And then I had a shock . . . There, neatly held together by a golden thread, lay a bunch of violets and carnations . . . They lay there as if inside a coffin. And when I picked the flowers up, a shiver ran down my spine. – I know how it came about that they arrived again today. She sensed her illness coming on and perhaps already had some inkling of her approaching death, but nevertheless put in her usual order at the flower-shop. I was not to forgo this mark of her affection. – Undoubtedly this is how their delivery is to be explained; something wholly natural, even perhaps a little touching . . . And yet, as I held the flowers in my hand, and they seemed to tremble and incline their heads, against all reason and my own resolve, I could not help finding them a little uncanny, as if they came direct from her, as if this were her greeting . . . as if even now in death she still wanted to tell me of her love, of her – belated faithfulness. Ah, we do not understand death, we never understand it; and every human being is really only dead once all those who knew him or her have died as well . . . Today I tended the flowers differently, more tenderly than usual, as if gripping them too firmly might make them suffer . . . as if their quiet souls might softly start to weep. And now as they stand before me on my desk in a slender, pale green crystal vase, it's almost as though they were sadly bowing their heads in thanks. All the pain of futile longing emanates towards me from their fragrance, and I can't help feeling that they could tell me something, if only one understood the language of all living things, and not merely of – all those that talk.

I have no wish to delude myself. They are merely flowers, nothing more. They are a retrospective greeting from the other side . . . They are not a cry, no, not a cry from within the tomb. – They are merely flowers, and some salesgirl in a flower-shop tied them together quite mechanically, put a bit of wrapping round them, laid them in the white box and then took them to the post. And now they are here, so why am I even bothering to think about it? –

I am out and about a lot, and go on long lonely walks. When I am in company, I feel no real affinity with anyone; the connecting threads break off. I notice it too when this sweet blonde girl is sitting in my room and chattering on about . . . to tell the truth, I have no idea what. For no sooner has she left than immediately, that very instant, she becomes utterly remote, as though she were far away, as though the tide of humanity had swept her off forever, as though she had disappeared without a trace. If she were never to return, I should scarcely be surprised.

The flowers are standing in the slender shimmering green vase, their stalks immersed in water, and their fragrance pervades the room. They are still exuding fragrance – even though they have now been in my room a week and have started wilting. And I understand all sorts of nonsense that I laughed at once. I understand how to cultivate a dialogue with natural objects . . . I understand that one can await an answer when one talks to clouds and springs; for I too am now gazing at these flowers and waiting for them to begin to speak . . . Or rather, I am aware that they are continuously talking . . . even now . . . this very minute . . . that they are talking and complaining incessantly, and that I am getting close to understanding them.

How relieved I am that this bleak winter is coming to an end. There is already a hint in the air of approaching spring. Time seems to pass of its own accord. I live much as I have always done, and yet I sometimes feel as though the parameters of my existence are now less sharply drawn. Yesterday is already dissolving, and everything that happened only a few days ago has assumed the quality of an obscure dream. Repeatedly, whenever Gretel leaves me, and especially when I don't see her for several days, I have this sense that the whole affair is something that was over long, long ago. She always approaches from so far, far away! Admittedly when she begins to chatter on, things soon get back to normal, and I have a clear sense of present actualities. Indeed words then become almost too loud and colours too glaring; and just as the dear girl recedes into an ineffable remoteness as soon as she has left me, so her presence too seems sudden and intense. Previously I always retained some echo or visual image of resonant or illuminating moments; but now everything fades or is obscured as in some gloomy grotto. And then I find myself alone with my flowers again. They have now completely wilted. They no longer give off any fragrance. Earlier Gretel took no notice of them, but today for the first time her gaze rested on them for some time, and I felt she wanted to question me about them. Then suddenly some secret shyness seemed to restrain her; – she did not say another word and shortly after took her leave.

The petals have begun to fall. I never touch them; they would turn to dust between my fingers. It grieves me beyond words that they have withered. Why I do not have the strength to make an end of the whole uncanny business I don't know. At times I cannot stand it any longer, and hasten out. And then in the middle of the street the old obsession seizes me again, and I feel compelled to return and see to them. And then of course I find them there in the same green vase, just as I left them, sorrowful and weary. Yesterday evening I wept beside them as one weeps beside a grave, yet without even thinking of the woman who had sent them. – I may be wrong! but I have the impression that Gretel too feels the presence of something uncanny in the room. She no longer laughs when she comes over. She no longer speaks out loud, in that fresh lively voice I have become accustomed to. Admittedly I don't receive her as often as I used to. I am also tormented by the ever-present fear that she might ask me after all; and I know that I should find such questions quite intolerable.

Often she brings her needlework, and if I am still absorbed in my books, she sits quietly at the table, embroidering or crocheting, and waits patiently until I put my books away, stand up, and coming over to her take her work out of her hand. Then I remove the green shade from the lamp she has been sitting by, and the soft friendly light pervades the room. I don't like it when the corners are in darkness.

Spring! – My window is wide open. Late in the evening Gretel and I were gazing down into the dark street. The air around us was warm and balmy. But when I looked over towards the street lamp emitting its pale light, suddenly there seemed to be a shadow standing there. I saw and yet didn't see it . . . I know I didn't really see it . . . I closed my eyes. And all at once I could see through my closed lids, and there the wretched creature stood in the wan light of the street lamp, and I saw her face with uncanny clarity, as though it were illuminated by a yellow sun, and saw those large bewildered eyes in her pale care-worn face . . . Slowly I retreated from the window and sat down at my desk, where the candle was flickering in the breeze. And I remained there motionless, for I knew that the poor creature on the corner was standing there and waiting; and had I dared to touch the dead flow-ers, I would have taken them out of the vase and brought them to her . . . I thought all this with complete conviction, yet at the same time knew that it was nonsense. Gretel too now left the window and stand-ing behind my chair a moment, touched my hair with her lips. Then she departed, leaving me alone . . .

I stared at the flowers. They are scarcely flowers at all now, no more than bare stalks, pitiful and dry . . . They are making me ill, driving me insane. – And yet it must somehow all make sense; other-wise Gretel would surely have asked me; but she can feel it too – and takes flight every so often, as though ghosts were in my room. –

Ghosts! – They exist, they exist! Dead things playing at being alive. And if wilting flowers smell of mould, it is only in memory of the time when they were blossoming and fragrant. And the dead return as long as we do not forget them. – What does it matter if she can no longer speak – I can still hear her! She is no longer visible, but I still can see her! – And the spring outside, and the sun streaming brightly across my carpet, and the fresh scent of lilac wafting in from the nearby park, and the people walking past below who mean nothing to me, is all that supposed to be alive? I can let down the curtains and the sun is dead. I decide to have nothing more to do with all these people, and they too are dead. When I close the window, no scent of lilac wafts about me any longer, and the spring is dead. I am might-ier than the sun, these people and the spring. But mightier than I is memory, for it comes as it wills and there is no fleeing from it. And these dry stalks in the vase are mightier than any spring or scent of lilac.

I was sitting over these pages when Gretel came in. She had never before come so early in the day, seldom before dusk. I was aston-ished, almost startled. She stood in the doorway for a few seconds, and I just stared at her without a word of greeting. Then she smiled and drew closer. She was holding a bunch of fresh flowers in her hand. Then without saying a word she came up to my desk and laid the flowers before me. A second later she reaches out for the withered flowers in the green vase. I felt as though my heart were being wrung – but I could say nothing . . . And as I try to rise and seize the girl by the arm, she looks at me and laughs. And holding the withered flowers aloft, she hurries behind the desk towards the window, and simply throws them out onto the street. I feel an impulse to follow in their wake; but the girl is standing there, leaning against the window-ledge, her face turned towards me. And the warm living sunlight streams in over her blond hair . . . And the rich scent of lilac enters from beyond. And I look at the empty green glass vase standing on the desk, and I don't know what I feel; freer I think – much freer than before. Then Gretel comes up to me, picks up her small bouquet and holds it out for me to smell; cool white lilac blossoms . . . Such a fresh healthy fragrance – so soft, so cool; I felt like burying my face in them. Laughing, white, kissing flowers – and I felt haunted no longer. – Gretel stood behind me and ruffled my hair with her wild hands. Dear fool, she said. – Was she fully aware of what she had done? . . . I took her hands and kissed them. And that evening we went out into the open air, into the spring. I have just this minute returned with her. I have lighted the candle; we walked a long way, and Gretel is so tired she has fallen asleep in the armchair by the stove. She looks very beautiful, smiling in her sleep.

In the slender green vase before me are the lilac blossoms. – Down there in the street – no, no, they are no longer lying there. The wind has long since swept them away in the dust.

The Wise Man's Wife

I propose to stay on here for some time. A sense of listlessness pervades this resort between the sea and the woods which does me good. Everything is motionless and tranquil. Only the white clouds drift slowly by; but the wind is blowing so high above the waves and tree-tops that the sea and trees don't stir. There is a deep solitariness about the place, and one is always conscious of it; even when one is among the crowds of people, in the hotel or on the esplanade. The spa's little band plays mainly melancholy Swedish and Danish songs, but even their lively pieces sound tired and muted. When the musicians have finished, they descend the bandstand steps in silence and slowly and disconsolately disappear with their instruments along the avenues.

I am putting all this down on paper while I am being rowed along the shore-line.

The shore is green and placid: simple rustic houses set in gardens; benches close to the water in the gardens, behind the houses the narrow white road, beyond the road the wood. This extends far inland, rising slightly, and ending where the sun is setting. Its evening radiance falls upon the extended yellow strip of island opposite. The boatman says it takes two hours to get there. I would like to go there some time. But this place has a strange hold on me; I always seem to find myself in the immediate vicinity of the little resort, down by the shore or on my terrace.

I am lying beneath the beech trees. The branches are drooping in the sultry afternoon; now and then I hear the approaching steps of people coming along the woodland path; but I cannot see them, since I do not stir and my eyes are gazing upward. I also hear children's light-hearted laughter, but the vast silence all about me quickly drinks up every sound, and scarcely a second after it has faded it seems to have been over long ago. If I close my eyes and then open them at once, I awake as though after a long night. And so I slip out of myself and float off into the vast tranquillity as if a part of nature.

My peace and quiet is over. And it will not return, either in the rowing-boat or beneath the beech trees. Everything suddenly seems changed. The tunes from the band sound intense and jolly; the people walking past all seem to talk a lot; the children laugh and shout. Even the beloved sea, which seemed so quiet, pounds thunderously against the shore at night. Life for me has become full of noise once again. Never before had I set out from home so light at heart; I had left nothing behind me uncompleted. I had finished my doctorate; I had finally buried the illusory artistic aspirations that had accompanied my youth, and Fräulein Jenny had become the wife of a watchmaker. So I had the unusual good fortune of setting out on a journey without leaving a mistress at home and without taking any illusions with me. I had felt secure and at ease in the sense of having closed a chapter of my life. And now it is all over; for Frau Friederike is here.

Late evening on my terrace; I have placed a lamp on my table and am writing. Now is the time to get everything clear. I am transcribing our conversation, the first with her for seven years, the first one since that hour . . .

It was on the esplanade, about midday. I was sitting on a bench. Now and then people would walk past me. A woman with a small boy was standing on the pier, too far away for me to have made out her features. Furthermore, I didn't notice her particularly; I was only aware that she had been standing there a long time, when she finally left the pier and came closer and closer to me. She was leading the boy by the hand. Now I could see that she was young and slender. Her face seemed familiar. She was still ten yards away from me. I got up and went towards her. She had smiled, and I knew then who it was.

'Yes, it's me,' she said and held out her hand.

'I recognised you at once,' I said.

'I hope that wasn't too difficult,' she replied. 'And you haven't really changed at all.'

'Seven years . . .' I said.

She nodded. 'Seven years . . .'

We both fell silent. She was very beautiful. Then a smile stole over her face, she turned to the boy she was still holding by the hand, and said: 'Give the gentleman your hand.' The little fellow held it out, but didn't look at me.

'This is my son,' she said.

He was a pretty child with auburn hair and light-coloured eyes.

'How nice, the way people meet again in life,' she began, 'I would never have thought . . .'

'Yes, it is strange,' I said.

'Why?' she asked, smiling and for the first time looking me full in the eye. 'It's summer time . . . everybody travels, don't they?'

Now it was on the tip of my tongue to ask about her husband, but I couldn't get it out.

'How long will you be staying?' I asked.

'A fortnight. Then I'm meeting my husband in Copenhagen.'

I gave her a quick glance; hers answered easily: 'Does that surprise you perhaps?' I felt uncertain, almost ill at ease. It suddenly struck me as incredible that one can forget things so completely. Only now did I realise that for some considerable time I had thought about that moment seven years ago so little, it might never have occurred.

'You must have many things to tell me,' she began again, 'a great many. No doubt you finished your doctorate long ago?'

'Not all that long – a month ago.'

'You've still got the same boyish face,' she said. 'Your moustache looks as though it's been pasted on.'

From the hotel the overly loud bell rang, summoning guests to dine.

'Adieu,' she said now, as though that was all she had been waiting for.

'Couldn't we go in together?' I asked.

'I'm dining in my room with the boy, I don't like being among so many people.'

'When shall we see each other again?'

Smiling with her eyes, she motioned toward the esplanade. 'People are bound to meet each other along here,' she said – and when she noticed that I was disagreeably affected by her answer, she added: 'Especially when they want to . – Good day.'

She gave me her hand, and without turning round again she walked away. The little boy however did look back at me again.

I wandered to and fro along the esplanade the whole afternoon and evening, but she failed to come. Can she have left again after all? I really ought not to be surprised.

A whole day has passed without my seeing her. All morning it rained, and apart from me there was almost no one on the esplanade. I've been past the house where she is lodging a few times, but don't know which are her windows. In the afternoon the rain abated and I took a long walk along the road beside the sea, as far as the next resort. It was overcast and sultry.

Along the way I was unable to think of anything but those bygone times. I could see everything clearly before me once again. The friendly house I had lived in, and the garden with green-painted chairs and tables. And the little town with its quiet white streets. And the distant hills, swathed in mist. And above it all, a patch of pale blue sky that so perfectly belonged as to seem as if here were the only spot on earth it was just this pale and blue. I could also see all the people from those days again; my fellow pupils, my teachers, and also Friederike's husband. I pictured him differently from the way he had appeared to me at that final moment. I envisaged him with the mild, rather tired expression his face wore, when after school he would stride past us boys with a friendly greeting on the street, and when he sat at table between Friederike and me, mostly in silence; I saw him as I had often caught sight of him from my window: sitting in the garden in front of the green-painted table, correcting work done by us pupils. And I remembered how Friederike had come into the garden, bringing him his afternoon coffee, and how as she did so she had looked up at my window smiling, with a look that at the time I did not understand . . . not until that final hour. Now I realise that I had often recalled all of this. But not as something living, rather as a picture hanging motionless and peaceful on a wall at home.

Today we sat on the beach beside each other, and talked to one another like strangers. The boy played with sand and pebbles at our feet. It was not as though anything were burdening us: we merely chatted like people who meant nothing to each other and whom life at the spa had chanced to bring together for a short time; about the weather, about the region, about the people, even about music and new books. While I was sitting next to her, I found this not unpleasant; but when she got up and walked away it was suddenly intolerable. I wanted to cry out after her: Leave me something at least; but she would not have understood. And when I think about it, what else could I expect? That she was so friendly when approaching me on our first meeting was evidently based only on surprise; perhaps also the pleasant feeling of encountering an old acquaintance again in a strange place. But now she has had time, like me, to remember everything; and what she had hoped to forget forever has powerfully resurfaced. I cannot possibly estimate, of course, what she may have had to tolerate on my account, and what today she perhaps still has to suffer. I can see that she has stayed with him, and the four-year-old boy is living proof that they have become reconciled again – but one can be reconciled without forgiving, and one can forgive without forgetting. – I should leave, it would be better for us both.

In its strange melancholy beauty, that whole year revives before me, and I relive everything again. Details come back to me. I remember the autumn morning when, accompanied by my father, I arrived in the little town where I was to spend my last year of secondary school. I can see the school building clearly before me, in the middle of the park with its tall trees. I remember studying quietly in the pleasant spacious room, the cordial conversations about my future I had at table with my teacher, and which Friederike listened to smiling; the walks with school friends out along the road to the next village; and all these trivialities moved me profoundly, as if they somehow contained the meaning of my youth. Probably these days would all be lying in the deep shadow of oblivion had they not been imbued with a mysterious radiance by that final hour. And the most remarkable thing of all is that, since Friederike has been near me, those days have seemed even closer than the ones this May when I was in love with the little Fräulein who married the watchmaker in June.

Early this morning I went to my window and looked down onto the broad terrace, and I saw Friederike sitting at a table with her little boy; they were the first guests down to breakfast. Her table was directly beneath my window and I called out good-morning to her. She looked up. 'Awake so early?' she said. 'Won't you come and join us?'

A minute later I was sitting at their table. It was a glorious morning, cool and sunny. We chatted about the same trivial things as last time, and yet everything was different. Behind our words memory was aglow. We went for a walk in the woods. Then she began to talk about herself and about her home.

'Everything is still exactly the same with us as it was then,' she said, 'except that our garden has become more beautiful; my husband takes a good deal of care over it, now we have the child. Next year we are going to get a greenhouse.'

She chattered on. 'For the last two years we have had a theatre, which plays all winter until Palm Sunday. I go two or three times a week, usually with my mother, it gives her a great deal of pleasure.'

'Me theatre too,' cried the little fellow, whom Friederike was leading by the hand.

'You too, of course. On Sunday afternoon,' she turned to explain to me, 'they sometimes put on shows for the children; then I take the boy. But I enjoy it all very much as well.'

I had to tell her something about myself. She didn't ask much about my profession and other serious matters; she was more interested to know how I spent my free time, and enjoyed hearing about the convivial amusements of city life.

The whole conversation flowed amiably along; not a word was mentioned about the memory we shared – and yet it was undoubtedly as continuously present in her thoughts as in mine. We walked about for hours, and the little fellow would come between us, and then our hands would touch above his locks. But we both pretended not to notice, and went on talking perfectly naturally.

When I was alone again, my good mood soon evaporated. For suddenly I again felt that I didn't know anything about Friederike. I found it incredible that this uncertainty had not tormented me during our entire conversation, and it seemed strange that Friederike herself had felt no need to talk about it. For even were I to suppose that between her husband and herself there had been no thought of that hour for years – she herself could surely not have forgotten it. Something serious must have followed my silent departure then – so how has she managed not to say anything about it? Has she perhaps been expecting that I would begin first? What has prevented me from doing so? The same shyness perhaps that forbade her asking? Are we both afraid of touching on the matter? – That could well be. And yet it must finally be done; for until then something will remain between us that divides us. And that anything should divide us pains me more than all else.

This afternoon I went for a stroll in the woods, along the same paths we walked this morning. I was filled with yearning, as for someone infinitely dear. Late in the evening I went past her house, after I had looked for her everywhere in vain. She was standing at the window. I called up to her, as she had done to me this morning: 'Won't you come down?'

She said, coolly, it seemed to me: 'I'm tired. Good night' – and closed the window.

In memory Friederike appears to me in two different guises. For the most part I recall her as a pale gentle woman, sitting in the garden wearing a white morning dress, who is like a mother to me, and strokes my cheek. If it had only been her that I had encountered again here, then my tranquillity would certainly not have been disturbed, and I should be lying in the afternoons under the shady beech trees as in the first days of my stay here.

But she also appears to me as a completely different woman, the way I saw her only once; and that was during the last hour I spent in the little town where I went to school.

It was the day I received my matriculation certificate. As on every other day, I had dined at midday with my teacher and his wife, and as I did not want to be accompanied to the station, we had said our farewells at once on getting up from table. I felt absolutely no emotion. It was only when I was sitting on my bed in the room I had cleared out, my packed suitcase at my feet, and looking out through the wide open window across the tender foliage of the little garden at the white clouds, which stood motionless above the hills, that the sorrow of parting came softly, almost affectionately upon me. Suddenly the door opened. Friederike entered. Hastily I got to my feet. She came closer, leaned against the table, supporting both hands behind her against the edge, and looked earnestly at me. Very softly she said: 'So today's the day?' I just nodded and for the first time felt, really deeply, how sad it actually was that I had to leave here. She looked at the floor for a while and remained silent. Then she raised her head and came still closer to me. She laid both hands very lightly on my hair, as indeed she had often done before, but I knew at that moment that it meant something different from usual. Then she let her hands glide slowly down over my cheeks, and gazed at me with infinite depth of feeling. She shook her head with a pained expression, as though it were something she simply could not grasp. 'Must you really go today?' she asked softly. 'Yes,' I said – 'For ever?' she cried out. 'No,' I answered. – 'Oh yes,' she said, her lips twitching painfully, 'it's for ever. Even if you visit us some time . . . in two or three years – today you will still be leaving us forever.' She said this with a tenderness that no longer had anything motherly about it. A shiver ran down my spine. And then suddenly she kissed me. At first I just thought: she has never done that before. But when her lips would not part from mine, I understood what that kiss meant. I was confused and happy; I felt like crying. She had flung her arms around my neck, I sank, as if she had pushed me, into the corner of the divan; Friederike prostrated herself before me on her knees and pulled my mouth down to her own. Then she took both my hands and buried her face in them . . . I whispered her name and was amazed how beautiful it was. The fragrance from her hair rose towards me; I breathed it in with rapture . . . At that moment – I thought I would die of fright – the door which had been left ajar opens softly, and there stands Friederike's husband. I feel like screaming but can't get out a sound. I stare him in the face – I don't manage to see whether his expression changes – for that same instant he has already disappeared again and closed the door. I try to get up, to release my hands in which Friederike's head is still resting, try to speak, again blurt her name out with an effort – when suddenly she herself leaps up – deathly pale – whispers to me almost peremptorily: 'Quiet!' and stands there for a second motionless, her face turned towards the door, as though listening. Then she opens it softly and looks out through the crack. I stand there breathless. Then she opens it fully, takes me by the hand and whispers: 'Go, go, quickly.' She pushes me out – I creep swiftly across the little landing to the stairs, then turn round once more – and see her standing at the door, with an expression of unspeakable anxiety, and an impatient gesture of the hand that says: Go! Go! And I rush away.

I think back on what happened next as on some insane dream. I hastened to the station, racked by mortal fear. I travelled through the night, sleeplessly tossing in my bunk. I arrived home expecting that my parents would already be informed of everything, and was almost astonished when they received me joyfully and warmly. Then I spent days in great trepidation, prepared for something terrible to happen; and every ring at the door, every letter made me tremble. At last came news that put me more at ease: it was a card from a school friend, whose home was in the little town, and who sent on harmless news and cheery greetings. So, nothing terrible had happened, or at least it had not come to an open scandal. I could assume that everything had been quietly resolved between man and wife, that he had forgiven her and she had repented.

Even so, this adventure lived on in my memory at first as something sad, almost depressing, and I felt like someone who without being to blame had destroyed the peace of a home. Gradually this feeling faded, and only later, when new experiences helped me to understand that hour better and more deeply, did a strange longing for Friederike occasionally come over me – as did the painful sense that such glorious promise should not have been fulfilled. But this longing also passed, and so it had come about that I had almost completely forgotten the young woman. – But now suddenly everything that at the time made the incident into an experience has revived; and everything is even more intense than then, for I am in love with Friederike.

Today everything that has been so puzzling over the last few days now seems quite clear to me. Late in the evening we sat on the esplanade, just the two of us; the boy had been put to bed already. I had asked her in the morning whether she would come; quite innocently; I just said something about the beauty of the sea at night, and how wonderful it would be, when everything around was quiet, to be beside the shore and gaze out into the immense darkness. She had said nothing, but I knew she would come. And then we sat on the esplanade, almost in silence, our hands clasped, and I felt that Friederike would be mine, whenever I desired. Why talk about the past, I thought – and I knew that from the very first moment of our reunion *she* had thought so too. Are we the same people anyway that we were at that time? We are so light-hearted, so free; our memories flutter high above us, like distant summer birds. Perhaps she has had other experiences during those seven years, as I have – what do I care? Now we are people of today and yearning for each other. Yesterday perhaps she may have been an unhappy woman, perhaps a rash one; today she is sitting in silence next to me beside the sea, and is holding my hand and longing to be in my arms.

I slowly accompanied her the few steps to her house. The trees cast long black shadows along the street.

'We could go sailing tomorrow morning,' I said.

'Yes,' she answered.

'I shall wait at the pier, at seven.'

'Where to?' she asked.

'To the island out there . . . where the lighthouse is, do you see it?'

'Ah yes, the red light. Is it far?'

'An hour – we can be back in good time.'

'Good-night,' she said and stepped into the hall.

I walked away. – In a few days you will have forgotten me again perhaps, I thought, but tomorrow at least will be a marvellous day.

I was on the pier earlier than she was. The little boat was waiting; old Jansen had hoisted the sails and was sitting at the tiller smoking his pipe. I jumped in with him and let the wavelets rock me. I imbibed those moments of waiting like a morning drink. In the street I kept my eye on there was still nobody about. After a quarter of an hour Friederike appeared. I could see her some way off, and had the impression that she was walking faster than usual: when she stepped onto the pier I stood up; only now could she see me and she greeted me with a smile. Finally she reached the end of the pier, I gave her my hand and helped her into the boat. Jansen let the rope go, and our craft slipped away. We sat close together; she clung to my arm. She was dressed all in white and looked like an eighteen-year-old girl.

'What is there to see on this island?' she asked.

I couldn't help laughing.

She blushed and said: 'The lighthouse, anyway?'

'Perhaps the church as well,' I added.

'Well, ask the man . . .' she pointed to Jansen.

I asked him. 'How old is the church on the island?'

But he didn't understand a word of German; and so after this one attempt we were able to feel more alone together than before.

'Over there,' she said and motioned with her eyes – 'is that another island ?'

'No,' I answered, 'That is Sweden itself, the mainland.'

'That would be even nicer,' she said.

'Yes,' I replied – 'but one would need to stay there . . . for some time . . . for good –'

If she had now said to me: Come, let's flee together to another country and never come back – I would have agreed. The way we were gliding along in the boat, the pure breeze playing about us, the bright sky above us and all around us the glittering water, it seemed to me a festive trip, we ourselves a royal couple, and all the previous constraints of our existence null and void.

Soon we could distinguish the little houses on the island; the white church on the gradually emerging hill which ran the length of the island stood out in sharper outline. Our boat flew straight towards the shore. Near us little fishing-boats appeared; a few which had withdrawn their oars drifted easily on the water. Friederike's gaze was mostly directed towards the island; but she wasn't *looking*. In less than an hour we sailed into the harbour, which was closed in all around by a wooden jetty, so that one could imagine oneself in a small pond.

A few children were standing on the jetty. We got out and slowly walked towards the shore; the children followed us, but soon dispersed. The whole village lay before us, consisting of at most twenty houses dotted about. We almost sank in the thin brown sand, washed here by the water. On a sunny open square which reached down to the sea, nets were hanging out to dry; a few women were sitting outside their front doors mending nets. After a hundred yards or so we were completely alone. We found ourselves on a narrow path that led away from the houses, towards the end of the island where the lighthouse stood. On our left, divided from us by a strip of poor farmland which gradually got narrower, lay the sea; on our right rose the hill, along the ridge of which we saw the path leading to the church which lay behind us. Over all this the silence and the sun lay heavily. – All this time Friederike and I had not spoken at all. Nor did I feel any inclination to do so; I felt infinitely contented, just strolling on with her like this through the vast silence.

But she began to speak.

'A week ago today,' she said . . .

'Well –?'

'I didn't know anything . . . not even where I would be travelling to.'

I said nothing.

'How lovely it is here,' she exclaimed, and took my hand.

I felt drawn to her; I should have liked to close her in my arms and kiss her eyes.

'Yes?' I asked softly.

She said nothing and became rather serious.

We had reached the little cottage that was built onto the light-house; here the path ended; we had to turn round. A narrow field path led up the hill quite steeply. I hesitated.

'Come on,' she said.

Now as we were walking, we could see the church. We were approaching it. I put my arm around Friederike's neck; she had to stay very close to me in order not to slip. I touched her warm cheeks with my hand.

'Why did we never hear from you all that time?' she asked suddenly – 'I at least,' she added, as she looked up at me.

'Why?' I repeated, nonplussed.

'Well then?'

'But how could I?'

'Oh, *that's* why,' she said; 'were you hurt?'

I was too astonished to be able to respond.

'Well, what did you think?'

'What did I – '

'Yes – or don't you remember anymore?'

'Certainly I remember. Why do you mention it now?'

'I've been wanting to ask you for some time,' she said.

'Well, go on,' I replied, deeply moved.

'You took it for a passing mood . . . Oh, I'm sure of it,' she added vehemently, when she noticed that I was about to demur – 'but I tell you, it wasn't. I suffered more during that year than anyone can know.'

'Which year?'

'Well . . . when you were staying with us . . . Why do you ask that?

– At first I said to myself . . . But why am I telling you this?'

I seized her arm impetuously. 'Tell me . . . Please . . . I love you so.'

'And I you,' she cried out suddenly; took both my hands and kissed them – 'and I shall always – always.'

'Please, tell me more,' I said; 'tell me everything, everything . . .'

She talked as we slowly walked on up the field path in the sun.

'At first I said to myself: he is a child . . . I'm fond of him as a mother might be. But the closer the time of your departure came . . .'

She broke off for a while, then continued:

'And finally it came. – I didn't intend to come to you – I don't know what drove me up there. And once I was with you, I didn't intend to kiss you either – but . . .'

'Go on, go on,' I said.

'And then I suddenly told you that you ought to leave – no doubt you thought the whole thing was a farce, didn't you?'

'I don't understand.'

'That's what I imagined the whole time. I even wanted to write to you . . . But what would have been the point . . . Anyway . . . the reason that I sent you away was . . . I was suddenly frightened.'

'I know that.'

'If you know that – why did I never hear from you again?' she cried out passionately.

'Why were you frightened?' I asked, beginning to understand.

'Because I thought there might be someone just outside.'

'You thought so? How was that?'

'I thought I heard footsteps on the landing. That was it. Footsteps! I thought, it could be *him* . . . Then I was gripped by fear – for it would have been frightful if he – oh, I don't want to think about it. – But no one was there – no one. He didn't come home until late in the evening when you had long, long since gone.'

While she was relating this, I felt something tightening within me. And when she had ended, I looked at her as though I were bound to ask her: Who are you? – Involuntarily I turned towards the harbour, where I could see the sails of our boat gleaming, and I thought: How long, how infinitely long ago is it, that we came to this island? I landed here with a woman whom I loved, and now a stranger is walking by my side. I found it impossible to utter even a single word. She hardly noticed; she had linked her arm round mine and took it no doubt for tender silence. But I was thinking about *him*. So he had never told her! She doesn't know, she has never known that he saw her lying at my feet. He crept away from the door, and only later . . . hours later, returned and said nothing to her! And all these years he has lived on by her side, without betraying himself by so much as a word! He has forgiven her and she has been unaware of it!

We had arrived near the church; it lay before us scarcely ten yards away. Here a steep path turned off, which must lead down to the village within a few minutes. I set out along it. She followed me.

'Give me your hand,' she said, 'I'm going to slip.' I gave it to her without turning round. 'What's the matter with you,' she asked. I couldn't answer and merely gave her hand a squeeze, which seemed to reassure her. Then, just for something to say, I remarked: 'What a pity, we could have visited the church.' – She laughed: 'We passed by it without noticing!'

'Do you want to go back?' I asked.

'Oh no, I'm looking forward to being on the boat again soon. One day I'd like us to go sailing like this alone together, without that man.'

'I can't sail.'

'Oh,' she said and paused, as though something had occurred to her that she did not want to say. I didn't ask. Soon we were on the jetty. The boat was waiting. The children who had greeted us on our arrival were there again. They stared at us with large blue eyes. We sailed off. The sea had become calmer; when one closed one's eyes, one scarcely noticed that one was in motion.

'I want you to lie at my feet,' said Friederike, and I stretched out on the bottom of the boat and laid my head in Friederike's lap. I was glad I did not have to look her in the face. She talked, and to me the sound of her voice seemed to come from a great way off. I understood everything and yet was able to pursue my own thoughts at the same time.

I shuddered as I looked at her.

'This evening we'll go out on the sea together,' she said. Something eerie seemed to have come over her.

'Out on the sea this evening,' she repeated slowly, 'in a rowing-boat. You can row, can't you?'

'Yes,' I said. I shuddered at the profound forgiveness that silently enveloped her, without her knowing.

She talked on. 'We will let ourselves be swept out to sea – and we will be alone. – Why aren't you saying anything?' she asked.

'I am happy,' I said.

I shivered at the silent destiny that had been hers for so many years, without her being aware of it.

We glided on.

For a moment the thought crossed my mind: Tell her. Remove this uncanny aura from her; then she will again be a woman to you like any other, and you will desire her. But I couldn't do it. – We moored the boat.

I leaped out and helped her disembark.

'My boy will be pining for me by now. I must hurry. Leave me alone now.'

There was quite a crowd on the esplanade; I noticed a few people watching us.

'And this evening,' she said, 'about nine I'll be . . . but what's the matter?'

'I'm very happy,' I said.

'This evening,' she said, 'at nine o'clock I'll be here on the esplanade, I'll be with you. – See you soon!'

And she hurried off.

'See you soon!' I said too and remained standing there. – But I shall never see her again.

As I write these lines, I am already far away – further with every second; I am writing in the compartment of a train that left Copenhagen an hour ago. It is just nine. At this moment she is standing on the sea-front waiting for me. When I close my eyes, I see the figure before me. But it is not a woman strolling to and fro along the shore in the twilight – it is a shadow gliding up and down.

Dead Men Tell No Tales

He couldn't bear sitting idly in the carriage any longer, so he got out and strode up and down. It was already dark; the few street lights in this quiet side-street flickered, swaying to and fro in the wind. It had stopped raining; the pavements were almost dry; but the unpaved roads were still damp, and water had gathered in little puddles here and there.

It's strange, thought Franz, how here, a hundred yards from the Praterstrasse, one could easily imagine oneself in some small Hungarian town. Anyhow, here we should at least be safe: she certainly won't meet any of her dreaded acquaintances out here.

He looked at his watch . . . Seven – and completely dark already. Autumn is here early this year. And this confounded storm as well!

He turned up his collar and walked up and down more briskly. 'Another half an hour,' he said to himself, 'and I can go. Ah, I almost wish things had come to a head already.' He stopped at the corner; from here he had a view along both the streets down which she might come.

Yes, she's sure to come today, he thought as he held on to his hat, which was threatening to blow away. Friday – the Professorial Board meeting – so she'll be able to risk slipping out and even staying a little longer . . . He could hear the jingling of a horse-drawn tram; then the bell from the nearby St Nepomuk Church began to toll. The street was becoming busier. More people walked past him – mainly, he thought, employees from the shops which closed at seven. They were all walking briskly, battling as it were against the storm, which made progress more difficult. No one took any notice of him; only the occasional shopgirl glanced up at him curiously. Suddenly he caught sight of a familiar figure rapidly approaching. He hurried towards her. Without a carriage? he thought. Can it be her?

She it was; and as she became aware of him, she quickened her pace.

'You've come on foot?' he said.

'I dismissed the carriage at the Carltheater. I had the impression I'd driven with the same coachman once before.'

A gentleman walking past them glanced fleetingly at the lady. The young man eyed him sharply, almost menacingly, and the gentleman hurried on. The lady stared after him. 'Who was that,' she asked anxiously.

'I don't know. But rest assured, there are none of your acquaintances round here. Well, come on, hurry; let's get in.'

'Is this your carriage?'

'Yes.'

'An open one?'

'An hour ago it was still fine.'

They hurried across and the young woman got in.

'Coachman!' shouted the young man.

'Where is he?' asked the young woman.

Franz looked about. 'This is unbelievable,' he exclaimed, 'I can't see the fellow anywhere.'

'Oh my God,' she cried softly.

'Wait a moment, dearest; he's sure to be here somewhere.'

The young man opened the door into the little tavern; the coachman was sitting at a table with a few other people; hastily he got to his feet.

'Coming at once, Sir,' he said, finishing off his glass of wine as he stood up.

'Whatever do you think you're doing?'

'So please Your Honour, I'm all set to go.'

Reeling a little, he hurried over to the horses. 'Where are we off to then, Your Honour?'

'Prater – the Amusement House.'

The young man got in. The young woman leaned back, concealing herself completely, almost cowering in the corner beneath the raised hood.

Franz took both her hands. She didn't stir. 'Won't you at least say good evening to me?'

'Please leave me alone a minute, I'm still quite breathless.'

The young man leaned back in his own corner. They both remained silent for a while. The coach had turned into the Praterstrasse, drove on past the Tegetthoff Monument, and in a few seconds was flying down the broad dark Praterallee. And now Emma suddenly flung both arms round her beloved. He gently drew back her veil, which still separated him from her lips, and kissed her.

'Are we really together again at last?' she said.

'Do you realise how long it's been since we saw each other?' he exclaimed.

'Since Sunday.'

'Yes, and even then only at a distance.'

'How do you mean? You were at our house!'

'Exactly . . . at your house! Look, things just can't go on like this. I am not going to come to your house ever again. But what's the matter now?'

'A coach just drove past us.'

'My dear girl, people who go out for a drive in the Prater these days really aren't going to worry about us.'

'That may be true. But someone could still glance across and see us.'

'They couldn't possibly recognise anyone.'

'Please let's drive on somewhere else.'

'As you wish.'

He called out to the coachman, who seemed however not to hear. So he leaned forward and shook him. The coachman turned round.

'We want to turn back. And why are you lashing the horses like that? We're not in any hurry, do you hear? We're going to . . . you know, the avenue that leads out to the Reichsbrücke.'

'To the Reichsbrücke?'

'Yes, but don't race along like this, there's no need for it at all.'

'Begging your pardon, Sir, it's the storm what's driving the horses a bit wild.'

'Yes, of course, the storm.' Franz sat back again.

The coachman turned the horses. They drove back.

'Why didn't I see you yesterday?' she asked.

'How could I possibly have managed it?'

'I thought you were invited to my sister's too.'

'Was I?'

'Why weren't you there?'

'Because I can't stand being with you in the presence of other people. Never again.'

She shrugged her shoulders.

'Where are we?' she asked.

They drove under the railway bridge into the Reichsstrasse.

'This is the way out to the Danube,' said Franz, 'we are on the road to the Reichsbrücke . . . No acquaintances out here!' he added mockingly.

'The coach is jolting terribly.'

'Yes, but we'll soon be back again on the paved road.'

'Why is he driving in this zig-zag way?'

'It just seems like it to you.'

But he too found that the coach was throwing them about more violently than necessary. He didn't want to say anything though, so as not to add to her anxiety.

'I have some serious matters to discuss with you today, Emma.'

'Then you'd better start soon, because I have to be home by nine.'

'Everything can be decided in a word.'

'God, what's happening? . . .' she cried. The carriage had got stuck in a tramline, and now, as the coachman tried to steer out of it, veered so sharply that it almost overturned. Franz seized the coachman by his cape. 'Pull up,' he shouted to him. 'You're drunk.'

With an effort the coachman brought the horses to a halt. 'But Sir . . .'

'Come, Emma, let's get out here.'

'But where are we?'

'At the bridge already. It's not so stormy now. Let's walk a little. We can't talk properly while we're being driven.'

Emma lowered her veil and followed him.

'You call this not so stormy?' she shouted, a gust of wind buffeting her as she alighted.

He put her arm in his. 'Follow us,' he shouted to the coachman.

They walked on ahead. As they proceeded up the bridge's gradual incline they said nothing; and when they could both hear the water rushing beneath them, they stood still for a while. Profound darkness lay all about them. The broad grey river stretched away towards uncertain margins, and in the distance they could see red lights that seemed to hover over the water in which they were reflected. From the bank the pair had just left, glittering patterns of light played across the water; on the other side, it was as though the river had got lost amid the pitch-black meadows. At this point there was a rumbling of distant thunder, which seemed to be coming nearer; involuntarily the couple gazed in the direction of the shimmering red lights; trams with brightly lit windows rolled along between the iron arches of the bridge which seemed suddenly to loom up out of the night and immediately sink back again. The thunder gradually subsided and all became quiet: only the wind still came in sudden gusts.

After a long silence Franz said, 'Perhaps we ought to go?'

'Yes,' replied Emma softly.

'Yes, let's go,' said Franz excitedly, 'I mean, go away for good . . .'

'But you know that's impossible.'

'Because we are cowards, Emma; that's the only reason it's impossible.'

'But what about my child?'

'He would let you have him, I'm quite sure.'

'And how would we go about it?' she asked softly. 'Just run away by night through mist and rain?'

'No, not at all. All you have to do is simply tell him that you cannot live with him any longer because you belong to someone else.'

'Are you in your right mind, Franz?'

'If you wish, I'll even spare you that – I'll tell him myself.'

'Franz, you will do nothing of the sort.'

He tried to look at her; but in the darkness all he could make out was that she had raised her head and turned towards him.

He remained silent for a while. Then he said calmly, 'Don't worry, I won't.'

They were approaching the far bank.

'Can you hear anything?' she said. 'What's that noise?'

'It's coming from over there,' he said.

Slowly the rattling drew near out of the darkness; a little red light swayed towards them; soon they saw that it came from a small lamp attached to the front shaft of a farm cart, but they could not see whether the cart was laden and whether there were people on it. Close behind came two more similar carts. On the last of these they could discern a man in peasant dress, who was just then lighting his pipe. The carts drove past. Then they could again hear nothing but the muffled sound of their *Fiaker*, which slowly trundled after them twenty yards behind. The bridge was now descending gently towards the far bank. They could see the road in front of them running on between the trees into the darkness. Below to right and left of them lay open fields: they peered as into an abyss.

After a long silence Franz said suddenly: 'Well then, this is the last time . . .'

'That what?' asked Emma in a tone of concern.

'That we shall see each other. Stay with him if you must. But I shall bid you adieu.'

'Are you serious?'

'Absolutely.'

'You see how it's always you, not me, who spoils the few hours we have together!'

'Yes, of course, you are right,' said Franz, 'Come, let's drive back.'

She clung to his arm more tightly. 'No,' she said tenderly, 'I don't want to go just yet. I won't let myself be dismissed like this.'

She drew him down to her and gave him a long kiss. 'Where would we end up,' she then asked, 'if we kept on driving along here.'

'It goes all the way to Prague, my love.'

'That might be a bit far,' she said smiling, 'but if you felt like it, we could go out along this road a little further.' She pointed into the dark.

'Hey, coachman!' cried Franz. There was no response.

'Stop, will you!' he shouted.

The carriage kept on going. Franz ran after him. Then he saw that the coachman was asleep. After much ado Franz managed to wake him. 'We want to drive on a little further – straight ahead, do you understand?'

'Right you are, Your Honour . . .'

Emma climbed back in, followed by Franz. The coachman applied the whip and as if maddened, the horses flew along the softened road. But inside the coach, rocked to and fro, the couple held one another in a close embrace.

'Isn't this rather nice too?' whispered Emma very close to his lips.

At that same moment the coach suddenly seemed to be flying through the air: Emma felt herself flung forward, tried to hold on to something, but found herself grasping at thin air; she felt as if she were spinning round at an insane speed, so that she was forced to close her eyes – then she found herself lying on the ground, and an immense weight of silence overwhelmed her, as though she were remote from the world and totally alone. She heard various confused noises: the sound of horses' hooves beating the ground close by, a soft moaning; but she could see nothing. An insane fear gripped her; she screamed; when she realised she could not hear her own scream, her terror increased. Then she knew exactly what had happened: the coach had hit something, perhaps one of the milestones, had turned over, and they had been flung out. Where is *he*? was her next thought. She called out to him by name. And now at last she could hear herself calling – very faintly, it was true, but she could distinctly hear herself. There was no answer. She tried to raise herself. She managed to sit up on the ground, and when she reached out with her hands she felt a human body next to her. And now, too, her eyes began to penetrate the darkness. Franz was lying beside her completely motionless. With her outstretched hand she touched his face: she could feel something moist and warm running down it. She caught her breath. Blood . . .? What had happened? Franz must be injured and unconscious. And the coachman – where was he? She called out to him. No answer. She was still sitting on the ground. There's nothing wrong with me, she thought, although she felt pain in every limb. What am I to do, what am I to do . . . it doesn't seem possible that nothing should be wrong with me at all. 'Franz!' she cried. A voice answered from very close at hand: 'Where are you, Fräulein, where's the worthy gentleman? Are you all right? Wait Fräulein – I'll light the lamp, then we can see something; don't know what's got into the horses today. I'm not to blame, upon my word . . . confounded horses ran into the haystack.'

Emma had by now recovered herself completely, even though all her limbs were aching, and the fact that nothing had happened to the coachman made her feel a little calmer. She heard the man opening the shutter of the lantern and striking matches. Anxiously she waited for the light. She did not dare touch Franz again as he lay there before her on the ground; when one can't see, everything seems more frightening, she thought; he is sure to have opened his eyes by now – it won't be anything serious.

A glimmer of light appeared to one side. She suddenly saw the carriage, which to her amazement was not lying on the ground but simply leaning over at an angle to the ditch, as though a wheel were broken. The horses were standing completely still. The lamp approached; she watched the light glide slowly over a milestone, then over the haystack into the ditch; then it crept up Franz's feet, slid over his body and came to rest on his face. The coachman had placed the lamp on the ground next to the prone man's head. Emma got down on her knees, and when she looked at her lover's face, she felt as though her heart would stop beating. It was pale and the eyes were half-open, so that she could see only the whites. From the right temple a trickle of blood ran slowly over the cheek and disappeared under the collar at the neck. The teeth had bitten into the lower lip. 'I simply can't believe it,' said Emma to herself.

The coachman, too, had knelt down and was staring into the prone man's face. Then he took hold of the head with both his hands and raised it. 'What are you doing?' cried Emma in a choking voice, frightened by this head which seemed to rear up of its own accord.

'I'm much afraid, Fräulein, there's been a great mishap.'

'It's not true,' said Emma. 'It can't be true. Has anything happened to you? Or me . . .?'

The coachman let the still man's head sink slowly back again – into the trembling Emma's lap: 'If only someone would come . . . if only those peasants had come by a quarter of an hour later . . .'

'What shall we do?' said Emma with quivering lips.

'Well, Fräulein, if the coach wasn't broken down . . . but the way it's damaged now . . . We'll just have to wait until someone comes along.' He talked on, without Emma's taking in his words; but as he did so, she seemed to come to her senses and recognise what had to be done.

'How far is it to the nearest village?' she asked.

'Not far, Fräulein, Franz Josefsland is just down the road . . . We'd be able to see the houses if it was light, we could be there in five minutes.'

'You go then. I'll stay here; go and fetch help.'

'Well, Fräulein, I almost think it would be wiser if I stayed here with you – it won't be all that long before someone comes along, after all, this is the Reichsstrasse and . . .'

'It will be too late, it could be too late. We need a doctor.'

The coachman looked at the face of the motionless figure, then he looked at Emma and shook his head.

'You can't be sure of that,' cried Emma, 'and neither can I.'

'Yes, Fräulein . . . but where am I to find a doctor out there in Franz Josefsland?'

'From there someone can go into town and –'

'Come to think of it, Fräulein, I believe they might just have a telephone there. Then we could telephone the Ambulance Brigade.'

'Yes, that might be best. Go on then, run, for Heaven's sake! And bring someone back with you . . . And . . . I beseech you, go, why are you still here?'

The coachman peered again into the pale face resting in Emma's lap. 'Ambulance Brigades and doctors are not much use no more.'

'Go! For God's sake! Go!'

'All right, I'm off – just so long as you don't get frightened, Fräulein, alone here in the dark.' And he hurried quickly off down the road. 'Nothing I can do about it, upon my word,' he muttered to himself. 'Who would have thought, on the Reichsstrasse in the middle of the night . . .'

Emma found herself alone with the motionless body on the dark road. What now? she thought. I can't believe it . . . the thought kept going through her head . . . I just can't believe it. Suddenly she had the impression that she could hear breathing beside her. She bent over the pale lips. No, not a sign. The blood on the temples and cheeks seemed to have dried. She stared at the eyes, those sightless eyes, and shuddered. But why won't I believe it – there's no doubt about it . . . this is death. And she was filled with horror. All she felt now was: a dead man. Me and a dead man, the dead man on my lap. And with trembling hands she pushed the head away, so that it fell back onto the ground. And now for the first time a terrible feeling of abandonment came over her. Why had she sent the coachman away? How stupid. What was she supposed to do with the dead man alone here on this country road? Supposing someone should come by . . . Yes, what should she do if anyone came by? How long would she have to wait here? And she looked at the dead man again. But I'm not alone with him, she said to herself: after all the lamp is here. And she felt as though this lamp were something dear and friendly, something she must thank. There was more life in this one little flame than in the whole expanse of night around her; yes, it was almost as though this lamp were a talisman against the pale, terrifying man lying beside her on the ground . . . And she gazed at the light so long that her eyes swam and it began to dance. Suddenly she felt as though she were waking up. She leapt to her feet. This won't do, this will never do, they mustn't find me here with him . . . She felt as though she could actually see herself standing there on the road, the dead man and the lamp at her feet, and pictured herself as a large strange figure looming out of the darkness. What am I waiting for, she asked, and her thoughts raced on . . . What am I waiting for? For help to come? What would they need me for any way? People are bound to come and start asking questions . . . and I . . . what am I supposed to have been doing here? They will want to know who I am. What should I reply? Nothing. I won't say a word when they arrive, I'll simply keep quiet. Not a word . . . they can't force me, after all.

Voices were approaching in the distance.

Already? she thought. She listened anxiously. The voices were coming from the bridge. So these could not be the people that the coachman had gone to fetch. But whoever they were – they would notice the light in any case – and that mustn't happen, then she'd be discovered.

She kicked the lamp over with her foot. It went out. Now she was standing in total darkness. She could see nothing. She could no longer even see him. Only the white haystack still gleamed faintly. The voices were drawing nearer. Her whole body began to tremble. If only she were not discovered here. For Heaven's sake, that's the only thing that matters, everything depends on that and that alone – she will be lost if anyone were to discover that she was the mistress of . . . convulsively she clasps her hands. She prays that the people on the other side of the road will pass by without noticing her. She listens intently: yes, the voices are coming from over there . . . but what are they saying? There are two or perhaps three women. They have noticed the carriage, because they are talking about it, as she can make out from the occasional word. A coach . . . overturned . . . but what else are they saying? She can't make it out. They are walking on . . . they have passed . . . thank God! And now what? Oh, if only she were dead like him. He is almost to be envied: for him everything is over . . . for him there is no more danger and no more fear. Whereas she has every reason to be trembling. She is terrified that she will be found here, that she will be asked who she is . . . That she will have to go to the police, that everyone will get to know about it, that her husband – that her child – ·

And she is quite unaware that she has been standing there so long, as if rooted to the spot . . . Of course she can go, she is of no use to anybody here, and she would only bring unhappiness upon herself. And she takes a first step . . . Carefully . . . she must get across the ditch . . . up one more step – oh, it is quite shallow! – then two more steps and she is in the middle of the road. There she pauses for a moment, gazing straight ahead of her, and can just make out the grey road leading off into the dark. The city must be over there. She can't see any sign of it . . . but she is sure of the direction. She turns round one last time. It is not really as dark as all that. She can distinctly see the coach; the horses too . . . and when she strains her eyes, she can even discern something resembling the outline of a human body lying on the ground. She opens her eyes wide: she feels sure something is trying to hold her back . . . it must be the dead man trying to detain her here, and she shudders at his uncanny power . . . But she wrenches herself free, and only now notices that the ground is sodden, that she has been standing on the slippery road and that the mud has been preventing her from moving. But now she is walking . . . walking faster . . . running . . . away from here . . . back towards the light, towards the noise and bustle, to other human beings. She runs along the road, holding her dress up so as not to trip. The wind is at her back, it feels as though it were driving her on.

She no longer really knows what she is fleeing from. She imagines she must be fleeing the pale man lying there, far behind her, by the ditch . . . but then she reflects that in fact she is trying to escape the living, who will soon be out there looking for her. Whatever will they think? Will they not come after her? But now they won't catch up with her since she will soon have reached the bridge, which will give her a good lead, then the danger will be over. They will not suspect who she is, not a soul will suspect who the woman was who drove down the Reichsstrasse with that man. The coachman does not know her, nor is he likely to recognise her should he see her again later. Nobody will worry about who she was. Whose business was it anyway? It was astute of her not to have waited there, and it was surely not dishonourable. Franz himself would have given his approval. After all she must go home, she has a child, she has a husband, and she would have been lost if they had found her there beside her dead lover. There's the bridge, the road seems lighter too . . . yes, she can already hear the water rushing as before: she has reached the spot where she walked arm in arm with him – but when exactly, when? How many hours ago? It surely can't have been long. But then again, perhaps it was! Perhaps she was unconscious for quite some time, perhaps it is well past midnight, perhaps morning is approaching and already she has been missed at home. No, no, that's just not possible, she is quite certain she never did lose consciousness; indeed she can now remember even more clearly than at the time how she fell out of the coach and was aware of everything immediately. As she runs across the bridge she can hear her footsteps echoing. She does not look round to left or right. Then she notices a figure coming in her direction. She slackens her pace. Who can this be coming towards her? Someone in uniform. She is now walking quite slowly: she must not attract attention. She thinks she can see the man staring hard at her. What if he should question her? She draws closer to him, recognises his uniform as a security guard's, and walks on past him. She hears him come to a halt behind her. With an effort she restrains herself from breaking into a run, since this would look suspicious. She continues to walk at the same pace as before. She can hear the jingling of a horse-drawn tram. It can't be anywhere near midnight. Now she is walking faster again; she hurries on towards the city, whose lights she can already see gleaming at her beneath the railway viaduct at the end of the street, and whose muffled sounds she is sure she can make out already. Just this lonely street to go, and deliverance is at hand. Now she hears the shrill sound of a siren in the distance, becoming shriller and drawing nearer by the minute until finally a vehicle races past. Involuntarily she stops and gazes after it. It belongs to the Ambulance Brigade and she knows full well where it is off to. How quick, she thinks . . . As if by magic. For a moment she feels an impulse to call out after it, as though she simply must go back with it, must return where she has just come from – for a moment she is seized by a sense of shame more terrible than she has ever felt before: she is conscious that she has been cowardly and wicked. But as she hears the rumbling and the siren recede into the distance, a wild elation overcomes her and she hurries on like someone on the point of being rescued. People come towards her, but she is afraid of them no longer – the worst has been overcome. The noise of the city is now more noticeable; it is getting ever brighter up ahead; already she can see the rows of houses on the Praterstrasse, where she imagines herself being greeted by a surging tide of people, permitting her to disappear without a trace. As she approaches a streetlamp, she is now sufficiently composed to consult her watch. It is ten minutes to nine. She holds the watch to her ear – no, it hasn't stopped. And she reflects: I am alive, healthy . . . even my watch is going . . . and he . . . he . . . dead . . . it's fate . . . She feels as though everything has been forgiven her . . . as though there had never been any offence at all on her part. This has been attested, yes it has been attested by events. She hears herself saying these words aloud. But what if fate had determined otherwise? What if she were now lying there in the grave and he had remained alive? He would not have fled, no . . . not he. But then, he is a man. She is a woman – and she has a child and husband to consider. She was right – it was her duty – yes, her duty. She knows quite well that she has not acted as she has out of a sense of duty . . . But she has done the right thing. Instinctively . . . as . . . good people always do. By now she would have been discovered. By now the doctors would have been questioning her. And your husband, dear lady? Oh God! . . . and the newspapers tomorrow – and her family – would have been destroyed for ever, and none of this would have been able to bring him back to life. Yes, that was the point: she would simply have condemned herself to ruination for nothing. – She is now under the railway bridge. Keep going . . . keep going . . . Here is the Tegetthoff Column, where all the streets converge. Today, on this rainy, wind-swept autumn evening, few people are still out of doors, but to her it feels as though the life of the city is surging tumultuously around her; for out there where she has come from was frighteningly quiet. She still has time. She knows that today her husband will not come home before about ten – she can even change her clothes still. Now it occurs to her to look at her dress. She notices with horror that it is caked with dirt. What will she say to the chambermaid? It flashes through her mind that tomorrow the story of the accident will be in all the papers. The story, too, about a woman who was with the coach and then could not be found will be everywhere for people to read, and at this thought she again begins to tremble – *one* careless slip and all her cowardice will have been in vain. But at least she has the key to the apartment with her, so she can unlock the door herself – she must take care not to be heard. Quickly she climbs into a cab, and is on the point of giving her address when it occurs to her that this might not perhaps be wise, and she calls out the name of the first street that comes to mind. Driving down the Praterstrasse, she tries to experience some emotion, but finds it is beyond her; all her feelings are concentrated on a single desire: to be safely at home again. Everything else is a matter of indifference. From the moment she decided to leave the dead man lying on the road alone, she has had to repress everything within her that wanted to lament and grieve for him. At present she can feel nothing beyond anxiety for herself. Not that she is heartless . . . not at all! . . . she knows full well that days lie ahead when she will be in despair; she will even succumb, perhaps; but at present she can feel nothing but a yearning to be sitting at home, dry-eyed and calm, at the same table as her husband and her child. She gazes out of the window. The cab is now driving through the Inner City; here it is all lit up brightly, and quite a lot of people are hurrying past. Suddenly she fancies that perhaps everything she has lived through in the last few hours might not be true. It all seems like a bad dream – hard to grasp as something real and unalterable. In a side street just past the Ringstrasse she has the cab pull up, gets out, quickly turns the corner, and there takes another cab, this time giving her real address. She still feels quite incapable of collecting her thoughts. Where is *he* now? passes through her mind. She closes her eyes, and pictures him lying on a stretcher before her in the ambulance . . . and suddenly she imagines herself sitting beside him as they are driven along. The ambulance begins to rock, and she is terrified that she might be flung out again – and screams aloud. The cab comes to a halt. With a start she realises that she is outside her own front door. Quickly she gets out and hurries through the entrance-hall, treading so softly that the porter behind his little window doesn't even look up, climbs the stairs, gently unlocks the door so nobody will hear . . . through the hall into her room – success! She lights a lamp, quickly throws off her clothes and hides them in a cupboard. They should dry overnight – tomorrow she will brush and clean them herself. Then she washes her face and hands and puts on a dressing-gown.

Outside the doorbell rings. She hears the chamber-maid go to the apartment door and open it. She hears her husband's voice; she hears him put his stick away. She is aware that she must now be strong, otherwise all could still have been in vain. She hurries into the dining-room, contriving to enter at the same moment as her husband.

'Ah, you are home already?' he says.

'Of course,' she replies, 'quite some time ago.'

'They obviously didn't see you come in.' She manages to smile without its appearing forced. But she finds it exhausting to have to smile as well. He kisses her on the forehead.

Her little boy is already at table; he has had a long wait and has fallen asleep. He has propped his book against a plate and his face is resting on the open book. She sits down next to him, while her husband opposite her picks up the newspaper and glances quickly through it. Then he lays it aside and says: 'The others are still in session, they're still deliberating.'

'What about?' she asks.

And he begins to tell her at great length a great deal about the day's proceedings. Emma pretends to be listening and occasionally nods.

But she takes nothing in, she has no idea what he is saying, her mood is that of someone who has had a miraculous escape from some appalling danger . . . All she can think is, 'I am saved, I am home again.' And while her husband talks on and on, she draws her chair closer to her little boy, takes his head and presses it to her bosom. An indescribable tiredness comes over her – she can't control herself, she feels overwhelmed by sleep; her eyes begin to close.

Suddenly a possibility crosses her mind, which she has not considered since that moment when she dragged herself out of the ditch. Supposing he wasn't dead! Supposing he . . . Ah no, there was no room for doubt . . . Those eyes . . . that mouth – and then – not a breath on his lips. But there is such a phenomenon as apparent death. There are cases where even practised eyes can err. And certainly she has no practised eye. What if he is alive, what if he has already regained consciousness, if he has suddenly found himself alone on that country road in the middle of the night . . . if he calls out to her . . . by name . . . eventually becomes worried that she might be injured . . . tells the doctors that a woman was with him and must have been thrown further out. And . . . and . . . well, what then? They will look around for her. The coachman will return from Franz Josefsland with help . . . he will explain . . . but when I left the woman was here . . . and then Franz will realise. Franz will understand at once . . . he knows her so well . . . he will realise that she has run away and a hideous rage will take possession of him, and he will announce her name in order to avenge himself. After all, he is lost . . . and he will be so deeply shaken by her abandonment of him in his final hour alone that he will recklessly declare: it was Emma, my mistress . . . both cowardly and stupid, for is it not the case, good doctors, that if one had appealed to your discretion you would certainly not have insisted on her name. You would have calmly let her go, and so of course would I – she had only to stay put until you arrived. But since she has behaved so wickedly, I shall tell you who she is . . . she is . . . Ah!

'What's wrong with you?' says the Professor very seriously, getting to his feet.

'What . . . how do you mean . . . what's wrong?'

'Well, what's the matter with you?'

'Nothing.' She hugs the boy more tightly to her.

The Professor looks at her long and hard. 'You were beginning to fall asleep you know, and –'

'And?'

'Then suddenly you cried out.'

'. . . Well?'

'As if you were having nightmares in your sleep. Were you dreaming?'

'I don't know. I really have no idea.'

And in the hall-mirror opposite her she catches sight of a face which is smiling hideously, with distorted features. She knows it is her own, and yet she shudders at it . . . She watches it becoming rigid; she cannot move her mouth; she knows that as long as she lives that smile will play about her lips. And she attempts to scream. Then she feels two hands being laid on her shoulders, and sees her husband thrust his face between her face and that in the mirror; questioning and menacing, his eyes sink deep into her own. She knows that if she does not survive this final test, then all is lost. She feels her strength returning; she regains control of her limbs and features; she can command them freely, at least for now; but she must take advantage of the moment lest it pass; so she reaches out with both hands to her husband, whose own hands are still resting on her shoulders, draws him to her, and looks at him brightly and tenderly.

And as she feels her husband's lips upon her forehead, she thinks: why of course . . . it's only a bad dream. He will never tell anyone, he will never seek revenge, never . . . he is dead . . . he is quite definitely dead . . . and dead men tell no tales.

'Why do you say that?' she suddenly hears her husband's voice asking. She recoils in horror. 'What did I say, then?' It occurs to her that she must suddenly have blurted everything out loud . . . that she must have told the whole story of her evening here at table . . . and cringing before his horrified gaze she again asks: 'What did I say?'

'Dead men tell no tales,' repeated her husband very slowly.

'Yes . . .' she says, 'yes . . .'

And in his eyes she discerns that she can no longer hide anything from him, and for a long time the two look steadily at one another. 'Put the boy to bed,' he then says to her; 'I think you have something more to tell me . . .'

'Yes,' she says.

And she knows that in a moment she will tell the whole truth to this man whom she has been betraying for years.

And as she walks slowly through the door with her little boy, still conscious of her husband's eyes upon her, a great tranquillity comes over her, as though all will once again be well . . .

Lieutenant Gustl

How much longer is this going to last? I'll just glance at my watch . . . not quite the done thing, perhaps, at such a highbrow concert. But who will notice? If anybody does, then he must be paying as little attention as I am, so I needn't feel embarrassed . . . Only a quarter to ten? It feels as though I've been sitting through this concert for a good three hours already. I'm just not used to it . . . What are they playing, I wonder? Must have a look at the programme . . . So it's an oratorio! I thought it might be a mass. Things like that really belong in church. The good thing about church is that one can leave at any time. If only I had a corner seat! – Ah well, patience, patience! Even oratorios come to an end! Perhaps it's really beautiful and I'm just not in the mood. But, what is there to put me in the mood. And to think that I came here expecting to be entertained . . . I should have given the ticket to Benedek instead, he enjoys this sort of thing; he even plays the violin himself. But then Kopetzky would have taken offence. After all, it was very kind of him, or at least he meant well. A good fellow, Kopetzky! The only one I can depend on . . . His sister is somewhere up there on the stage. At least a hundred virgins, all dressed in black; how am I supposed to pick her out? It was because she is singing that Kopetzky had the ticket . . . So why didn't he come himself? After all, they sing quite nicely. And it's all very uplifting. Bravo! bravo! . . . I suppose one should clap too. The fellow next to me is clapping like mad. Wonder whether he really enjoyed it all that much? The girl in the box up there is very pretty. Is she looking at me or the man with the blond beard over there? . . . Ah, now we have a solo! Who is it, I wonder? Alto: Fräulein Walker; soprano: Fräulein Michalek . . . it's probably the soprano . . . I haven't been to the opera for ages. I always enjoy going to the opera though, even when the show is boring. Perhaps I'll go again the day after tomorrow, to *La Traviata*. But the day after tomorrow I may be a dead man already! Oh, nonsense, I don't really believe that for a minute. Just you wait, Herr Doktor, you'll laugh on the wrong side of your face for making remarks like that. I'll slice off the tip of your nose . . .

If only I could get a proper look at that girl in the box. I'd like to borrow an opera-glass from the gentleman next to me, but he'd eat me alive if I disturbed his raptures. Where in the choir might Kopetzky's sister be? Wonder if I'll recognise her? I've only met her two or three times, the last time in the Officers' Mess . . . Wonder whether they are all respectable young girls, all hundred of them? Alas! . . . 'In collaboration with the Choral Society!' – Choral Society . . . funny! I always imagined them as something like the Vienna Chorus Girls, that is, even though I knew that they were different! . . . Fond memories! That time at the 'Green Gate' . . . but whatever was her name? Later she sent me a postcard from Belgrade . . . pretty country round there too! – Kopetzky's lucky, sitting in some tavern all this time and smoking his Virginia cigars! . . .

Why does that fellow over there keep looking at me? I think he's seen I'm bored and don't belong here . . . Take my advice and don't stare at me so rudely, or you'll answer for it later in the foyer! He's already turned the other way! . . . Strange how they always get frightened when I glare at them. 'You have the most beautiful eyes I've ever seen,' Steffi told me recently . . . Oh, Steffi, Steffi, Steffi! It is actually Steffi who's to blame for my having to sit here through hours of lamentation. – All those letters of Steffi's too, calling off our meetings, they're getting on my nerves. How delightful this evening could have been. I'm itching to read Steffi's little note. I've got it with me. But if I take my wallet out, the fellow next to me will eat me alive! – I already know what's in it . . . she can't come because she has to go and dine with 'him' . . . Ah, that was really funny last week when she was with him at the Horticultural Society, and Kopetzky and I were sitting opposite; she kept making eyes at me about our meeting later, and he didn't notice a thing – incredible! I think he must be Jewish! He's with a bank, and then the dark moustache . . . He's also supposed to be a lieutenant in the Reserves! Well, in my regiment he'd never get as far as basic weapons training. When all's said and done, it's amazing that they are still commissioning so many Jews – though they can keep their anti-Semitism! That party at the Mannheimers' recently, where the whole business with the doctor started . . . the Mannheimers themselves are supposed to be Jews too, baptised of course . . . but in their case one would never notice – especially with the wife . . . so fair, and a stunning figure too . . . Very entertaining, all in all. Capital food, splendid cigars . . . Ah well, need one ask who has the money?

Bravo, bravo! Surely it will soon be over now? – Yes, the whole company is rising . . . it all looks splendid – very impressive! – Even an organ? . . . I'm very partial to the organ . . . I enjoyed that – mar-

vellous! It's really true, one should go to concerts much more often
. . . I'll tell Kopetzky how wonderful it was . . . Wonder whether I'll
meet him at the coffee-house today? – Ah, I don't fancy going there;
yesterday really was infuriating. Lost a hundred and sixty guilders at
one sitting – stupid, really! And guess who won the lot? Ballert – the
very man who doesn't need it . . . It's all Ballert's fault that I had to
come to this stupid concert . . . otherwise I could have gone and
played another round today, and perhaps won something back. But
perhaps it's as well I gave my word of honour not to touch cards
again for a whole month. Mama will make a long face again when
she gets my letter! Well, let her go and see my uncle, he's rolling in
money; the few hundred guilders won't make any difference to him.
If I could only persuade him to give me a regular allowance . . . but
no, every time you need a few pennies you have to beg for them. It's
always the same old story: last year the harvest was bad! . . . Wonder
whether I should go down to my uncle's again this summer for a fortnight? Actually one gets bored to death out there . . . But if I could . . .
what was her name . . . It's odd, I can never remember names! . . . Oh
yes, Etelka! . . . She didn't understand a word of German, but that
wasn't necessary . . . We didn't need to talk! . . . Yes, it would be quite
pleasant, fourteen days of country air, and fourteen nights of Etelka,
or someone else . . . But I really ought to spend a week or so with
Papa and Mama again . . . Last Christmas she looked terrible. But by
now she should have got over her indisposition. In her place I'd be
pleased that Papa has taken his retirement. – And Klara is still sure
to find a husband . . . Uncle can give her something . . . Twenty-eight
is not really all that old . . . Steffi is certainly no younger . . . But it's
amazing how *those* women seem to preserve their youthful looks so
much longer. When you think of it, that Maretti recently in *Madame
Sans-Gêne* – she must be thirty-seven at least, and looks . . . Well, I
wouldn't have said no! – Pity she didn't ask me . . .

It's getting hot. Still no end in sight? I'm looking forward to a bit
of fresh air! I'll go for a stroll along the Ringstrasse . . . The order of
the day is: early to bed so as to be fresh for tomorrow afternoon!
Funny how little I think about that, it doesn't worry me at all. The
first time I did get a little agitated. Not that I was afraid; but I was a
bit restive the night before . . . Of course, Lieutenant Bisanz was a
formidable opponent. – And yet nothing happened to me! . . . A year
and a half ago already. How time flies! And if Bisanz didn't do me
any harm, the lawyer certainly will not. And yet, it's precisely these
amateurish fencers who can be the most dangerous. Doschintzky
told me that one fellow, who had never had a sword in his hand

before, only missed cutting him down by a hair; and today Doschintzky is a fencing instructor with the Territorials. Mind you, who knows whether he was quite as skilled at that time . . . The main thing is: keep cool. I don't even feel particularly angry any more, and he certainly had a cheek – incredible! If he hadn't been drinking champagne, he wouldn't have had the gall . . . What insolence! Sure to be a Socialist! The people who manipulate the law are all Socialists these days! What a mob . . . they'd abolish the whole army right away if they had half the chance; but they don't give a thought to who would help them if the Chinese were to invade. Idiots! – One has to make an example of people like that now and then. I was quite right. I'm glad I didn't let him off after that remark. I get absolutely furious every time I think about it. But I behaved impeccably; even the Colonel said it was all absolutely correct. The whole affair should stand me in good stead. I know there are those who would have let the matter drop. Müller of course would have looked at it 'objectively' or something. Plenty of people are fooled by this so-called objectivity . . . 'Lieutenant!' . . . even the way he said 'Lieutenant' was impertinent . . . 'You will surely admit . . .' – How did we get onto the whole subject? How did I get involved in a discussion with the Socialist? How did it all start? . . . As I recall, the dark woman I had escorted to the bar was there too . . . and then that young man who paints those hunting scenes, what's his name now? . . . Upon my word, he was the one to blame for the whole thing! He had been talking about army manoeuvres, and it was then that this lawyer joined us and said something or other about playing at soldiers that annoyed me – but I didn't get a chance to have my say . . . Yes, and then the conversation turned to the Cadet Schools . . . yes, that's it . . . and I told them about some patriotic rally . . . and then the lawyer said – not immediately, but following on from what I'd said about the rally – 'Lieutenant, you will surely admit that not all your comrades joined the army solely to defend the Empire!' What impudence! For a man like that to have the affrontery to say that to an officer! I wish I could remember what I answered! . . . Oh yes, something about people not meddling in matters they don't understand . . . Yes, that's right . . . and then there was somebody there who tried to smooth it all over, an older gentleman with a cold in the nose . . . but I was much too angry. It was absolutely clear from the tone in which the lawyer said it that he meant me personally. He might as well have gone on to say that they threw me out of high school and that's why I ended up in the Cadet School. People like that don't understand us military types, they're too stupid . . . When I remember the first time

I wore my uniform, well, not everyone experiences a thrill like that
. . . Last year on manoeuvres – I'd have given a good deal for things
suddenly to have begun in earnest . . . And Mirovic told me he felt
exactly the same way. And then, when His Highness inspected the
troops on horseback, and the Colonel addressed us – well, a fellow
would have to be a real lout for his heart not to beat faster . . . And
then this pen-pusher comes along, who has never done anything in
his life but pore over his books, and feels at liberty to make insolent
remarks! . . . Ah, just you wait, my good fellow, we'll go on until you
can't fight back . . . I can assure you, you won't be able to fight
another stroke . . .

Now what's happening? Surely it must be over soon? . . . 'Ye, his
angels, praise the Lord' . . . – Yes, that sounds like the final chorus . . .
Marvellous, there's no denying it, marvellous! – I'd completely forgotten about the girl in the box who started flirting with me earlier.
Where is she, now? . . . Must have left already . . . The one over there
seems rather nice too . . . Stupid not to have an opera-glass with me!
Brunnthaler is really clever, he always leaves his opera-glass with the
cashier in the coffee-house where it's safe and sound . . . If only the
little lady in front of me would turn round just *once!* Sitting through it
all as good as gold. The woman next to her must be her Mama. –
Wonder whether I shouldn't think seriously about getting married?
Willy was no older than I am now when he took the plunge. Something to be said for having a pretty little woman ready to hand at
home . . . What a bore that today of all days Steffi should have no
time! At least if I knew where she was, I could go and sit opposite her
again. But I'd be in a pretty pickle if he were to catch her out, because
then *I'd* have her round my neck . . . When I think how much Fliess's
affair with the Winterfeld woman is costing him! And yet she betrays
him left and right. That will all end in disaster one day . . . Bravo,
bravo! Over, finally! . . . Good to be able to stand up and move about
again . . . If one's lucky! How much longer is this fellow going to take
putting his opera-glass in its case?

'Excuse me, excuse me, mind letting me out?'

What a crush. Better let people through . . . Elegant figure . . .
wonder if they are real diamonds? . . . She is really rather nice . . .
What a look she gave me! . . . Yes indeed, dear lady, I'd be delighted
. . . Oh, the nose! – a Jewess . . . There's another . . . It's really amazing, half of them are Jews . . . one can't even enjoy an oratorio in
peace these days . . . Well, better join the queue . . . What's the idiot
behind me pushing for? I'll soon teach him a lesson . . . Ah, an older
gentleman! . . . Who's that greeting me over there? . . . Good evening

to you! Good evening! I've no idea who that was . . . the easiest thing
would be to go to Leidinger's for supper . . . or should I go to the Horticultural Society: perhaps Steffi will be there as well? Why didn't she
write and tell me where she was going with him? She wouldn't have
known herself beforehand. Terrible, really, such a dependent existence . . . Poor thing! – Ah, here's the exit . . . Well, now she really is
a beauty. All alone? She's smiling at me. That's an idea, I'll follow
her! . . . Now down the stairs . . . Oh, the Major from the Ninety-Fifth
. . . Very courteous, the way he thanked me . . . So I wasn't the only
officer attending . . . But where's the pretty girl? Ah, there she is . . .
standing by the balustrade . . . And now for the cloakroom. Mustn't
let the little creature get away . . . She's found someone already!
What a miserable hussy! She lets herself be picked up by another
man and now she smiles at me! – None of them are any good . . . My
God, what a crowd outside the cloakroom! . . . Better wait a little . . .
There! Is the idiot going to take my counter? . . .

'Excuse me, number two hundred and twenty-four! It's over there!
What's wrong with your eyes? It's over there! Well, thank God for
that! Here's my counter.' This fat fellow is blocking the whole cloak-
room.

'My coat, please! . . .'

'Patience, patience! . . .'

What did the fellow say?

'Just have a little patience!'

I can't let that one go . . . 'Move over, there!'

'You're not going to lose it.'

What did he say? He actually said that to me? That's really a bit
much. I won't put up with it! 'You just be quiet!'

'What was that?'

And in that tone of voice as well? This really is the limit!

'Stop shoving!'

'Shut your mouth!' I shouldn't have said that, it was a bit crass . . .
Well, it's done now!

'What did you say?'

Now he's turning round . . . But I know this fellow! – Good God,
it's the master-baker who is one of the regulars at the coffee-house.
What's he doing here? No doubt he has a daughter in the Choral
Society or something . . . But what's happening? What's he up to? I
do believe . . . yes, by God, he's grabbed my sword-hilt . . . Is the fellow mad? . . . You, Sir . . .'

'You, Lieutenant, just calm down!'

What did he say? My God, did anybody hear? No, he spoke quite softly . . . But why won't he let go of my sword? Lord almighty . . . He must be raving mad . . . I can't get his hand off the hilt . . . Must avoid a scandal! . . . Could the Major be behind me? Has anybody noticed him holding the hilt of my sword? But he's talking to me. What's he saying?

'Listen, Lieutenant, if you make the slightest fuss, I'll draw your sword out of its sheath, break it and send the pieces to your regimental commander. Do you understand, you young fool?'

What did he say? I must be dreaming. Is he really talking to me? I ought to reply . . . But the fellow is serious – he's really going to draw my sword. My God – he's actually doing so! . . . I can already feel him tugging at it. What's he saying? For God's sake, there must be no scandal. What's he saying now?

'But I don't want to ruin your career . . . So, behave yourself! . . . No need to worry, nobody has heard . . . everything's all right . . . there we are! And so that nobody will think that we've been quarrelling, I shall now be very courteous to you. Good evening, Lieutenant, it has been a pleasure.'

My God, have I been dreaming? . . . Did he really say all that? . . . Where's he gone? . . . There he goes . . . I ought to draw my sword and cut him down – My God, can anyone have overheard? . . . No, he spoke very softly, right into my ear . . . So why don't I go over and crack his skull open? . . . No, it wouldn't do, it wouldn't do . . . I should have done so at once . . . Whyever didn't I do so at once then? . . . Well, I couldn't . . . he wouldn't let go of the hilt; and he's ten times as strong as I am . . . If I'd said another word, he really would have broken my sword . . . I must be thankful that he didn't speak out loud! If anyone had heard, I'd have been obliged to shoot myself there and then . . . Perhaps it really was a dream . . . Why is the man by the pillar over there looking at me like that? – did he hear anything perhaps? . . . I'll go and ask him . . . Ask him? – I must be mad! – How do I look? – Is there anything they'd notice? – I must be deathly pale. – Where is the dog? . . . I'll have to kill him! . . . He's disappeared . . . Place is already quite empty . . . Where's my coat? . . . I'm already wearing it . . . Didn't even notice . . . Who was it gave me a hand? . . . Ah, the attendant over there: I must tip him . . . there! . . . But what's it all about? Did it really happen? Did someone really talk to me like that? Did someone really call me a 'young fool'? And I failed to strike him on the spot? . . . But there was nothing I could do . . . after all, he had a fist of iron . . . I just stood there as if nailed to the floor . . . No, I must have taken leave of my senses, otherwise I could have used my other hand . . . But then he would have drawn my sword and broken it, and that would have been the end – that would have been the end of everything! And afterwards, when he was leaving, it was too late . . . I couldn't have run my sword through him from behind.

What, I'm already in the street? How did I manage to get out of there? – How cool it is . . . ah, the breeze feels good . . . Who's that over there? Why are they looking across at me? Could they possibly have overheard anything? . . . No, no one could have heard a thing . . . I'm sure of it because immediately after, I looked round! No one was paying any attention to me, no one had noticed anything . . . But he did say it, even if no one heard it; he said it nonetheless! And I just stood there and put up with it, as if someone had knocked me on the head! . . . But there was nothing I could say, nothing I could do; the only thing to do was to keep calm, keep calm! . . . it's frightful, it's intolerable; I'll kill him when I meet him! . . . Fancy anyone saying that to me! 'Young fool', a dog like him saying that to me! And to cap it all, he knows me . . . Oh, my God, he knows me, he knows who I am! . . . He can tell everybody what he said to me! . . . No, no, he won't do that, otherwise he wouldn't have spoken so softly . . . he just wanted me to hear it! . . . But there's no guarantee that sooner or later he won't mention it to someone – to his wife, his daughter, or some acquaintance in the coffee-house! Good God, I'll be seeing him again tomorrow! When I enter the coffee-house tomorrow, he'll be sitting there as usual playing taroc with Herr Schlesinger and the florist . . . No, no, that won't do, that won't do at all . . . I'll cut him to pieces when I see him. No, no, I can't do that . . . I should have done it then and there! If only it had been possible! I shall go to the Colonel and report the matter to him . . . yes, straight to the Colonel . . . The Colonel is always very friendly – and I shall report to him: Sir, he gripped my sword by the hilt and wouldn't let it go; I was effectively disarmed . . . – And what will the Colonel say? – I know what he will say. There is no other option but dishonourable discharge! . . . Are those volunteer troops over there? How disgusting, at night they look like officers . . . Yes, they are saluting! – What if they knew – what if they knew! . . . – There's the Café Hochleitner . . . Sure to be a few fellow officers inside . . . perhaps even somebody that I know . . . What if I were to tell the first fellow I run into the whole story, but as if it had happened to somebody else? . . . I really am quite mad already . . . Why am I wandering about like this? What am I doing on the street? – Where am I trying to get to? Didn't I intend to go to Leidinger's? Haha, and sit down among a whole crowd of people . . . I'm sure everyone would notice . . . Yes, something would be bound to happen . . . But what on earth could happen? . . . Nothing, absolutely nothing – no one heard anything . . . no one knows anything . . . so far, no one knows anything at all . . . What if I were now to go to his apartment and beg him to tell no one? . . . – I'd rather put a bullet through my head at once than that! . . . That would be the best solution! . . . The best? The best? But there's absolutely no other option . . . none at all . . . If I were to ask the Colonel, or Kopetzky – or Blany – or Friedmair – they would all say: you have no other choice! . . . What if I were to have a word with Kopetzky? . . . Yes, that would be the most sensible idea . . . about tomorrow . . . Yes, of course – about tomorrow . . . I'm supposed to fight a duel at four o'clock tomorrow . . . out at the Cavalry regimental barracks . . . and yet I'm not allowed to any more, I am no longer fit to render satisfaction . . . Nonsense! Nonsense! Nobody knows about it, nobody at all! – There are plenty of people about whom worse things have happened to than me . . . All those stories they told about Deckener and his exchange of fire with Rederow . . . in that case the Court of Honour decided that the duel could take place . . . But how would the Court of Honour decide in my case? – 'Young fool – young fool' . . . and I just stood there! Heavens above, it makes no difference whether anybody else knows! . . . *I* know, that's what counts! *I* feel I'm not the same person that I was an hour ago. *I* know I'm not fit to give satisfaction, and that's why I must shoot myself . . . otherwise for the rest of my life I would never have another moment's peace . . . I would always be living in fear that someone would find out about it somehow . . . and that one day someone would confront me with what occurred this evening! – How happy I was an hour ago . . . Kopetzky *would* have to give me the concert ticket, and Steffi, the slut, *would* go and stand me up! – One's fate can turn on things like that . . . This afternoon everything was still fine and dandy, and now I am a doomed man and have to shoot myself . . . Why am I running like this? Nothing's going to run away from me . . . What time is the clock striking? . . . 1, 2, 3, 4, 5, 6, 7, 8, 9, 10, 11 . . . eleven, eleven . . . I really ought to go and have some supper! After all, I must go somewhere . . . I could go and sit in some restaurant where no one knows me – after all, a man must eat, even if he is to shoot himself straight after . . . Haha, death is certainly no child's play . . . who was it said that recently? Oh, what does it matter . . .

I wonder who would be the more upset? . . . Mama or Steffi? . . . Steffi . . . My God, Steffi . . . she can't afford to let anybody notice, otherwise 'he' will show her the door . . . poor thing! No one in the regiment would have a clue why I had done it . . . they would all be racking their brains: whatever made Gustl commit suicide? – It would never occur to anyone that I had to shoot myself because of a miserable baker, a common fellow like that, who just happened to have stronger fists . . . it's just too stupid, too stupid for words! – And all because of this, a fine-looking young fellow like me has to . . . Afterwards everyone is bound to say: he really didn't have to do it over a stupid thing like that; it's such a shame! . . . But if I were to ask anyone right now, they would all give me the same answer . . . the same as I'd give, if I were to ask myself . . . devil take it, we are utterly defenceless against these civilians . . . People think we are better off because we wear a sword . . . but if ever one of us makes use of it, all hell breaks loose, as though we were born murderers one and all . . . No doubt it would be in the papers too: 'Suicide of a young officer . . .' What are the catch-phrases? . . . 'Motive shrouded in mystery . . .' – Haha! . . . 'The mourners at his coffin were . . .' – But of course it's true . . . I keep feeling I'm telling myself stories . . . but it's true . . . I have to commit suicide, there is no other choice – I cannot risk Kopetzky and Blany returning their mandate tomorrow and declaring: We cannot be your seconds! . . . I'd be stupid to give them the chance . . . How could a fellow like me just stand there and let himself be called a young fool! . . . by tomorrow everyone will know . . . How stupid of me to imagine for a moment that with a person like that it wouldn't go any further . . . he'll talk about it everywhere . . . his wife will know by now already . . . tomorrow the whole coffee-house will know . . . the waiters . . . Mr Schlesinger – the lady at the cash-register – And even if he has promised not to mention it, the day after tomorrow he is sure to let it out . . . and if not, then in a week's time . . . And unless he should have a stroke today, then I know . . . I just know . . . and I'm not the man to go on wearing my uniform and sword with a curse like that hanging over me! . . . So, it must be done, and there's an end of it! What's there to it anyway? – Tomorrow afternoon the lawyer may kill me with his sword . . . that sort of thing has been known to happen . . . Bauer, poor chap, caught a brain fever and was dead within three days . . . and Brenitsch fell from his horse and broke his neck . . . no, when all is said and done: there is no way out – not for me, at least, not for me! – No doubt there are men who would take it all more lightly . . . God, the things people will stoop to! Ringheimer had his ears boxed by a butcher who caught him with his wife, resigned his commission, and now has married and lives somewhere in the country . . . Astonishing that there are women who will marry a man like that! . . . – I swear, I'd refuse to shake hands with him if he came back to Vienna . . . So there you have it, Gustl: your life is over, finished, dust to dust! . . . Now I see that, the whole

thing is utterly straightforward . . . Indeed, I'm actually quite calm
. . . Of course I always knew that in the event I would be completely
calm . . . but I never imagined that it could come to this . . . that I
would have to kill myself because of such a . . . Perhaps I didn't
understand him properly . . . perhaps after all he said something
completely different . . . I was quite stupefied by all the singing and
the heat . . . could I have been temporarily insane and none of it be
true? . . . Not true, ha ha, not true! – I can still hear it . . . it's still ringing in my ears . . . and in my fingers I can still feel how I tried to get
his hand off my sword . . . He's a brawny fellow, a real Hercules . . .
Though I'm no weakling myself . . . Franziski is the only one in the
regiment stronger than me . . .

    The Aspernbrücke . . . How much further am I going? – If I keep
on like this, I'll be in Kagran by midnight . . . Haha! – My God, how
happy we were last September when we marched into Kagran. Only
two hours more, and then Vienna . . . I was dead tired when we
arrived . . . I slept like a log all afternoon, and by the evening we were
at Ronacher's . . . Kopetzky, Ladinser and . . . who else was with us?
That's right, the fellow from the Volunteers who told us those Jewish
anecdotes during the march . . .

    Sometimes they're quite nice chaps, these one-year Volunteers . . .
but they should only be given 'acting' status – otherwise, where's the
sense in it? We regulars have to slog on for years, while one of those
fellows can serve one year and finish up with the same rank . . . it's
sheer injustice! – But what do I care about all that now? Why should
I be bothered with such things? – A private in the Catering Corps is
more important now than I am . . . I'm no longer even of this world
. . . I'm done for . . . Honour lost, all's lost! . . . There's nothing left for
me to do but to load my revolver and . . . Gustl, Gustl, it seems to me
you still really don't believe it? Just come to your senses . . . there's no
alternative . . . however much you rack your brains, there's no alternative! It's all a matter of behaving decently, in one's final hour, like
an officer and a gentleman, so that the Colonel will say: he was a fine
fellow, we will hold him in fond remembrance! How many platoons
turn out for a lieutenant's funeral? . . . I ought to know that . . . Haha!
even if the whole battalion or the entire garrison turns out and fires a
twenty-gun salute, even that'll never wake me! – This is the coffee-
house where I sat outside with Herr von Engel once last summer,
after the army steeplechase . . . Funny, I've never seen the man again
since then . . . Wonder why he had his left eye bandaged? I always
wanted to ask him, but it wouldn't have been proper . . . There go
two artillerymen, they probably think I'm following that woman . . .

Must get a look at her . . . Oh, hideous! – I'd like to know how one like that manages to earn a living . . . I'd rather . . . Although the devil will eat flies when desperate . . . that time in Przemysl – afterwards I was so disgusted I thought I'd never touch a woman again . . . That was a grim time up there in Galicia . . . a real stroke of luck our returning to Vienna. Bokorny is still out there in Sambor, and could well stay there growing old and grey for another ten years . . . But if I'd stayed out there, what happened today would never have happened to me . . . and I'd rather grow old and grey in Galicia than . . . than what? than what? – what's the matter with me? – Am I mad, the way I keep forgetting? – My God, I seem to be forgetting every other minute . . . whoever heard of anyone about to put a bullet through his head in a few hours, mulling over all sorts of things that don't concern him any longer? My God, it's almost as though I were drunk! Haha! How absurd! Drunk on death! Drunk on suicide! I'm even making jokes, would you believe it! Yes, I'm in quite a cheerful mood – must be something I was born with . . . Indeed, if I were to tell anyone, he wouldn't believe me . . . – I think that if I had the thing with me . . . I'd squeeze the trigger now – it would all be over in one second . . . Not everyone's that fortunate – people sometimes suffer for months. My poor cousin, she was bed-ridden for two years, couldn't move, had the most hideous pains – utter misery! . . . Isn't it better to see to things oneself? It's just a matter of taking care, aiming well, and avoiding disasters like what happened to that Reserve cadet last year. Poor devil, he didn't die but he was left blind . . . Wonder what happened to him? Where is he living now? Terrible to be running around like that – that is: he can't run around but must be led – such a young fellow too, even today he can't be more than twenty . . . in the case of his mistress his aim was rather better . . . she died at once . . . Incredible the things people kill themselves over! How can anyone be jealous? I've never in my life felt anything like that. At this very moment Steffi is sitting at her ease in the Horticultural Society; later she'll go home with 'him' . . . It doesn't mean a thing to me, not a thing! She's well set up – that little bathroom with the red lamp. – The way she came in recently in her green silk dressing-gown . . . I won't see that green dressing-gown again – or Steffi either . . . and I'll never climb those fine broad stairs in the Gusshausstrasse again either . . . And Miss Steffi will go on amusing herself as if nothing had happened . . . she won't even be able to tell anyone that her beloved Gustl committed suicide . . . But at least she'll weep – oh yes, she'll weep all right . . . Indeed, quite a lot of people will be weeping . . . Oh my God, poor Mama! – No, no, I mustn't think about it. – Ah no,

that's absolutely unthinkable . . . Don't start thinking about home,
Gustl, do you understand? – don't even begin to think about it . . .

Well fancy that, here I am in the Prater already . . . in the dead of
night . . . this morning it would never have occurred to me that
tonight I'd be walking in the Prater . . . Wonder what the policeman
over there is thinking? . . . Well, might as well keep walking . . . it's
really quite agreeable . . . Forget about supper and the coffee-house;
the air is pleasant, and it's peaceful . . . very . . . But then I'll soon be
at peace anyhow, as much at peace as I could ever wish. Haha! – but
I'm completely out of breath . . . I've been tearing along like mad . . .
slow down, Gustl, slow down, you won't miss anything, you don't
have anything to do – absolutely nothing at all! – Wonder why I feel
so cold? – It must be all the excitement . . . and then I haven't eaten
anything . . . What's that curious smell? . . . can the blossoms be out
yet? . . . What's the date today? – the 4th of April . . . true, it's rained
a lot these last few days . . . but the trees are still almost completely
bare . . . and how dark it is: gives one the creeps . . . The only time in
my life I've ever been afraid was in a wood once as a small boy . . .
though I wasn't really all that small . . . fourteen or fifteen . . . How
long ago was that? – nine years . . . that's right – at eighteen I was an
'acting' and at twenty a regular lieutenant, and next year I'll be . . .
What will I be next year? What does that mean anyway: next year?
What does next week mean? What does the day after tomorrow
mean? . . . Why are my teeth chattering? Well, let them chatter . . .
Lieutenant, you are now on your own, you don't have to impress anyone . . . and that's the bitter truth . . .

I'll just sit down on the bench here . . . Ah! – how far have I come,
I wonder? – Incredible how dark it is! That coffee-house over there
behind me must be the second one . . . I was there once last summer
too, when our band was giving a concert . . . with Kopetzky and with
Rüttner – and a few others . . . – God, I'm so tired . . . I feel as if I've
just been on a ten-hour route-march . . . Yes, that would be quite
something, to fall asleep here. – Haha! a vagrant lieutenant . . . Well,
I suppose I ought to be going home . . . though what would I do at
home? But then, what am I doing in the Prater? – Ah, what I would
like most is not to have to get up again – just to fall asleep here and
never to wake up again . . . How comfortable that would be. – No,
things are not going to be made comfortable for you, Lieutenant . . .
But in what way and when? . . . I really ought to think the whole matter through properly . . . everything must be considered . . . that's how
it is in life . . . Well now, let's consider . . . but consider what? . . . How
good the air is . . . one ought to go for walks in the Prater at night

more often . . . Yes, that should have occurred to me before, no more Prater and walks in the fresh air now . . . What's the matter with me? – Off with this cap; it feels as though it's pressing on my brain . . . I can't think straight . . . That's better! . . . now pull yourself together, Gustl . . . there are final arrangements to be made. Tomorrow morning everything is going to end . . . tomorrow morning at seven o'clock . . . a beautiful hour, seven o'clock. Haha! – so when school begins at eight it will all be over . . . Kopetzky won't be able to take his classes, he'll be so badly shaken . . . Though perhaps he won't have heard by then . . . after all, it's possible not to hear a thing. They didn't find Max Lippay until the afternoon, and he had shot himself in the morning, and no one had heard anything about it . . . But what do I care whether Kopetzky takes his classes or not? . . . Well then, seven o'clock it is! – Good . . . now, what next? . . . There's really nothing else to be considered. I'll shoot myself in my room, and that'll be the end of it! On Monday, there will be my corpse . . . I know one person who will be very happy, and that's the lawyer . . . Duel cannot take place, due to suicide of one of combatants . . . Wonder what they'll say at Mannheimer's – He won't make much ado over it . . . but the beautiful blonde wife . . . she would have been worth it . . . Yes, I think I might have had a chance with her, if I'd taken myself in hand a little . . . yes, with her it would have been quite different from a wench like Steffi . . . But it would have kept one on one's toes: paying court, sending flowers, talking seriously . . . no question of saying to her: Come and see me in the barracks tomorrow afternoon! . . . Yes, a respectable woman like that would have been really something . . . The wife of the major in Przemysl now, she was hardly what you'd call respectable . . . I could swear to it that Libitzky and Wermutek and even that miserable acting lieutenant had all had her . . . But Mrs Mannheimer . . . yes, that would have been quite different, that would have been a genuine relationship, it might almost have made another person of one – one would have acquired a little polish – been able to respect oneself a little more. – But with me it's always been those common hussies . . . I started so young too – I was still a lad that time when I was on my first leave and at home with my parents in Graz . . . Riedl was there as well – it was a Bohemian woman . . . must have been twice my age – I didn't get home till morning . . . what a look my father gave me . . . Klara too . . . It was facing Klara that I felt most ashamed . . . At the time, she was engaged . . . wonder why nothing ever came of it? Actually I never worried much about it . . . Poor thing, she never had much luck – and now she's going to lose her only brother . . . Yes, you will never see me again,

Klara – it's the end! Did you ever imagine, little sister, when you accompanied me to the station on New Year's Day, that you'd never set eyes on me again? – and Mama . . . my God, Mama . . . no, I mustn't think about that . . . when I think about that, I feel I might do something utterly contemptible . . . But what if I were to go home first . . . tell them I had one day's leave . . . see Papa, Mama and Klara one last time before I make an end of everything . . . Yes, I could catch the first train to Graz at seven, and be there by one o'clock . . . Greetings, Mama . . . Hello, Klara! Well, how are you all? . . . Now, this is a surprise! . . . But they might notice something . . . if the others don't, then Klara's sure to . . . Klara is such a clever girl . . . What a nice letter she wrote me recently, and I still owe her a reply – and all that good advice she always gives me . . . such a kind-hearted creature . . . Wonder whether everything would have turned out differently if I'd stayed at home? I might have studied economics, might have joined my uncle . . . they all wanted this when I was a lad . . . By now perhaps I'd be already married to some good sweet girl . . . perhaps to Anna, who was so fond of me . . . even now, I noticed, when I was home last time, although she already has a husband and two children . . . I noticed how she looked at me . . . And she still affectionately calls me 'Gustl' as she used to . . . She'll get a shock when she hears what sort of end I came to – though her husband will say: I saw it coming – what a scoundrel! – Everyone will think it was because I was in debt . . . and it simply isn't true, I've repaid everything . . . except the last hundred and sixty guilders – and anyway they'll be there tomorrow . . . Yes, I still have to arrange for Ballert to get those hundred and sixty guilders . . . I must jot it down before I shoot myself . . . It's terrifying, absolutely terrifying! . . . Supposing I were to pack up and leave instead – for America where no one knows me . . . In America no one will know anything about what happened here this evening . . . no one will bother about it there . . . In the paper recently there was something about a Count Runge, who was obliged to leave the country because of some sort of shady dealings, and how he now has a hotel over there and doesn't give a hoot about the swindling. And in a few years one could come back again . . . not to Vienna of course . . . or even to Graz . . . but I could settle on the farm . . . and Mama and Papa and Klara would be infinitely happier if I were to stay alive . . . And what do I care about all the others? Who else has my welfare at heart? – Apart from Kopetzky, I could be robbed by any of the others . . . Kopetzky is really the only one . . . And he was the one who had to go and give me that ticket . . . the ticket is to blame for everything . . . without the ticket I would not

have gone to the concert, and all this would never have occurred . . .
But what *has* happened, when all is said and done? . . . I feel as
though a hundred years have passed, yet it can't be more than a
couple of hours . . . Two hours ago a fellow called me a 'young fool'
and threatened to break my sword . . . My God, I'm going to start
screaming in the middle of the night! Why did it all have to happen?
Could I not have waited a bit longer until the cloak-room was completely empty? And why on earth did I say: 'Shut your mouth' to
him? How did that slip out? I'm normally a courteous fellow . . . even
with my men I'm not usually so crude . . . mind you, I was a little on
edge – all the things that seem to have come at the same time . . . bad
luck at cards and Steffi forever crying off – and the duel tomorrow
afternoon and lately I haven't been getting enough sleep – and all
that toiling in the barracks – one can't take it in the long run! . . . Yes,
sooner or later I'd have fallen ill – and had to apply for sick-leave . . .
Now it won't be necessary – I'm now coming up for extended leave –
after the required qualifying period, haha! . . .

How much longer am I going to sit here? It must be past midnight
. . . didn't I hear the clock strike earlier? – What's this, a carriage driving past? At this hour? Rubber tires – I can well imagine . . . They
are better off than I am – perhaps it's Ballert with his Bertha . . . Why
particularly Ballert? – Ah well, drive on! His Highness had a smart
little gig in Przemysl . . . he always used to drive into town to see the
Rosenbergs in it . . . Very sociable, His Highness – a true comrade,
on familiar terms with everyone . . . Those were good times . . .
although . . . the region was pretty desolate and sweltering in summer
. . . in a single afternoon once three men were overcome by sunstroke . . . even the corporal from my platoon – such a useful fellow
. . . In the afternoon we would lie down naked on our beds. – Once
Wiesner suddenly burst in on me; I must have been in the middle of
a dream just then, because I leaped to my feet and drew my sword,
which was lying by my side . . . I must have looked a sight . . . Wiesner nearly died laughing – he's already a captain in the Cavalry now
. . . – Pity I didn't join the Cavalry . . . but the old man wouldn't have
it – that would have been far too expensive a proposition – and now
of course it's all the same to me . . . How so? – Yes, I remember,
because I have to die, of course, that's why it's all the same to me –
because I have to die. Well then, how? – Look, Gustl, you've made
this extra trip out to the Prater in the middle of the night, where not
a soul is going to disturb you – so now you can reconsider everything
at leisure . . . That's all nonsense about America and resigning your
commission, and you are much too stupid to take up something else

– and what if you live to be a hundred, and have to think back on how that fellow threatened to break your sword, calling you a young fool, and you just stood there and did nothing – no, no, there is nothing at all to reconsider – what has happened has happened – even all that about Mama and Klara is just nonsense – they will get over it – people get over everything . . . How Mama lamented when her brother died – and after four weeks she scarcely thought about it . . . she would drive out to the cemetery . . . once a week at first, then once a month – and now only on the anniversary of his death. – Tomorrow, the 5th of April, will be the anniversary of my death! – Wonder if they will transport me back to Graz? Haha! the worms in Graz will be delighted! – But that's no concern of mine – others can bother their heads about that . . . Well then, what should I be concerned about? . . . The hundred and sixty guilders for Ballert – that's all – aside from that I have no final arrangements to make. – What about writing letters? Whoever to? Whatever for? . . . Just to bid everyone farewell? – But surely, devil take it, when a man shoots himself, the message is quite clear! – People will notice soon enough that one has made one's exit . . . And if people only knew how little I care about the whole business, they would not feel sorry for me either – anyway, I'm no great loss . . . After all, what have I had out of life? – There is one thing I would gladly have participated in: a war – but I'd have had a long wait for that . . . As for the rest, I know it all . . . Whether a wench is called Steffi or Kunigunde is neither here nor there. – I've seen the finest operettas too – and I've been to *Lohengrin* twelve times – and this evening I was even at an oratorio – and a baker called me a young fool – upon my sword, that's more than enough! – Besides, I'm no longer even curious . . . – So, slowly, very slowly, I shall make my way home . . . I'm really in no hurry. – Just a few more minutes' rest here in the Prater, on a bench – without shelter. – I shall never go to bed again – but I'll have time enough to sleep. – Ah, the air! I shall miss the air . . .

What's happening? – Hey, Johann, bring me a fresh glass of water . . . What's up? . . . Where on earth? . . . Am I dreaming? . . . My poor head! . . . Confound it . . . Fischamend . . . I can't open my eyes! – But I'm fully dressed! – Where am I then? – Good Heavens, I must have fallen asleep! How could I possibly have slept; it's already dawn! – How long have I been sleeping? – Must look at my watch . . . Can't see a thing! . . . Where are my matches.? . . . Surely, one will catch? . . . Three o'clock . . . and at four I'm supposed to fight a duel – no, not a duel – I'm supposed to shoot myself. – The duel is of no importance; I have to shoot myself because a baker called me a young fool . . . But did it really happen? My head feels very strange . . . my neck feels as though it's in a vice – I can't move at all – my right leg has gone to sleep. – Must get up! Must get up! . . . Ah, that's better! – It's already getting lighter . . . And the breeze . . . just like that morning when I was on patrol and camping in the woods . . . That was quite a different awakening – I had another day before me then . . . I still can't quite believe it all – there's the road, grey, deserted – I must be the only person in the Prater. I was out here once before at four o'clock, with Pausinger – we were out riding – I was on Captain Mirovic's horse and Pausinger on his old nag – that was in May last year – everything was in bloom already – everything was green. Now everything's still bare, but spring will soon be here – in just a few more days – lilies of the valley, violets – pity I won't be able to enjoy them any more – every man and his dog is free to enjoy them, but I must die! It's a crying shame! And all the others will sit around in the little wine-garden over supper as though nothing untoward had happened, just as we all sat in that wine-garden the same evening, the day they carried Lippay out . . . And Lippay was extremely popular . . . more popular than I am with the regiment – so why shouldn't they sit in some little wine-garden when I kick the bucket? – It's really warm – much warmer than yesterday – and so fragrant – some flowers must be out . . . Wonder whether Steffi will bring flowers? – It won't even occur to her! She'll go out for a drive instead . . . Now if it were still Adele . . . Goodness, Adele! I don't believe I've thought of her for at least two years . . . never in my life have I seen a woman cry so much . . . It was really the most beautiful thing I have experienced . . . How modest, how undemanding she was – I could swear that she was really fond of me. – She was quite different from Steffi . . . Can't imagine why I gave her up . . . what an ass! I just got bored, I suppose, that was all . . . Going out every evening with the same girl like that . . . Then I got worried that I might never escape – all that grumbling. – Well, Gustl, you could still have waited – she was the only one who was really fond of you . . . What's she doing now? Well, what would one expect? – By now she'll have found somebody else . . . It's true the arrangement with Steffi is more convenient – since we only see each other now and then and someone else has all the inconvenience, while I just have the pleasure . . . So I can't really expect her to come out to the cemetery . . . Who would come anyway, if he didn't have to! Kopetzky perhaps, and then that would be it! – It's really sad to have absolutely no one . . .

But what nonsense! there's Papa and Mama, and there's Klara . . .
True, and I'm their son and her brother . . . but what else do we have
in common? They're fond of me no doubt – but what do they know
about me? – That I'm serving in the army, that I gamble and that I
go around with sluts . . . but what else? I never wrote and told them
that I was sometimes disgusted with myself – but then I don't think I
fully realized it myself. – Anyway, why are you bringing all this up,
Gustl? Next thing, you'll begin to weep . . . for shame! Keep in step,
now . . . that's the way! Whether going on duty, to a rendez-vous or
into battle . . . who was it said that? . . . ah, yes, Major Lederer, in the
canteen, when they were talking about Wingleder and how before
his first duel he went pale and vomited . . . Yes: whether he is going
to a rendez-vous or certain death, a true officer does not reveal it
either on his face or in his stride. So, Gustl – it was Major Lederer
who said it!

It's getting lighter . . . light enough to read . . . What's that
whistling? . . . Ah yes, the Northern Line Station's over there . . . The
Tegetthoff Column . . . never seen it look so tall . . . Some carriages
are standing waiting over there . . . But the streets are deserted,
except for the street-cleaners . . . my last street-cleaners . . . haha! I
can't help laughing when I think about it . . . can't quite take it in . . .
Wonder whether everyone's like this, once they know for certain?
The station clock says half-past three . . . the question is, should I
shoot myself at seven by the railway clock or by Vienna time? Seven
. . . yes, but why specifically at seven? . . . As if no other time would do
. . . I'm really hungry – God, I'm hungry – no wonder . . . how long
since I had anything to eat? . . . Not since – since six yesterday
evening in the coffee-house . . . that's right! When Kopetzky gave me
the ticket – white coffee and two rolls. – Wonder what the baker will
say when he hears about it? . . . the accursed dog! – Ah, he'll know
why – the penny'll drop all right – and then he'll realise what it
means to be an officer! – That sort of fellow can brawl in the open
street and get away with it, while one of us, even when privately
insulted, is as good as dead . . . If only the scoundrel would stand and
fight a duel – but no, he would be far too canny, he wouldn't risk anything like that . . . And now the fellow lives on, lives calmly on, while
I – must perish! It's he who's killing me . . . Yes, Gustl, don't you see?
– he's the one who's killing you! But he won't get away with it that
easily! – No indeed! I will write a letter to Kopetzky explaining everything, telling the whole story . . . or, better still: I'll write to the
Colonel, I'll make a report to the Regimental Commander . . . just
like an official report . . . Just you wait, do you think something like

this can remain a secret? – You are mistaken – it will be recorded in immemorial remembrance, and then I'd like to see whether you will dare show your face in the coffee-house again – Haha! – 'I'd like to see,' that's a good one! There are lots of things I'd like to see, but alas that won't be possible – it's curtains for me!

At this moment Johann is entering my room, and he'll notice that his Lieutenant has not slept at home. – He'll imagine all sorts of things, but not, I'll wager, that his Lieutenant spent the whole night in the Prater . . . Ah, there goes the Forty-fourth! they are marching out to the shooting range – better make way for them . . . I'll stand here to one side . . . – Up there a window's opening – good-looking wench – though if I were going to the window at least I'd put a towel around me . . . Last Sunday was the last time . . . I never would have dreamed that Steffi of all people would be my last. – Ah God, that's the only real pleasure . . . Well, in two hours or so the Colonel will ride out after them in the grand manner . . . the top brass have an easy time of it – Yes, yes, eyes right! – That's the way . . . If only you knew that I don't give a damn for any of you! – Well I'll be blowed: there's Katzer . . . since when has he been transferred to the Forty-fourth? – Good morning, good morning! What's he grimacing about? . . . Why is he pointing at his head? – My dear fellow, your skull is of very little interest to me . . . Oh, I see! No, my dear fellow, you are quite mistaken: I simply spent the night out in the Prater . . . you will read all about it in the evening paper. – 'Impossible!' he will say, 'I saw him in the Praterstrasse only this morning, as we were on our way out to the shooting-range!' – Who will take over my platoon, I wonder? – Will they give it to Walterer? That will put them in a pretty pickle – the fellow lacks pluck, he should have been a cobbler . . . What, the sun coming up already? – It looks like being a lovely day – a real spring day . . . Devil take it! That cab-driver will still be in this world at eight o'clock, while I . . . Come, come, now that really would be too absurd – to lose countenance at the very last minute on account of some miserable cab-driver . . . What's this, why is my heart pounding like this all of a sudden? – Not because of all this, surely . . . No, of course not . . . it's simply because I haven't eaten for so long. – Come on, Gustl, be honest with yourself: you are frightened – frightened because you've never tried anything like this before . . . But that won't help you, fear never helped anyone: everyone must face up to it sooner or later, and your turn happens to be sooner . . . You were never worth much anyway, so at least behave decently until the end, that much I demand of you! – Well then, let's think things through – but what? I keep wanting to think everything through . . .

but it's really all quite simple: – the pistol is lying in the night-safe and is loaded, so all I have to do is pull the trigger – hardly something calling for great skill.

   She is off to her shop already . . . poor girls! Adele worked in a shop too – I would pick her up in the evening occasionally . . . When they're with a shop they don't become such sluts . . . If Steffi were willing to be mine alone, I'd have her become a milliner or something . . . Wonder how she'll come to hear about it? – From the paper! . . . She'll be angry that I never wrote to her about it . . . I think I must be going mad . . . What do I care whether or not she will be angry . . . How long has our affair been going anyway? . . . Since January? . . . No, it must have been before Christmas . . . because I brought her back some sweets from Graz, and at New Year she sent me a little thank-you note . . . Which reminds me, all those letters that I have at home – are there any that I ought to burn? . . . Hm, there's the one from Fallsteiner – if they found that letter . . . the fellow could be in for trouble . . . Why should I bother about that! – Well, it's not really that much trouble . . . but I can't go hunting down a single scrap of paper . . . Best to burn the lot . . . who needs them anyway? Just waste-paper really. – And my few books I could leave to Blany. – *Through Night and Ice* . . . pity I won't ever finish reading that . . . haven't got round to reading much lately . . . An organ – ah, from the church . . . Early mass – haven't been for ages . . . last time was in February, when my platoon was ordered to attend . . . But that doesn't count – I was keeping an eye on my men, to make sure they paid due respect and were behaving properly . . . – I'd like to go inside the church . . . perhaps there's something to it all . . . Well, after supper today I shall know for certain . . . 'After supper,' that's a good one! . . . Well, how about it, shall I go in? – I think it would be a comfort to Mama if she knew that I had done so! . . . Klara sets much less store by these things . . . Well, here we go, it can't do any harm!

   An organ – singing – hm! – wonder what it is? – I feel quite giddy . . . Oh God, oh God, oh God! if only there were someone I could talk to first! – That's an idea, I could go to confession! How the priest would gape if I were to say at the end: my respects to you, Father, now I'm off to kill myself! . . . – What I really feel like doing is lying down on the stone floor and howling . . . No, no, one can't do that! Though a good cry can sometimes do one good . . . Let's sit down a moment – but mustn't fall asleep again as in the Prater! . . . – People who have religion are more fortunate . . . Oh God, now even my hands have begun to tremble! . . . If things go on like this, I will end up being so disgusted with myself that I'll kill myself out of pure shame! – That

old woman there – what is she praying for, I wonder? . . . Would be
an idea to go up to her and say: please include me in your prayers –
I never learned to do it properly . . . Haha! I think dying must make
one simple-minded! – Must get up! – What does that melody remind
me of? – Good Heavens! yesterday evening! – Out of here, I don't
think I can stand this! . . . Sh! less noise, don't clatter with your sword
– mustn't disturb people at their prayers – there we are – feels better
in the open air . . . light . . . Ah, it keeps drawing nearer – if only it
were already over! – I should have done it at once – in the Prater . . .
one should never go out without a revolver . . . If I'd had one yesterday evening . . . Oh God, oh God! – I could go to the coffee-house
and have some breakfast . . . I'm so hungry . . . Before, it always used
to strike me as very odd, that on their last morning the condemned
should still drink their coffee and smoke their cigars . . . Confound it,
I've never smoked! never had any urge to smoke! – But funnily
enough, I do feel the urge to go along to my coffee-house . . . It
should be open by now, and none of our lot will be there – and even
if they are . . . when all is said and done it will be seen as a sign of coolness. 'At six he was still having breakfast in the coffee-house, and he
shot himself at seven . . .' – I'm quite calm again . . . it's so pleasant
walking – and the beauty of it is that no one's forcing me. – If I
wanted to, I could still wash my hands of the whole shebang . . .
America . . . What on earth does that mean: 'shebang'? What *is* a
shebang? I think I must have sunstroke! . . . Aha, is that perhaps why
I'm so calm, because I still imagine I don't need to go through with
it? . . . But I must, I must! No, I want to! Can you, Gustl, ever imagine yourself taking off your uniform and making a run for it? That
accursed dog the baker would split his sides laughing, and even
Kopetzky would not shake hands with you again . . . I believe I'm
blushing at the very thought. – The policeman is saluting me . . . I
must respond . . . 'Good morning!' – There, now I've greeted him!
A poor devil like that always appreciates it . . . Well, no one has ever
had much to complain about in me – off duty I've always been a
companionable fellow. When we were on manoeuvres, I gave cigars
to all the non-commissioned officers in the company; and once during drill, I heard a man behind me muttering something about
'damned drudgery,' but did not report him – I simply said: 'You,
watch out, one of these days someone else might hear – and then
you'd be in trouble! . . .' The palace courtyard . . . Who's on sentry
duty today? – The Bosniacs – they certainly look smart – our Lieu-
tenant-Colonel said recently that when we were down there in '78,
no one believed they would hold us off the way they did! . . . My God,

I wish I could have taken part in something like that. – They're all getting up from the bench. – Good morning, good morning! – It's really disgusting that fellows like me miss all the action. – It would have been better to die in defence of the realm on the field of honour than like this . . . Yes, Herr Doktor, you're going to escape scot-free after all! . . . Couldn't someone else stand in for me? – By God, that's what I should do: arrange for Kopetzky or Wymetal to fight the fellow in my place . . . He shouldn't get away with everything so lightly. – Ah well, does it really matter what happens afterwards? I'll never hear about it! – Those trees are budding . . . I once picked up a girl here in the Volksgarten – she was wearing a red dress – lived in the Strozzigasse – afterwards Rochlitz took her over . . . I think he's still seeing her, but he's ashamed of it . . . Steffi will still be sleeping now . . . She looks so sweet when she's asleep . . . as if she couldn't count to five! – Well, they all look like that when they're asleep! – I really ought to write her a few words . . . after all, why not? It's what everybody does, they write farewell letters beforehand. – I should also write to Klara, so she can comfort Papa and Mama – the usual sentiments! – and to Kopetzky as well of course . . . Come to think of it, it would have been much easier if one had said a few goodbyes personally . . . And then there's the report to Regimental Command – and the hundred and sixty guilders for Ballert . . . still quite a lot to do, in fact . . . Well, no one is insisting that I do it by seven . . . after eight there'll still be time enough for dying! . . . Yes, and about dying – as the saying goes – there's nothing can be done.

The Ringstrasse – now I'll soon be at my coffee-house . . . I'm actually looking forward to my breakfast . . . hard to believe. – Yes, and after breakfast I'll light myself a cigar, and then I'll go home and write . . . Yes, first I'll prepare the report to the Regimental Commander; next will be the letter to Klara – then the one to Kopetzky – then one to Steffi . . . What am I to say to the little hussy . . . 'My dear girl, doubtless you never thought . . .' – Ah, what nonsense! – 'My dear girl, how can I thank you . . .' – 'My dear girl, before I depart this world, I don't want to forgo the opportunity . . .' – Ah well, letter-writing never was my strong point . . . 'To my dear girl, a last farewell from your loving Gustl . . .' I can see her fearful eyes already! Just as well I wasn't in love with her . . . it must be really sad when one is fond of someone and then . . . Come now, Gustl, be a good fellow: it's sad enough as it is . . . After Steffi there would have been others, and perhaps even someone who was worth while – a young girl from a good family with assets – that would have been really nice . . . – I must write to Klara in more detail and explain why I could not have acted otherwise . . . 'You must forgive me, dear Sister, and please comfort our dear parents too. I know I have been a worry to you and caused you all some pain, but believe me, I have always loved you all most dearly, and I hope you will again be happy, my dear Klara, and not forget your unfortunate brother altogether . . .' Ah, I'd rather not write to her at all! It just makes me want to cry . . . my eyes begin to water when I think about it . . . I'll just write to Kopetzky – a comradely farewell, and he can report it to the others . . . – Is it six already? – Not yet: between half past and a quarter to. – What a charming little face! . . . that little rogue with the dark eyes I see so often in the Florianigasse! – What will she say? – But then she doesn't even know me – she will merely wonder why she never sees me any more . . . The day before yesterday I decided to speak to her next time. – She has certainly been playing the coquette enough . . . how young she was – perhaps even still a virgin! . . . Yes, Gustl! Don't put off till tomorrow what you can do today! . . . That fellow probably hasn't slept all night either. – Well, now he'll go quietly home and lie down – like me! – Haha! Yes, Gustl, but now things are getting serious! . . . Ah well, if there weren't that edge of fear, there'd be nothing to it – and all in all, though I say it myself, I've behaved extremely well . . . Where are we? Ah, there's my coffee-house . . . they're still sweeping the place out . . . Well, let's go in . . .

There's the table at the back where they always play taroc . . . Strange, I find it hard to believe that the fellow who always sits there against the wall could be the same fellow that . . . – No one's here yet . . . Where's the waiter? . . . Ah, there he comes, out of the kitchen . . . he's quickly slipping into his tailcoat . . . That's really no longer necessary! . . . ah, but for him it is, he will have to serve others too today!

'We are honoured, Lieutenant!'

'Good morning.'

'Very early today, Lieutenant?'

'Ah, don't bother about my coat – I don't have much time and I'll sit here with it on.'

'And your order, Lieutenant?'

'A white coffee, please.'

'At once, Lieutenant!'

Ah, there are the papers . . . today's papers already? . . . Could there be any mention? . . . What am I thinking of? – I do believe I wanted to check and see whether they mention that I've committed suicide! Haha! – Why am I still standing? . . . I'll take a seat there by the window . . . He's already brought my coffee . . . I'll just draw the curtain; I don't like people peering in . . . Though nobody is passing

by yet . . . Ah, the coffee tastes good – no mad delusion, breakfast! . . .
One feels like a new man – how stupid of me not to have had an
evening meal . . . What's the fellow here again for? – Ah, he's brought
the rolls . . .

'Has the Lieutenant heard yet?' . . .

'What about?' Good Heavens, does he know about it? . . . Nonsense, that's utterly impossible!

'About Herr Habetswallner . . .'

What? That's the name of the master-baker . . . what's coming
next? Could he perhaps have been here already? Could he possibly
have come by yesterday and reported everything? . . . Why doesn't
the fellow spit it out? Well, give him a chance . . .

' . . . who had a stroke at twelve o'clock last night.'

'What? . . .' I mustn't shout like that . . . no, no, I mustn't draw
attention to myself . . . but perhaps I'm dreaming . . . I must ask him
once again . . . 'Who was it had a stroke, you say?' Splendid, splendid! I made that sound innocent enough!

'The baker, Lieutenant! You must know him, Sir . . . the fat fellow
who made up a little taroc party next to the officers every afternoon . . . along with Herr Schlesinger and Herr Wasner the florist
opposite!'

I'm wide-awake – it all makes sense – and yet I still can't believe it
– I must ask him once again . . . but very casually . . .

'So he's had a stroke, has he? . . . Now fancy that. How do you
know about it?'

'But Lieutenant, who should know about it earlier than people like
us – the rolls you are eating, Sir, come from Herr Habetswallner's.
The lad who delivers them from the bakery every morning at half
past four informed us.'

Good Heavens, I mustn't betray myself . . . I feel like shouting . . . I
feel like laughing . . . I feel like giving Rudolph here a kiss . . . But I must
ask him one more thing! . . . Having a stroke does not mean dying . . .
I must ask whether he is dead . . . but very quietly, for what do I care
about the baker – I must look at the paper while I ask the waiter . . .

'Is he dead?'

'Why certainly, Lieutenant; he died on the spot.'

How marvellous, how marvellous! Perhaps all this is because I
went into the church . . .

'He'd been to the theatre in the evening; he collapsed on the stairs
– the house porter heard the noise . . . well, and then they carried him
into his apartment, and by the time the doctor got there it was all
over.'

'But that's really sad. He was still in the prime of life.' – I said that brilliantly – no one would have noticed anything amiss . . . I really must restrain myself, so that I don't start shouting, or leap onto the billiard table . . .

'Yes, Lieutenant, very sad; he was such a nice man, and has been coming here for twenty years – a good friend of the proprietor. And his poor wife . . .'

I don't believe I've ever been so happy in my life . . . He's dead – he's dead! No one knows a thing, and nothing ever happened! – What incredible luck my coming by the coffee-house . . . otherwise I would have shot myself for nothing – it's like a decree from fate . . . Where's Rudolph gone to? Ah, he's talking to the stoker . . . So he's dead – he's dead – I still can't believe it! I'd really like to go over and take a look at him myself. Perhaps the stroke was brought on by anger, suppressed fury . . . Anyway, I don't care how it happened! The main thing is he's dead, and I can live, and the world is all before me once again . . . Funny, how I keep crumbling these rolls Herr Habetswallner baked! They taste quite good, my dear Habetswallner! Capital, in fact! – Well, now I could really do with a cigar . . .

'Rudolf! I say, Rudolf! Don't spend all day there with the stoker.'

'Coming, Lieutenant!'

'I'll have a Trabucco . . .' I'm so happy, so happy! . . . What shall I do? . . . What shall I do? I must do something, or else I too am liable to have a stroke from sheer joy! . . . In a quarter of an hour or so I'll go over to the barracks and have Johann give me a cold rub-down . . . there's weapons handling at half past seven and drill at half past nine. – And I'll write and tell Steffi to keep this evening free, even if it means not going to Graz! And this afternoon at four . . . just you wait, my good fellow, just you wait! I'm in fine fettle . . . I'll make mincemeat out of you!

Andreas Thameyer's Farewell Letter

There is no way that I can go on living. Because as long as I remain alive people would jeer and no one would acknowledge the truth. But the truth is that my wife has been faithful to me – I swear to it by all that I hold sacred and I shall seal it with my death. Besides, I've looked it all up in a whole lot of books that deal with these difficult and puzzling matters, and while there are some authors who doubt the facts themselves, on the other hand there have been leading authorities who are quite convinced of them, and I myself intend to cite examples that must appear incontrovertible to any impartial judge. Malebranche for instance relates how during the festivities for the canonisation of Pope Pius, one woman studied his portrait so closely that the boy she brought into the world shortly afterwards precisely resembled the saint: indeed, his countenance showed exactly the same tired features of old age, his arms were crossed over his breast, his eyes turned towards heaven, and even the shape of the Pope's hanging cap appeared in a birthmark on one shoulder. Whoever considers this account insufficiently attested, however, despite the authority of the witness who was a disciple of the famous philosopher Descartes, will perhaps be satisfied with Martin Luther as an alternative authority. Luther, it will be recalled – and this can be checked in his *Table Talk* – knew a citizen of Wittenberg who had the features of a death's-head, and it was established that during her pregnancy the mother of this unfortunate man had been terrified out of her wits by the sight of a corpse. But the case that seems most significant to me, and which there are no rational grounds for doubting, is one reported by Heliodorus in his *Libri aethiopicorum*. According to this esteemed author, after ten years of childless marriage Queen Persina bore her husband, the Ethiopian king Hydaspes, a white daughter, and in fear of the anger she foresaw from her spouse, she had the child exposed immediately after the birth. But she provided her with a belt on which the true cause of the fateful event was stated, namely that in the garden of the royal palace where the queen had received the embraces of her dusky husband, magnificent marble statues of Greek gods and goddesses had been placed, and towards these Persina had directed her ecstatic gaze. But the powers of the spirit go well beyond this, and it is not only the ignorant or superstitious who hold this view, as the following incident which occurred in France in the year 1637 attests. It so happened that a woman, after the four-year absence of her husband, gave birth to a boy, and swore that at the corresponding time beforehand she had had the most extraordinarily vivid dreams of her husband's passionate embrace. The doctors and midwives of Montpellier declared under oath that the facts as stated were indeed possible, and the town court of Le Havre granted the child the full rights of legitimate birth. Further to the above, I find in Hamberg's *Mysterious Natural Events*, page 74, the case of a woman who gave birth to a child with a lion's head, having earlier attended the performance of a lion-tamer with her husband and her mother. Furthermore, I have read of a case – it may be found in Limböck's *On Lapses in Women*, Basel, 1846, page 19 – in which a child was born with a large red birthmark on its cheek because a few weeks before the birth the mother had seen the house opposite go up in flames. This volume contains many other highly remarkable things. It lies before me on the table as I write, I've just been leafing through it again, and the facts that are reported there are all well-attested and scientifically authenticated, and equally well-attested is the event experienced by myself, or rather by my good wife who has been true to me, as surely as I am at this moment still alive! Will you forgive me, dear wife, for having resolved to die? Look, you must forgive me. It is entirely out of love for you that I am going to die, for I cannot tolerate people jeering and laughing both you and me to scorn. Now they will certainly stop laughing, now they will understand as I too understand. Those of you who find me, who find this letter, should know that, as I write, she is asleep in the next room, peacefully asleep as one can only sleep with a clear conscience; and her child – our child, who is now fourteen days old, is lying in the cradle next to the bed and sleeping likewise. And before I leave the house, I shall go in and kiss my wife and child on the forehead without waking them. The reason I am writing all this down so precisely is so that no one can say that I am mad . . . no, all has been carefully considered and I am completely calm. As soon as I have finished this letter, I shall go out in the deep of night, through the empty streets, on and on down the road I so often walked along with my wife during the first year of our marriage, to Dornbach – and on into the wood. And so matters stand. My name is Andreas Thameyer, I am an official at the Austrian Savings Bank, thirty-four years old, residing at Hernalser Hauptstrasse No. 64, and have been married for the past four years. I knew my wife for seven years before we married, and she turned down two other suitors because she loved me and was willing to wait for me – a commissioned officer with an income of 1,800 guilders and a very handsome medical student from Trieste who lived as a lodger, be it noted, with her parents – both turned down for my sake, even though I was neither rich nor handsome, and though our marriage had been postponed from year to year. And now people are maintaining that this woman, who waited patiently for me for seven years, has actually betrayed me! People are miserably stupid, and cannot, if I may so express myself, look into one's inner life; they are malicious and gross in the extreme. But now they will all be silenced . . . yes, now they will all say: we did you an injustice, we acknowledge that your wife was true to you, and there was no need for you to kill yourself . . . But I say to you all: it *is* necessary! Because as long as I remained alive, you would all continue jeering. Only one person has been high-minded and considerate, and that's old Dr Walter Brauner . . . Indeed he explained everything to me at once; before bringing me in he said to me, 'My dear Thameyer, don't be shocked and don't excite your wife. Such things have often occurred before. Tomorrow I'll lend you a book by Limböck and others on lapses in pregnant women.' These books are lying in front of me now, you may rest assured! and I would kindly request my relatives to arrange for their return to this excellent man, Dr Brauner, with my most humble thanks. I have no further testamentary dispositions to attend to. My will was made long ago, and I have no reason to change it, since my wife has been faithful to me, and the child she has presented me with is my child. Why it should have such an unusual skin colour I shall now explain to you quite simply. Only malevolence and ignorance can remain impervious to my explanation, and I would go so far as to assert that if we were living among people who were less vulgar and spiteful I would be able to continue living, since everybody would accept it. But as things are no one will accept it, people just laugh and snigger. Even Herr Gustav Rengelhofer, my wife's uncle, to whom I have always shown the greatest respect, winked at me in a most offensive manner when he saw my child for the first time; and my own mother . . . she pressed my hand in a very strange way, as though I were in need of her sympathy. And my colleagues at the office started whispering together when I arrived at work yesterday, and the house porter, to whose children I gave my old broken watch for Christmas – a watch-case like that has its uses as a toy at least . . . the house porter choked back his laughter as I passed him yesterday; and our cook made such a droll face, as if

she were quite drunk, and the grocer on the corner looked round at
me three or four times at least . . . the other day he was standing outside his shop and said to an old lady: 'That's him.' And as evidence
of how rapidly the most nonsensical rumours spread: there are people I don't know at all who seem to know all about it, I have no idea
how. The day before yesterday, as I was coming home on the stage-
coach, I heard three old women inside talking about me; I heard my
Christian name quite distinctly as I was standing on the platform.
And so I ask aloud (I use this expression deliberately, although these
notes are written) – I ask out loud: What can I do? What else can I
do? I can't say to everyone: read Hamberg's *Mysterious Natural Events*
and Limböck's splendid work *On Lapses in Pregnant Women*. I cannot
kneel before them pleading, 'Don't be so remorseless . . . can't you see
. . . my wife has always been faithful to me!' True, she became dis-
tracted last August when she went to the zoo with her sister, down
where those wierd men, those creepy blacks, were camped. But I can
swear it was a momentary attention lapse because the incident came
about as follows. On that day – and for some days previously – I had
been with my parents in the country – my father, I should explain,
was ill . . . This might be concluded from the fact that he did indeed
die a few weeks later. But I digress. So, Anna was alone. And when I
returned I found my wife lying in bed – yes, she lay there in agitation,
pining . . . Heaven knows what! And yet I had only been away three
days. So deeply did my dear wife love me. And so I had to sit at her
bedside at once and have her tell me how she had spent the last three
days. And without my enquiring, she told me everything. I shall
record it all here with the precise details that are necessary in this
case. On Monday she had been at home the whole morning. In the
afternoon she went with Fritzi – as we call her unmarried sister, who
was christened Friederike – she went with Fritzi to the town centre to
do some shopping. Fritzi is engaged to a very fine young man, who
now has a position in Germany, in Bremen, with a large trading
house, and Fritzi is supposed to follow him quite soon and become
his wife . . . But again I am digressing, I'm well aware of that. My wife
spent the whole of Tuesday at home, as it was raining. It was raining
too, on that particular day, out in the country where my parents live,
as I can remember quite distinctly. Then came Wednesday. On that
day, towards evening, my wife and Fritzi went to the zoological gardens, where some negroes were camped. Here I should add that I
saw these people myself later, in September, when I went down there
with Rudolf Bittner and his wife one Sunday evening; Anna refused
to come, so strong was the feeling of horror that had remained with

her ever since that Wednesday. She told me that never in her life had
she felt such horror as when she found herself alone with the negroes
that evening . . . Alone, for Fritzi had suddenly slipped away . . . I
find it impossible to pass over this fact in silence. Now I don't want
to say anything against Fritzi, since this is my last letter. But it does
seem to me in order at this point to issue Fritzi with a stern admon-
ishment not to do anything to offend her bridegroom, since he as a
decent man would be most upset by it. Unfortunately the fact
remains that on that particular evening Herr . . . but what's the point
in mentioning names here . . . well, in short, that on that evening
Fritzi slipped away with this gentleman whom I know only too well,
and who does not enjoy the best of reputations, even though he is
married, and my poor wife suddenly found herself alone. It was one
of those misty evenings that sometimes occur in late summer; I for
my part never go out into the Prater without an overcoat . . . I recall
that often grey wisps of mist lie on the meadows there, in which the
varying play of light is mirrored . . . Well, it was just such an evening
that Wednesday, and Fritzi was suddenly gone, and my Anna was
alone . . . suddenly alone . . . now who can fail to understand that
under these circumstances she must have felt an overwhelming horror at those giant men with glowing eyes and great black beards? . . .
For two hours she waited for Fritzi in the hope that she would return,
until at last the gates were closed and she had to leave. That is how it
was. Anna related all this to me early in the morning as I sat at her
bed, as I mentioned above . . . She had thrown her arms around my
neck, trembling, and her eyes were very sad, and I grew afraid
myself, even though I did not yet know, that day, what I learned later,
any more than she did. For had I known that she was already carrying our child beneath her heart, then I would never for a single
moment have permitted her to go out with Fritzi into the Prater on a
misty evening exposing herself to God only knows what dangers. For
a woman in her condition everything is dangerous . . . Certainly if
Fritzi had not slipped away, my wife would never for a moment have
got herself into such a frightful state, but that is precisely where the
whole misfortune lay, that she was left quite alone and trembling for
Fritzi . . . Well, now it's all over and I won't cast a stone at anybody.
But I have written all this down because I consider it necessary to
clear up this whole matter. Were I not to do so, who knows whether
those wretched people wouldn't in the end still say: he killed himself
because his wife betrayed him . . . No, no all you people, once again
I tell you my wife is true to me and the child she has had is my child!
And I shall love them both to the very last. It is all of *you* who are

hounding me to death, you who are too small-minded or spiteful to believe or understand. And the more I were to talk to you and try to explain the case scientifically . . . I know, the more you would jeer and laugh, if not to my face then behind my back – or you might even say: 'Thameyer is mad.' Well, I've deprived you of that, my worthies, I am dying for my convictions, for the truth and above all for the honour of my wife; and when I am dead you won't be able to scorn my wife or laugh at me; you will have to acknowledge that such things as Hamberg, Heliodorus, Malebranche, Welsenburg, Preuss, Limböck and others have reported do actually occur. As for you, dear Mother – you really did not have to press my hand, as though I were to be pitied! Now you will surely ask my wife's forgiveness, I know you will . . . And now, I think, I have nothing more to say. The clock has just struck one. Good night, dear friends. Now I shall go into the next room and give my wife and child one last kiss – then I shall make my exit. Farewell.

Success

Engelbert Friedmaier, police constable number seventeen thousand nine hundred and twelve, stood at his post between the Kaiser Josef- and the Taborstrasse and brooded over the failure of his life. Three years had elapsed since he had left the army with the rank of sergeant and joined the police force, full of the noblest enthusiasm for his new profession, burning with zeal to maintain security and order in the city; his sweetheart Kathy, the daughter of the second-hand dealer Anton Wessely, was waiting to be led home as his bride; but Engelbert's prospects for promotion were extremely bleak, not to say desperate. Three years had gone by without yielding him a single arrest. A case like his had never been known since the founding of the police force in Vienna. Engelbert's superiors doubted his commitment, his comrades respected him no longer, and Kathy, once his solace in despondent moments, had begun to ridicule him bitterly. And yet he felt he was simply not to blame. He was unlucky! Within a thousand paces round him all criminal impulses mysteriously ceased. He had stood on busy intersections where normally dozens of coachmen were pulled up for reckless driving, and in especially propitious cases for running someone down; at night on public holidays he had been on duty in the suburbs outside dens of ill repute, where in the past several people had come crashing through the door crying: 'I've been stabbed!' . . . Once he had even been transferred to a street where bicycling was forbidden, and where on one justly famous day his predecessor had actually managed to haul sixty-seven cyclists off to the police station – and yet no sooner had Engelbert Friedmaier taken over this responsible position than everything had changed. The most restive trotters slowed to an even pace, the most notorious pimps failed to do anything provocative, and the wildest cyclists, whom Engelbert with pounding heart watched hurtling down towards the interdicted street, would deliberately dismount and wheel their bicycles on to the next corner.

Engelbert could only look on dumbfounded as each and every regulation remained inviolate and the entire system of security unthreatened. Even small gratifications that his colleagues enjoyed from time to time were invariably denied him. Not once had he caught a glimpse of some young lady through a window at her all-too-early morning toilet, no pleasure-loving street-walker had ever dreamed of behaving improperly in his vicinity, no coach had ever driven past him with suspiciously drawn blinds, nor was it granted him to surprise some excessively amorous couple on his nightly beat through public gardens. And even on important occasions, such as those on which in the past so many of his comrades had plucked immortal laurels, things went off without a hitch. He had been one of those chosen to stand outside parliament when a yelling mob of Socialists marched past, and he strained his ears in case any of them should dare to utter some treasonable remark or even curse the universally revered Mayor . . . But all those closest to him held their tongues, as if forewarned by some good or evil spirit. – On another occasion he had been standing among a crowd lining the Ringstrasse to watch a procession with some royal personage. He was obliged to look on as, not ten paces away, a younger colleague arrested a harmless passer-by, who was deaf and had no idea what was wanted of him, for causing a disturbance – whereas behind Engelbert a wall of people stood for hours without so much as shoving or breaking out of line.

But the worst thing that happened to him was an occasion when he thought he had almost reached his goal; it was then that his dream of success was transformed into bitter disillusionment. It had been a gorgeous afternoon, just like today, and Engelbert was standing at his post in the Rotenturmstrasse when some way off he saw an elegant gentleman approaching, leading a young girl by the hand. The little creature seemed fatigued, and the gentleman was dragging her along after him. She collapsed on the ground; the gentleman pulled her to her feet; the little girl began to scream and cry, and the gentleman cursed so loudly that Engelbert could make out every word, the obscenity of which sounded extremely promising. The girl cried out: 'Dear kind Papa, I'm so very tired!' and sank to her knees; the gentleman then raised his stick and struck her on the head, so that she collapsed, apparently dead. People gathered round and Engelbert, eyes sparkling, hurried to the scene. The incident was particularly felicitous, for at the time public interest had been aroused by several cases of child abuse, and now he could be man of the hour at one fell swoop. What did he care about reckless drivers or trivial stab wounds? Here, he hoped, a defenceless child had just been murdered, and he was on the spot. With formidable dignity he strode through the crowd that had built up . . . But what should he behold?

The very people whom he expected to find profoundly shaken were convulsed with laughter, the elegant gentleman was saying: 'Allow me, ladies and gentlemen, to invite you all to my début, which will take place in the Floral Rooms this evening', and there on the ground before him lay – a wooden puppet! But Engelbert did not yet want to give the matter up: perhaps some particularly sophisticated crime might be entailed, in which the murderer had subtly made himself out to be a ventriloquist and the child a puppet. But when Engelbert got down on one knee and found himself staring into the glass eyes of a wooden doll, the general hilarity reached a climax. There was still of course the tempting option of taking the ventriloquist to the police station on a charge of public mischief, but at that moment two cavalry officers came past and became engaged in friendly conversation with the artist. – With a start, Engelbert recognised one of the officers as an archduke, and sensing that there was nothing in it at all for him, he slunk away.

From that day on, Engelbert Friedmaier was utterly convinced that he was being pursued by a malignant fate. He could not help envying some of his comrades who were stricter than the regulations and more punctilious than the law, and the vague temptation stirred in him to emulate these eager beavers. He became even more acutely aware of the incomparable order and morality around him, as if it were a form of contempt directed at him personally, and the entire population of his district seemed to him a band of conspirators who with all their respectability had no other object in mind than to destroy him.

And so today too he stood at his post, miserably aware of his own superfluousness and his absurdity. – Evening was approaching and tardy pedestrians were making their way towards the Prater, from which the noise of the Sunday crowds surged confusedly towards him. Engelbert paced up and down, up and down. Every so often he would stop short and look along the street, his gaze sweeping from the Westbahnhof . . . to the Praterstern – and then he would resume pacing up and down, up and down. Suddenly he became aware of a familiar figure rapidly approaching along the Taborstrasse. It was Katharina decked out in a blue, white-spotted foulard dress with a little white straw hat and crimson sunshade, and as she drew closer Engelbert could see that she was smiling. She knew that he was on duty here . . . had she come to visit him? He hardly dared to hope so, for recently she had not been at all kind to him, indeed she had often positively made fun of him. She was approaching fast. At this point he also noticed that a young man in a light grey suit, a cigarette in his

mouth and twirling a walking-stick between his fingers, was saunter-
ing along some ten paces behind her, which might well of course be
mere coincidence.

Engelbert, who had been standing in the middle of the street,
crossed over to the pavement. Katharina stopped short before him
and with the same sweet smile asked: 'Constable, would you mind
telling me the way to the Prater?'

'Kathy,' he exclaimed, 'Kathy, have you really come to see me?'

'Whatever are you thinking of, Constable . . . that wouldn't be permitted! You're on duty now! I've merely stopped to ask the quickest
way to the Prater.'

The young gentleman in the grey suit with a walking-stick had
stopped on the pavement opposite. It was quite conceivable that he
was waiting for a tram.

'Kathy,' said Engelbert, 'look, it's very good of you . . .'

'What is very good of me? I could just as well have asked somebody else, but as I happened to be passing and as I generally have so
much respect for the police and as you seemed so amiable . . . Indeed
it's true, anyone can see at once that you wouldn't hurt a fly.'

The corners of Engelbert's mouth trembled slightly. What was she
up to? Had she merely come to provoke him again? – Just then a
horse-drawn omnibus came by, and the young gentleman in grey did
not get on. But perhaps what he had to do lay in the opposite direction.

'Why don't you say something, Superintendent?' Kathy now
asked him. 'Are you not duty-bound, according to instructions, to
respond with information to the enquiries of all parties in a polite
and proper manner?'

'Kathy, I beg you, don't make fun of me! Don't you see I can't bear
it any longer?'

'Well then,' said Katharina, as she raised herself on tiptoes and
then sank back again, 'I shall simply have to ask somebody else.
Would you do me the honour, Sir . . .' – 'Kathy!'

'What's the matter? Don't look at me so crossly, you might really
frighten me.'

A tram drove by – in the opposite direction; the young gentleman
did not get on. He just stood there opposite, twirling his walking-
stick, as if rooted to the spot. – 'Kathy, someone's following you!'

'Really?' She turned her head and looked at the young gentleman
across the street with an expression which was decidedly not
unfriendly. The young gentleman was evidently watching some mysterious object which happened just then to be slowly ascending

through the air; perhaps it was a swallow, perhaps a fly, perhaps a balloon . . . at all events Engelbert himself could see nothing whatsoever.

'Well, arrest him then, Constable . . . for . . . Let me see, if we had only had more experience, we'd soon know the charge . . . I've got it! . . . for malicious damage to other people's property! . . . And so, Superintendent, I remain your humble servant, and will find my own way to the Prater!' – 'Kathy!' – 'What now?' – 'Are you really off?'

'Do you imagine I came by just to disturb you while on duty? That would never do now, would it? Adieu!'

She began to walk away. He followed her. 'Kathy!' he cried, 'don't go! don't go!' – She turned round and looked at him wide-eyed.

'I beg you, Kathy, stay a little longer. You can't just go off like this. At least tell me . . .' – 'Tell you what?'

'That you're still fond of me . . . Kathy, please!'

'No fear! I hold the service in far too high esteem for that . . . And so goodbye – I'm off to the Prater!' – 'Kathy, are you serious?'

'How could I presume to joke with a constable on duty? Of course I'm serious! First I'm going on the round-about, then I'm going on the big dipper, then I'm going on the helter-skelter, then I'm going on the crazy rocker, then I'll watch the harlequins in one of the sideshows . . . Can you think, Superintendent, of anything else . . .' – 'Kathy!'

He was trembling to his very finger-tips. The young gentleman opposite was leaning against the lamp-post and gazing at his shoes. Kathy nodded farewell a couple of times and turned again to go. Engelbert seized her hand. Kathy stared at him.

'What do you think you're doing?' she asked, suddenly quite serious.

'Kathy, I won't allow it! Do you understand? . . . I won't allow you to go to the Prater! Next Sunday I've got the day off and we can go together.'

'It would just have to be you to be given the day off! How could they do without you for an entire day . . . the whole of Vienna would be topsy-turvy, you could kiss goodbye to law and order, people would do exactly as they pleased as soon as they knew that Engelbert Friedmaier was off duty . . . Goodbye, Engelbert. I'll drop past again on my way home; perhaps by then you'll have been promoted. Adieu!'

'Kathy, don't you dare go to the Prater, or you'll regret it!'

'Just let go of me!' – 'Kathy!' he said hoarsely, 'if you go to the Prater, it's all over between us – understand?'

'Really now, is that a promise? In that case, I can't wait to go!' She stalked off. For a moment Engelbert stood there as if hamstrung. Then he saw the young man opposite waken from his dreams and, casually swinging his walking-stick, set off in the same direction as Kathy. A moment later Engelbert had caught up with Kathy and seized her by the arm . . . She gave a little scream and said: 'Tell me, have you been drinking?'

'You'll stay right here!' He said this in a completely expressionless voice, and the whites of his eyes went red. – 'Let go!' said Kathy. 'Let go of me at once! I've never been treated like this in all my life!'

He let go of her arm. 'I'll ask you one last time . . .'

'Will you ever leave me in peace? No, it's all over, I'm going to the Prater!' – 'Kathy!' – 'You're just a surly ape!' – 'Kathy . . . what did you say?'

She looked at him cheekily and repeated: 'I said that you're a surly ape!'

Engelbert stared at the half-open lips, from which these words had just issued. For a moment he was on the point of answering, his fingers twitched and everything began to swim before his eyes, so that Kathy's figure seemed to dissolve in a strange mist and the young gentleman to be prancing in the air. Yet the very next moment he was again able to see clearly, more clearly than he ever had before, and a calm that he himself could not quite comprehend came over him. He was no longer Engelbert the lover. He was a policeman on duty, and the figure before him no longer his adored bride-to-be but a female personage who had insulted him. A mad but meaningful smile transformed his face and, putting his hand on the girl's shoulder, he announced in a firm, utterly changed, loud voice such as no one had ever heard from him before: 'In the name of the law, you are under arrest!'

Kathy looked at him wide-eyed and did not know at first whether to laugh or to feel vexed; but his expression and the tone of his voice were so determined that it was hard to doubt that he was serious.

'Engelbert, are you . . .' – 'No more of that Engelbert business . . . I am Constable Friedmaier to you!' – A few passers-by had stopped to watch.

'Engelbert,' said Kathy softly, giving him an imploring look.

'Follow me to the police station at once, Fräulein, where you will soon learn that a police constable is no surly ape!'

More passers-by stopped to watch. One of them had heard what Engelbert had said and passed it on to those around him; the amazement of the little circle knew no bounds.

'No assembling on the street!' said Engelbert, turning majestically toward the bystanders. 'I request you to disperse immediately. Fräulein, kindly follow me!'

Kathy stared at him . . . she still did not know quite how to take it.

'What are you waiting for, Fräulein?' said Engelbert. 'Quick march!'

And with a gesture which permitted no gainsaying he instructed her to move along. The other people had fallen back and were watching the arrest of the pretty girl with deferential awe.

'Why are you arresting this lady?' someone asked suddenly from immediately behind Engelbert. Greatly surprised, Engelbert turned round. The person who had spoken was of course the young gentleman in the grey suit.

'What?' asked Engelbert in a tone which betrayed justifiable doubts as to his interlocutor's sanity.

'Why are you arresting this lady,' repeated the young gentleman, looking at Engelbert with insufferable insolence. An expression of gratitude, to say the least, appeared on Kathy's face. Engelbert now felt he could not stop half-way.

'You come along too,' he shouted. 'I arrest you in the name of the law.' – 'I shall be only too pleased to come along, my dear Constable,' said the young gentleman with a smile.

'And I'm not your dear Constable! Quick march!'

'Pardon me,' said the young gentleman, 'but that's not for you to judge; to my mind you are a very dear Constable indeed.'

'Be quiet and follow me! Kindly disperse, the rest of you,' he said, turning to the crowd that had again closed in. 'This is not a theatre!'

He walked down the middle of the pavement, with Kathy on his right and the young gentleman on his left. So finally he had brought it off, now there would be an end to the mockery of his comrades, the suspicion of his superiors, and the contempt of his beloved . . . yes, even that! even that! Everything else between them was over too, of course . . . But that was neither here nor there, that was and could be no concern of his.

The two under arrest beside him had begun to chat; he tried not to listen in but to no avail. The young man said: 'Fräulein, I am really very sorry that your walk has been so rudely interrupted.'

Kathy replied: 'Don't mention it, I'm sorry too that for my sake, for the sake of a complete stranger . . .'

'I assure you, Fräulein, that even were I to be sentenced to many years' hard labour, for me it would be a pleasure.'

Engelbert was obliged to listen to all this and walk on between them in silence. Without looking at his prisoners he could sense that the couple's glances expressed much more than their words did; that an ever stronger bond forged by a common destiny was linking them, against which he was powerless.

Kathy was walking so close beside him that her dress brushed against him. They were nearing the police station. When he caught sight of the familiar building in the distance, a seductive thought ran through his mind. What if he were to make an end of the whole business? What if he were to let the couple go free and beg Kathy to forgive him . . .?

But immediately he dismissed this temptation as unworthy, and with a firm step crossed the threshold of the police-station, followed by the couple under arrest.

Without looking up, the superintendent asked: 'What's the charge?'

'Superintendent, Sir,' said Engelbert, 'insulting an officer on duty and impeding the course of justice.'

The superintendent looked up. When he recognised Engelbert, a look of mild surprise appeared on his face. Then he said amiably, 'Well, well, well!'

Engelbert knew that this was a form of recognition already, but he felt none of the joy that he had formerly always anticipated he would feel at the first sign of such satisfaction with his work. The superintendent proceeded to personal particulars. 'If you don't mind, Fräulein . . .'

'Katharina Wessely, second-hand dealer's daughter, twenty-two years old . . .'

'And you, Sir?'

'Albert Meierling, medical student.'

'Now – insulting an officer on duty . . . what form did this insolent behaviour take?'

'Superintendent, Sir,' replied the constable, 'the girl called me a surly ape.'

'I see, I see,' said the superintendent. 'And what about the young man?'

'He presumed to question the arrest of the young lady.'

'I see, I see. Well, we can't proceed any further here. This is a matter for the District Court. Thank you both,' he said turning to the two under arrest. 'You will receive a summons in due course.'

'Can we go then?' asked the young man, and when he said 'we' Engelbert saw red.

'Certainly, wherever you want,' said the amiable superintendent.

Kathy glanced at Engelbert as though he were a stranger. The young man opened the door and departed with the girl. Engelbert was on the point of following them when the superintendent called out to him:

'Oh, Friedmaier!'

'Yes, Superintendent?'

'Congratulations. It was high time of course. By the way, how did the girl happen to call you a surly ape?'

'Superintendent, Sir, it is my duty to report, Sir, you see, she is my bride.'

The superintendent rose from his seat. 'What?' Then he looked long and hard at Engelbert, and slapped him on the shoulder. 'Splendid! I like that, I must say.'

'Or rather, she was my bride, Superintendent,' said Engelbert, tears streaming from his eyes. The superintendent looked at him kindly. Then he said: 'Well, back to your post now. And by the way, I shall be recommending you for special commendation.'

Engelbert hastened out onto the street. He was just in time to see Kathy and the young man getting into a *Fiaker* on the next corner, and to hear the young man call out to the coachman: 'To the Prater, Hauptallee.'

The hearing took place a few weeks later. The counsel for the prosecution paid tribute to the honourable character and dedication to duty of the constable, who had not allowed himself to be restrained by any personal attachments from letting justice take its course. The defence counsel denounced his outrageous attempt to use official channels to get a mistress he had grown tired of off his back, and expressed the hope that only isolated instances of such Machiavellian conduct were to be found among the city's fine constabulary. The prosecuting counsel, undeterred, maintained in his response that the foundations of the state would begin to totter if in this case an example were not set. And so it was to be: Kathy was sentenced to a fine of twenty-five guilders, the medical student Albert Meierling to ten; he put up the money for both of them. Sentence was passed on a beautiful day in July: that same evening the two of them again drove out to the Prater.

But the curious thing is that from that day forth the jinx that had weighed so heavily on Engelbert Friedmaier vanished. Now the criminal urges all about him are awakened: in his vicinity order and propriety have vanished; daily he escorts miscreants to the station, and his comrades look up to him admiringly. Indeed, they hardly recognise him. He has become a grim, hard man, and all the protestations of respectable people are just so many despicable lies when confronted by the dark power of his professional oath, to which judges and superintendents bow.

The Green Cravat

A young gentleman by the name of Cleophas led a secluded life in his house close to the city. One morning he felt the urge to be out among his fellow human beings. So he dressed respectably as he always did, put on a new green cravat and went out into the park. People greeted him politely, found his green cravat very becoming, and for some days talked appreciatively all about the green cravat Herr Cleophas was wearing. Some attempted to emulate him and they too put on green cravats – though admittedly theirs were of poorer quality and tied with very little flare.

Not long afterwards, Herr Cleophas again went for a walk through the park in a brand new suit but wearing the same green cravat. Some people shook their heads doubtfully and said: 'He's wearing that green cravat again . . . It's probably the only one he's got . . .' Others who were a little irritable exclaimed: 'He'll drive us to distraction with that green cravat!'

The next time Herr Cleophas went out and about he wore a blue cravat. Some exclaimed: 'What an idea, going about in a blue cravat all of a sudden.' But the more irritable called out loudly: 'We have got used to seeing him in a green cravat! We really don't need him to appear now in a blue one!' But a few who were particularly shrewd exclaimed: 'Oh, no, he's not going to persuade us that that cravat is blue. Herr Cleophas is wearing it, and so of course it must be green.'

The next time Herr Cleophas appeared, as respectably dressed as ever, he was wearing the most beautiful purple cravat. When they saw him coming from a distance, people shouted out contemptuously: 'Here comes the gentleman with the green cravat!'

There was one particular group of people whose means did not allow them to wear anything beyond string ties around their necks. They declared that string ties were more elegant and more distinctive, and hated anyone who wore cravats, especially Herr Cleophas who was always immaculately dressed, and wore more beautiful and better tied cravats than anybody else. Once the most vociferous of these people, when he saw Herr Cleophas coming by, yelled out: 'Gentlemen who wear green cravats are lechers!' Herr Cleophas paid no attention and simply continued on his way.

The next time Herr Cleophas went out walking in the park, the man with the string tie around his neck yelled out: 'Gentlemen who wear green cravats are thieves!' And several others now joined in. Herr Cleophas shrugged his shoulders and reflected that for gentlemen who wore green cravats these days, things were really getting out of hand. When he came by a third time, the whole crowd, led by the loud fellow with the string tie about his neck, yelled out: 'Gentlemen who wear green cravats are back-stabbing murderers!' Cleophas noticed that many eyes were turned towards him. He remembered that he too had often worn green cravats, and going up to the fellow with the string tie he asked: 'Who exactly do you have in mind? Me, I suppose?' The fellow replied: 'But Herr Cleophas, whatever makes you think so – ? You're not wearing a green cravat!' And he shook his hand and assured him of his sincere esteem.

Cleophas bade him good-day and left. But when he was a respectable way off, the man with the string tie clapped his hands and shouted: 'You see how that struck a raw nerve with him! Who can now be in any doubt that Cleophas is a lecher, a thief and a back-stabbing murderer?!'

An Eccentric

I was sitting in the coffee-house last night when suddenly a voice behind me exclaimed: '*Ah non – ça –* never again!'

I scarcely needed to look up: it was of course Augustus. He was as handsome and debonair as ever. With that splendid nonchalance that I have always secretly envied in him, he sat down opposite me at the little table without removing the yellow top-coat from around his shoulders, pulled the stiff little black bowler-hat – about which I shall have more to say – well down over his eyes, and summoned the waiter who was lying on the billiard table reading the paper.

The waiter came over hastily. 'Good evening, Herr von Witte.'

'Good evening, he says – crikey – are you pulling my leg? Bring me something to eat or drink, there's a good fellow.'

'Certainly, Herr von Witte – black coffee – or would you like a brandy . . .?'

Augustus glowered at the waiter. 'Coffee be damned,' he said, 'bring me two sardines, two soft-boiled eggs in a hard glass, a ham roll and a bottle of beer.'

The waiter vanished. Augustus snatched the paper out of my hand and tossed it onto another table. 'I do exist, you know!'

'I'd noticed,' I replied cheerfully. 'Where the devil have you come from at this hour?'

'Where from . . .?' said Augustus and gazed at me with a demonic melancholy look. 'I would never ask a fellow such a question at three in the morning, unless he happened to be in evening dress. But then, you are and will always be a lout,' he added, attempting, not without success, to imitate poor Mitterwurzer, 'an unmitigated lout!'

I made no reply but picked up a paper and read a while. Suddenly a strange heat started radiating from my paper, and almost at once the review of a new operetta by Charles Weinberger began to glow and blacken, and the end of a freshly lighted cigarette appeared at its exact centre. But I only smiled a little, for over our years of fraternising Augustus had spoiled me with a surfeit of such jokes – and occasionally rather better ones.

'Shall I give you a bit of advice?' he asked suddenly. 'Please do,' I answered courteously.

Augustus looked at me and said clearly and distinctly: 'Take on anything, do you understand, my dear fellow, absolutely anything, except an eccentric singer!'

'I'll make a point of it,' I said.

'Anything,' Augustus reiterated; 'flower-girls, ladies travelling from Romania alone, flute-players, wives of chimney-sweeps, or tragic actresses. *Les dernières des dernières* . . . anything at all, my dear fellow, except a genuine eccentric!'

I nodded archly. The waiter brought what Augustus had ordered, and my friend set to. But no sooner had he taken his first sip of beer than he continued. 'You see, one is utterly defenceless against such creatures, that's the awful thing. Look, I'll explain. One can come to blows with a good friend one catches with one's mistress, one can shoot a passing acquaintance right there on the spot, and one can simply tan the hide of a complete stranger, provided, that is, he isn't the epitome of elegance. In all these cases one knows how to behave because one is dealing with normal people. But the things I've had to endure from the very first moment I fell in love with Mademoiselle Kitty de la Rosière until . . .' Here he took his fob-watch from his waistcoat pocket – 'until one hour ago precisely.'

'I think I'd better say goodnight,' I said and stood up.

'Oh, waiter,' Augustus called out, 'lock that door, will you!'

'Certainly, Sir, at once,' replied the waiter, who was almost as much of a wag as Augustus himself, and hurried across and locked the door.

'Sit down, my dear fellow,' said Augustus, 'and I'll tell you a tale that . . .' (here he rolled his eyes and comically assumed the melodramatic tone of a Lewinsky), 'that will chill you to the very marrow. *Les amours de Monsieur Auguste Witte et de la très-jolie Kitty de la Rosière.* – Henry, a Virginia cigar, if you would!' He leaned back in his corner, propping his elbow against the upholstered window-seat; he was still wearing the stiff little black bowler-hat – about which I shall have more to say – and with his top-coat still draped around his shoulders he looked more beguiling than ever. I was feeling very drowsy and only the hope that my friend was going to tell me about some disgraceful escapade kept me upright.

'She betrayed me,' he began.

'Ah!' I said, my interest pleasantly aroused.

'Not that I'm telling you this as if it were anything out of the ordinary, which would scarcely be in good taste. Of course I was prepared for it, as you may well imagine: but at least in the beginning I hoped I would avoid actually making the discovery. Indeed, I have acquired a certain virtuosity in that regard. I never, for instance, visit my fair ones (Augustus sometimes went in for such old-fashioned expressions) at an unexpected hour, I never read the letters that I happen to find upon their dressing-tables, I immediately leave any club where I might chance to hear their names mentioned by some stranger at the next table, and if despite all these precautions I still get wind of something, I simply refuse to give it any credence. But with Kitty all these prophylactic measures were to no avail. Do you remember Little Pluck?'

'I certainly do, the little monster.'

'Kitty evidently didn't find him so. Let me begin by saying that for about two weeks we had been blissfully happy together. Each evening I would call on her after the performance; she made her entry at eleven, I made mine at one. And on each occasion she received me very warmly. That evening too, no other arrangements had been made.'

'Which evening?'

'The one on which Little Pluck made his début, all two-foot-three of him and anywhere between eighteen and fifty-nine years old, the little monster. I entered Kitty's dressing-room as usual on the dot of one, and whom should I find . . .? Little Pluck – how should I put it? – at her feet. I was speechless. Even though any misunderstanding was virtually out of the question, I still expected some word from her that would redeem the situation – for instance: "You're making a mistake . . ." But none was forthcoming. She simply looked at me with saucer eyes and said quite unforgettably: "*N'est-il pas drôle?*" In immediate response my hand gave a reflexive jerk, so deeply rooted are our instincts; but when I looked at Little Pluck, an utterly ludicrous object – far more ludicrous at that moment than one can describe in words – my anger vanished, and I said to myself: "You really can't beat up a dwarf, and shooting it out with him would be even more preposterous." And so I merely picked up on Kitty's remark and said: "*Bien drôle! Bien drôle!*" nodded, smiled and left.'

'And all this occurred today?'

'Today? – No, no, this was two months ago. Anyway, I forgave her. And for a few weeks we were again supremely happy.'

'Did Little Pluck remain part of the ensemble?' I asked with a sardonic smile.

'I understand your impertinent little innuendo,' replied Augustus. 'But I can assure you that even though Little Pluck continued to perform at Ronacher's for a whole month, he was never again received

by Kitty when I wasn't there. And on the evening of his last performance I even arranged a little celebration for him at Kitty's, and
although he was blind drunk he behaved with such irreproachable
propriety that I permitted Kitty to give him a farewell kiss. Next
morning he left for Trieste; we accompanied him to the station, and
Kitty wept. But I was happy he was leaving. At Ronacher's, as you
are well aware, the programme changes.'

'Aha!' I said.

Augustus cannot have found my expression very flattering at that
moment, as he responded by flinging a bread-roll in my face – in jest
admittedly, but not without a touch of malice. I replaced it in the
bread-basket, and Augustus continued with his tale.

'In place of Little Pluck a feature appeared on their programme
which justifiably created a sensation. The enterprising management
– devil take them – engaged the "Two Darlings", two giants from
Tibet, and the largest pair of brothers ever seen.'

'Two!' I exclaimed, without meaning to insinuate anything in particular. But Augustus must have misunderstood me, because he
called me a miserable blackguard. 'Nevertheless,' he went on, 'your
surmise is correct. On the evening the Two Darlings made their first
appearance, I called as usual on Kitty. Need I say more . . .? Only one
of the two giants was there, but that was enough for me.'

'For you,' I said with such a cynical expression that I was startled
at myself. Augustus stared at me at first and then got up, his lips
curled in an obscene curse. But since as no doubt has already been
noticed he belonged to the best society, he controlled himself, sat
down again and in a tone almost of resignation continued. 'Kitty was
as self-possessed as ever. The giant grinned at me and seemed at first
to be mildly embarrassed. But when he noticed Kitty's calmness, he
construed the situation in a humorous manner, so to speak, gave a
hearty laugh which sounded rather like thunder in the distance, and
then said to me in English: "Good evening, Sir. I am very glad to see
you. What can I do for you?" – I won't deny that at first I was close to
boiling point, but just in time the astounding feats I had witnessed
not two hours earlier flashed through my mind: this was after all the
Darling who had lifted seven men at once above his head, broken
iron bars in two and juggled with three-hundred-kilo weights. So I
suppressed my indignation and gave Kitty a look which she probably
misunderstood. For instead of apologising, with that indescribable
composure of hers she said: "*Tu sais, mon chéri, je ne comprends pas un mot
de ce, ce qu'il dit!*" – 'You must admit that even for a more patient man
than I am, that was beyond a joke. My blood was seething, and feel-

ing that the situation was liable to end disastrously, I left without saying goodbye to her.'

'What a lout,' I said.

'When next day,' Augustus went on without heeding my rebuke, 'I
paid Kitty my customary visit, she received me as cordially as ever. I
was much too considerate to touch on the embarrassing scene the
previous evening, and Kitty seemed to have forgotten all about it.
Perhaps she even thought she had been dreaming – who knows! all
women are a mystery – all I know is, that day we made love more
ardently than ever. The same evening I was back in my box at
Ronacher's. The Two Darlings made their appearance, and as they
were as alike as two peas, I had no idea which one I had met at
Kitty's. I suspect even Kitty was never quite sure herself. But then
that's another matter. All I know is that from then on her relationship
with the two giants remained purely a friendly and innocent affair.'

'What!' I exclaimed so loudly that the windows rattled.

Without wavering Augustus continued: 'Never again did I
encounter either one of them alone with Kitty. They would have tea
with her before the performance, and I too would sometimes be
invited. And as neither giant understood a word of French and Kitty
not a syllable of English, I was so to speak the go-between.'

'And when you were not up there with them,' I asked cheerfully,
'how did they communicate?'

Augustus looked at me. 'Despite your air of childlike innocence,'
he answered with dignity, 'I can see full well that you are trying to
cast aspersions upon Kitty, but I assure you that I never had the
slightest reason to doubt her after that encounter. At any rate as far
as the giants were concerned, that is. It had been a mere caprice – my
God, I too have my caprices! And who knows how I would behave
confronted with a lady giant. I assure you, the Two Darlings were like
children; once I arrived and the two of them were playing ball with
Kitty . . . one giant was standing in one corner of the room, the other
in the other . . . or vice versa – I never could tell those fellows apart –
and Kitty was flying to and fro across the table.' Augustus smiled a
little foolishly as he recalled the jolly little scene. Suddenly however
his countenance darkened and he continued: 'Yesterday was their
last performance. At six this morning, Kitty and I accompanied the
two giants to the station. On the platform there was a great hulla-
baloo, especially when the Two Darlings waved goodbye from their
compartment window with two linen sheets. I took Kitty home by
carriage. I felt obligated to console her, and she showed herself so
grateful that it was midday before I reached the office. When I think

that all this was just this very morning . . . how utterly things have changed since then!'

'Among other things,' I remarked, full of presentiment, 'the programme at Ronacher's, no doubt.'

Augustus looked at me like an expiring deer. 'What do you expect,' he said, 'the public demands variety.'

'Who was it?' I asked simply.

'The Osmond Troupe,' Augustus answered blushing.

'How many?' I asked in a constricted voice.

'Seven,' replied Augustus.

'Seven!' I repeated with enthusiasm.

'Don't start that,' he replied quietly. 'I won't conceal from you that even during the performance unpleasant presentiments were troubling me. The Osmonds are people of incredible agility, great wit and enormous talent musically speaking. They don't have much that's new to offer, but everything was done with greater virtuosity than I have ever seen before. In general they do the familiar routines: they enter making the devil of a racket, do somersaults, break double-basses over one another's heads, tear off table-legs and blow the march from *Tannhäuser* on them, seat themselves on satin couches and croon "You are my one and only love", and so on. As I now watched the fellows clowning about and leaping over one another, I was overwhelmed by a sort of jealousy on credit, as it were' (I stick punctiliously to my friend's mode of expression, which did not always permit one to forget his occupation); 'for after my experiences so far with Kitty, I had no doubt that there was again something distressing in store for me tonight. But suddenly a thought occurred to me that brought me comfort, peace and even a kind of satisfaction. This was that these were all full-grown people, not dwarves, not giants, they were so to speak ordinary men like you and me.' I bowed, acknowledging the compliment. 'In that case I was released from all constraint. I could dispatch each of these seven fellows without making myself ridiculous. – At midnight the performance ended. From twelve to one I went for a walk; in the course of that hour the hope awoke in me afresh that this time her door would perhaps be locked. It was a vain hope indeed; the door was on the latch and behind it I could hear laughing conversation; I entered, and as you have rightly guessed, it was one of the dread Seven.

'No doubt the ring-leader,' I said without much thought.

'How on earth should I know!' Augustus retorted. 'At Ronacher's they were all of them made up and wearing fancy costumes, which was not the case with the fellow I caught with that miserable hussy.

He was, as I expected, a handsome young man, not unlike myself.' – He made no reference to me this time. 'The unfathomable Kitty looked at me with the most enchanting smile and said: "*Si je ne compte pas mal, c'est la troisième fois.*" – "*Et la dernière, je t'assure,*" I said in a tone she had certainly never heard from anyone before. Then I turned to the Osmond fellow, who despite having been caught in the act, shall we say, calmly continued smoking his cigarette, and seizing him by the arm said: 'Sir, you are a cad, and I intend to tan your hide. Not that I'm jealous of women of her ilk, but because I'm piqued – a good word, don't you think, on the spur of the moment? – to find you here.' And with this I raised my hand to slap him across the face. But that very same instant I suddenly blacked out – in the literal sense of the word; I couldn't see a thing, for with one mighty blow of his fist the Oswald Seventh had crammed my top hat over my eyes, and all I was conscious of were the words I had heard on the stage an hour before, as he had battered one of his six companions over the head with a hoe – German words in an English accent: "My dear fellow, you do look funny!" When I finally managed to raise my hat again, Kitty, the sweet little thing, was rolling about on the floor in a veritable fit of laughter, and the clown was sitting cross-legged on the arm of the divan and smoking his cigarette as though nothing untoward had happened. But for me this was really the last straw! I was completely drained and felt neither love, nor jealousy, nor pain, nor pride, nor hate. I simply said: 'Good night, Kitty', ignored the Osmond fellow, left the room, hung my squashed top hat on the peg in the hall, put on this nice new crisp black bowler hat belonging to the clown, and then made my way over here posthaste to warn you never to take up with an eccentric singer.'

'My dear Augustus,' I said, 'you are unjust. In my view you have reaped nothing but profit from the whole affair. I won't mention the hat, which suits you splendidly, but just think of the fund of experience you have garnered. How else are the likes of you and me to associate with dwarves and giants on so intimate a footing?' (Augustus shook his head in a deprecating manner.) I became more insistent: 'If I were in your shoes, I certainly wouldn't neglect to call on Kitty for tea tomorrow, where you will doubtless become acquainted with the entire troupe.' Augustus looked at me suspiciously. 'You see,' I continued, 'I can't help imagining it might be highly entertaining. Just as the two giants were playing ball with her, well perhaps the Osmonds will be having a flutter on the flute with her or something.'

'You're an idiot,' replied Augustus. He simply couldn't stand it when someone else made a good joke.

The waiter came. We paid and strode out into a glorious spring morning. 'I'm just pleased,' said Augustus, 'that the fellow won't laugh long over his little joke when, instead of his new hat in the hall . . .'

All of a sudden Augustus fell silent. I noticed that his features suddenly grew tense and his eyes started from his head. I followed his gaze and saw a young man coming towards us, dressed with consummate elegance except that the top hat he was wearing was completely crumpled. Augustus stopped short and waited for the young man to approach. The latter raised his hat and said: 'Good morning, Sir.'

'Good morning,' we both replied and doffed our hats, intending of course to put them on again immediately. I succeeded, but not so my friend Augustus. Deftly the stranger snatched Augustus's hat out of his hand, put it on and with a cordial smile handed him back the battered top hat in exchange. Then turning to me, as though I were the one to whom he owed an explanation, he observed: 'I misplaced this little hat when with a little lady friend a little while ago. Good morning, Sir.' And with that he left.

I would be lying if I claimed that I had ever seen a more foolish-looking face than that of my friend Augustus at that moment. He had gone deathly pale and seemed to be gasping for air, or at least for words. He waited until the gentleman was a respectable way off, and then with a sort of gloomy resoluteness he observed: 'What should one do? Stab him or simply laugh uproariously?'

'Stab him,' I said quickly. I gave him this advice not out of sheer bloody-mindedness, but rather out of curiosity, since I had never seen anybody stabbed before.

Whether because he was too good-hearted or simply didn't have a dagger on him, Augustus did not follow my advice, but merely emitted a short and not as he had at first proposed particularly uproarious laugh. I looked at him with some concern, as I knew of people who under similar circumstances have suddenly gone mad. Augustus did not do so. A strange spasm passed over his face, as though some terrible inner turmoil were subsiding, and in a dreamy voice he muttered something about 'a good straightening out'.

I am firmly convinced he was referring to the hat.

The Grecian Dancer

People may say what they like, I don't believe Frau Mathilde Samodeski died of a heart attack. I know better. Nor am I prepared to enter the house they bore her from to her eternal rest today. I have no desire to meet the man who knows as well as I do why she died, to shake his hand and to say nothing.

I shall go round another way; admittedly it's quite far, but it is a lovely still autumn day and it will do me good to be alone. Soon I shall be standing in front of the garden railings where last spring I saw Mathilde for the last time. The shutters of the villa will all be closed, the gravel will be strewn with russet leaves, and at some point I am sure to glimpse the Grecian statue, carved from white marble, gleaming through the trees.

Today I cannot help brooding a good deal over that evening. It almost seems as though my decision to accept the Wartenheimers' invitation at the very last moment was fated, particularly since over the years I have ceased to take any pleasure in such social gatherings. Perhaps it had something to do with the warm breeze which came wafting down from the hills into the city of an evening, enticing me out into the country. Moreover, the Wartenheimers had decided on a garden-party to celebrate the opening of their villa, so there was no fear of things being too constrained. It was also strange how on the drive out I scarcely thought about the possibility that I might meet Mathilde there. And yet I was well aware that Herr Wartenheimer had purchased the statue of the Grecian dancer from Samodeski to adorn his villa – and equally aware that Frau von Wartenheimer was in love with the sculptor like all the other women. Yet quite apart from that, I might well have thought of Mathilde, because in the days when she was still a girl I spent many a pleasant hour with her. There was one summer in particular by Lake Geneva seven years ago, exactly one year before her engagement, that I shall not easily forget. It would even appear that at the time, despite my grey hair, I had fancied my own chances, because when the following year she became Samodeski's bride, I felt some disillusionment and was utterly convinced – or fervently hoped – that she could not be happy with him.

It was not until the party that Gregor Samodeski gave, shortly after their return from their honeymoon, in his studio in the Gusshausgasse, where absurdly all the guests had to appear in Japanese or Chinese costume, that I saw Mathilde again. She greeted me quite unself-consciously; her whole being gave the impression of serenity and cheerfulness. But later while she was in conversation with others I occasionally caught a strange look in her eye, and after some deliberation I understood what it meant. It said, 'My dear friend, you think he married me for my money; you think he doesn't love me; you think I am unhappy – but you are mistaken . . . you are certainly quite mistaken. Look what a good mood I'm in, how my eyes are shining.'

I met her again later, several times, but always only very briefly. Once on a journey our paths crossed while changing trains; I dined with her and her husband in the station restaurant, and he told all sorts of jokes which did not particularly amuse me. I also talked to her in the theatre once: she was there with her mother, who is still, in fact, even more beautiful than she is . . . the devil only knows where Herr Samodeski was on that occasion. And last winter I saw her in the Prater, on a clear cold day. She was walking over the snow with her little girl beneath the bare chestnut trees. The carriage was slowly following them. I was on the opposite side of the carriageway and didn't even cross over. Probably I was inwardly preoccupied with other things; besides I was no longer particularly interested in Mathilde. Even today I should perhaps not be giving any further thought to her and her sudden death had it not been for that last encounter at the Wartenheimers'. I remember that meeting today with remarkable, even painful clarity, much as I do some of those days by Lake Geneva. It was already dusk when I got out there. The guests were strolling through the avenues and I greeted the host and several acquaintances. From somewhere hidden in the shrubbery came the sound of music from a string ensemble. Soon I came to the little pond under its half-circle of tall trees; in the middle on a dark pedestal, so that it appeared to hover above the water, gleamed the Grecian dancer; indeed it was a little theatrically illuminated by electric lighting from the house. I remember the sensation it had caused in the Secession the year before, and I must admit it made an impression on me too, although I find Samodeski singularly odious, and despite my strange feeling that it is not he who creates these beautiful objects so successfully, but something else within him, something inexplicable, fiery, demonic one might even say, which will quite certainly be extinguished once he ceases to be young and popular. I believe there are quite a few artists of this kind, and this fact has always filled me with a certain satisfaction.

Near the pond I came across Mathilde. She was walking on the arm of a young man who looked like a fraternity student and introduced himself to me as a relation of the family. The three of us strolled up and down chatting amicably in the garden, where lights had now come on everywhere. The hostess came towards us accompanied by Samodeski. We all stood there for a while and to my own astonishment I said a few highly commendatory words to the sculptor about the Grecian statue. Actually I spoke quite innocently; for that blithe tranquil feel was in the air one gets occasionally on such spring evenings: people who are normally on indifferent terms greet one another cordially, while others who are already bound by a certain sympathy feel moved to make all kinds of effusive confidences. When for example a short while later I was sitting on a bench smoking a cigarette, a gentleman whom I knew only slightly joined me and suddenly began praising people who knew how to make such elegant use of their wealth as did our hosts. I agreed with him completely, even though normally I think of Herr Wartenheimer as a simple-minded snob. Then I in turn confided my views on modern sculpture to him, a subject about which I don't know very much, and which normally would not have held the slightest interest for him; yet under the influence of that seductive spring evening he agreed with me enthusiastically. Later I met the nieces of our host, who declared the festivities utterly romantic, principally because the lights were shining through the leaves and music was playing in the distance. All this while we were standing right next to the string ensemble; yet even so I did not find the observation ludicrous. So completely was I too under the spell of the prevailing mood.

Supper was served at little tables which, so far as space permitted, were set out on the broad terrace, and the remainder in the adjacent drawing-room. The three large French windows stood wide open. I was seated at a table in the open air with one of the nieces; Mathilde had sat down next to me with the gentleman who looked like a fraternity student but was actually a bank employee and a reserve officer. Opposite us but inside the room sat Samodeski, between our hostess and some other beautiful lady whom I did not know. He blew his wife a playfully exaggerated kiss; she nodded in response and smiled. Without any particular purpose I observed him fairly carefully. He was really handsome, with his steel-blue eyes and long black pointed beard, which he stroked now and then raising two fingers of his left hand to his chin. But I also don't think I have ever in my life seen a man basking so, one might say, in the warm radiance of words, looks and gestures as he was on that evening. At first it seemed that he was simply allowing it all to flow over him. But soon I could see from the way he whispered softly to the women, from his intolerable looks of triumph, and especially from the lively animation of his fair neighbours, that their apparently innocent conversation was being nourished by some secret fire. Naturally Mathilde was bound to notice all this as well as I; but she chatted alternately with her neighbour and with me in apparent unconcern. Gradually she turned more exclusively to me, enquired about various external circumstances of my life, and asked me to tell her about my trip to Athens the previous year. Then she talked about her little girl who remarkably could already sing songs by Schumann she had picked up by ear; about her parents who had just purchased a little house for their old age in Hietzing; about some antique church fabrics she had obtained herself the previous year in Salzburg, and a hundred other things. But beneath the surface of this conversation something quite different was going on between us; an embittered silent struggle: she was trying to persuade me by her calmness that her happiness was unalloyed – and I was making every effort not to believe her. I could not help recalling that Chinese-Japanese evening in Samodeski's studio, when she had made the same attempt. This time she obviously felt that she was making little headway against my reservations, and that she would have to think up something very special in order to dispel them. And so she hit upon the notion of herself drawing my attention to the amorous and ingratiating behaviour of the two beautiful women towards her husband, and began to talk about his luck with women, as though she could take pleasure in this as a friend as well as in his looks and in his genius without the slightest disquiet or suspicion. But the more she strove to appear tranquil and contented, the darker the shadows that clouded her brow. Once when she raised her glass to her husband her hand was trembling. She tried to repress and hide it; but as a result not only her hand but her arm and her whole body became so tense that I was almost apprehensive. She pulled herself together, gave me a quick sidelong glance, evidently noticed that she was on the point of losing the game, and said suddenly, as if making a last desperate attempt: 'I bet you think I'm jealous.' And before I had time to respond, she added hastily: 'Oh, many people think that. At first Gregor thought so himself.' She deliberately spoke quite loud, so that at the table opposite every word could be heard. 'Ah well,' she said with a glance across at them, 'when one has a husband like that – handsome and famous . . . and is not thought to be particularly beautiful oneself . . . Oh, you don't have to reply . . . I'm aware of course that since I had my daughter I've become a little prettier.' Possibly she was right, but to her husband – I'm quite convinced of this – her noble features never meant especially much, and as far as her figure was concerned, its only charm had probably been lost for him with the passing of her youthfulness. But naturally I agreed in exaggerated terms; she seemed pleased and continued with increasing confidence: 'But I don't have the least propensity for jealousy. I didn't realise that at first and only gradually came to understand it, particularly in Paris a few years ago . . . you know we were there?'

I remembered.

'Gregor did the busts of Princess La Hire and Minister Chocquet there and various other works. We had such an agreeable life there as young people . . . of course, we are both still young . . . I mean, as a couple when we occasionally went out into society . . . we were at the Austrian ambassador's a few times, and called on the La Hires and others. In general though we did not set much store by high society. We even lived out in Montmartre in a fairly shabby house, where Gregor also had his studio. I assure you, many of the young artists with whom we associated there had no idea that we were married. I trudged round everywhere with him. Often at night I would sit with him in the Café Athénés, together with Léandre, Carabin and many others. Indeed, all sorts of women were often in our company, whom I would probably never associate with in Vienna . . . although admittedly –' She cast a hasty glance across at Frau Wartenheimer and quickly continued: 'And many of them were very beautiful. Several times Henri Chabran's last mistress was there too, after his death she always went about in black and had a new lover every week, all of whom during this period she insisted had to dress in mourning too . . . strange, the people one meets. You can imagine that women there ran after my husband no less eagerly than elsewhere; it made one laugh. But because I was always with him – or mostly, they didn't dare approach him, particularly since I was taken for his mistress . . . Had they only known that I was merely his wife! And then once I hit upon a curious notion, which you would certainly never have expected of me – and to be honest, today I am surprised myself at my audacity.' She looked straight ahead and spoke more softly than before: 'Moreover, it's possible that it was also connected with – well, you know what I mean. For some weeks I had known that I was expecting a child. This made me enormously happy. At the beginning I was not only more cheerful but also surprisingly much more free and easy than ever before. Just imagine, one fine evening I actually dressed up in men's clothes and went out like that with Gregor as an adventure. Naturally I made him promise beforehand not to feel in any way constrained, otherwise the whole affair would have had no point. Furthermore, I looked quite stunning – you would not have recognised me – no one would have recognised me. A friend of Gregor's, someone called Léonce Albert, a young painter and a hunchback, called for us on this particular evening. It was very beautiful . . . May . . . quite warm . . . and you have no idea how brazen I was being. Imagine, I simply took off my coat – a very elegant yellow topcoat – and carried it over my arm . . . exactly the way gentlemen usually do . . . Admittedly it was already fairly dark . . . We dined in a small restaurant on the outer Boulevard, and then we went to the Roulotte, where Legay and Montoya were singing . . . '*Tu t'en iras les pieds devant*' . . . You heard it here recently in the Wiedener Theater, I believe?' Here Mathilde cast a quick glance at her husband, who paid no attention. It was as though she were taking leave of him for an extended period. And now she talked on, ever more urgently, forging ahead as it were. 'In the Roulotte,' she said, 'there was a very elegant lady sitting just in front of us; she flirted with Gregor, but in a way which . . . well, believe me, it would be hard to imagine anything more indecent. I will never understand why her husband didn't strangle her on the spot. I could have done so. I believe she was a duchess . . . You mustn't laugh, she was certainly a lady from high society, despite her conduct . . . one can tell . . . And actually I wanted Gregor to respond . . . naturally! – I would have liked to see how one started an affair like this . . . I wanted him to pass her a note – or something of the kind – as he may well have done in such situations before I became his wife . . . Yes, that's what I wanted, even though it would not have been without some danger for him. Evidently we women are imbued with a terrible curiosity . . . But Gregor, thank God, was not interested. Indeed we left quite soon, out into the beautiful May night again, and Léonce continued to accompany us. He, by the way, had fallen in love with me that evening, and contrary to his usual manner was positively gallant. Normally he was a very diffident person – because of his appearance . . . I even said to him: 'It would seem one has to have a yellow top-coat before you will pay court to one.' We strolled on as contentedly as three students. And now came the interesting part: we repaired to the Moulin Rouge. This was part of the evening's programme. It also seemed necessary that at last something should happen. So far we had not had any adventures . . . except that I – just imagine: I myself – was proposi-

tioned by a woman on the street. But that after all had not been the
intention . . . By one o'clock we were in the Moulin Rouge. You probably know the kind of thing that goes on there; actually, I imagined it
would be a lot worse . . . Here too nothing very much happened
at first, and it looked as though my prank was going to come to nothing. I was a little annoyed. 'What a child you are,' said Gregor. 'What
did you imagine? That we'd arrive and everyone would fall at our
feet?' He said 'we' out of courtesy to Léonce; there was no question
of anyone falling at Léonce's feet. But just as we were all seriously
thinking of returning home, things took an unexpected turn. My
attention was caught . . . yes, truly, mine . . . by a person who quite by
chance had walked past us several times . . . She seemed very serious
and looked rather different from most of the other ladies present . . .
She was not in the least gaudily dressed – but in white, completely in
white . . . I had noticed how she did not respond at all to two or three
gentlemen who addressed her, but simply walked on without favour-
ing them with so much as a glance. She just watched the dancing,
very quietly, with interest, one might even say matter-of-factly . . .
Léonce asked a few acquaintances – as I had urged him to – whether
they had encountered the lovely creature anywhere before, and one
of them remembered having seen her the previous winter at one of
the Thursday night balls in the Latin Quarter. Léonce then
addressed her at some distance from us and to him she did respond.
Then he came over with her and we all sat down at a little table and
drank champagne. Gregor paid no attention to her, as though she
had not been there . . . He chatted exclusively with me . . . She
seemed to find this especially provoking. She became more and more
lively and loquacious and less inhibited, and as these things happen,
gradually told us her entire life story. Incredible what such poor creatures sometimes go through – or are obliged to go through, possibly!
One reads about these things so often, but when one suddenly hears
of them as something absolutely real from someone sitting next to
one, it all seems really quite bizarre. I can still remember some of it.
When she was fifteen years old, someone seduced and then abandoned her. Then she became a model. She had also been an extra in
a small theatre. The things she told us about the director! . . . I would
have got up and left had I not already become a little tipsy with
champagne . . . Then she had fallen in love with a medical student
who worked in a dissection room, and sometimes she would pick him
up at the morgue . . . or more often stayed there with him . . . I simply can't repeat the things she told us! The medical student left her
too of course. And it was this particularly that she couldn't reconcile

herself to. So she resolved to take her own life, that is, she made the attempt. She herself made light of it . . . with expressive gestures! I can still hear her voice . . . it didn't sound at all as vulgar as it was. And she adjusted her dress a little to reveal a small reddish scar above her left breast. And as we are all very earnestly examining this scar, she suddenly says – or rather, shouts at my husband: 'Kiss it!' I've already told you that Gregor had been paying no attention to her. Even when she was telling her story, he hardly listened, gazing across the room, smoking cigarettes, and now when she shouted at him like that he scarcely smiled. But I nudged and pinched him, for I was really quite tipsy by now . . . at all events, it was the strangest mood I'd been in in my life. And so whether he wanted to or not, the scar had to be . . . that is, he had to pretend to touch it with his lips. Well, and then things became even merrier and more abandoned. Never have I laughed so much as I did that evening – and without having the least idea why. And never would I have thought it possible that any woman – and especially a woman of her kind – could in the course of an hour fall so madly in love with anyone as this creature did with Gregor. Her name was Madeleine.'

I don't know whether Mathilde deliberately spoke louder when she mentioned this name – at all events I had the impression that her husband heard it because he looked across at us; strangely enough, he didn't look at his wife, but our eyes met and rested on one another a good while, and not with any special sympathy. Then he suddenly smiled at his wife, she nodded in response, he continued his conversation with his fair neighbours, and she turned again to me.

'Of course I can no longer remember everything Madeleine said later,' she observed, 'it was all rather confusing. But I'll be honest: there was one split second I did feel a little piqued! That was when Madeleine took my husband's hand and kissed it. But it was over almost at once. For in that same instant, you see, I couldn't help thinking of our child. And then I felt how indissolubly Gregor and I were bound to one another, and how everything else could never be more than shadows, trifling and laughter, as on that evening. And so everything was all right again. We then all sat in a café on the boulevard till dawn. Then I heard Madeleine ask my husband to accompany her home. He simply laughed at her. And then to end the fun on a light and in a sense propitious note – you know what egoists all artists are . . . that is, as far as their art is concerned . . . in short, he told her he was a sculptor and invited her to come to his studio in the near future, as he would like to use her as a model. She replied: 'If you're a sculptor I'll be hanged! But I'll come anyway.'

Mathilde fell silent. But never have I seen a woman's eyes express – or conceal – so much sorrow. Then, when she had steadied herself for the last thing she had to say to me, she continued: 'Gregor was most insistent that I should be there in his studio the following day. Indeed, he even made the suggestion that I should remain hidden behind the curtains if she came. Well, there are women, many women, I know, who would have agreed to this. But to my mind, either one has faith or one does not . . . And I decided to have faith. Am I not right?' And she looked at me with large questioning eyes. I simply nodded and she went on: 'Madeleine of course came the very next day and from then on very frequently . . . as many others have come before and since . . . and believe me, she was one of the most beautiful. Only today you yourself stood before her full of admiration, out there by the pond.'

'The Grecian dancer?'

'Yes, Madeleine posed for it. And now just imagine, if in that or any other case I had become mistrustful! Would I not have made both my own and his existence miserable? I'm so happy I have no reason to be jealous.'

Someone was standing in the open middle French window and had started to deliver an evidently very witty toast to our hosts, as people were all laughing heartily. But I was watching Mathilde, who was paying no more attention than I. And I saw her gazing across at her husband with a look that not only betrayed infinite love but simulated an unshakeable faith, as though it really were her highest duty not to disturb his enjoyment of life in any way. And he acknowledged even this look – smiling, undeterred, even though he knew as well as I that she was suffering and had suffered her whole life like an animal.

And that is why I don't believe the story of the heart-attack. I got to know Mathilde too well that evening, and for me the matter is beyond doubt: just as she played the happy wife for her husband from the first moment to the last, while he lied to her and drove her to insanity, in the same way she feigned a natural death for him when she threw away her life because she could no longer bear it. And he had accepted this last sacrifice as well, as though it were his due.

Here I am, standing in front of the railings . . . the shutters are securely closed. The little villa stands there white and as if enchanted in the evening light, and the marble statue gleams between the russet branches . . .

Perhaps, by the way, I am being unjust to Samodeski. When all is said and done he is so obtuse that he may really not suspect the truth.

But it is sad to think that there should have been no greater bliss for Mathilde in death than the knowledge that her last heavenly deception had succeeded.

Or might I be mistaken? Could it have been a natural death? . . . No, I won't be deprived of the right to hate the man whom Mathilde loved so much. That is likely to be my only pleasure for some considerable time to come . . .

The Prophecy

I

Not far from Bozen, at a moderate altitude, as though submerged in the forest and scarcely visible from the country road, lies the small estate of Baron von Schottenegg. A friend of mine, a doctor who has been living in Meran for the last ten years and whom I met there again last autumn, introduced me to the Baron. The latter was fifty years old at the time and dabbled in the arts. He composed a little, was competent on the violin and the piano, and he was not bad at drawing either. But what he had taken most seriously early in life was acting. It was said that as a youth he had done the rounds of the small theatres in outposts of the Empire for several years under an assumed name. Now whether the persistent opposition of his father, insufficient talent or lack of opportunity was the reason, in any event the Baron had given up this career early enough to be able to enter the civil service without significant delay, and thus to follow the profession of his forefathers, which he then pursued faithfully though without enthusiasm for some twenty years. Only when, immediately after the death of his father and scarcely over forty years of age, he left the service, did it become apparent how fondly he still clung to the object of his youthful dreams. He had the villa on the slopes of the Guntschnaberg put in order, and there, especially in summer time and autumn, he assembled a gradually expanding circle of gentlemen and ladies who would perform all manner of easily staged playlets and tableaux. His wife, from an old bourgeois Tirolean family, without any real affinity for things artistic, but clever and attached to her husband in tender companionship, regarded his hobby with some amusement, but all the more good-naturedly since the Baron's interests fitted in with her own inclinations for society. The company met with at the villa might not have appeared select enough to severe judges, but even guests who from birth and upbringing were normally disposed toward class prejudice took no exception to the voluntary assembly of a circle which seemed sufficiently justified by its artistic pursuits, and from which moreover the name and reputation of the baronial couple removed any suspicion of more free and easy ways. Among several others whom I can no longer call to mind, I met at the villa a young count from the Innsbruck district headquarters, a hunting official from Riva, a general staff captain with wife and daughter, an operetta singer from Berlin, a Bozen liqueur manufacturer with two sons, Baron Meudolt just back from his world tour, a retired court actor from Bückeburg, a widowed Countess Saima, who as a young girl had been an actress, with her daughter, and Petersen the Danish painter.

Only a few of the guests stayed at the villa. Some took quarters in Bozen, others in a modest inn which lay below at the crossroads, where a narrower road branched off to the estate. But usually by early afternoon the whole circle had assembled up at the villa, and then, sometimes under the direction of the former court actor, occasionally under that of the Baron, who never actually played a part himself, rehearsals would take place late into the evening, initially amid jokes and laughter, but with gradually greater seriousness, until the day of the performance approached, and depending on the weather, their mood and preparations, as far as possible taking account of where the action of the play was set, the performance took place either on the open meadow bordering on the wood behind the little garden of the villa or in the drawing-room, with its three large bay windows, on the same level.

The first time I visited the Baron I had no further intention than to spend an agreeable day in a new place among new people. But as so often happens when one is wandering about aimlessly and in total freedom, and when furthermore with youth gradually fading one has no remaining ties urgently summoning one back home, I allowed myself to be talked into staying on longer by the Baron. One day became two, then three and so on, and so to my own amazement I stayed on late into the autumn up there at the villa, where a very comfortably furnished room was prepared for me in a tiny tower with a view down into the valley. This first sojourn on the Guntschnaberg will always remain for me a pleasant and, despite all the jollity and noise around me, a very quiet memory, since I did not associate more than fleetingly with any of the guests, and furthermore spent a great deal of my time, stimulated equally to reflection and to work, on solitary woodland walks. Even the fact that, out of courtesy, the Baron once arranged to have one of my little plays put on did not disturb the peace of my stay, since no one took any notice of me in my capacity as the author. Indeed, the evening was a most delightful experience for me, since with this performance on the green lawn under the sky a modest dream going back to my early years found a fulfilment as unexpected as it was belated.

The lively activity in the villa gradually abated, the leave of the
gentlemen who held professional positions had in the main run out,
and only occasionally were visits made by friends who resided in the
area. Only now did I myself develop a closer relationship with the
Baron, and to my surprise found in him more personal modesty than
normally tends to characterise such dilettantes. He was under no
illusion that what went on at his villa was anything more than a
refined form of social entertainment. But since in the course of his
life he had been denied the opportunity of entering into a serious and
enduring relationship with his beloved art, he contented himself with
the radiance which, as if from a remote distance, illuminated the
harmless theatrical activities at the villa, and rejoiced moreover that
here at least no trace of the mean-spiritedness which accompanies
professionalism everywhere was to be felt.

On one of our walks, without being in the least importunate, he
mentioned an idea he had of one day seeing a play performed on his
open-air stage written expressly with the unlimited space and natural
setting in mind. This remark so perfectly coincided with a plan I had
been brooding over for some time that I promised the Baron to fulfil
his wish.

Soon afterwards I left the villa.

Early next spring, along with a few friendly words recalling the
pleasant days of the previous autumn, I sent the Baron a play which
seemed as though it might well suit the occasion. Soon afterwards I
received an answer, containing the Baron's thanks and a warm invitation for the coming autumn. I spent the summer in the mountains,
and early in September with the onset of cooler weather I travelled
to Lake Garda, without reflecting that I was now quite near Baron
von Schottenegg's villa. Indeed, today it seems to me that at the
time I had completely forgotten all about the villa and everything
going on there. Then on the 8th of September I received a letter
from the Baron, forwarded from Vienna. This expressed mild
astonishment that they had heard nothing from me, and contained
the announcement that the performance of the little play I had sent
him in the spring would take place on the 9th of September, and that
I should on no account be absent. The Baron promised I should be
especially delighted with the children, who were busy with the play
and already could not be prevented, even outside rehearsal hours,
from running about and playing on the lawn in their decorative costumes. The principal role – so the letter went on – had been assigned,
after a series of coincidences, to his nephew, Herr Franz von

Umprecht, who – as I would no doubt remember – had only twice taken part in tableaux the previous year, but who now showed surprising talent for acting.

I set off, by the evening was in Bozen, and on the day of the performance arrived at the villa, where the Baron and his wife received me warmly. There were other acquaintances to greet as well: the retired court actor, Countess Saima and her daughter, Herr von Umprecht and his beautiful wife, as well as the forester's fourteen-year-old daughter, who was to recite the prologue to my play. A large company was expected in the afternoon, and for the performance in the evening more than a hundred spectators would be present, not only the Baron's personal guests, but also people from the region all around, to whom today, as often before, admission to the play was free. This time furthermore a small musical ensemble had been engaged, consisting of professional musicians from an orchestra in Bozen and a few amateurs, who were to play an overture by Weber, as well as some incidental music which the Baron had himself composed.

Everyone was very convivial at table, only Herr von Umprecht seemed to me a little quieter than the others. I had hardly been able to remember him at first, and I noticed that he often looked across at me, sometimes with sympathy and then again a little shyly, but without ever speaking to me. Gradually the features of his face grew more familiar, and suddenly I recalled that the previous year he had been in one of the tableaux, sitting in a monk's habit with his arms resting on a chess-board. I asked him whether I was not mistaken. He became almost embarrassed when I addressed him; the Baron answered for him and then smilingly remarked on his nephew's recently discovered acting talent. At this Herr von Umprecht laughed out loud in a rather strange way, then cast a quick glance across at me, which seemed to express some kind of understanding between the two of us, yet which I could not comprehend. But from that moment on he avoided looking at me again.

II

Soon after the meal I had withdrawn to my room. There I stood at the open window once again, as I had so often done the previous year, and enjoyed the charming view down into the sunlit valley, which, narrow at my feet, gradually expanded and in the distance opened up completely, incorporating town and fields.

After a short while there was a knock. Herr von Umprecht stepped in, remained standing at the door and said with some embarrassment: 'I apologise if I'm disturbing you.' Then he entered the room and continued: 'But as soon as you have granted me a quarter of an hour's hearing, I am convinced you will consider my visit sufficiently excused.'

I invited Herr von Umprecht to sit down, but he disregarded this and continued with some animation: 'I have, you see, in the strangest way become indebted to you, and I feel obliged to thank you.'

Naturally all that occurred to me was that Herr von Umprecht must be referring to his role in the play, and as this seemed to me unduly civil, I started to protest. But Umprecht interrupted me immediately: 'You cannot know everything that my words imply. Could I ask you to hear me out?' He sat down on the window-seat, crossed his legs, and with an evidently deliberate attempt to appear as calm as possible, began: 'I am now a landowner, as you perhaps know, but earlier I was an officer. And at that time, ten years ago – ten years ago *today* – I met with the incredible adventure under the shadow of which I have in some sense lived until today, and which today has been resolved through you, without your knowledge or involvement. Between the two of us, you see, there is some demonic connection, which you will probably be as little able to explain as I am; but at least you should hear of its existence.

'My regiment at the time was stationed in a desolate Polish back-water. By way of entertainment outside military duties, which were not always arduous enough, there was only drink and gambling. Moreover, we faced the possibility of having to stay put out there for years, and not all of us knew, with such bleak prospects, how to bear life with composure. One of my best friends shot himself during the third month of our stay. Another comrade, up to now the most charming of officers, suddenly started to drink heavily, became unmannerly, irascible, scarcely responsible for his own actions, and had some row with a lawyer which cost him his commission. The captain of my company was married and, I don't know whether with or without good reason, he was so jealous that one day he threw his wife out of the window. Incredibly, she remained sound and healthy; the husband died in a lunatic asylum. One of our cadets, hitherto a very nice but exceptionally stupid lad, suddenly imagined he could understand philosophy, studied Kant and Hegel and learned whole passages from their works by heart, as children do their primers. As for me, I was nothing if not bored, so excruciatingly so in fact that some afternoons as I lay there on my bed, I was afraid of going mad.

Our barracks stood outside the village, which consisted of at most thirty scattered huts; the next town, a good hour's ride away, was dirty, repulsive, stinking and full of Jews. By force of circumstance we sometimes had to deal with them – the hotelier was a Jew, and so were the coffee-shop owner and the cobbler. As you can imagine, we behaved as insolently towards them as we could. We were all the more hostile to these people because a prince, who was assigned to our regiment with the rank of major, responded to the Jews' greetings – whether just as a joke or out of partiality I don't know – with extreme politeness; and furthermore he conspicuously and deliberately extended his patronage to our regimental doctor, who was quite obviously of Jewish descent. I should not of course have told you all this if it had not been precisely this whim of the Prince's that had brought me into contact with the very person who, in so unaccountable a way, was destined to establish the connection between myself and you. He was a conjurer, and furthermore the son of a Jewish wine and spirit merchant from the neighbouring Polish town. As a young lad he had gone to Lemberg, then to Vienna, and had once picked up a few card tricks from somebody or other. He went on learning on his own, mastered all kinds of other conjuring tricks, and gradually reached the stage where he could roam the world and perform successfully in variety theatres and clubs. Every summer he came back to his home town to visit his parents. There he never performed in public, and so I first saw him on the street, where I was immediately struck by his appearance. He was a little skinny beardless fellow, who at the time might have been about thirty, and dressed with an utterly ridiculous elegance that was completely inappropriate for the time of year: he strolled about in a black frock-coat and steamed top hat, and wore waistcoats of the most magnificent brocade; on a sunny day he would have a dark pince-nez upon his nose.

'Once, fifteen or sixteen of us were sitting round our long table in the casino after supper as usual. It was a sultry night, and the windows stood open. Several comrades had started to play cards, others were leaning against the window chatting, and still others drinking and smoking in silence. Then the day-duty corporal entered and announced the arrival of the conjurer. We were at first a little taken aback. But without further ado, the gentleman in question entered with great composure, and with a slight accent said a few words of introduction, in which he thanked us for the proffered invitation. He then turned towards the Prince, who advanced towards him and – for the sole purpose of annoying us, of course – shook hands with him. The conjurer accepted this as a matter of course, and then observed that he would first show us a few card tricks and afterwards introduce us to a bit of mesmerism and chiromancy. He had scarcely finished speaking when several of the company, who were sitting playing cards in the corner, noticed that their chips were missing: at a sign from the magician however, they came flying in through the open window. The conjuring tricks he followed on with were very entertaining too, and surpassed almost everything of the kind that I had seen. The experiment in mesmerism that he then conducted struck me as even more amazing. We all looked on aghast as the philosophical cadet was put to sleep and, obeying the magician's orders, then leapt out of the open window, climbed up the bare wall onto the roof, and, keeping close to the edge, hastened round the entire quad before sliding back down into the courtyard. When he was down again, still in this somnambular condition, the Colonel said to the magician: "You Sir, if he had broken his neck, I assure you, you would not have left the barracks alive." Never will I forget the look of silent contempt with which the Jew responded to this remark. Then he said slowly: "Should I read your palm, Colonel, and tell you when *you* will leave the barracks, dead or alive?" I don't know what the Colonel or the rest of us would have normally replied to this audacious remark – but the general atmosphere was so excited and confused that no one was surprised when the Colonel held out his palm to the conjurer and, mimicking his accent, said: "Go on then, read away."

'All this had taken place in the courtyard; the cadet, still fast asleep, was standing with arms outstretched like one crucified against the wall. The magician had grasped the Colonel's hand and was attentively studying the lines of his palm. "Seen enough, Jew?" asked a lieutenant, who was rather drunk. The magician turned round briefly and said solemnly: "My professional name as an artiste is Marco Polo." The Prince laid his hand on the Jew's shoulder and said: "My friend Marco Polo has sharp eyes." – "Well, what can you see?" asked the Colonel more courteously. "Must I speak?" asked Marco Polo. "We cannot force you to," said the Prince. "Speak!" cried the Colonel. "I would prefer not to," replied Marco Polo. The Colonel laughed aloud. "Out with it, it can't be that serious. And if it's serious, it still need not be true." "It's very serious," said the magician, "and it's also true." Everyone fell silent. "Well?" asked the Colonel. "You will no longer have to suffer from the cold," replied Marco Polo. "What?" exclaimed the Colonel, "is our regiment finally going to get to Riva?" – "I read nothing about the regiment, Colonel. All I see is that, come the autumn, you will be a dead man."

The Colonel laughed, but everyone else kept quiet; I assure you, we all felt as though at that moment the Colonel had become a marked man. Suddenly someone deliberately laughed especially loud, others followed suit, and amid noise and merriment there was a general return to the casino. "Now then," cried the Colonel, "I've been seen to. Aren't any of you other gentlemen at all curious?" Someone jestingly exclaimed: "No, we'd rather not know." Somebody else suddenly decided that this way of having one's fate predicted ought to be regarded as unacceptable on religious grounds, and a young Lieutenant vehemently declared that people like Marco Polo should be locked away for life. I saw the Prince standing in a corner smoking with one of our older comrades and heard him say: "When is the miracle going to begin?" Meanwhile I went over to Marco Polo, who was just getting ready to leave, and without anybody hearing said to him: "Read my fortune." Almost automatically he reached for my hand. Then he said: "It's impossible to see properly in here." I noticed that the oil lamps had begun to flicker, and that the lines of my palm seemed to tremble. "Come out into the courtyard, Lieutenant. I prefer the moonlight." He held me by the hand, and I followed him through the door out into the open air.

'Suddenly I had a strange idea. "Listen, Marco Polo," I said, "if you can't do anything besides what you have just shown our Colonel, then let's call it off." Without further ado the magician let go of my hand and smiled. "So you are afraid, Lieutenant." I quickly turned round, to see if anyone had heard us; but we had already stepped through the barracks gate and found ourselves on the road that led to the town. "I wish to know something specific," I said, "that's what it is. Words can always be interpreted in different ways." Marco Polo looked at me. "What is your wish, Lieutenant? . . . To see a picture of your future wife perhaps?" – "Could you . . . do that?" Marco Polo shrugged his shoulders. "Maybe . . . it might be possible . . ." – "But that's not what I want," I interrupted. "I want to know what will be happening to me later on, for example in ten years' time." Marco Polo shook his head. "That I cannot say . . . but I could do something else instead perhaps." – "What?" – "I could show you a picture, Lieutenant, of some moment from your future life." I did not immediately understand him. "What do you mean?" – "This is what I mean: I can conjure a moment from your future life into the world, down to this very spot where we are standing now." – "How?" – "You have only to tell me what sort of moment, Lieutenant." I didn't fully understand him, but I was tense with expectation. – "Very well," I said, "if you can show me, I want to see what will be happening to me

in ten years to the minute from now. Do you follow me, Marco Polo?"
– "Perfectly, Lieutenant," said Marco Polo and looked hard at me.
And already he was gone . . . but the barracks too was gone, which I
had just seen gleaming in the moonlight – gone were the squalid huts
that had been lying scattered on the plain in the moonlight – and I
saw myself as one sometimes sees oneself in dreams . . . saw myself
looking ten years older, with a full brown beard, a scar on my forehead, stretched out on a bier in the middle of a meadow – a beautiful woman with red hair at my side, her hand over her face, a boy and
a girl beside me, a dark wood in the background and two huntsmen
with torches near at hand . . . You are amazed – are you not,
amazed?'

I was indeed amazed, for what he had described to me was exactly
the scene with which my play was to close at ten that evening, and in
which he was to play the dying hero. 'You doubt me,' Herr von
Umprecht continued, 'and I am far from resenting that. But your
doubts should be put to rest at once.'

Herr von Umprecht reached into his coat pocket and pulled out a
sealed envelope. 'Please look at what it says on the back.' I read
aloud: 'Sealed by a notary on the 4th of January 1859, to be opened
on the 9th of September 1868.' Beneath it was the signature of a
notary well known to me personally, Dr Artiner in Vienna.

'That is today,' said Herr von Umprecht. 'And today it is just ten
years since my mysterious encounter with Marco Polo, which is
being resolved in this manner, without however being explained. For
year by year, as though fickle fortune were playing a game with me,
the possible outcomes of that prophecy wavered in the strangest way,
sometimes seeming to become a threatening reality, fading into
nothing, turning into relentless certainty, fluttering, retreating again
. . . But let me now come back to my story. The vision itself could certainly not have lasted more than a split second; for from the barracks
the same loud peal of laughter from the Colonel still rang in my ear
that I had heard before the vision had appeared. And now too Marco
Polo again stood before me, with a smile on his lips, whether of dis-
tress or contempt I cannot say, doffed his top hat, said: 'Good
evening, Lieutenant, I hope you have been satisfied,' turned round
and walked slowly off down the road in the direction of the town.
The next day, moreover, he set off once more on his travels.

'My first thought, as I returned towards the barracks, was that
what I had seen must have been a phantasmagoric image which
Marco Polo, perhaps with the aid of an unknown assistant, using
some reflective device or other, had been able to project. As I came

through the courtyard, to my horror I saw the cadet still leaning against the wall in cruciform position. Evidently they had forgotten all about him. I could hear the others inside talking and quarrelling with the utmost animation. When I grabbed the cadet by the arm, he woke up immediately, was not in the least astonished, and could not understand why the entire regiment was so excited. I myself at once joined in, albeit rather grimly, with the animated but hollow joviality which had been generated by the strange happenings we had witnessed, and no doubt talked no more sense that anybody else. Suddenly the Colonel shouted: "Well, gentlemen, I'm prepared to bet that I shall live to see next spring! Forty-five to one!" And he turned to one of our gentlemen, a lieutenant, who enjoyed a certain reputation as a gambler and a betting man. "Nothing doing?" Although it was clear that the gentleman addressed found it difficult to resist the temptation, nevertheless he appeared to consider it unseemly to make a bet on the death of his Colonel with the man himself, so he smiled and remained silent. He probably regretted it. For barely six weeks later, on the second morning of the great imperial manoeuvres, our Colonel fell from his horse and was killed instantly. And when it happened, we all realised that we had not expected anything else. From then on I began to think with a certain uneasiness about the nocturnal prophecy, which through some strange reluctance I had never mentioned to a soul. Only at Christmas, in the course of our journey to Vienna on vacation, did I confide in one of my comrades, a certain Friedrich von Gulant – you may have heard of him, he wrote charming verse and died very young . . . Anyway, it was he and I together who devised the plan that you will find enclosed in this envelope. You see, he was of the opinion that such incidents should not be lost to science, whether in the end one's hypotheses about them turn out to be true or false. With him I went to Dr Artiner's, before whose eyes the plan inside this envelope was sealed. Up to now it has been held in the notary's chambers, and only yesterday, in compliance with my wishes, was it delivered to me. I have to admit that the seriousness with which Gulant handled the whole affair vexed me a little at first; but when I stopped seeing him and especially when he died soon after, the whole business began to strike me as utterly ridiculous. Above all it was clear to me that I had my own fate firmly in hand. Nothing in the world could force me into lying on a bier with a full brown beard at ten o'clock in the evening on the 9th of September 1868; I could simply avoid woods and meadow landscapes, marrying a woman with red hair and having children. The only thing I could not avoid was an accident, a duel say, which could leave me with a scar on my forehead. So for the time being I was reassured. – A year after the prophecy, I married Fräulein von Heimsal, my present wife; soon afterwards, I left the army and devoted myself to agriculture. I visited various small estates and – funny though it may sound – made sure that no scenic spots were to be found within these properties that in any way resembled the grass clearing in the dream (as I liked to call the content of that vision to myself). I was on the point of concluding a purchase when my wife received an inheritance, and a property in Karinthia with a fine hunting-preserve fell to our lot. On my first walk through the new estate I reached a meadow which, bordered by woods and forming a slight hollow, in a strange way seemed to resemble the spot I perhaps had every reason to be wary of. I had a bit of a fright. I had not told my wife about the prophecy; she is so superstitious that by confessing I should undoubtedly have poisoned her whole life' – he smiled as if relieved – 'until today, at least. So naturally, I could not communicate my doubts to her either. But I reassured myself with the reflection that I would under no circumstances spend September 1868 on my estate.

'In the year 1860 a boy was born to us. Even during his first few years I thought I could recognise in his features a similarity to the boy's features in the dream; sometimes it would seem to fade, sometimes it would appear more pronounced – and today I am able to acknowledge to myself that the boy who will be standing by my bier at ten o'clock tonight is indeed the spitting image of the boy in the dream. – I have no daughter. Then three years ago it so happened that the widowed sister of my wife, who before that had lived in America, died and left behind a little daughter. At my wife's request I went overseas to fetch the girl, so as to take her into our own home. When I first set eyes on her, I thought I noticed that she looked exactly like the girl in the dream. It crossed my mind to leave the child with strangers there in that foreign country. Of course I dismissed this ignoble idea at once, and we took the child into our home. I again reassured myself completely, despite the growing resemblance of the children to the children of that prophetic vision, for I imagined that my memory of the children's faces in the dream perhaps might be deceiving me. My life flowed on in complete tranquillity for quite some time. Indeed, I had almost ceased to think about that strange evening in the Polish backwater, when two years ago I was very understandably shaken by a new warning from fate. I had been obliged to travel away from home for several months; when I returned, my wife came towards me with red hair, and her resemblance to the woman in the dream, whose countenance of course I had not seen, seemed to me complete. I thought it as well to conceal my terror by a show of anger; indeed, I deliberately became more and more heated, for suddenly an idea bordering on madness came to me: if I were to separate from my wife and the children, then all the danger would perforce disappear, and I would have made a fool of fortune. My wife wept, sank to the ground as though completely broken, begged my forgiveness and explained to me the reason for her transformation. A year earlier, on the occasion of a trip to Munich, I had been particularly delighted by the portrait of a red-haired woman in the exhibition, and there and then my wife had conceived the plan of making herself look like this portrait when the opportunity arose, by having her hair dyed. Of course I beseeched her to restore her hair to its natural colour as soon as possible, and when this had been done everything seemed to be all right again. Did I not see clearly that my fate was as always in my power? . . . Didn't everything that had happened so far have a natural explanation? . . . Didn't a thousand others have estates with woods and meadows and a wife and children? . . . And only one thing that might perhaps frighten the superstitious was still unaccounted for – until this winter: the scar which you now see on my forehead. I am not, if you'll permit me to say so, entirely without courage; while I was an officer I twice fought a duel, moreover on fairly dangerous terms – and again eight years ago, shortly after my marriage, when I had already left the army. But when last year on some trifling pretext – a less than absolutely courteous greeting – a gentleman called me to account, I preferred' – Herr von Umprecht blushed slightly – 'to offer my apologies. The matter was of course settled with complete decorum, but I'm absolutely certain that on that occasion too I would have fought, had not an insane fear come over me that my opponent might inflict a wound on my forehead, and thereby play another trump into the hands of fate . . . But as you see, it was all to no avail: the scar is there. And the moment when I received this wound was perhaps the one occasion in the entire ten years that brought home to me my defencelessness most deeply. It was this winter, towards evening; I was travelling with two or three people I didn't know at all, on the train between Klagenfurt and Villach. Suddenly the window-pane shattered, and I felt a pain in my forehead; at the same time I heard something hard drop to the floor; first I reached up to the place that hurt – it was bleeding; then I quickly stooped down and picked up a sharp stone from the floor. The people in the compartment were quite startled. "Has anything happened?" cried one of them. They noticed I was bleeding and tried to be of some assistance. One gentleman however – I could see quite clearly – had shrunk back into his corner. At the next stop water was brought, and the station doctor supplied me with a makeshift dressing, but of course I wasn't afraid of dying from this wound: I knew that it would become a scar. A discussion had developed in the carriage, people wondered whether an attempt on someone's life had been intended, or whether it was a case of some mean schoolboy prank; the gentleman in the corner remained silent and stared straight in front of him. At Villach I got out. Suddenly the man was at my side, saying: "It was me it was intended for." Before I could answer, or even reflect, he had vanished; I have never been able to discover who he was. Someone suffering from persecution mania perhaps . . . or perhaps someone who rightly believed himself persecuted by an injured husband or brother, and whom I had possibly saved, because I was destined to receive the scar . . . who can tell? . . . After a few weeks there it was gleaming on my forehead in the same spot where I had seen it in the dream. And it became more and more clear to me that I was locked in an unequal struggle with some unknown contemptuous power, and I looked towards the day when my destiny would be fulfilled with growing apprehension.

'In the spring we received my uncle's invitation. I was firmly resolved not to take it up, for without my being able to picture anything precisely, it nevertheless seemed to me possible that the infamous spot was perhaps to be found on his estate. My wife would not have understood a refusal, and so I decided after all to travel down with her and the children as early as the beginning of July, with the firm intention of leaving the villa again as soon as possible and going further south, to Venice or the Lido. On one of the first days of our visit, the conversation came round to your play, my uncle mentioned the small children's roles it contained and asked me to let my little ones take part. I had no objection. At the time it was arranged that the hero would be portrayed by a professional actor. Several days later I was seized by the fear that I might become dangerously ill, and not be able to set out again. So one evening I announced that the following day I intended to leave the villa for a few days and go seabathing. I had to promise to be back by the beginning of September. The same evening a letter arrived from the actor, who on some slight pretext put off his engagement with the Baron. My uncle was very annoyed. He asked me to read the play – perhaps I would be able to suggest someone from among our acquaintance who might be suitable to play the part. And so I took the play with me to my room and read it. Now try to imagine how I felt when I came to the ending and there found the scene, recorded word for word, that had been prophesied to me for the 9th of September of this year. I could hardly wait for morning to tell my uncle that I wanted to play the part. I was afraid that he might raise objections; having read the play I felt I had found safe haven, and if the chance to act in your play eluded me I would again be exposed to that unknown power. My uncle agreed at once, and from then on everything took its simple and propitious course. We have been rehearsing daily for some weeks, I have been through the scene that lies ahead of me today some fifteen or twenty times already: I lie on the bier, the young Countess Saima with her beautiful red hair kneels before me, her hands covering her face, and the children stand beside me.'

As Herr von Umprecht spoke these words, my eye fell on the envelope lying still unopened on the table. Herr von Umprecht smiled. 'Very true, I still owe you the evidence,' he said and broke the seal. A folded piece of paper came to light. Umprecht unfolded it and spread it out on the table. Before me lay a perfect stage-plan, as though drawn up by me, of the final scene of the play. The background and wings were schematically indicated and labelled 'Woods'; a line had been drawn roughly in the middle of the plan under a male figure, above which was written: 'Bier' . . . Next to the other figure sketches was written in small letters in red ink: 'Woman with red hair', 'Boy', 'Girl', 'Torch-bearer', 'Man with hands raised'. I turned to Herr von Umprecht. 'What does that mean: "Man with hands raised"?'

'Well,' said Herr von Umprecht hesitating, 'I had almost forgotten about that. As regards that figure the situation is as follows: the vision did indeed include an old man, garishly illuminated by the torches – completely bald, clean-shaven, bespectacled, a green scarf around his neck, with hands raised and wide staring eyes.'

This time I was dumbfounded.

We remained silent for a while, then, strangely perturbed, I asked: 'What do you suspect? Who should that be?'

'I assume,' said Umprecht calmly, 'that someone or other from the audience, perhaps from among my uncle's servants . . . or one of the peasants might become especially excited at the end of the play and rush onto the stage . . . or perhaps fate will have it that, in one of those coincidences that have ceased to surprise me, just at the moment when I am lying on the bier, an escapee from the lunatic asylum should come running across the stage.'

I shook my head.

'What was it you said? . . . Bald – bespectacled – a green scarf . . .?'
Now the whole business seems to me stranger than ever. The figure
of the man you saw on that occasion was indeed one I had intended
for my play, but I decided against it. It was the wife's mad father, who
is mentioned in the first act, and who at the end was to have come
storming onto the stage.'

'But what about the scarf and spectacles?'

'The actor could well have seen to those himself – don't you
think?'

'Quite possibly.'

We were interrupted. Frau von Umprecht had sent for her husband, as she wanted to talk to him before the performance, and he
took his leave of us. I stayed on for a while and attentively examined
the stage-plan that Herr von Umprecht had left lying on the table.

III

I soon found myself drawn to the spot where the performance was to
take place. It lay behind the villa and separated from it by a charming garden. At the point where it ended in a low hedge, about ten
plain wooden benches had been set up; the front rows were covered
with dark red rugs. Facing the first row there were a few music stands
and chairs; there was no curtain. The partition of the stage from the
audience was indicated by two tall fir trees on either side; immediately to the right were some wild bushes, behind which, invisible
to the audience, stood a comfortable armchair intended for the
prompter. To the left the ground was clear and left the view open into
the valley. The background to the scene was made up of tall trees;
they only stood closer together in the middle, and off to the left narrow footpaths emerged out of the shadows. Further into the wood,
within a small artificial clearing, a table and chairs had been set up,
where the actors could await their cues. For lighting, to the side of the
stage and audience tall antique church candlesticks with giant candles had been placed, functioning like sets. Behind the bushes on the
right there was a sort of open-air storage room for props; here next to
other smaller pieces of equipment that were required in the play, I
saw the bier on which Herr von Umprecht was to die in the final
scene.

Now as I strode across the meadow, it was suffused with soft
evening sunlight . . . Naturally, I had reflected on Herr von
Umprecht's story. I thought it not impossible at first that Herr von

Umprecht belonged to that breed of fantastic liars who plan some elaborate mystification well in advance, just to make themselves interesting. I even thought it conceivable that the notary's signature was forged, and that Herr von Umprecht had let others into the secret in order to carry out the matter systematically. I was particularly dubious about the as yet unknown man with his hands raised, with whom Umprecht might have reached an understanding. But my doubts were undermined above all by the role this man had played in my original plan, which no one could have known about – and especially by the favourable impression I had formed of Herr von Umprecht's character. And however improbable, indeed monstrous his whole narrative appeared to me – something in me craved to be allowed to believe him; perhaps it was the foolish vanity of feeling that I was the executor of some inexorable will prevailing over us.

Meanwhile around me things had begun to move; servants came out of the villa, candles were lit, and people from the surrounding region, some of them in peasant costume, slowly climbed the hill and seated themselves modestly on the end of the benches. Soon the lady of the house appeared with several gentlemen and ladies, who casually assumed their places. I joined them and chatted with acquaintances from the previous year. The members of the orchestra had appeared and made their way to their seats; the ensemble was a little unusual: there were two violins, a cello, a viola, a double-bass, a flute and an oboe. They began at once, evidently too early, to play an overture by Weber. Very near the front, close to the orchestra, stood an old peasant, who was bald-headed and had flung a sort of dark cloth around his neck. Perhaps he was destined, I thought, later to take out a pair of spectacles, to go mad and rush onto the scene. Daylight had vanished completely, and the tall candles were flickering a little as a light breeze had arisen. Behind the bushes things were livening up, the participants having reached the vicinity of the stage along concealed paths. Only now did I think again about the others who were going to take part, and it occurred to me that I had not yet seen anyone apart from Herr von Umprecht, his children and the forester's daughter. Now I heard the loud voice of the director and the laughter of the young Countess Saima. The benches were all full, the Baron was sitting in one of the front rows and talking to the Countess Saima. The orchestra began to play, the forester's daughter stepped forward and delivered the prologue. The plot concerned the fate of a man who, seized by a sudden longing for adventuring in distant parts, leaves his loved ones without a word of farewell, and in the course of one day experiences so much pain and misery that he decides to return before his wife and children miss him; but one last incident on the way back, close to the door of his house, results in his being murdered, and only as he expires is he able to bid farewell to those he has abandoned, who are confronted with his flight and death as the most inexplicable of riddles.

The play had begun and the gentlemen and ladies played their parts very nicely; I thoroughly enjoyed the simple performance of the simple events and at first thought no more about Herr von Umprecht's story. After the first act the orchestra played again, but no one listened, so lively was the conversation on the benches. I myself did not remain seated but stood unnoticed by the others, quite close to the stage, on the left side where the open road dipped toward the valley. The second act began; the wind had become a little stronger, and the flickering lights contributed not a little to the play's effectiveness. Again the players disappeared into the wood, and the orchestra struck up again. Then quite by chance my eye fell on the flautist, who was clean-shaven and wearing spectacles; but he had long white hair, and there was no sign of any scarf. The orchestra ceased and the players returned to the scene. Then I noticed that the flautist, who had placed his instrument on the music stand in front of him, reached into his bag, pulled out a large green scarf and wound it round his neck. I was utterly taken aback. Seconds later Herr von Umprecht came on. I could see how his gaze was suddenly arrested by the flautist, how he noticed the green scarf and halted for a moment; but he quickly regained his composure and delivered his lines without a flaw. I asked a plainly dressed young lad next to me whether he knew the flautist, and learned that he was a school-teacher from Kaltern. The play continued and the dénouement approached. The two children, as prescribed by the text, wandered across the stage, noises in the wood came closer and closer, shouts and calls were heard; that the wind was growing stronger and the branches were moving didn't fit in badly either; and at last Herr von Umprecht as the dying adventurer was carried in on a bier. The two children rushed over, and the torch-bearers stood motionless at his side. The wife entered later than the others, and with a look consumed by fear sinks down beside the murdered man; the latter tries to open his lips again, tries to raise himself, but – as prescribed in the text – is no longer able to. Then all at once a freakish gust of wind arises, which threatens to put out the torches; I see someone in the orchestra leap up – it is the flautist – and to my amazement he is bald, his wig has blown away; with his hands raised, the green scarf fluttering about his neck, he rushes towards the stage. Involuntarily my eyes turn towards Umprecht; he is gazing fixedly at the man, as if entranced; he tries to say something – evidently he cannot manage it – he sinks back . . . Many still imagine that all this belongs to the play; I myself am not sure how this second collapse is to be interpreted; meanwhile the man has passed the bier, still in pursuit of his wig, and disappears into the wood. Umprecht does not rise; another gust of wind extinguishes one of the two torches; several people close to the front become uneasy. – I hear the Baron's voice: 'Quiet! Quiet!' – things calm down again – even the wind no longer stirs . . . but Umprecht remains outstretched, without stirring or moving his lips. The Countess Saima screams – naturally people think this too is part of the play. I however thrust my way through the audience, rush onto the stage, hear the commotion behind me – people get up, others follow me, the bier is surrounded . . . 'What's the matter, what has happened?' . . . I seize a torch out of the hand of one of the torch-bearers, light up the face of the outstretched figure . . . I shake him, tear open his waistcoat; meanwhile the doctor has arrived at my side, he feels for Herr Umprecht's heart, he takes his pulse, he asks everybody to move back, he whispers a few words to the Baron . . . the wife of the figure on the bier has forced her way through, she screams, throws herself upon her husband, the children stand there as though devastated and unable to grasp the situation . . . No one can believe what has happened, and yet they relay it to each other; – and a minute later everyone all around the circle knows that Herr von Umprecht has suddenly died on the bier that he was carried in on . . .

I myself hurried down into the valley the same evening, shaken with horror. Overcome by a strange dread, I could not bring myself to set foot inside the villa again. I spoke to the Baron the following day in Bozen, and there I told him Umprecht's tale, as he himself had imparted it to me. The Baron would not believe it, so I reached into my briefcase and showed him the mysterious sheet of paper; he looked at me disconcerted, even a little fearful, and handed the sheet back to me – it was blank, with no writing and no sketch . . .

I have made several attempts to trace Marco Polo; but all I could find out about him was that he last appeared three years ago, in a Hamburg entertainment establishment of the lower sort.

But what remains the most baffling thing about the whole mysterious business is the fact that the schoolteacher who ran after his wig with hands raised on that occasion was never seen again, nor was his body ever discovered.

EDITORIAL POSTSCRIPT

I did not know the compiler of the above account personally. He was in his time a fairly well-known author, all but lost sight of, however, after he died about ten years ago, scarcely sixty years of age. His total estate went, without any special stipulation, to the friend of his youth in Meran mentioned in these pages. And he in turn – a doctor with whom, during my stay in Meran last winter, I had discussed all manner of dark questions, particularly ghosts, telepathy and fortune-telling – handed the manuscript printed here over to me for publication. I should have been very willing to regard its contents as a freely invented story, had not the doctor, as indeed emerges from the account, attended the theatrical performance with its uncanny outcome, described at the end, and been personally acquainted with the schoolteacher who vanished so mysteriously. As regards the magician Marco Polo, I remember very well in my earliest youth having seen his name printed on a poster at a summer resort on the Wörthersee; it lodged in my memory because just at that time I was reading the travel accounts of the famous voyager of the same name.

Fräulein Else

'Are you sure you won't play another set, Else?' – 'No, Paul, I've really had
enough. Adieu. – Good day to you, Madam.' – *'My dear Else, do call
me Frau Cissy – or preferably just Cissy.'* – 'Very well then, good day Frau
Cissy.' – *'But why are you off so early, Else? It's a good two hours before supper.'*
– 'I'm afraid you'll have to play singles with Paul, Frau Cissy, I'm
really not in the mood today.' – *'Let her go, Madam, today is one of her
ungracious days. Ungraciousness becomes you capitally, Else, by the way. – And
that red sweater even more so.'* – 'Perhaps you'll find grace from someone
wearing blue then, Paul. Adieu.'

That wasn't a bad exit. I hope they don't both think I'm jealous.
But I could swear there is something going on between cousin Paul
and Cissy Mohr. Though there is nothing in the world I could care
less about. Now I'll just turn round once more and wave goodbye.
I'm waving and smiling. Do I appear gracious now, I wonder? – Oh
God, they're playing again already. Actually I play rather better than
Cissy Mohr; and Paul isn't exactly a matador on court. He looks
impressive, though, with that open collar and devil-may-care expres-
sion. If only he were less affected. No need for you to worry, Aunt
Emma . . .

What a glorious evening. Today the weather would have been just
right for the walking-tour up to the Rosetta Hut. How splendidly
Mount Cimone towers against the sky! – We would have set out at
five in the morning. At first I would have felt unwell as usual, of
course. But that would have passed. – Nothing more delightful than
walking in the grey light of dawn. – The one-eyed American at the
Rosetta Hut looked like a boxer. Perhaps someone knocked his eye
out in a boxing match. I rather fancy the idea of getting married and
going to America – though not to an American, unless, that is, I were
to marry an American and we were to live in Europe. A villa on the
Riviera perhaps. Marble steps out into the sea. I would lie naked on
the marble. – How long is it since we were in Menton? Seven or eight
years perhaps. I must have been thirteen or fourteen. Ah yes, we were
much better off in those days. – It was really a little stupid to have
postponed the outing. We'd certainly have been back by now. At four

when I went to play tennis the express letter that Mama sent by telegraph had not arrived. I might just as well have played another set.
Why are those two young people greeting me? We aren't even
acquainted. They've been staying at the hotel since yesterday and at
meal-times they sit by the window on the left where the Dutchmen
used to sit. Did I respond to them ungraciously? Even a little haugh-
tily perhaps? I'm not like that at all really. What was it Fred called me
on the way home from *Coriolanus*? It wasn't proud. No, spirited. You
are not haughty, Else, you are spirited. A good word. He always had
a way with words. – Why am I walking so slowly? Am I afraid of
Mama's letter after all? Well, it can hardly contain anything agreeable. Sent express! Perhaps I shall have to return home. Oh dear,
how tiresome life is – despite my red sweater and silk stockings.
Three pairs of them! The poor relation, here on the invitation of her
rich aunt. No doubt she is regretting it already. My dear aunt, must I
put it in writing that I'm not dreaming about Paul? Or anyone else
for that matter. I am not in love with anyone. I've never been in love.
Not even with Albert, although for a whole week I imagined that I
was. I don't believe I'm capable of falling in love. Odd, really.
Because I'm certainly quite sensual. But thank God I'm also spirited
and just a bit ungracious. Perhaps the only time I was truly in love
was when I was thirteen. It was with Van Dyck – or rather with the
Abbé Des Grieux, and also with Madame Renard. And then at sixteen on the Wörthersee. – No, no, that was nothing really. Anyway
why think back, I'm not writing my memoirs. I don't even keep a
diary, unlike Bertha. I no longer find Fred attractive. Perhaps if he
were a bit more elegant. So after all I am a snob. Papa thinks so too,
and teases me about it. Alas, dear Papa, you worry me a lot. I wonder whether he has ever been unfaithful to Mama? No doubt about
it. Frequently. Mama is rather stupid. She hasn't the least suspicion
what I'm really like. Nor has anybody else. Fred perhaps? But no
more than a suspicion. – What a glorious evening. How festive the
hotel looks. You sense at once that here is a host of people having a
good time and without a care in the world. Like me for instance.
Haha! If only I'd been born to a carefree life. It could have been so
wonderful. Such a shame! – There's a red glow on the peaks of the
Cimone. Paul would say: an Alpenglow. But it's not a true Alpenglow
yet. I could weep, it's all so beautiful. Or, why do I have to go back to
town!

    'Good evening, Fräulein Else.' – 'Good evening, Madam.' – *'Been play-
ing tennis?'* – She can see I have, so why ask? 'Indeed, madam. We've
been playing for nearly three hours. – And Madam is taking another

stroll?' – *'Yes, my usual evening walk. Out along the coach-road. It winds so pic-turesquely through the meadows, but during the day it's almost too hot.'* – 'Indeed, the meadows here are splendid. Especially by moonlight from my window.'

'Good evening, Fräulein Else. – *Your humble servant, Madam.'* 'Good evening, Herr von Dorsday.' – *'Been playing tennis?'* – 'How observant of you, Herr von Dorsday.' – *'Don't mock me, Else.'* – Why doesn't he say "Fräulein Else?" – *'When someone looks so lovely with a racquet, one might almost regard it as a fashion accessory.'* – What an ass! I won't respond to that at all. 'We've been playing all afternoon. Unfortunately there were only three of us. Paul, Frau Mohr and myself.' – *'I was once an enthusiastic tennis player myself.'* – 'And now you've given it up?' – *'Now I'm too old.'* – 'Too old! In Marienlyst there was a Swede of sixty-five who played from six o'clock to eight each evening. And the year before he even took part in a tournament.' – *'Well, I'm not yet sixty-five, thank God, but unfortunately I'm no Swede either.'* – Why unfortunately? No doubt that's meant to be a joke. Best to smile politely and move on. 'Your humble servant, Madam. Adieu, Herr von Dorsday.' How low he bows and how he eyes me. Positively ogling. Did I hurt his feelings over the sixty-five-year-old Swede? Wouldn't be a bad thing. Frau Winawer must be an unhappy woman. Must be getting on for fifty. Those bags under her eyes – as though she'd been crying a lot. How terrible to be as old as that. Herr von Dorsday is being very attentive, strolling by her side. He still looks quite impressive with his greying moustache. But I don't take to him. He gives himself such airs. What good is your first-class tailor, Herr von Dorsday? Dorsday! No doubt you had a different name once. – Here comes Cissy's sweet little girl, together with her nanny. – 'Hello there, Fritzi. Bonsoir, Mademoi-selle. Vous allez bien?' – *'Merci, Mademoiselle. Et vous?'* – 'What's this I see, Fritzi, you've got a walking-stick. Are you off to climb the Cimone then?' – *'Of course not, I'm not allowed as high as that yet.'* – 'But you'll be allowed to next year. Bye, Fritzi. A bientôt, Mademoiselle.' – *'Bonsoir, Mademoiselle.'*

An attractive woman. Why is she in service, I wonder? Especially with Cissy. A bitter fate. Oh God, the same could happen to me. No, I know how to do better than that. Better? – What an exquisite evening. "The air is like champagne," Doctor Waldberg said yester-day. The day before that someone said the same. – How can people lounge about the foyer in glorious weather like this? Incomprehens-ible. Could they all be waiting for letters by express? The porter has already seen me – if I had an express letter, he'd have brought it over to me straightaway. So there can't be anything. Thank Heaven for that. I'll go and lie down for a while before dinner. Why does Cissy always say *"dîner"*? Stupid affectation. They suit one another, Paul and Cissy. – If only the letter had arrived. It's bound to get here in the middle of the *dîner*. And if it doesn't, I'll have a restless night. Last night too I slept so miserably. Admittedly it's the time of the month as well. That's why my legs seem to drag so. Today is the third of September. So probably on the sixth. I'll take some Veronal this evening. Oh, I won't become addicted. No, my dear Fred, you needn't be concerned. Mentally I always use *Du* when I address him. – One should try everything – even hashish. It was Brandl, the naval ensign, I believe, who brought hashish back with him from China. Does one drink hashish or smoke it? It's supposed to give one marvellous visions. Brandl invited me to drink – or smoke – hashish with him – cheeky devil. But very handsome.

'Excuse me Fräulein, there's a letter for you.' The porter! So it has come after all! I'll turn round quite naturally. Might it not be a letter from Caroline or Bertha, or from Fred or from Miss Jackson? 'Thank you.' So it's from Mama. Sent express. I'll wait and open it upstairs in my room where I can read it in peace. – Here comes the Marchioness. How young she looks in the half-light. Must be forty-five. Where will I be at forty-five? Already dead perhaps. I hope so. She smiles at me pleasantly, as she always does. I make way for her, nodding slightly, – though not as if I felt especially honoured being smiled on by a Marchioness. – *'Buona sera.'* She said *"buona sera"* to me. Now I shall at least have to bow to her. Was that too low? She's so much older. How splendidly she walks. Is she divorced? I walk well too. But – I'm aware of it. Yes, that's the difference. With an Italian I could well find myself in danger. Pity the dark handsome one with the Roman head has gone off again. "He looks like a libertine," Paul said. Dear God, I have nothing against libertines, quite the contrary. – Well, here I am. Number seventy-seven. A lucky number, come to think of it. Pretty room. Pinewood. There's my virginal bed. – Now that really is an Alpenglow. But with Paul I'll argue about it. Paul is actually quite shy. A doctor, a gynaecologist! Perhaps that's why. He could have been a bit more forward in the forest the day before yesterday, when we were so far ahead. But I'd have made sure that he regretted it. So far no-one has ever been really forward with me. Unless it was in the pool that time on the Wörthersee three years ago. Forward? No, he was simply indecent. But handsome. A regular Apollo Belvedere. Actually, I didn't fully understand it at the time. But then – at sixteen! My heavenly meadows! Mine! If only I could take them back to Vienna with me. Such a delicate mist. Autumn already? Well, it's

the third of September and high up in the mountains.

Well, Fräulein Else, are you finally going to bring yourself to read the letter? After all, it needn't be about Papa at all. Couldn't it equally be about my brother? Perhaps he has become engaged to one of his young flames? To some chorus-girl or milliner? Oh no, he's surely too intelligent for that. But then I really don't know all that much about him. For a time when I was sixteen and he was twenty-one we were on friendly terms. He talked a lot about a certain Lotte. Then suddenly he stopped. This Lotte must have done something to him. And since then he has stopped confiding in me. – There, the letter's opened, and I didn't even notice I was doing it. I'll sit here on the windowsill and read it. Must be careful not to fall. According to a report just received from San Martino, an unfortunate accident has occurred at the Hotel Fratazza. A stunningly beautiful young girl, Fräulein Else T., daughter of the well-known lawyer . . . Naturally it would claim that I had killed myself over an unhappy love affair or because I'd fallen pregnant. An unhappy love affair, no alas.

"My dear child" – I'll have a look at the end first. – "Well, once again, don't be angry with us, my dear good child, and may a thousand" – Heavens above, they can't have committed suicide! No, no, if that were the case I would have received a telegram from Rudi. – "My dear child, you can imagine how sorry I am to burst in on your precious few weeks' holiday" – As if I were not permanently on holiday, worse luck – "with such unpleasant news!" What an atrocious style Mama has – "But on mature reflection I really can see no alternative. Well, in short, this business with Papa has become pressing. I don't know where to turn for advice or help!" – Why does she go on so? – "A ridiculous sum is entailed, comparatively speaking, thirty thousand guilders," – ridiculous? – "which must be found within three days, or all is lost." For goodness sake, what is that supposed to mean? – "Just think, my dear child, Baron Höning" – what, the public prosecutor? – "summoned Papa this morning. You know how highly the Baron esteems, indeed one might almost say loves Papa. That time when everything hung by a hair eighteen months ago, it was he personally who spoke to the principal creditors and set matters right at the very last moment. But this time if the money is not forthcoming nothing can be done. And quite apart from the fact that we shall all be ruined, there will be an unprecedented scandal. Just think, a lawyer, and a famous lawyer at that – who, – no, I can't bring myself to write it. I'm fighting back my tears. You know, child, clever creature that you are, that we have already been in a similar situation several times before, alas, and that the family has always helped us out. Indeed last time it was a matter of a hundred and twenty thousand guilders.

"But on that occasion Papa had to sign an undertaking never to approach the relatives again, particularly Uncle Bernhardt!" – Come on, come on, where is all this leading? What can I do about it? – "The only person one might conceivably think of turning to would be Uncle Victor, but unfortunately he is away on a trip to Scotland or North Cape" – Yes, he's all right, the disgusting old fellow – "and is impossible to contact, at least for the moment. As to Papa's colleagues, and more specifically Dr Sch. who has often helped him out before" – My God, what a predicament – "he can no longer be considered now that he is remarried" – so what now, what now, what do you want me to do? – "And then your letter arrived, dear child, where among other things you mention that Dorsday is also staying at the Fratazza, and that struck us as a sign from fate. You know how often Dorsday used to visit us in years gone by" – well, frequently enough – "it is pure chance that we have seen less of him over the last two or three years; he is reputed to have made a fairly firm attachment – not a model of refinement between you and me" – what's this, "between you and me"? – "Papa still meets him for a round of whist at the Residenz Club every Thursday, and last winter Papa saved him a considerable amount of money in a lawsuit against another art dealer. Besides, why shouldn't I tell you, he helped Papa out once before!" – I thought as much – "On that occasion it was a mere bagatelle, eight thousand guilders, – but after all – for Dorsday even thirty would amount to nothing. So I wondered whether you would be so kind as to have a word with Dorsday" – What? – "After all, he was always very fond of you" – I never noticed it. Once when I was twelve or thirteen years old he stroked my cheek: "Quite the young lady already." – "And since Papa has fortunately not approached him again since the eight thousand, he won't refuse him this one favour. Recently he is said to have made eighty thousand on one Rubens alone which he sold in America. You mustn't mention that of course." – Do you think I'm that much of a goose, Mama? – "But otherwise you can speak to him quite openly. You can also mention that Baron Höning sent for Papa, should occasion arise. And that with the thirty thousand catastrophe will in fact be averted, not just for the moment but, God willing, for ever!" – Do you really believe that, Mama? – "Because the Erbesheimer case, which is proceeding splendidly, is sure to bring Papa a hundred thousand, though it goes without saying that he can't ask the Erbesheimers for anything at this stage in the proceedings. So, I beg you, dearest child, speak to

Dorsday. I assure you, there's nothing to it. Papa could have simply sent him a telegram, indeed we did seriously consider it, but talking to someone personally, child, is quite a different thing. The money must be there on the sixth at noon; Dr F. "– Who is Dr F.? Oh yes, Fiala – "is quite implacable. Personal rancour also comes into it, of course. But as securities are unfortunately involved" – Heavens above! What have you done, Papa? – "there is nothing we can do. And if the money isn't in Fiala's hands by noon on the fifth, an arrest warrant will be issued: that is as long as Baron Höning can hold off. So Dorsday would need to have his bank send the money to Dr F. by telegraph. Then we will be saved. Otherwise God knows what will happen. Believe me, my dear child, you will not lose face in any way. Papa was reluctant at first. He even explored two other quite separate avenues. But he returned home in complete despair!" – Is Papa ever capable of despair? – "Not so much about the money perhaps, but because of the shameful way people behaved towards him. One of them was once Papa's best friend. You can guess who I mean!" – I can't possibly imagine. Papa has had so many best friends and in reality not one. Warnsdorf perhaps? – "Papa came home at one o'clock, and now it's four in the morning. He has fallen asleep at last, thank goodness." – The best thing for him would be if he were never to wake up. – "I'll post the letter myself first thing in the morning by express, then you should receive it on the morning of the third." – How has Mama managed to think all this through? In matters like this she never knows how to go about things. – "So have a word with Dorsday, I beseech you, and let us know the outcome by telegram at once. And for goodness sake don't let Aunt Emma notice anything; it is sad indeed that in such circumstances one can't turn to one's own sister, but one might just as well try talking to a stone. My dear dear child, I'm so sorry that you should have to be involved in such matters at your tender age, but believe me, Papa himself is only the tiniest bit to blame." – Who else then, Mama? – "Well, let's hope to God the Erbesheimer trial turns out to be in all respects a watershed in our existence. It's just a matter of getting through the next few weeks. It would be truly a disgrace were some misfortune to occur because of the thirty thousand guilders." – She doesn't seriously mean that Papa might commit . . . But wouldn't – the alternative be even worse? – "Well I must stop here, my child, and hope that whatever happens" – Whatever happens? – "you will be able to stay on over the holidays in San Martino, at least until the ninth or tenth. As far as we are concerned, there is no need for you to return. Greetings to your aunt, and just continue to be nice to her. Once again, don't be angry with us, my dear good child, and a thousand" – yes, I know all that.

So, I'm to pump Herr Dorsday . . . What lunacy. How does Mama imagine it? Why didn't Papa simply catch a train and come here? – It would have been just as quick as an express letter. But perhaps if he were suspected of attempting to escape, at the station they might have – Frightful, simply frightful! Even the thirty thousand wouldn't help us all that much. One crisis after another! For the last seven years! No – longer. Who would have suspected? No one could tell from my behaviour, nor from Papa's. And yet everybody knows. It's a mystery how we've managed to hold out. But one gets used to everything! And yet we seem to live quite well. Mama is a real genius. That supper last New Year's Day for fourteen people – incredible. On the other hand, my two pairs of ballroom gloves caused quite a song and dance. And when Rudi needed three hundred guilders recently, Mama very nearly wept. And yet Papa is invariably in a good mood. Invariably? Well, no. His expression during *Figaro* at the opera recently – suddenly quite vacant – I was really shocked. For a moment he was like a completely different person. But then we had dinner at the Grand Hotel and he was in as genial a mood as ever.

And now here I am with this letter in my hand. It's an insane proposal. Speak to Dorsday? I would die of shame. – But why should I feel shame? After all it's not my fault. Supposing I were to speak to Aunt Emma? Useless. She probably doesn't have that much money at her disposal anyway. Uncle is an absolute miser. Oh God, why don't I have any money? Why have I still not earned any? Why haven't I learned anything? Oh, but I have learned something! Who says I haven't learned anything? I can play the piano, speak French, English and a little Italian, I've even attended lectures on Art History – Haha! And even if I'd studied something more practical, how would that have helped? I couldn't possibly have saved thirty thousand guilders. –

The Alpenglow has faded. The evening has lost its radiance. The landscape looks so sad. No, not the landscape, it's life itself that's sad. And here I am, calmly sitting on the window-ledge. And Papa is about to be locked up. No, never. It must not be allowed to happen. I shall save him. Yes, Papa, I shall save you. It's perfectly simple. A few nonchalant words, in keeping with my "spirited" nature – haha, I'll treat Herr Dorsday as if it were an honour for him to lend us money. As indeed it is. – Herr von Dorsday, could you spare a moment? I've just received a letter from Mama, and she – or rather Papa – is in a spot of bother financially at the moment. – "But of course, my dear Fräulein, it will be a pleasure. How much is involved, by the way?" – If only I didn't dislike him so much. Especially the way he looks at me. No, Herr Dorsday, I don't believe in your elegance, or in your monocle, or in your nobility. You could just as well be a dealer in old clothes as in old pictures. – But Else! Else, what are you thinking of? – Oh, I can get away with it. No one would suspect me. I've even got blond, reddish blond hair, and Rudi looks the perfect aristocrat. With Mama admittedly one can tell at once, when she speaks at least. But not with Papa. Anyway, let them notice for themselves. I'm not in the least disposed to deny it and Rudi even less so. What would Rudi do if Papa were locked away? Would he shoot himself? What nonsense! Shootings and criminals, such things don't really exist, they're just something in the papers.

The air is like champagne. In an hour dinner will be served. *Dîner.* I can't stand Cissy. She doesn't pay any attention to her little girl. What shall I wear? The blue dress or the black? Today black might perhaps be more appropriate. Too low-cut? What in French novels they call *toilette de circonstance.* At all events, I must look enchanting when I speak to Dorsday. And after dinner, nonchalant. He'll be forever peering down my dress. Disgusting fellow. I hate him. I hate everyone. Must it be specifically Dorsday? Is Dorsday really the only person in the world with thirty thousand guilders? What if I approached Paul? What if he were to tell Auntie that he had gambling debts – surely she'd then be able to procure the money.

Almost dark already! Night, quiet as the grave. I wish I were dead. – No, that's not true. What if I were to go down straight away and speak to Dorsday before dinner? Oh, how horrible! Paul, if you can get me the thirty thousand, you may have your way with me. Again that's straight out of a novel. High-born daughter sells herself for beloved father and thoroughly enjoys herself into the bargain. Disgusting. No Paul, you shan't have me, not even for thirty thousand guilders. No one will. But for a million? – For a palace? For a string of pearls? Once I'm married, I'll probably do it for less. After all, is it really all that wicked? Fanny sold herself, when all is said and done. She told me herself that she was revolted by her husband. Well, Papa, how would it be if I were to auction myself off this morning? To save you from imprisonment. Sensation! – I'm feverish, without a doubt. Or perhaps I'm sick already? No, it's just a touch of fever. From the air perhaps. Like champagne. – If Fred were here, could he advise me? No, I don't need any advice. There is nothing to be advised about. I shall speak to Herr Dorsday d'Eperies, I shall pump him, I the spirited aristocrat, the marchioness, the beggar, the daughter of a swindler. How have I come to this? How have I come to this? No one climbs as well as I can, no one has my nerve – I'm a sporting girl, I should have been born in England, or a countess.

There are my clothes, hanging in the wardrobe. Has the green loden cloak been paid for yet, Mama? Only a deposit, I suspect. I'll wear the black one. Yesterday everybody stared at me. Even the pale little gentleman with the gold pince-nez. I'm not really beautiful perhaps, but striking. I should have gone on the stage. Bertha has already had three lovers, and no-one thinks the worse of her . . . In Düsseldorf it was the Director. In Hamburg she was going with a married man and living in the Hotel Atlantic – a suite with its own bathroom. I do believe she's proud of it. What fools they all are. I shall have a hundred lovers, why not a thousand? The neckline isn't low enough; if I were married it could of course be lower. – Nice to see you, Herr von Dorsday, I've just received a letter from Vienna . . . I'll take the letter with me, just in case. Should I ring for the chambermaid? No, I'll get ready by myself. I don't need any help with the black dress. I would never travel without a maid if I were rich.

I must light the lamp. It's getting chilly. Must close the window. Draw the curtains too? – Not really necessary. There's no-one over on the mountain with a telescope. The more's the pity. – I've just received a letter, Herr von Dorsday. – Perhaps after dinner would be better. People are in a better mood then. Dorsday too – and I could drink a glass of wine beforehand. But if the matter were resolved before dinner, I would enjoy the meal more. Pudding *à la merveille, fromage et fruits divers*. And what if Herr von Dorsday should say no? – Or if he should become impertinent? Alas, no one has ever been impertinent with me. Well, there was that naval lieutenant Brandl, but he did not mean to be offensive. – I've got a little thinner. It suits me. – The twilight is peering in at me. Like a ghost. Like a hundred ghosts. Ghosts are rising from my meadow. How far is Vienna? How long have I been away already? How alone I am here! I have no girlfriend or protector. Where are they all? Who will I marry? Who will marry a swindler's daughter? – I've just received a letter, Herr von Dorsday. – "Don't mention it, Fräulein Else. I sold a Rembrandt yesterday, you put me to shame, Fräulein Else! And then he'll tear a cheque from his cheque-book and sign with his gold fountain-pen; and tomorrow morning I'll return to Vienna with the cheque. Whatever happens; even without the cheque. I won't stay here any longer. I couldn't anyway, it wouldn't be right. Here I am living the life of an elegant young lady and Papa is standing with one foot in the grave – or rather, in the

dock. My second last pair of silk stockings. Nobody will notice the little tear just below the knee. Nobody? You never know. Now don't be
frivolous, Else. – Bertha is just a little hussy. But is Christine really any
better? I wish her future husband joy. Mama was certainly always a
faithful wife. I shall not remain faithful. I may be spirited, but I won't
be faithful. I'm at risk when it comes to libertines. The Marchioness
is sure to have some libertine for a lover. If Fred really knew what I
was like, that would put an end to his adoring. – "You could have
become any number of things, Fräulein, a pianist, an accountant, an
actress, you have so much potential. But then you've always had
things too easy. Too easy! Haha. Fred overestimates me. Actually I
don't have real talent for anything much. – Who knows? Perhaps I
might have gone as far as Bertha. But I lack energy. A young lady of
good family. Good family, indeed! With a father who embezzles.
Why are you doing this to me, Papa? If you had something to show
for it at least! But then to risk everything on the stock-exchange! Was
that worth it? And even the thirty thousand won't help stem the tide.
For three months perhaps. But in the end he is bound to go under.
Eighteen months ago things had almost come to such a pass. Then
help arrived in time. But one day it won't – and what will happen to
us then? Rudi will go to Rotterdam to work in the bank under old
Vanderhulst. But what about me? A wealthy catch. If I could only
make up my mind to it. I'm really quite beautiful tonight. It's probably the effect of all the excitement. But who is all my beauty for?
Would I be happier if Fred were here? Ah, when all is said and done,
Fred is nothing to me. He's no libertine! But if he had money, I'd
accept him. And then a libertine would come along – and our misery
would be complete. You'd like to be a libertine, would you not, Herr
von Dorsday? – From a distance you sometimes even look the part.
Like a dissolute viscount, or a Don Juan – with your absurd monocle
and your white flannel suit. But you are far from being a libertine. –
Have I got everything? All ready for the *dîner*? – But what am I going
to do for a whole hour, if I don't meet Dorsday? If he's out walking
with the unhappy Frau Winawer? Oh, she's not in the least unhappy,
she doesn't need thirty thousand guilders. Well, I shall go down to the
foyer, settle grandly in an armchair, and look through the *Illustrated
News* and *Vie Parisienne* – the tear won't show if I cross my legs. Perhaps some billionaire has just arrived. – She it must be, or no one. –
I'll take the white shawl, I look good in that. I'll throw it casually over
my splendid shoulders. Who are they intended for, these splendid
shoulders? I'm sure I could make some man happy. If only the right
man would appear. But I don't want to have children. I'm not

remotely motherly. Now, Marie Weil is motherly. Mama is motherly, and Aunt Irene is motherly. But I have a noble brow and a splendid figure. – "If only I could paint you as I should like, Fräulein Else." – Yes, I'm sure that would suit you down to the ground. I can't even remember his name now. It certainly wasn't Titian, the cheeky fellow. – I've just received a letter, Herr von Dorsday. – A dash more powder on my throat and neck, a drop of vervain in my hanky, lock the box, open the window again, ah, how marvellous! Makes me want to cry. I'm rather on edge. Difficult to avoid being on edge under the circumstances. The box of sleeping tablets is among my blouses. I really need new blouses too. That will create another song and dance. Oh God.

How uncannily gigantic the Cimone looks, as though it was about to fall on me! Not a star in the sky as yet. The air is like champagne. And what fragrance from the meadows! I shall live in the country. I shall marry a landowner and have children. Dr Froriep was perhaps the only one I'd have been happy with. How marvellous those two evenings were, one straight after the other, first at Kniep's and then the Artists' Ball. Why did he vanish so suddenly – at least from me? Because of Papa perhaps? Quite likely. I feel like shouting a greeting out into the night before going down to join the company. But who should my greeting go to? I'm utterly alone. No-one can imagine how terribly alone I am. Greetings, my beloved. But who? Greetings, my bridegroom! Who? Greetings, my friend! Who? – Fred? – Not for a moment. There, I'll leave the window open. Even though it may get cold. Must turn the lamp out. There. – Oh yes, of course, the letter. I must take it with me just in case. That book on the bedside table: tonight I shall continue reading *Notre Coeur*, without fail, whatever happens. Good evening, lovely lady in the mirror, remember me kindly, won't you, farewell . . .

Why am I locking the door? Nothing is ever stolen here. Wonder whether Cissy leaves her door unlocked at night? Or does she wait and unlock it when he knocks? All clear? Yes, of course. And then they lie in bed together. How distasteful. I won't share a bedroom with my husband, or with my thousand lovers. – The main stairwell is deserted! Always the case at this hour. My footsteps echo so. I've been here three weeks now. I left Gmunden on the twelfth of August. Gmunden was a bore. Where did Papa find the money to send Mama and me off to the country? And Rudi went on a trip for four whole weeks. God knows where. He didn't write more than once all that time. I'll never understand our lives. Mama certainly has no more jewellery. – Why did Fred only stay two days in Gmunden? He has a mistress too, no doubt. Though I somehow can't imagine it. It's been eight days since he wrote to me. He writes such lovely letters. – Who is that sitting at the little table? No, it isn't Dorsday. Thank Heaven for that. It would be quite impossible to approach him now, before dinner. – Why is the porter looking at me so strangely? Did he perhaps read the express letter from Mama? I think I'm going mad. I must tip him again at the very next opportunity. – The blonde lady over there is also already dressed for dinner. How can one get as fat as that? – I'll go outside for a while and stroll up and down in front of the hotel. Or should I go into the music room? Isn't that someone playing? A Beethoven sonata! How can anyone play Beethoven sonatas in a place like this! I've been neglecting my piano exercises. In Vienna I shall do regular practice again. Begin a new life altogether. That's what all of us must do. Things can't go on like this. I must have a serious talk with Papa – if there's still time for that. There will be, there will be. How is it I've never done so before? Everything in our household is passed off with a joke, yet no one is in the mood for jokes. In reality we are all afraid of one another, and everyone's alone. Mama is alone because she isn't clever enough and doesn't understand any of us, neither me nor Rudi nor Papa. But she isn't aware of this and nor is Rudi. Of course he's an elegant and agreeable enough fellow, but at twenty-one he showed greater promise. Going to Holland will do him good. But where am I to go? I want to leave and do whatever I like. If Papa escapes to America, I shall go with him. Oh dear, I'm getting quite confused . . . The porter will think I'm mad, sitting here on the arm of this chair and staring into space. I shall light a cigarette. Where's my cigarette case? Upstairs. But where? The sleeping tablets are in among my linen. But where did I put the cigarette case? Here come Paul and Cissy. Yes, of course, she has to change for *dîner*, otherwise they could have continued playing in the dark. – They haven't seen me. Why is she laughing in that idiotic way? It would be amusing to write an anonymous letter to her husband in Vienna. Would I be capable of such a thing? Never. And yet, who knows? Now they've seen me. I'll nod to them. She's annoyed that I am looking so attractive. How put out she is.

'*What's this, Else, dressed for dinner already?*' – Why does she now pronounce it dinner rather than *dîner*? She's not even consistent. – 'As you see, Frau Cissy.' – '*You really look enchanting, Else, I feel a wild desire to court you.*' – 'Save yourself the bother, Paul, and let me have a cigarette. *I'd be delighted.*' – 'Thank you. How did the singles go?' – '*Frau Cissy beat me three times in a row.*' – '*Of course he wasn't concentrating. By the way, Else, did you know the Crown Prince of Greece is expected here tomorrow?*'

– What do I care about the Crown Prince of Greece. 'Really, is that
so?' O God – Dorsday with Frau Winawer! They greet me. Then
continue on. I responded much too politely. Yes, quite differently
from normal. O, what a dreadful person I am. *'I think your cigarette has
gone out, Else.'* – 'Well then, give me another light. Thank you.' –
*'Your shawl is very beautiful, Else, it goes splendidly with your black dress.
Which reminds me, I too must go and change.'* I wish she wouldn't leave, I'm
afraid of Dorsday. *'I've ordered the hairdresser to come at seven: she is
absolutely marvellous. She spends the winter in Milan. Well, adieu then, Else,
adieu, Paul.'* – *'Your servant, Madam.'* – 'Adieu, Frau Cissy.' She's gone.
Thank goodness Paul at least has stayed. *'May I sit down beside you for a
moment, Else, or would that be intruding on your dreams?'* – 'Why on my
dreams? On my realities perhaps.' That doesn't make any sense at
all. I wish he'd leave. After all, I simply have to speak to Dorsday.
He's still over there with the unhappy Frau Winawer: he's bored, I
can tell, he wants to come across to me. – *'So there are realities, are there,
on which you don't want anybody to intrude?'* – What's he saying? To hell
with him. Why am I smiling so coquettishly at him? It isn't meant for
him. Dorsday is watching us out of the corner of his eye. Where am
I? Where am I? – *'What's the matter with you today, Else?'* – 'Why, what
should be the matter?' – *'You seem mysterious, demonic, utterly seductive'.* –
Don't talk nonsense, Paul.' – *'One could go mad just looking at you.'* –
What's he got in mind? Why is he talking to me like this? How handsome he is. The smoke from my cigarette has got caught up in his
hair. But I could do without his being around at the moment. – *'You
seem to be gazing straight past me, Else. Why is that?'* – I won't reply to that.
I don't need him around just now. I'll put on my most forbidding
look. As long as I avoid further conversation. – *'Your thoughts are miles
away.'* – 'That could be true.' He is giving me a breathing space. Has
Dorsday noticed that I'm waiting for him? I'm not looking at him,
but I know he's looking over here. – *'Well, goodbye then, Else.'* – Thank
God for that. He's kissing my hand. He never does that normally.
'Adieu, Paul.' Where have I acquired that melting voice? Off he goes,
the two-faced rascal. He probably still has to make arrangements
with Cissy for tonight. I'll wrap the shawl round my shoulders, get up
and take a turn in front of the hotel. Of course it will be a little chilly
by now. Pity my coat is – ah, yes, of course, I handed it in at the
porter's lodge this morning. I can feel von Dorsday's gaze on my
neck through the shawl. Frau Winawer is now on her way up to her
room. How is it I know that? Telepathy. 'Porter, I wonder whether –'
'Fräulein would like her coat?' – 'If you wouldn't mind.' – *'The evenings
are already rather chilly, Fräulein. It sets in quite suddenly in these parts.'* –

'Thank you.' Should I really go outside? Of course, why not? Well, at least make towards the door. Now they are assembling one after the other. The gentleman with the gold pince-nez. The tall fair-haired man with the green waistcoat. They're all watching me. How beautiful that little Genevan is. No, she's from Lausanne. Actually, it's not that chilly.

'*Good evening, Fräulein Else.*' – Heavens, it's him. I won't say anything about Papa. Not a word. Not until after supper. Or rather, I'll leave for Vienna first thing tomorrow. I'll go and see Dr Fiala personally. Why didn't I think of that in the first place? I'll turn round and pretend I don't know who is standing behind me. 'Ah, Herr von Dorsday.' – '*You are thinking of going for another walk, Fräulein Else?*' – 'Oh, not a walk exactly, just strolling up and down a little before dinner.' – '*That is still almost an hour away.*' – 'Really?' It's not that chilly at all. How blue the mountains are. It would be amusing if he were suddenly to take my hand. – '*There isn't a finer spot on earth than this.*' – 'You think so, Herr von Dorsday? But I beg you, don't go on to tell me that the air here is like champagne.' – '*No, Fräulein Else, I would only say that above two thousand metres. And here we are standing no more than six hundred and fifty metres above sea level.*' – 'Does it make all that much difference?' – '*It does indeed. Have you ever been to Engadine?*' – 'No, never. Is the air there really like champagne?' – '*One might almost say that. But champagne is not my favourite drink. I much prefer this region. Not least because of its magnificent woods.*' – What a bore he is. Doesn't he realise it himself? Clearly he doesn't quite know what to say to me. It would be easier with a married woman. A small indecency and the conversation proceeds. – '*Are you staying much longer here in San Martino, Fräulein Else?*' – How stupid. Why must I look at him so archly? He's already smiling in that knowing way. How stupid men are. 'That partly depends on my aunt's inclinations.' That isn't true at all. I can return to Vienna on my own. 'Probably until the tenth.' – '*Your Mama is still in Gmunden?*' – 'No, Herr von Dorsday, she is already in Vienna. She's been there for the past three weeks. Papa is also in Vienna. This year he barely took a week's vacation. I believe the Erbesheimer trial is keeping him extremely busy.' – '*I can imagine. But your Papa is the only one who can get Erbesheimer off. . . Indeed it's already an achievement that it's become a civil case at all.*' – This is good, this is good. 'I am pleased to hear that you too have positive presentiments.' – '*Presentiments? How do you mean?*' – 'I mean that Papa will win the case for Erbesheimer.' – '*I do not wish to maintain that with any certainty.*' – What, already in retreat? He mustn't get away with that. 'Oh, I firmly believe in presentiments and premonitions. Just think, Herr von Dorsday, this very morning I received a letter from home.' That was not very clever. He looks a little astonished. Keep going, don't start sobbing. He's a good friend of Papa's of old. Forwards. Forwards. Now or never. 'Herr von Dorsday, you've just spoken so well of Papa that it would be positively hateful of me if I were not completely open with you.' Why is he making sheep's eyes? Oh God, he suspects something. Keep going, keep going. 'That is, in the letter you too are mentioned, Herr von Dorsday. It's a letter from Mama.' – 'I see.' – 'It's a very sad letter, as a matter of fact. Of course you know the circumstances of our household, Herr von Dorsday.' Good Heavens, my voice is beginning to sound tearful. On with it, on with it, there's no turning back now. Thank God for that. 'In short, Herr von Dorsday, things have come to a pass again.' – Now he'd much prefer to disappear. 'It's a matter of – a mere bagatelle. Really just a bagatelle, Herr von Dorsday. And yet, according to Mama, everything's at stake.' I'm prattling on so, like a silly cow. – *'Calm down now, Fräulein Else.'* – He said that very kindly. But that doesn't mean he had to touch my arm. – *'Well now, what's the matter, Fräulein Else? What's in the sad letter from Mama!'* – 'Herr von Dorsday, Papa' – My knees are trembling. 'Mama writes to say that Papa' – *'In Heaven's name, Fräulein Else, what is wrong with you? Shouldn't you perhaps – ah, here's a bench. Would you like to take my coat? It is a little chilly.'* – 'Thank you, Herr von Dorsday, oh, it's nothing, nothing in particular.' So, here I am all of a sudden, sitting on a bench. Who is that lady coming past? Don't know her at all. If only I didn't have to go on. The way he's looking at me. How could you ask this of me, Papa? It wasn't right of you, Papa. Well, now it's happened. I should have waited until after the *dîner*. – *'Well, Fräulein Else?'* – His monocle is dangling. How absurd it looks. Should I answer him? I simply have to. Quickly then, so it's over and done with. What can happen to me anyway? He is Papa's friend. 'Oh God, Herr von Dorsday. You are an old friend of our family.' I said that very nicely. 'And you will hardly be surprised when I tell you that Papa again finds himself in a rather embarrassing situation.' How strange my voice sounds. Is that really me who's prattling on? Could I be dreaming? I'm sure my face too looks quite different from normal. – *'I am certainly not altogether surprised. You are quite right about that, my dear Fräulein Else, even though I'm very sorry to hear it.'* – Why am I looking up at him so pleadingly? Smile, smile. That's better. – *'I feel such sincere friendship for your Papa, indeed for all of you.'* – He shouldn't look at me like that, it's quite indecent. I'll try a different approach and avoid smiling. I must behave with greater dignity. 'Well, Herr von Dorsday, this would be an opportunity for you to prove your friendship with my father.'

Thank Heavens, I've recovered my normal voice. 'It would appear, Herr von Dorsday, that all our relatives and friends – most of them have not returned yet to Vienna – otherwise it would never have occurred to Mama of course. – You see, in a recent letter to Mama I happened to mention – among other things of course – that you were in San Martino.' – *'I assumed, Fräulein Else, that I would not constitute the sole topic of your correspondence with Mama.'* – What's this, he's pressing his knee against mine as he stands in front of me. Ah well, so be it. What does it matter! Once one has sunk as low as this. – 'The situation is as follows. This time it is Fiala who is making things particularly difficult for Papa.' – *'Ah, Dr Fiala.'* – Evidently he too knows what to make of this Dr Fiala. 'Yes, and the amount in question must be paid by noon on the fifth, that is, the day after tomorrow – or rather, it must be in his hands if Baron Höning is not to – yes, just imagine, the Baron called Papa over privately, being so very fond of him.' Why am I talking about von Höning, that surely wasn't really necessary. – *Do you mean to say, Else, that otherwise he will be arrested?'* – Why is he saying that so harshly? I won't answer, I'll just nod. 'Yes.' There, now I've gone and said yes after all. – *'Hm, that is serious, that is indeed very – such a brilliantly gifted fellow. – And what was the actual sum in question, Fräulein Else?'* – Why is he smiling? He considers the matter serious and yet he smiles. What does his smile mean? That it is of no consequence how much? And what if he says no! I'll kill myself if he says no. Well then, I shall have to name the sum. 'What, Herr von Dorsday, I've not yet said how much? A million.' Whyever am I saying that? Surely this is not the moment to be joking? But if I then tell him how much less it really is, he will be relieved. Is he wide-eyed with astonishment? Does he really think Papa would ask him for a million? – 'Forgive me, Herr von Dorsday, for joking at a moment like this. I am not really in the mood for jokes.' Go on, press your knee up close, indulge yourself by all means. 'Of course there is no question of a million, Herr von Dorsday, the total amount is a mere thirty thousand guilders, Dorsday, and it has to be in the hands of Dr Fiala by noon the day after tomorrow. Indeed it has. Mama writes that Papa has explored every avenue, but as I mentioned, the relatives who might be considered are not in Vienna at the moment.' – Oh God, how humiliating. – 'Otherwise it would never have occurred to Papa, of course, to turn to you, Herr von Dorsday, that is, to ask me –' – Why is he so silent? Why is his expression so impassive? Why doesn't he say yes? Where is the chequebook and the fountain-pen? Surely for Heaven's sake he won't say no? Ought I to throw myself on my knees before him? Oh God! Oh God –

'On the fifth, did you say, Fräulein Else?' – Thank God, at last he's saying something. 'Yes indeed, Herr von Dorsday, at noon the day after tomorrow. So it would be necessary – I believe it could now hardly be sorted out by post.' – *'Of course not, Fräulein Else, we would have to telegraph.'* – "We," he said, that's good, that's excellent. – *'That would be of least concern. How much was it you said, Else?'* – He heard what I said, why is he tormenting me? 'Thirty thousand, Herr von Dorsday. a ridiculous amount really.' Why did I say that? How stupid. But he's smiling. He's thinking what a stupid girl I am. He is smiling really kindly. Papa is saved. He would have lent him fifty thousand even, and we would have been able to purchase all sorts of things. I could have bought myself new blouses. How contemptible I am. That's how one becomes. – *'Not quite so ridiculous, dear child,'* – Why does he say "dear child"? Is that good or bad? – *'as you might imagine. Even thirty thousand guilders have to be earned.'* – Forgive me, Herr von Dorsday, I didn't mean it quite like that. I just thought how sad it is that Papa, for want of such a sum, a mere bagatelle' – Oh God, I'm getting all tangled up again. 'You can't imagine, Herr von Dorsday, – even though you have some acquaintance with our circumstances, how terrible it all is for Mama and me.' – He has put one leg up on the bench. Is that a mark of poise – or what? – *'Oh, I can well imagine, my dear Else.'* – Now his tone has changed completely; how strange. – *'I myself have often thought: unfortunate, most unfortunate for all these brilliant people.'* – Why does he say "unfortunate"? Is he not going to hand the money over? No, he means it only in a general sense. Why won't he finally say yes? Or does he take all that for granted? The way he looks at me! Why doesn't he go on? Ah, because the two Hungarian ladies are strolling past. At least he is now standing respectably, no longer with his foot up on the bench. His cravat is too loud for an older gentleman. Did his mistress choose it for him? Not a model of refinement, "between you and me", as Mama put it. Thirty thousand guilders! And yet I'm smiling at him. Whyever am I smiling? Oh, I'm such a coward. – *'If one could at least assume, my dear Fräulein Else, that this sum would make any difference? But – you are a clever creature, Else, what would these thirty thousand guilders amount to? A drop in the bucket.'* – For Heaven's sake, is he not going to give the money? I mustn't look so frightened. Everything's at stake. I must now say something sensible and with conviction. 'O no, Herr von Dorsday, it wouldn't be just a drop in the bucket this time. Don't forget, Herr von Dorsday, the Erbesheimer trial is pending, and even today it is as good as won. You yourself had that feeling, Herr von Dorsday. And Papa is also involved in other trials. And besides, I have every intention, and you mustn't laugh, Herr

von Dorsday, of giving Papa a very serious talking to. He depends on me a little. Indeed I would go so far as to say that if anyone is in a position to wield some influence over him, it would probably be me.' – *'You are certainly a moving, an enchanting creature, Fräulein Else.'* – His voice has assumed that insinuating tone again. How I detest it when men adopt that tone. Even with Fred I don't like it. – *An enchanting creature indeed.'* – Why does he say "indeed" like that? It's really in poor taste. They only use such innuendos in the Burgtheater. – *'But much as I'd like to share your optimism – once a man is up to his ears in debt . . .'* – 'He isn't, Herr von Dorsday. If I didn't believe in Papa, if I were not absolutely convinced that this thirty thousand guilders' – I don't know what more to say. I can't literally start begging. He is considering evidently. Perhaps he doesn't know Fiala's address? Nonsense. The situation is quite impossible. Here I sit like some miserable sinner, while he stands before me, gazing piercingly at me through his silly monocle and saying nothing. The best thing to do is to get up and go. I won't let myself be treated in this way. Papa can go and kill himself. I shall kill myself as well. Life like this is a disgrace. The best thing would be to throw myself off that cliff over there and it would all be over. Serve you right, all of you. I'm getting up. – *'Fräulein Else'* – 'Forgive me, Herr von Dorsday, for having troubled you at all under these circumstances. Naturally I can fully understand your negative reaction' – there, it's done, I'm going – *'Wait a minute, Fräulein Else.'* – Wait, he says? Why does he want me to wait? He's going to hand over the money. Yes. Without a doubt. He has to. But I won't sit down again. I shall remain standing, as though it will only take half a second. I'm a little taller than he is. – *'You did not wait to hear my answer, Else. Forgive me, Else, for mentioning it in this connection,'* – there's no need for him to say Else quite so often – *'but I was in a position once before to help your Papa out of an awkward situation. Admittedly over an – even more ridiculous sum than on this occasion, and I did not for a moment flatter myself with the expectation that I should ever see the money again – so that there would in fact be no grounds for refusing my help again on this occasion. The more so when a young lady like you, Else, when you yourself approach me as an intercessor –'* – What's he getting at? His voice no longer sounds insinuating. Or in a different way! What's behind the way he's looking at me? He'd better watch out!! – *'Well then, Else, I am prepared – Dr Fiala shall have his thirty thousand guilders at noon the day after tomorrow – on one condition.'* – He mustn't, he mustn't go on. – 'I myself, Herr von Dorsday, I personally, will undertake to guarantee that my father will reimburse you that amount as soon as he has received his fee from Erbesheimer. So far the Erbesheimers have not paid anything at all.

Not even a deposit – according to Mama.' – *'Spare yourself the trouble, Else, one should never undertake guarantees on behalf of other people – or even of oneself.'* – What does he want? His voice has that insinuating tone again. No one has ever looked at me like this before. Woe betide him! – *'An hour ago I would scarcely have thought it possible I would ever permit myself to fall into the trap of imposing a condition. And yet now I'm doing so. Yes Else, one is only human after all, and it is not my fault, Else, that you are so lovely.'* – What does he want? What does he want –? – *'Today or perhaps tomorrow, I would have made the same request of you that I am now about to make, even if you had not asked me for a million – pardon me, thirty thousand guilders. Admittedly, under different circumstances you would scarcely have granted me the opportunity to talk to you alone for quite so long.'* – 'Indeed, Herr von Dorsday, I have imposed on you for far too long.' That was well said. Fred would have approved. What's this? Trying to take my hand? What does he think he's up to? – *'Surely, Else, you have long been aware . . .'* – He had better let go of my hand! Thank God for that, he's let go. Keep your distance, keep your distance. – *'You would not be a woman, Else, if you had not noticed.* Je vous désire.' – He could have said it just as well in German, our fine Herr Vicomte. – *'Need I say more?'* – 'You have said too much already, Herr Dorsday.' And yet I am still standing here. Why? I'm off, I'm off without bidding him good evening. – *'Else, Else!'* – He's at my side again. – *'Forgive me, Else. I too was merely joking, just like you over the million guilders. I too will not raise my demand as high – as you had feared, for that alas seems to be the appropriate word – so that my lesser demand may perhaps come as an agreeable surprise. I beg you, stay a moment, Else.'* – I have actually stopped walking. Whatever for? We are now facing one another. Shouldn't I simply have slapped him in the face? Wouldn't there still be time to do so now? The two Englishmen are coming past. Now would be the moment, since they are present. So why then don't I do it? Because I am a coward. I'm broken, I'm humiliated. What will he want instead of the one million? A kiss perhaps? That would be negotiable. A million is to thirty thousand as – Strange equations! – *'If you should ever really need a million, Else, – I am not a rich man, but we shall see. This time, however, like you I shall be modest. This time I want nothing more, Else, than – to see you.'* – Is the man mad? He can see me at the moment. – Ah, so that's what he means. Why don't I slap him in the face, the scoundrel? Have I turned red or pale? So you want to see me naked? You're not the only one. I'm beautiful naked. Why don't I slap him in the face? How huge his face is. Don't come so close, you scoundrel! I don't want you breathing on my cheek. Why don't I simply walk away from him? Am I spellbound by his gaze? We are looking one another in the eye like mortal enemies. I feel like calling him a scoundrel, but I can't. Or don't I want to? – *'You are staring at me, Else, as though I were deranged. Perhaps I am a little, Else, for a magic emanates from you that you yourself are unaware of. You must surely realise, Else, that my request is not an insult. Yes, I say "request", even though it looks damnably like blackmail. But I am no blackmailer, I am simply a man who has learned from experience – amongst other things that everything in the world has its price, and that anyone who gives away his money when he is in a position to receive something in return is an utter fool. And – as to what I want to buy on this occasion, Else, however valuable it is, you will be none the poorer for selling it. And that it would remain a secret between yourself and me, Else, I swear to you by – by all the charms you would delight me with by unveiling.'* – Where did he learn to talk like that? It sounds like something out of a book. – *'I also swear to you that – I will not make any use of the situation not foreseen in our agreement. I ask no more of you than to be permitted to stand for a quarter of an hour in reverence before your beauty. My room is on the same floor as yours, Else, number sixty-five, quite easy to remember. Wasn't the Swedish tennis player you spoke of earlier exactly sixty-five years old?'* – He's mad! Why do I allow him to continue? I'm completely paralysed. – *'But if for any reason it does not suit you to visit me in room number sixty-five, Else, I propose a little walk after the* dîner. *There is a clearing in the wood, which I recently discovered quite by chance, scarcely five minutes away from our hotel. It is a glorious summer night, almost sultry, and the starlight will clothe you splendidly.'* – It's as if he were talking to a slave. I could spit in his face. – *'You shouldn't answer me at once, Else. Consider the matter. After the* dîner *perhaps you would be good enough to announce your decision.'* – Why does he say "announce"? How pompous: "announce your decision" indeed. – *'Consider the matter at your leisure. You will perhaps realise that it is not simply a trade-off that I am proposing.'* – What else, you unmitigated scoundrel! – *'You may conceivably apprehend that the man addressing you is rather lonely and not especially happy and deserves some consideration.'* – Affected scoundrel. Talks like a third-rate actor. His manicured fingers look like claws. No, no, I won't do it. So why do I not say so. Go on and kill yourself, Papa! What's he up to with my hand? My arm's quite limp. He's raising my hand to his lips. Hot lips. Disgusting! My hand is cold. I'd like to blow his hat off. Haha, how funny that would be. Finished kissing, you scoundrel? – The lamps in front of the hotel are already lighted. Two windows on the third floor are open. Mine's the one where the curtain is moving. There's something gleaming on top of the wardrobe. No, not on top of it, just one of the brass fixtures. – *'Well then, goodbye, Else.'* – I'm not saying anything. Just standing there motionless. He looks me in the eye. My face is quite inscrutable. He can't tell anything. He doesn't know whether I will come or not. I don't know either. All I know is that everything is over. I am half-dead. He turns to go. He stoops a little. Scoundrel! He can feel my gaze on his neck. Who's he greeting? Two ladies. He greets them as though he were a count. Paul ought to challenge him and shoot him dead. Or Rudi. Who does he think he is? Impertinent fellow! No, never ever! You have no alternative, Papa, you will just have to kill yourself. – The couple over there are clearly returning from a longer walk. Both she and he are quite good-looking. Do they still have time to change for the *dîner*? No doubt they are on their honeymoon, or perhaps not even married. I shall never have a honeymoon. Thirty thousand guilders. No, no, no! Are thirty thousand guilders nowhere to be found on earth? I'll go and see Fiala. I shall sort things out. Mercy, mercy, Herr Doktor Fiala. With pleasure, my dear young lady. Proceed into my bedroom. – Do me this one favour, Paul, ask your father for thirty thousand guilders. Say that you have gambling debts, and otherwise will have to shoot yourself. I'll be happy to, dear cousin. My room number is such and such, I'll be expecting you at midnight. Ah, Herr von Dorsday, you are indeed modest. For the moment. Right now he must be dressing. Dinner jacket. Well then, let's decide. The meadow by moonlight or room number sixty-five? Will he wear his dinner jacket to escort me to the woods?

There is still a little time before dinner. I'll take another turn and consider matters calmly. I'm a lonely old man, haha! Heavenly air, like champagne. Not in the least bit chilly – thirty thousand . . . thirty thousand . . . I must look ravishing against this sweeping landscape. Pity almost no one's out of doors now. The gentleman at the edge of the wood there evidently finds me most appealing. Yes, my good sir, and naked I am even more beautiful, and the price is ridiculous, thirty thousand guilders. Perhaps you could bring your friends along, then it would work out cheaper. I hope you have a lot of handsome friends, younger and handsomer at least than Herr von Dorsday. Do you know this Herr von Dorsday? He's a scoundrel – an unmitigated scoundrel . . .

Come on now, think, consider . . . a man's life is at stake. Papa's life. Nonsense, he won't kill himself, he'd rather go to prison. Three years' hard labour, five at most. He has been living in perpetual fear of this for five or ten years already . . . Securities . . . And Mama just as much so. And me as well. – Who will I be obliged to strip naked for next time? Or will we stick to Herr von Dorsday, just to keep things simple? His current mistress is not a model of refinement, "between you and me". He's sure to prefer me. But it's none too certain that

I'm any more refined. Don't put on airs, Fräulein Else, I could tell tales about you . . . about a certain dream for instance, which you've already had three times – and which you didn't confide even to your friend Bertha. And what was all that about, earlier this year in Gmunden at six one morning on the balcony, my high and noble Fräulein Else? Perhaps you didn't even notice the two young men in the boat who were staring at you? Of course they couldn't make out my face distinctly from the lake, but they certainly noticed that I was in my nightgown. And it gave me pleasure. Ah, more than pleasure. I was intoxicated. I ran both hands over my hips, and pretended to be unaware that anyone was watching me. Yes, that's the way I am, that's the way I am. Really just a slut. They all can tell. Even Paul can tell. Naturally, since he's a gynaecologist. But the naval lieutenant could tell as well and so could the painter. Only Fred, the stupid fellow, is unconscious of it. That is why he loves me. Yet it's precisely by him that I wouldn't want to be seen naked, no, never. It would give me no pleasure. I would feel ashamed. But by the rogue with the Roman head – how willingly. By him more readily than by all the others. Even if I then had to die immediately. But would I really need to die immediately. One survives these things. Bertha has survived much more. No doubt Cissy too lies naked, while Paul steals along the hotel corridors to her, as I tonight will steal across to Herr von Dorsday.

No, no. I refuse to do it. I'll go to anybody else, but not to him. To Paul if need be. Or I'll choose someone this evening during *dîner*. It's all the same to me. But then I can't tell just anyone that I want thirty thousand guilders in return! Then I'd be like some common harlot from the Kärntnerstrasse. No, I will not sell myself. Never. I shall never sell myself. I shall give myself to someone. Yes, when once I find the right man, I shall give myself to him. But I will never sell myself. I may be a slut, but I refuse to be a whore. You have miscalculated, Herr von Dorsday. And Papa as well. Yes, he too miscalculated. He must have foreseen everything. He knows how people are. He knows what Herr von Dorsday's like. He must have recognised that Herr von Dorsday would not intervene again and again for nothing. – Otherwise he could have sent a telegram or travelled here himself. But this way was easier and safer, wasn't it Papa? Why should one need to go to prison when one has such an attractive daughter? And Mama, being the fool she is, sits down and writes the letter. Papa didn't dare to do it himself. I would have seen through him at once. But you will not succeed, either of you. No, you have speculated too confidently on my childish affection, Papa, been too

ready to assume that I would rather endure any ignominy than let
you bear the consequences of your criminal recklessness. Of course
you are a genius. Herr von Dorsday says so, everybody says so. But
what good is that to me. Fiala is a nonentity, but he does not embezzle shares, even Waldheim can't be mentioned in the same breath
as you . . . Who was it that said that? Ah yes, Dr Froriep. Your Papa's
a genius. – And yet I've only heard him speak once! – At court
last year before a jury – that was the first and last time! He was magnificent! Tears streamed down my cheeks. And the miserable fellow
he defended was acquitted. Perhaps he wasn't such a miserable fellow. He at least had only stolen, not embezzled securities to play Bac-
carat and speculate on the Exchange. And now Papa himself will be
standing before the jury. It will be in all the papers. Second day of the
proceedings, third day of the proceedings; the counsel for the
defence got to his feet to reply. But who will take on his defence? Not
another genius. Nothing will save him. Unanimously found guilty.
Sentenced to five years. Rocks, convict uniform, shaven head. Once
a month he'll be allowed a visit. Mama and I will travel third class to
see him. For of course we won't have any money. No one will lend us
anything. A little apartment in the Lerchenfelderstrasse, like the one
where I visited the seamstress ten years ago. We'll bring him things to
eat. But how? When we ourselves have nothing. Uncle Victor will
pay us an annuity. Three hundred guilders a month. Rudi will be in
Holland under Vanderhulst – if he's still well thought of. The Children of the Convict! A novel by Temme in three volumes. Papa
receives us in his striped convict's uniform. He doesn't look angry,
simply sad. He's incapable of looking angry. – Else, if only you'd
obtained the money for me then, he'll be thinking to himself, but he
won't say anything. He won't have the heart to reproach me. He's a
good soul at heart, just reckless. His fatal flaw is his passion for gambling. But he can't help it, it's a kind of madness. Perhaps they will
acquit him on the grounds of insanity. He didn't think about the letter beforehand either. Perhaps it never even occurred to him that
Dorsday might exploit the opportunity and demand something so
ignoble of me. He is a good friend of the family, and lent Papa eight
thousand guilders once before. How should one imagine such a
thing of anyone? No doubt Papa first tried every alternative. Imagine
what he must have gone through, before persuading Mama to write
that letter! He would have run from one friend to another, from
Warsdorf to Burin, from Burin to Wertheimstein and God only
knows who else. No doubt he also went to Uncle Karl. And they all
left him in the lurch. All his so-called friends. And now Dorsday is his

one and only hope. And if the money doesn't come through he'll kill himself. Of course he'll kill himself. He won't let himself be locked away. Inquest and arrest, proceedings, trial by jury, convict clothes. When the warrant for his arrest arrives, he will shoot or hang himself. He'll be hanging from the window. They'll send across from the house opposite, the locksmith will have to open up and I shall have been to blame. And right now he's sitting with Mama in the very room where in two days' time he'll hang himself, and smoking a Havanna cigar. How come he is still supplied with them? I can hear him talking to Mama and reassuring her. Depend upon it, Dorsday will remit the money. Don't forget, I saved him a tidy sum this winter by my intervention. And then there is the Erbesheimer trial . . . Yes, I can hear his very words. Telepathy! Amazing. I can see what Fred's doing at the moment too. He is walking past the spa-house in the Stadtpark with a young lady. She is wearing a light blue blouse and dainty shoes and sounds a little husky. I'm absolutely certain of all this. When I get back to Vienna, I'll ask Fred whether on the third of September between seven-thirty and eight in the evening, he was in fact in the Stadtpark with his mistress.

Where to now? What's the matter with me? It's almost completely dark. How nice and quiet. Not a soul about. Now they are all already sitting down to dinner. Telepathy? No, that's hardly telepathy. I heard the gong strike earlier. Where is Else, Paul will say to himself. Everyone will notice if I'm still not there for the hors d'oeuvres. They will send up for me. What's happened to Else? She is normally so punctual. Even the two gentlemen by the window will wonder: where is the beautiful young lady with the reddish-blond hair today? And Herr von Dorsday will be gripped by fear. He's undoubtedly a coward. Rest assured, Herr von Dorsday, nothing is going to happen to you. I despise you too much. If I so wished, you would be a dead man tomorrow evening. – I'm quite sure Paul would challenge him, if I were to tell him the whole story. I grant you your life, Herr von Dorsday.

How immensely wide the meadows are and how gigantic the black mountains. Almost no stars. Oh yes, three, four – soon there will be more. And the forest behind me is so quiet. Lovely, just sitting here on the bench at the edge of the forest. How far, far away the hotel seems and how magically its lights are twinkling. And what scoundrels are lodging there. Ah no, just people, poor wretched people, I feel so sorry for them all. I even feel sorry for the Marchioness, I don't know why, and for Frau Winawer and for the nanny of Cissy's little girl. She never sits at the main table and she used to eat with

Fritzi. What has happened to Else, Cissy asks. Is she not in her room either? They are all undoubtedly concerned about me. I'm the only one who's unconcerned. Yes, here I am in Martino di Castrozza, sitting on a bench at the edge of the forest where the air is like champagne, and yet I do believe I'm crying. Why should I be crying? There is no reason for tears. It must be nerves. I must control myself. I mustn't let myself go like this. But crying is not at all unpleasant. A good cry always does me good. That time I visited our old French servant in the hospital, who later died, I remember crying then. I also cried at Granny's funeral, and when Bertha left for Nuremberg, and when Agatha's baby died, and over *The Lady of the Camellias* at the theatre. Who will weep when I die? Oh, how marvellous it would be to be dead. Laid out in the drawing-room, the candles burning. Tall candles. Twelve tall candles. Downstairs the hearse is already waiting. People have gathered outside the front door. How old was she? Only nineteen. Really, only nineteen? – Just imagine, her father is in prison. Why did she kill herself? An unhappy affair with a roué. You can't be serious? She was going to have a baby. No, no, she fell climbing the Cimone, it was an accident. Good day Herr Dorsday, so you too have come to pay your last respects to little Else? Little Else, says the old woman. – Why not? Of course I must pay my last respects to her. After all, I also paid her the ultimate insult. Ah, but it was well worth it, Frau Winawer, never before have I seen such a lovely body. It only cost me thirty million. A Rubens costs three times that much. She poisoned herself with an overdose of hashish. All she wanted was to see beautiful visions, but she took too much and never woke up. Why is Herr von Dorsday's monocle red? Who is he waving to with his handkerchief? Mama is coming down the stairs and she kisses his hand. Disgusting. Now they are whispering to one another. I cannot understand a word because I'm laid out on the bier. The crown of violets round my forehead is from Paul. The ribbons are so long they reach the floor. No one ventures into the room. I might as well get up and look out of the window. What a large blue lake! A hundred boats with yellow sails. The waves are sparkling. The sun's intense. The gentlemen are all in rowing-vests. The ladies are in swimming costumes. That's indecent. They imagine I am naked. How stupid they are. I'm all dressed up in black because I'm dead. I'll prove it to you. I shall go back at once and lie down on the bier again. But where is it? It has vanished. It's been misappropriated. That is why Papa's in prison. And yet they released him for three years on bail. The jurymen have all been bribed by Fiala. Now I shall go to the cemetery on foot, so Mama will be saved the funeral expenses. We have to tighten our belts. I'm walking so fast that no one will be able to come after me. How fast I'm walking. In the street everyone stops short and marvels at me. Why are they allowed to stare at someone who is dead like that! It's quite importunate. I'd better cut across the fields, which are blue with forget-me-nots and violets. The naval officers have formed a guard of honour. Good morning, gentlemen. Open the door, Herr Matador. Don't you recognise me? I'm the dead girl . . . So you'd better not kiss my hand . . . Where's my grave? Has that been misappropriated too? Heaven be praised, this is not the cemetery at all. Of course this is the park in Menton. Papa will be so happy that I've not been buried. I'm not afraid of snakes. So long as they don't bite my foot. Oh dear.

What's happening? Wherever am I? Did I fall asleep? Yes, I must have nodded off. I even seem to have been dreaming. My feet are so cold. Especially the right foot. Why is that? Ah, there's a small hole in my stocking near the ankle. Why am I still sitting out in the forest? The gong for dinner must have sounded long ago. Dinner.

But my God, wherever was I? It all seemed so far away. What was it I was dreaming? I seem to remember that I was already dead. And that I had no more worries and didn't have to rack my brains. Thirty thousand, thirty thousand . . . I still don't have the money. I have to earn it first. And yet here I am sitting alone at the edge of the forest. I can still see the hotel lights from here. I must get back. It's awful to have to go back. But there's not a moment to be lost. Herr von Dorsday is awaiting my decision. My decision. Well, my decision is no! No, Herr von Dorsday, the short answer is no. You were joking, Herr von Dorsday, that goes without saying. Yes, that's what I'll say to him. That will do splendidly. Your jest was not in particularly good taste, Herr von Dorsday, but I'm willing to forgive you. I'll send Papa a telegram tomorrow morning, saying that the money will be in Dr Fiala's hands on time. Marvellous. That's what I'll say to him. Then he'll have no choice, he will be obliged to send the money off. Obliged to? Will he really be obliged to? Whyever should he be obliged to? And if he did so he would be sure to find some way to get his revenge. He would arrange things so that the money came too late. Or he would send the money and then go around saying he had had me. But of course he will not send the money off. No, Fräulein Else, that was not our bargain. Telegraph whatever you like to your Papa, I will not dispatch the money. Don't imagine, Fräulein Else, that I shall permit myself to be duped by a slip of a girl like you, I the Vicomte d'Eperies.

I must watch my step. The path is completely dark. Strange, I feel better than before. Nothing at all has changed and yet I do feel better. What was I dreaming about? About a matador? What sort of matador was it then? It's further than I thought back to the hotel. They are all certain to be at dinner still. I shall sit down quietly at the table and say I had a migraine, and have them serve my dinner late. Eventually Herr von Dorsday himself will come across to me and say the whole thing was merely a joke. Forgive me, Fräulein Else, forgive me for the poor joke, I've already telegraphed my bank. But he won't say that at all. He hasn't sent a telegram. Everything is still exactly as before. He's waiting. Herr von Dorsday is waiting. No, I will not see him. I cannot bear to see him any more. I don't want to see anyone any more. I don't want to go back to the hotel, I don't want to go home, I don't want to return to Vienna, I don't want to contact anyone, neither Papa nor Mama, nor Rudi nor Fred, nor Berta nor even Aunt Irene. She is still the best and would understand everything. But I'll have nothing more to do with her or anybody else. If I could wave a magic wand, I'd rather be in some completely different corner of the world. On some magnificent ship in the Mediterranean perhaps, though not all by myself. Together with Paul for instance. Yes, I can imagine that quite well. Or I might live in a villa on the sea, and we would lie on the marble steps leading down into the water, and he would hold me tightly in his arms and bite my lips, the way Albert did two years ago during my piano lesson, the shameless fellow. No, I'd rather lie waiting on the marble steps by the sea alone. And at long last one or perhaps many men would come, and I would take my pick, and the others whom I had scorned would all throw themselves into the sea in despair. Or else they would wait patiently until the following day. Ah, what a delightful life that would be. Otherwise what's the point of having splendid shoulders and beautiful long legs? And what am I here on earth for anyway? And it would serve them right, all of them, since after all they did bring me up to sell myself, one way or another. They wouldn't hear of my going on the stage. They only laughed at me. And yet last year they would have been quite happy for me to have married the Director, Wilomitzer, who is nearly fifty. Except that they could not persuade me. Papa at least was too embarrassed. But Mama made several broad hints. – How huge the hotel looks, like a gigantic illuminated fairy castle. Everything's so huge. The mountains too. Quite terrifying. I've never seen them so black. There's no moon yet. It won't rise till the performance, the grand performance on the meadow, when Herr von Dorsday has his slave dance naked. What do I care about Herr Dorsday? Come now, Mademoiselle Else, why are you making such a fuss? You were ready enough to go off and become the mistress of those strangers, one after another. And yet you are bothered by this trivial thing that Herr von Dorsday asks of you? You are prepared, are you not, to sell yourself for pearls, for beautiful clothes, for a villa on the sea? And is your father's life worth less than that to you? It would provide the perfect start. It would also be the justification for everything that followed. It was you, I could then say, you are all to blame for what I have become, not just Papa and Mama. Rudi too is to blame and Fred as well, and everybody, everybody, because no-one really cares about one. They show a little affection if you're really pretty, a little concern if you have a fever, and they send you off to school, and at home you learn French and the piano, and in summer they take you to the country and you get presents for your birthday and at table they talk about all sorts of things. But as to what is going on inside me, what I'm worrying and brooding over, have any of them ever bothered about that? Occasionally there was a hint of awareness in Papa's eye, but only fleetingly. And then immediately it would be replaced by professional matters – his worries and his speculations on the stock exchange – and probably a secret affair with some woman or other, "not a model of refinement, between you and me" – and I would be alone again. Well now, what would you do, Papa, what would you do now, if I weren't here?

Here I am, yes, here I am outside the hotel. – Dreadful to have to go on in, with everybody staring, Herr von Dorsday, my aunt and Cissy. How beautiful it was before, on the bench at the edge of the forest when I was already dead. A matador – if I could only recall – that's right, there was a regatta, and I was watching from the window. But who was the matador? – If only I were not so tired, so frightfully tired. And yet I'm supposed to stay up till midnight and then slip into Herr von Dorsday's room? Perhaps I'll meet Cissy in the passage. Does she have anything on under her dressing-gown when she visits him? It's hard when one has no experience in such matters. Should I perhaps ask Cissy for advice? Of course I wouldn't say that Dorsday was involved, and she would imagine I had a nocturnal rendezvous with one of the handsome young men here in the hotel. For instance the tall blond fellow with those sparkling eyes. But then he's no longer here. He disappeared suddenly. I haven't thought about him once until this moment. But unfortunately it is not the tall blond man with sparkling eyes, nor is it Paul, it's Herr von Dorsday. Well then, how am I to go about things? What should I say to him? Simply yes? But I can't possibly go to Herr von Dorsday's room. He's bound to have an array of elegant bottles on his dresser, and the whole room

will reek of French perfume. No, not there, not for the world. Better
in the open air. There he won't affect me. The sky is so high and the
meadow so broad, I won't have to think about Herr Dorsday. I won't
even have to look at him. And if he dared to touch me, I'd kick him
with my bare feet. Ah, if only it were someone else, anybody else. He
could have everything, everything from me tonight, anybody else
except Dorsday. He, he of all people! How he'll stare and ogle. He'll
stand there grinning with his monocle. No, no, he won't grin, he'll
adopt a formal air. Elegance personified. After all, he's accustomed
to such things. How many others has he seen like this? A hundred
maybe, or a thousand? But could any one of them compare with me?
No, that's certain. I shall tell him that he's not the first to see me like
this. I shall tell him that I have a lover. But only after the thirty thousand guilders have been sent off to Fiala. Then I'll tell him that he has
been a fool, that he could have had me for the same amount. – That
I've already had ten, twenty, a hundred lovers. – But of course he
won't believe me. – And even if he does, what good would that do
me? If only I could somehow ruin his enjoyment. What if someone
else were present? Why not? After all, he didn't say he had to be
alone with me. Oh, Herr von Dorsday, I'm so afraid of you. Would
you be so good as to allow me to bring along a friend? But that does
not in any way contravene our bargain, Herr von Dorsday. If I so
pleased, I would invite the whole hotel along, and you would still be
obligated to send the thirty thousand guilders. But I'll be satisfied
with just bringing my cousin Paul along. Or perhaps you would prefer somebody else? The tall blond man is unfortunately no longer
here, neither is the rake with the Roman head, alas. But I'm sure I
can find somebody else. You're afraid of some indiscretion? But that
isn't an issue. I don't care about discretion. When one has gone as far
as I have, nothing matters any longer. Today is just the beginning. Or
do you imagine I shall be returning home from this adventure a
respectable girl of good family just the same? No, neither respectable
nor of a good family. All that is over and done with. I must now stand
on my own two feet. I have beautiful legs, Herr von Dorsday, as you
and the other participants at our little celebration will soon have the
opportunity to observe. So everything is settled, Herr von Dorsday.
At ten o'clock, while everyone is still sitting in the foyer, we shall walk
across the meadow in the moonlight, through the forest to this
famous clearing you've discovered. You must bring the telegram to
the bank with you, just in case. After all, I'm entitled to demand some
security from a scoundrel like yourself. And at midnight you may
return home, and I shall stay on in the moonlight with my cousin or

the other person. You surely have no objection, Herr von Dorsday? You have no right to. And if tomorrow morning I should happen to be dead, you should not be too surprised. In the event, Paul will send the telegram. That will all be seen to. But for Heaven's sake, don't imagine that it was you, miserable fellow, who drove me to my death. I have known for some time now that this is how everything would end for me. Just ask my friend Fred whether I have not often said so to him. Fred, that is to say Herr Friedrich Wenkheim, the only decent person I have met in my entire life, by the way. The only one I could have loved, if he had not been quite such a decent fellow. Yes, that's how depraved a creature I am. I'm not made for a bourgeois existence, and I don't have any talent either. Anyway it would be best if our family were to die out. Some disaster or other is going to befall Rudi too. He'll probably plunge into debt for some Dutch chorus girl and embezzle money at Vanderhulst's. That's the way things are in our family. My father's youngest brother shot himself when he was fifteen years old. No one knows why. I never knew him. Have them show you his photograph, Herr von Dorsday. We have it in an album . . . They say I look like him. Not a soul knows why he took his own life. And no one will know why I did either. Certainly not because of you, Herr von Dorsday. I wouldn't pay you the compliment. Whether one goes at nineteen or at twenty-one doesn't really make much difference. Or should I perhaps become a maid or a telephonist, or marry a Herr Wilomitzer or allow myself to be kept by you? It's all equally disgusting, and I absolutely refuse to go out across the meadows with you. No, it's all too tiring and too stupid and objectionable. When I am dead, I trust you will be good enough to send off the few thousand guilders to Papa, as it would really be too tragic if he were to be arrested on the same day that my body were brought back to Vienna. But I shall leave a letter behind with my last will and testament: that Herr von Dorsday has the right to see my corpse. My beautiful naked maiden corpse. So you won't be able to complain, Herr von Dorsday, that I turned round and slapped you in the face. You will have had something for your money. There is nothing in our contract to say that I must be alive. O no. Nothing is there in writing. To the art dealer Herr von Dorsday, then, I bequeath a good look at my corpse, to Herr Fred Wenkheim I bequeath the diary of my seventeenth year – I didn't keep one after that – and to Cissy's nanny I bequeath the five twenty-franc pieces I brought back from Switzerland some years ago. They are in the bureau next to all the letters. And to Bertha I bequeath my black evening dress. And to Agatha my books. And to my cousin Paul I bequeath one kiss on my pale lips.

And to Cissy I bequeath my racquet, because I am high-minded. And I am to be buried here in San Martino di Castrozza in the pretty little graveyard. I don't want to go home again. Even when I'm dead. And Papa and Mama are not to get upset, since I am better off than they. And I forgive them. And no one is to pity me. – Haha, what a funny will. I'm really quite affected by it. What will it be like this time tomorrow, when all the others are sitting at *dîner*, with me already dead? Aunt Emma will not of course come down to dinner, nor will Paul. They will have the meal served in their rooms. I'm curious how Cissy will behave. Except that sadly I will not be aware of anything any more. Or perhaps one is conscious of everything, so long as one is not yet buried? And until then I shall only look as though I were dead. And when Herr von Dorsday approaches my corpse, I shall awake and open my eyes, and he'll be so frightened his monocle will fall out.

But none of this is true, alas. I won't just appear dead or be dead either. I won't kill myself at all, I'm much too cowardly for that. Even though I am a hardy climber, I'm still a coward for all that. And perhaps I don't even have enough Veronal. How many tablets does it take, I wonder? Six I believe. But ten is safer. I think there are ten left. Yes, that should be enough.

How many times have I walked round the hotel? What now? Here I am in front of the main entrance. No one's in the foyer yet. But of course – they are all at dinner still. The foyer looks strange, so empty. There's a hat on that chair, very smart, a tourist's hat. Fine chamois. An old gentleman is sitting in the armchair over there. He's probably lost his appetite. He's reading the paper. He's all right. He has no worries. He's quietly reading the paper, while I have to rack my brains how to procure thirty thousand guilders for Papa. What nonsense. Of course I know how. It's all so frightfully simple. What do I want? What do I really want? What do I intend to do here in the foyer? They will all be back from dinner shortly. What should I do? Herr von Dorsday is bound to be on tenterhooks. Why isn't she here, he will be thinking. Has she killed herself after all? Or is she engaging someone to kill me? Or is she inciting her cousin Paul to come after me? Don't be alarmed, Herr von Dorsday. I am not that dangerous. I'm really just a little slut, that's all. You shall have your reward for the anxiety you have endured. Twelve o'clock, room sixty-five. I would find it much too chilly out of doors. And from there, Herr von Dorsday, I shall go directly to my cousin Paul. Surely you have no objections, Herr von Dorsday?

'Else! Else!'

What? What was that? That was Paul's voice surely. Is dinner over already? – *'Else!'* –

'Oh, Paul; what's the matter, Paul?' I'll play the innocent. – *'Where on earth have you been, Else?'* – 'Where should I have been? I went for a walk.' – *'At this hour, during dinner?'* – 'Well, what of that. After all, it's the nicest time to go for one.' I'm talking nonsense. – *'Mama has been imagining all sorts of things. I went up to your room and knocked.'* – 'I didn't hear anything.' – *'But seriously, Else, how could you let us all get so upset! You might at least have let Mama know you were not going to be at dinner.'* – 'Of course you're quite right, Paul, but if you knew what a terrible headache I had.' My voice is all soft and melting. O, what a slut I am. – *'Do you at least feel better now?'* – 'I couldn't really say.' – *'I'll take you to Mama'* – 'Wait Paul, not just yet. Please convey my apologies to Auntie, but I must just pop up to my room for a few minutes to tidy myself up a little. Then I'll come down at once and have them serve me a late bite of something.' – *'Why are you so pale, Else? Should I send Mama up to you?'* – 'Don't make such a fuss over me, Paul, and don't look at me like that. Have you never seen a woman with a headache before? I'll be down directly. In ten minutes at the latest. See you soon, Paul.' – *'Well, goodbye then, Else.'* – Thank Heavens, he's going. Stupid fellow, but endearing. What does the porter want? What, a telegram? 'Thank you. When did it arrive?' – *'A quarter of an hour ago, Fräulein.'* – Why is he looking at me like that – as if he felt sorry for me. For Heaven's sake, what does it say? I'll wait and open it upstairs, otherwise I might fall down in a faint. Perhaps after all Papa has – If Papa is dead, then everything is fine, then I won't have to go with Herr von Dorsday out into the meadow . . . Oh, what a wretched person I am. Dear God, let there be no bad news in the dispatch. Dear God, let Papa be still alive. Under arrest, if needs must be, but please not dead. If it contains no bad news, I'll make a sacrifice. I'll become a chambermaid, I'll take an office job. Don't be dead, Papa. I am prepared. I'll do anything you want . . .

Thank God I'm back upstairs. Must turn on the light, must turn on the light. It's grown quite chilly. The window was open too long. Courage, courage. Perhaps it says that everything has been sorted out. Perhaps Uncle Bernhard has made over the money and they are telegraphing me to say don't speak to Dorsday. But how can I see what the telegram says while I'm staring at the ceiling? Trala, trala. Courage. What will be, will be. "Repeat urgent request speak to Dorsday. Amount not thirty but fifty. Otherwise all is lost. Address remains Fiala." – Fifty! Otherwise all is lost. Trala, trala. Fifty. Address remains Fiala. Of course, whether it's thirty or fifty makes no difference. Even to Herr von Dorsday. The Veronal is among my underwear, just in case. Why didn't I say fifty in the first place. After all, it did cross my mind! Otherwise all is lost. Well then, dash downstairs, don't just sit here on the bed. Forgive me, Herr von Dorsday, there's been a small mistake. Not thirty, but fifty, otherwise all is lost. Address remains Fiala. "Do you take me for a fool, Fräulein Else?" Not at all, Herr Vicomte, how could I? For fifty, Fräulein, I would have to demand significantly more. Otherwise all is lost. Address remains Fiala. As you wish, Herr von Dorsday. You have only to command. But first write out the telegram to your banking house, otherwise I will have no security. –

Yes, that's how I'll do it. I'll go to his room, and only after he has made out the telegram before my eyes – will I undress. And I'll hold on to the telegram. Oh, how unappetising. And where am I supposed to put my clothes? No, no, I'll undress here first and put on my long black coat which will cover me completely. That will be the most convenient. For both parties. Address remains Fiala. My teeth are chattering. The window is still open. There, that's better. Out of doors? I could have caught my death. The villain! Fifty thousand. He can't possibly say no. Room sixty-five. But first I'll tell Paul to wait in his room for me. From Dorsday's I'll go straight to Paul and tell him everything. And then Paul will challenge him. Yes, this very evening. Quite an eventful programme. And then comes the Veronal. No, whatever for? What's the point in dying? None at all. Let's have lots of fun, life is only just beginning. May you all enjoy yourselves. May you be proud of your little daughter. I shall become the greatest slut the world has ever seen. Address remains Fiala. You shall have your fifty thousand guilders, Papa. But with the next lot I earn I shall buy myself new nighties trimmed with lace, and lovely silk stockings you can see through. One only lives once. What's the point of being good-looking. Must have more light – I'll turn on the light above the mirror. How beautiful my reddish-blond hair and shoulders look; my eyes are not bad either. How large they are. Pity to throw myself away. No need to rush things with the Veronal. – But I must hurry downstairs. All the way down. Herr Dorsday is waiting, and he doesn't yet know that the amount has gone up to fifty thousand. Yes, I have gone up in price, Herr von Dorsday. I must show him the telegram, otherwise he won't believe me and will think I want to make a profit out of the whole business. I'll send the telegram over to his room with a note of explanation. To my deep regret, Herr von Dorsday, the figure has now become fifty thousand, though to you of course this will be a matter of indifference. Moreover, I'm convinced that your counter-proposal was not intended seriously. After all, you are a Vicomte and a gentleman. Tomorrow morning you must send the fifty thousand, on which my father's life depends, without delay to Dr Fiala. I am counting on you. – "But of course, Fräulein, I'll send a hundred thousand to make sure, without requiring any service in return; and furthermore from this day on I undertake to provide an allowance for your entire family, to pay your Papa's debts off on the stock exchange, and to make good all the securities that he embezzled." Address remains Fiala. Hahaha! Yes, that's exactly the kind of man the Vicomte d'Eperies is! The whole thing is nonsense. But what else can I do? It has to be, I shall have to do it, I shall have to do everything Herr von Dorsday demands, so that Papa will have the money by tomorrow – so that he won't be locked away, so that he won't commit suicide. And I intend to do it too. Yes, I'll do it, even though it will all be completely thrown away on him. In six months we'll be back to square one. In four weeks more likely! – But then it will no longer be any concern of mine. I shall make this one sacrifice – and then that's it. Never, ever again. Yes indeed, I shall make that clear to Papa as soon as I get back to Vienna. Then off out of the house, who cares where to. I shall ask for his advice. He is the only one who is really fond of me. But I'm forgetting that things have not yet reached that point. I'm not in Vienna, I'm still in Martino di Castrozza. Nothing has happened yet. So what am I to do? There's the telegram. What should I do about the telegram? But I have already decided. I must send it to him in his room. But what else? I must add a little note. Well then, what shall I say to him? Expect me at twelve o'clock. No, no, no! He mustn't have that satisfaction. I won't, I won't, I won't. Thank god I have those tablets. That's the only way out. Where are they though? For Heaven's sake, surely they haven't been stolen. Ah no, here they are. In their little box. Are they all still there? One, two, three, four, five, six. Yes, all of them are there. I'm just looking at them, dear little pills. That doesn't commit me to anything. Even shaking them into a glass doesn't commit me to anything. One, two – but I'm quite sure I would never kill myself. I wouldn't dream of it. Three, four, five – still not enough to kill me. It would be terrible if I didn't have the Veronal with me. Then I'd have to throw myself out of the window, and I'm sure I wouldn't have the courage to do that. Whereas with Veronal – you slowly fall asleep and don't wake up again, no worry, no pain. You get into bed; then in one gulp you drink it down, dream, and everything is over. I took one pill the day before yesterday, and then two more. Ssh! don't tell anybody. Today of course it will be a little more. But only just in case. In case I should simply be too utterly revolted. But why should I be revolted? If he touches me, I'll spit in his face. Quite simple.

But how am I to get the letter to him? I can't very well send Herr von Dorsday letters via the chambermaid. The best thing would be to go downstairs and talk to him and show him the telegram. I have to go downstairs anyway. I can't just stay here in my room. I simply couldn't stand it for three whole hours – until the moment arrives. I must go down too because of Auntie. Oh, what do I care about Auntie. What do I care about society? Behold, ladies and gentlemen, here is the glass of Veronal. Now I am taking it in my hand. And now I am raising it to my lips. Yes, any minute now I may be on the other side, where there are no Aunties and no Dorsday and no father who embezzles shares . . .

But I don't intend to kill myself. There's no need for that. Nor do I intend to go to Herr von Dorsday in his room. I'm not going to expose myself naked before an old roué for the sake of fifty thousand guilders, just to save a good-for-nothing criminal. No and no, on both counts. Whatever led Herr von Dorsday to imagine I would? Is he so special? If one person is to see me, then others may as well. Yes! – Splendid idea! – All of you shall see me. The whole world shall see me. And then for the Veronal. No, not the Veronal, – what would be the point!? then comes the villa with the marble steps and the handsome youths and the freedom of the whole wide world! Good evening, Fräulein Else, that's the way I like you. Haha. Downstairs they will all think I have gone mad. But I've never been more sane. For the first time in my life I am genuinely sane. All, all of you must see me! – Then there will be no turning back, no going home to Papa and Mama, to my uncles and aunts. Then I will no longer be the Fräulein Else they want to marry off to some Director Wilomitzer or other; this way I shall make fools of all of you – especially that scoundrel Dorsday – and I shall be reborn . . . otherwise all is lost – Address remains Fiala. Haha!

No more wasting time, mustn't get cold feet again. Off with my dress. Who is going to be first? What about you, Cousin Paul? Lucky for you the fellow with the Roman head is no longer here. Are you going to kiss these lovely breasts tonight? Ah, how beautiful I am. Bertha has a black silk blouse. Sophisticated. I shall look even more sophisticated. What a glorious life. Off with my stockings, otherwise it might look indecent. Naked, completely naked. How Cissy will envy me! Other women too. But they wouldn't dare. Even though they would all love to. Why not follow my example? I'm a virgin and yet I dare to do it. I shall die laughing over Dorsday. Feast your eyes,

Herr von Dorsday. Now quickly, to the post office. Fifty thousand guilders. Is it really that much?

How beautiful, how beautiful I am! Look at me, O Night! O Mountains, look at me! O Sky, behold how beautiful I am. But then of course you're blind. The crowd downstairs have eyes though. Should I let my hair down? No, then I'd look like a madwoman. You must not think of me as mad. You must only think of me as shameless. As a hussy. Where's the telegram? Oh my God, where have I put the telegram? Ah there it is, lying quietly beside the Veronal. "Urgently repeat – fifty thousand – otherwise all is lost. Address remains Fiala." Yes, that's the telegram. There it is, words on a piece of paper. Posted in Vienna at four thirty. No, I'm not dreaming, it's all quite true. And at home they're waiting for the fifty thousand guilders. And Herr von Dorsday too is waiting. Let him wait. There's plenty of time. Ah, how marvellous it is, walking stark naked up and down the room like this. Am I really as beautiful as in the mirror? Do come closer, beautiful Fräulein. I want to kiss your blood-red lips. I want to press your breasts against my own. What a pity the glass stands between us, the cold glass. How well we would get along. Don't you think so? We wouldn't need anybody else. Perhaps there are no other people. There are telegrams and hotels and mountains and railway stations and forests, but no other people. We only dream them. Only Dr Fiala exists with that address of his. That always remains constant. I'm not in the least bit mad. I'm just a little excited. That is perfectly understandable when one is about to be reborn. For the former Else has already died. Yes, certainly I'm dead. One doesn't need Veronal for that. Shouldn't I pour it away? The chambermaid might drink it inadvertently. I'll put a card beside it and write: poison; no, perhaps: medicine, – so that nothing will happen to the chambermaid. See how high-minded I am. There. Medicine, underlined twice with three exclamation marks. Now nothing can go wrong. And if I come up afterwards and don't feel like killing myself and just want to sleep, then I simply won't drink the whole glass, just a quarter perhaps, or even less. Quite simple. Everything is under control. The simplest thing would be for me to run straight downstairs – just as I am, along the hall and down the stairs. No, no, then I might be detained before I reached the bottom – and I must be absolutely certain that Herr von Dorsday will be there! Otherwise of course he won't send off the money, the dirty old man. – But I still haven't written to him yet. And yet that's the most important thing. Oh, how cold the back of the chair feels, but not unpleasantly. When I have my villa on the Italian coast, I shall always stroll naked in my

park . . . When I finally die, I shall bequeath my pen to Fred. But in
the meantime I have something more intelligent to do than dying.
"Most esteemed Vicomte" – now then, be sensible, Else, no flowery
preambles, neither most esteemed nor most despised. "Your condition, Herr von Dorsday, has been fulfilled" – "This very moment as
you read these lines, Herr von Dorsday, your condition has been fulfilled, albeit not quite in the manner you expected." – "Well I never,
how well the girl writes", Papa will say. – "And so I am counting on it
that you on your part will keep your word and telegraph the fifty
thousand guilders without delay to the agreed address, yours, Else."
No, not Else. No signature at all. There we are. My lovely yellow
writing-paper! Given to me for Christmas. What a waste. There –
now in go both the telegram and letter into the envelope. – "Herr
von Dorsday," room number sixty-five. Why put the number? I'll
simply place the letter outside his door as I go past. But I don't have
to. I don't have to do anything at all. If I so please, I can still just lie
down on the bed and go to sleep and not worry about anything. Neither about Herr von Dorsday nor about Papa. A striped convict suit
is not inelegant. Many people have shot themselves before. And all of
us must die.

But for the time being none of that applies to you, Papa. You have
your splendidly well developed daughter, and the address remains
Fiala. I shall take a collection. I'll go round with a plate. Why should
Herr von Dorsday be the only one to pay? That would be unjust.
Each according to his means. How much will Paul put into the plate?
And how about the man with the gold pince-nez? Only, don't imagine that your enjoyment is going to last for very long. I shall wrap
myself up again immediately, run up the stairs to my room, lock
myself in and, if I so please, swig the whole glass down in one gulp.
But I shall not so please. That would just be cowardice. It would be
simply cowardice. They don't deserve that much respect, the
scoundrels. Feel ashamed in front of you? Why should I feel ashamed
in front of anyone? I hardly think that's called for. Look into your eyes
once more, my lovely Else. What huge eyes you have when I
approach. I wish someone would kiss me on my eyes, on my blood-
red mouth. My coat scarcely reaches to my ankles. People will notice
that my feet are bare. Who cares, they are going to see a lot more
than that! But I'm not as yet committed. I can still turn back, even
before I get downstairs. I can turn back on the first floor. I don't have
to go downstairs at all. But I want to though. I'm looking forward to
it. Haven't I been longing for something like this all my life?

So what am I waiting for? I'm set to go. The performance can begin. Don't forget the letter. Aristocratic handwriting, Fred says. Good-bye, Else. You look lovely in that coat. Florentine ladies had themselves painted dressed like this. Their pictures hang in galleries and that does them honour. No one need notice anything, if I have my coat on. Except my feet, except my feet. I'll wear my black patent-leather shoes, then they'll think I'm wearing flesh-coloured stockings. I can walk across the hall downstairs like that, and no one will suspect that under my coat there's nothing except myself. And then I can always come back up again . . . – Who is that playing the piano so beautifully downstairs? Chopin? – Herr von Dorsday will be a little nervous. Perhaps he's afraid of Paul. Patience, patience, all in good time. I don't know what will happen either, Herr von Dorsday, I'm terribly on edge too. Must turn the light out. Is everything in order in my room? Farewell, Veronal, goodbye. Farewell, my passionately beloved mirror-image. How radiant you are in the dark. I've already got quite used to being naked underneath my coat. Very pleasant. Who knows whether others aren't sitting like this in the hall downstairs, without anybody knowing? Whether some fine lady doesn't go to the theatre and sit in her box like this – either as a joke or for other reasons.

Should I lock my door? What's the point? Nothing's ever stolen here. And if it were, I no longer need anything. So there's an end . . . Now where is number sixty-five? No one's in the corridor. Everybody's still downstairs at dinner. Sixty-one . . . sixty-two . . . what enormous climbing-boots outside that door. There's a pair of trousers hanging on a hook here. How indecent. Sixty-four, sixty-five. Here we are. So this is where he's staying, this Vicomte . . . I'll just prop the letter against the door like this. He should see it there at once. Surely no one will steal it? There, that's done . . . It doesn't matter . . . I can still do just what I want. I will simply have made a fool of him . . . As long as I don't now meet him on the stairs. Here he comes . . . no, it isn't him. This gentleman is much handsomer than Herr von Dorsday, very elegant with his little black moustache. When did he arrive? I could stage a brief rehearsal – and open my coat the slightest bit. I have a strong desire to do so. Take a good look at me, sir. Little do you realise whom you are passing. Pity you've come upstairs at just this moment. Why don't you stay downstairs in the foyer? You are going to miss something. A spectacular performance. Why don't you stop me? My fate lies in your hands. If you greet me, then I shall turn back. Well come on, greet me. I'm giving you such an inviting look . . . He isn't going to. He has walked straight past. He's turning round, I can feel it. Call out to me, greet me! Save me! You may be responsible for my death, good sir! Though you will never know it. Address remains Fiala . . .

Where am I? In the main hall already? How did I get here? So few people and so many of them strangers. Or is my sight that bad? Where is Dorsday? He isn't here. Is that a sign from fate? I shall go back. I shall write Dorsday another letter. I shall await you in my room at midnight. Bring along the order to your bank. No, he might consider it a trap. It might be one too. I might have concealed Paul in my room, and he might force him to make over the order to us at the point of a revolver. Extortion. A couple of criminals. Where is Dorsday? Dorsday, where are you? Could he have killed himself out of remorse over my death? He'll be in the games room. That must be it. He'll be sitting at a card-table. I'll signal to him from the doorway with my eyes. He will stand up at once. "Here I am, my little Fräulein." His voice will be insinuating. "Shall we go for a little stroll, Herr Dorsday?" – "As you like, dear Fräulein Else." We cross the Marienweg towards the forest. We are alone. I open my coat. The fifty thousand guilders are now due. The air is cold, I catch pneumonia and die . . . Why are those two ladies looking at me like that? Have they noticed anything? What am I doing here? Have I gone mad? I'll go back to my room, quickly put my blue dress on, and then the coat over it, exactly as it is now, but open, then no one will suspect that I had nothing on before . . . No, I can't go back. Nor do I want to. Where is Paul? Where is Aunt Emma? Where is Cissy? Where are they all: none of them will notice anything . . . Nothing shows at all. Who is playing so beautifully? Chopin? No, Schumann.

I'm flitting about the foyer like a bat. Fifty thousand guilders! Time is running out. I must find this accursed Herr von Dorsday. No, I must go back up to my room. I shall drink some Veronal. Just a little sip, then I shall sleep well . . . It's good to rest after a task well done . . . But the task is not yet done. If the waiter serves the black coffee to that old gentleman over there, everything will be all right. If he takes it to the young married couple in the corner, all is lost. How is that? What is that supposed to mean? He is taking it to the old gentleman. Triumph! Everything is going to be all right. Ah, Cissy and Paul! They are strolling up and down outside in front of the hotel. They are talking quite cheerfully to one another. He is not especially concerned about my headache. What a fraud! . . . Cissy's breasts are not as nice as mine. Admittedly of course she has a child . . . What are they both saying? If only one could hear. What do I care what they are saying? But I could go outside too, wish them good evening and then on across the meadows to the forest, climb higher and higher to the very top of the Cimone, lie down, fall asleep and freeze to death. Mysterious suicide of young lady from Vienna high society. Dressed only in an evening coat, the beautiful girl was found in an inaccessible spot on Mount Cimone della Pala . . . But perhaps they won't find me . . . Or not until next year. Or even later. Decomposed. A mere skeleton. Better after all to be here inside the heated hall than out there freezing. Now then, Herr von Dorsday, where can you have got to? Am I obliged to wait for you? It's up to you to look for me, not me for you. I'll just have another look in the games room. If he's not there, he will have forfeited his rights. And I shall write and say to him: you were nowhere to be found, Herr von Dorsday, you have voluntarily abstained; but that does not release you from your obligation to send the money off at once. The money. What money? What do I care? I don't give two hoots whether he sends the money off or not. I no longer feel the slightest compassion for Papa. I don't feel compassion for any one at all. Not even for myself. My heart is dead. I don't think it's even beating any longer. Perhaps I've drunk the Veronal already . . . Why is the Dutch family staring at me like that? It's impossible for anyone to tell. The porter is looking at me suspiciously too. Has another telegram arrived perhaps? Eighty thousand? A hundred thousand? Address remains Fiala. If a telegram had come, he would surely tell me so. He is looking at me very respectfully. He doesn't know that under my coat I have nothing on. No one knows. I'm going back up to my room. Back, back, back! There would be a fine to-do if I were to stumble on the stairs. On the Wörthersee three years ago a lady swam out completely naked. But she left that same afternoon. Mama said she was an operetta singer from Berlin. Schumann? Yes, it's *Carnaval.* She or he plays quite well. But the games room is to the right. Your last chance, Herr von Dorsday. If he's there, I'll signal him over with my eyes and say, I'll be in your room at midnight, you scoundrel. – No, I won't call him a scoundrel. But afterwards I'll tell him so . . . Someone's following me. I won't turn round. No, no. –

'*Else!*' – Good heavens, it's my aunt. Keep going, keep going! '*Else!*' – I'll have to turn round, it can't be helped. 'Oh, good evening, Auntie.' – '*But Else, whatever is the matter with you? I was on the point of coming up to see you. Paul told me – What a sight you look!*' – 'Well, how do I look then, Auntie? I feel much better already. I've even had a bite to eat.' She's noticed something, she's noticed something. – '*Else – you haven't – any stockings on!*' – 'What was that you said, Auntie? Goodness me, I haven't any stockings on. Oh no – !' – '*Are you sure you are all right, Else? Your eyes – you've got a fever.*' – 'A fever? I don't think so. I just had this terrible headache, worse than I've ever had before.' – *'You must go to bed at once, child, you are as pale as death.'* – 'That's the effect of the lighting, Auntie. Everybody looks pale here in the main hall. She's looking at me so strangely. Surely she can't have noticed anything? So long as I can keep my head. Papa is lost if I don't keep my head. I must say something. 'Do you know what happened to me in Vienna earlier this year, Auntie? I walked down the street wearing one yellow shoe and one black one.' Not a word of it is true. I must keep talking. But what on earth shall I say? 'You know, Auntie, after my migraine attacks I do sometimes have these fits of absent-mindedness. Mama used to be the same.' Not a word is true. – *'All the same, I'm going to send for the doctor.'* – 'But Auntie, I beg you, there isn't one in the hotel. They would have to fetch one from some other resort. He would be sure to have a good laugh at us for summoning him because I'm not wearing any stockings. Haha.' I mustn't laugh so loud. My aunt's face is distorted with anxiety. She finds it all a little eerie. Her eyes are starting out of her head. – *'By the way, Else, you don't happen to have seen Paul?'* – Ah, she wants to summon some assistance. Keep your head, everything's at stake. If I am not mistaken, he is strolling up and down with Cissy Mohr in front of the hotel'. – *'In front of the hotel? I'll go and fetch them in. Then we'll all take tea together, shall we?'* – 'With pleasure.' What a stupid face she's making. I'll just give an innocent and friendly nod. There, she's gone. Now I'll go up to my room. No, what should I do back in my room? The time has come, the time has come. Fifty thousand, fifty thousand. Why am I running like this? Slow down, slow down . . . What am I doing? What's the man's name? Herr von Dorsday. Curious name . . . Ah, there's the games room. Green curtain across the door. Can't see anything. I'll stand on tiptoes. A whist party. They play every evening. Over there two men are playing chess. Herr von Dorsday isn't there. Victory! I'm saved! How so? I've got to keep on looking. I'm condemned to look for Herr von Dorsday until my dying day. He is sure to be looking for me too. We shall keep on missing one another for ever and ever. Perhaps he's looking for me upstairs. We will meet each other on the stairs. The two Dutch ladies are looking at me again. The daughter is quite pretty. The old gentleman is wearing glasses, wearing glasses, wearing glasses . . . Fifty thousand. It isn't really all that much, Herr von Dorsday, fifty thousand. Schumann? Yes, *Carnaval* . . . I once studied that piece too. She's playing beautifully. Why she? Perhaps it's a he? Perhaps it's a female virtuoso? I'll just have a quick look in the music room.

Here's the door. – Dorsday! I think I'm going to faint. Dorsday! There he is standing by the window listening. How can this be possible? I'm distraught – I'm going mad – I'm at death's door – and here he is listening to a lady, a perfect stranger, playing the piano. Two gentlemen are sitting over there on the divan. The blond one arrived only today. I saw him getting out of the carriage. The lady is certainly no longer young. She's been here a few days already. I didn't know she played the piano quite so well. She is fortunate. Everyone is fortunate . . . only I am damned . . . Dorsday! Dorsday! Is that really him? He hasn't seen me! At this moment he looks like any ordinary respectable gentleman. He's listening to the music. Fifty thousand

guilders! Now or never. I'll open the door softly. Here I am, Herr von Dorsday! He hasn't seen me yet. I'll just signal to him with my eyes, and then open my coat a little, that will be quite enough. After all, I'm only a young girl. I'm a respectable young girl from a good family. I'm not a whore . . . I must get out. I shall take my Veronal and sleep. You are mistaken, Herr von Dorsday, I am not a whore. Adieu, adieu! . . . Wait, he's looking up. Here I am, Herr von Dorsday. The way he's eying me! His lips are trembling. He's staring at me with that penetrating gaze. But he doesn't suspect I'm naked underneath my coat. Let me go, let me go! His eyes are glowing. His eyes are threatening. What do you want from me? You are a scoundrel. No one else is looking at me. They are all listening to the music. Come on then, Herr von Dorsday! Don't you notice anything? Who's that in the armchair over there – good God, it's the Roman-headed rogue

– sitting in the armchair! Heaven be praised. He has come back, he has come back! He was only away on a walking-tour! And now he has come back. My Roman-head is here again. My bridegroom, my beloved. But he hasn't seen me. Nor should he see me. What is it you want, Herr von Dorsday? You are gazing at me as though I were your slave. I am not your slave. Fifty thousand guilders! Does our bargain still hold, Herr von Dorsday? I am ready. Here I am. I am completely calm. I am smiling. Can you read my face? His eyes are speaking to me: Come! His eyes say: I want to see you naked! Well then, you scoundrel, here I am, naked. What more do you want? Send the telegram . . . Immediately . . . My skin is tingling all over. The lady is continuing to play. My skin is tingling deliciously. How wonderful being naked is. The lady is continuing to play, she doesn't

know what's happening here. No one knows. Still nobody has noticed me. Dear rogue, dear rogue! I'm standing here stark naked. Dorsday's eyes are open wide. At last he actually believes it. The young rogue is getting to his feet. His eyes are sparkling. We understand each other, handsome stripling. 'Haha!' The lady has stopped playing. Papa is saved. Fifty thousand guilders! Address remains Fiala! 'Ha, ha, ha!' Who's that laughing? Is it me? 'Ha, ha, ha!' What are all these faces round me staring at? 'Ha, ha, ha!' How stupid of me to be laughing like this. I've no desire to laugh, indeed not. 'Ha, ha!' – *'Else!'* – Who's calling Else? It's Paul. He must be behind me. I

can feel a draught all down my bare back. There's a ringing in my
ears. Am I perhaps already dead? What do you want, Herr von
Dorsday? Why are you so large and why are you hurling yourself on
me? 'Ha, ha, ha!'

What have I done? What have I done? What have I done? I'm
going to faint. It's all over. Why has the music stopped? Someone has
placed an arm around my neck. It's Paul. What has happened to the
young rogue? I'm lying on my back. 'Ha, ha, ha!' My coat has been
flung down over me. And I'm just lying here. Everyone thinks that
I'm unconscious. No, I'm not unconscious. I'm in full possession of
my senses. I'm a hundred times awake, I'm a thousand times awake.
I just can't help laughing. 'Ha, ha, ha!' Now you have had your way,
Herr von Dorsday, you must send the money for Papa. Immediately.
Haaaah! I don't want to scream, and yet I can't help screaming. Why
do I have to scream. My eyes are closed. No one can see me. Papa is
saved. – *'Else!'* – That's my aunt. *'Else! Else!'* – *'A doctor, a doctor!'* –
'Hurry, tell the porter!' – *'What's happened?'* – *'This is incredible.'* – *'The poor
child.'* – What is it they're murmuring? I'm not a poor child at all. I'm
happy. The rogue saw me stark naked. Oh, I'm so ashamed. What
have I done? I will never open my eyes again. – *'Close the door, please.'* –
Why do they want to close the door? What are they all murmuring
about? A thousand people have gathered round me. They all think
I'm unconscious. I'm not unconscious. I'm only dreaming. – *'Calm
down, madam.'* – *'Have they sent for the doctor?'* – *'It's a fainting fit.'* – How
far away they all are. They are talking from the top of the Cimone.
'She can't just be left here lying on the floor.' – *'Here's a tartan rug.'* – *'It's a blanket.'* – *'Rug or blanket, what's the difference!'* – *'Please be quiet everyone.'* – *'Onto
the divan.'* – *'Could somebody please shut the door.'* – *'Don't be so impatient,
it's already shut.'* – *'Else!* – If only Auntie would be quiet! – *'Can you hear
me, Else?'* – *'But Mama, you can see she's unconscious.'* – Yes, thank God, to
you I am unconscious. And unconscious I shall remain. – *'We must
take her to her room.'* – *'What has happened? Heavens above!'* – Cissy. How
come Cissy is out here on the meadow? Ah, but of course, it is not the
meadow. – *'Else!'* – *'Quiet, please.'* – *'Everyone stand back a little.'* Hands.
Hands underneath me. What is it they want? How heavy I am. Paul's
hands. Get away. The rogue is close to me, I can sense it. And Dorsday has disappeared. Somebody must go and look for him. He must
not be allowed to kill himself before he has sent off the fifty thousand
guilders. Ladies and gentlemen, he owes me money. Arrest him.
'Have you any idea who the telegram was from, Paul?' – *'Good evening, ladies
and gentlemen.'* – *'Else, can you hear me?'* – *'Best leave her alone, Cissy.'* – *'Ah,
Paul.'* – *'The Manager says it could be four hours before the doctor gets here.'* –

'She looks just as though she were asleep.' I'm lying on the divan, Paul is holding my hand and feeling my pulse. Of course, he is a doctor. – *'There is absolutely no danger, Mama. She has merely fainted.'* – *'I won't stay a day longer in this hotel.'* – *'Mama, I beg you.'* – *'We are leaving first thing tomorrow morning.'* – *Just carry her up the back stairs. The stretcher will be here shortly.'* Stretcher? Wasn't the bier a sort of stretcher earlier today? Haven't I already died? Do I have to die again? – *'Sir, as Manager, perhaps you would see to it that the doorway is cleared of people.'* – *'Don't get all worked up, Mama.'* – *'People are so inconsiderate.'* – Why is everybody whispering? Just like round a death-bed. The bier will be here shortly. Open the door, Herr Matador! – *'The hall is clear.'* – *'People might at least show some consideration.'* – *'Please, Mama, do calm yourself.'* – *'Madam, I beg you.'* – *'Would you mind seeing to my mother for a while, Frau Cissy?'* She is his mistress, but she is not as beautiful as I am. What's the matter now? What's happening? They are bringing in the stretcher. I can see it with my eyes closed. It's the stretcher they use to carry accident victims on. Dr Zigmondi who fell on the Cimone was laid out on it as well. And now I shall be lying on it too. I've fallen too. 'Ha!' No, I'm not going to scream again. They're whispering. Who is that bending over my head? Pleasant smell of cigarettes. His hand is underneath my head. Hands underneath my back, hands underneath my legs. Get away, don't touch me. Can't you see I'm naked. Disgusting, disgusting. What do you all want? Leave me in peace. It was only for Papa. – *'Careful, easy does it.'* – *'What about the rug?'* – *'Yes, thank you, Frau Cissy.'* – Why is he thanking her? What is it she's done? What are they doing with me? Ah, how nice, how nice. I'm floating, I'm floating. I'm floating along. They're carrying me, they're carrying me, they're carrying me to my grave. – *'But I'm used to it, Doctor. We've had heavier people on the stretcher before. Once last autumn two together.'* – *'Shush, shush.'* – *'Perhaps you would be good enough to go ahead, Frau Cissy, and see that everything is ready up in Else's room.'* – What business has Cissy in my room? The Veronal, the Veronal! So long as she doesn't pour it away. Then I would have to throw myself out of the window. *'Thank you very much, Sir, for managing everything so smoothly.'* – *'I shall take the liberty of enquiring again later.'* – The stairs are creaking, the bearers must be wearing heavy climbing-boots. Where are my patent leather shoes? Left behind in the music room. They will be stolen. I wanted to bequeath them to Agatha. Fred will get my fountain-pen. They are carrying me. A funeral procession. Where is Dorsday, the murderer? He's left. The rogue has also left. He immediately set out on his walking-tour again. He only came back for one look at my white breasts. And now he's gone again. He's following a dizzy path with a cliff on

one side and a sheer drop on the other; – farewell, farewell. – I'm
floating, I'm floating. Let them bear me on and on, up to the roof, up
to the sky. How peaceful that would be. – *'I could see it coming, Paul.'* –
What did Auntie think she could see coming? – *'For the past few days I
could see something like this coming on. She simply isn't normal. Of course she
will have to be placed in an institution.'* – *'But Mama, this really isn't the time to
talk about it.'* – Institution –? Institution–?! – *'Don't imagine, Paul, that I'm
going to travel back to Vienna in the same compartment as this person. Who knows
what scenes we might be letting ourselves in for.'* – *'Nothing of the sort will happen, Mama, I guarantee that you won't be in any way embarrassed.'* – *'How can
you guarantee any such thing?'* – No, Auntie, you won't be embarrassed.
No one will be embarrassed. Not even Herr von Dorsday. Where are
we? We've come to a halt. We must be on the second floor. I'm going
to blink. Cissy is standing by the door and talking to Paul. – *'Over here,
please. Good, that's right, here. Thank you. Bring the stretcher close up to the bed.'*
– They are raising the stretcher. They're lifting me off. How nice.
Now I'm at home again. Ah! – *'Thank you. That will do nicely. Please close
the door. – If you would be so good as to give me a hand, Cissy.'* – *'Oh, with pleasure, Doctor.'* – *'Slowly does it. Take hold of her like this, please, Cissy. Here, by
her legs. And then – Else? – Can you hear me, Else?'* – Of course I can hear
you, Paul. I can hear everything. But what's that got to do with any of
you. It's so marvellous lying here unconscious. Very well, do as you
please. – *'Paul!'* – *'Yes, Madam?'* – *'Do you think she's really unconscious,
Paul?'* – What? She used the intimate form of address to him! I've
caught you out, both of you! She said *Du* to him! – *'Yes, she's completely
unconscious. That's usually the case with fits like this.'* – *'Don't, Paul! You're
such a scream when you adopt your grown-up doctor's manner.'* – There, I've
caught you out, you deceitful couple, can you now deny it? – *'Be quiet,
Cissy.'* – *'Whatever for, if she can't hear?!'* What's happened? I'm lying in
bed naked underneath the blanket. How have they managed that? –
'Well, how is she? Better?' – That's Auntie. What does she want now? –
'Still unconscious?' – She is approaching me on tip-toes. Devil take her,
I shall not let myself be put in any institution. I'm not mad! – *'Can't
she be brought back to consciousness?'* – *'She will soon come round, Mama. At the
moment all she needs is rest. Moreover, you do too, Mama. Won't you go to bed?
There is absolutely no danger. Frau Cissy and I will watch over Else during the
night.'* – *'Yes, indeed, Madam, I shall be the night-watchwoman. Or Else will,
depending which way you take it.'* – Miserable hussy. Here I am unconscious and she's cracking jokes. – *'And I can depend upon it, can I Paul, that
you will have me woken the moment the doctor arrives?'* – *'But Mama, he won't
be here before tomorrow morning.'* – *'She looks as though she were asleep. Her
breathing is completely regular.'* – *'Well, it is a kind of sleep, Mama.'* – *'I'm still*

beside myself, Paul, such a scandal! You'll see, it will get into the papers!' –
'Mama!' – *'But she can't hear anything if she's unconscious. And we're talking
very softly.'* – *'In this condition the senses are sometimes uncannily acute.'* – *'You
have such a learned son, Madam.'* – *'Please, Mama, do go to bed.'* – *'Tomorrow,
though, we're leaving, come what may. And in Bozen we'll engage an orderly to
take charge of Else.'* – 'What? An orderly! You had better think again. –
'We'll talk about all that tomorrow, Mama. Good night, Mama.' – *'I'll have a
cup of tea brought up to my room, and I'll look in again in quarter of an hour.'* –
'That really isn't necessary, Mama.' – No, of course it isn't necessary. You
can go to the Devil, as far as I'm concerned. Where's the Veronal? I
must wait a little longer. They are accompanying Auntie to the door.
Now nobody can see me. The glass of Veronal must still be on the
dressing-table. If I drink it all, then everything will be over. I'll drink
it at once. Auntie has gone. Paul and Cissy are still standing at the
door. Ha. She's kissing him. She's kissing him. And here I am naked
underneath the blanket. Aren't you the least bit ashamed of yourselves? She's kissing him again. Aren't you ashamed of yourselves? –
*'You see, Paul, now I know she's unconscious. Otherwise she would undoubtedly
have seized me by the throat.'* – *'Would you very kindly be quiet, Cissy?'* – *'But
what's the matter with you, Paul? Either she really is unconscious: in that case she
cannot see or hear a thing. Or else she is making fools of us: in that case it jolly well
serves her right.'* – *'Cissy, that was someone knocking.'* – *'I thought so too.'* – *'I'll
open quietly and see who it is. – Good evening, Herr von Dorsday.'* – *'Excuse me,
but I just wanted to enquire after the patient.'* – Dorsday! Dorsday! How
dare he? The beasts of hell have broken loose. I can't quite see him.
But I can hear them whispering at the door. Paul and Dorsday. Cissy
is posing in front of the mirror. What do you think you are doing
there in front of the mirror? It's my mirror. Doesn't it still contain my
image? What are Paul and Dorsday talking about outside the door?
I can feel Cissy's gaze. She's looking at me out of the mirror. What is
she after? Why is she coming up to me? Help! Help! I'm screaming
out, yet nobody can hear me. What are you doing beside my bed,
Cissy? Why are you bending over me? Are you going to strangle me?
I can't move. – *'Else!'* – What's she up to? – *'Else, Can you hear me, Else?'*
Of course I can but I'll keep quiet. I'm unconscious, so I must keep
quiet. – *'Else, you gave us quite a nasty fright.'* – She's talking to me. Talking to me as if I were awake. What's she up to? – *'Do you know, Else,
what you did? Just imagine, you came into the music room dressed only in your
coat, and suddenly were standing there stark naked in front of everybody, and then
you fell down in a faint. A case of hysterics, they're claiming. I don't believe a word
of it. I also don't believe you're unconscious. I bet you can hear every word I'm saying.'* – Yes, I can hear, yes, yes, yes. But she can't hear me saying yes.

How is that? I can't move my lips. That's why she can't hear me. I can't move at all. What's the matter with me? Am I dead? Am I in a state of suspended animation? Am I simply dreaming? Where's the Veronal? I want to drink my Veronal. But I can't stretch out my arm. Go away, Cissy. Why are you bending over me? Go, go! She will never know I heard her. No one will ever know. I shall never speak to anyone again. I shall never wake again. She's going over to the door. She's turning round towards me one last time. She is opening the door. Dorsday! He's standing there. I can see him even with my eyes closed. No, I can really see him. My eyes are open after all. The door is ajar. Cissy is outside too. Now they're all whispering. I am all alone. If only I could move.

Ah, but I can, I can. I can raise my hand, I can move my fingers, I can stretch my arm, I can open my eyes wide. I can see, I can see. There's my glass. Quick, before they come back inside the room. Were there enough tablets, I wonder?! I must never wake up again. I have done what I had to do on earth. Papa is saved. I could never show my face in company again. Paul is peeping round the door. He thinks I'm still unconscious. He can't see that my arm is almost stretched out. Now they are all outside the door again, the murderers! – They're all murderous. Dorsday and Cissy and Paul, and Fred is a murderer too and Mama is a murderess as well. All of them have murdered me and are pretending they know nothing. She killed herself, is what they'll say. It's you who've killed me, all of you, all of you! I can almost reach it now. Quick, quick! I have to do it. Mustn't spill a drop. There. Hurry now. It tastes quite nice. Drink up, drink up. It isn't really poison after all. I've never tasted anything so good. If you only knew how good death tastes! Good night, my glass. Clink, clink! What's that? The glass is lying on the floor. It's down there somewhere. Good night. – '*Else! Else!*' – What do you want? – '*Else!*' – Have you all come back again? Good morning. I'm lying here unconscious with my eyes closed. You shall never see my eyes again. – '*She must have moved, Paul, how else could it have fallen?*' – '*A reflex movement, that's quite possible.*' – '*Supposing she's awake.*' – '*You're imagining things, Cissy. Just look at her.*' – I've taken Veronal. I'm going to die. And yet I feel just the same as I did before. Perhaps there wasn't enough . . . Paul has taken my hand. – '*Her pulse is regular. Cissy, don't laugh at the poor child.*' – '*Would you call me a poor child if I had exposed myself stark naked in the music room?*' – '*Do stop it, Cissy.*' – '*As you wish, Sir. Perhaps I should withdraw and leave you and our naked Fräulein alone together. Please don't feel embarrassed. Carry on as if I were not here.*' – I've drunk the Veronal. It was so nice. I'm going to die. Thank God for that. – '*Besides, do you know what I think? That this*'

Herr von Dorsday is in love with our naked Fräulein. He was very agitated, as if the matter were of personal concern to him.' – Dorsday, Dorsday! That's of course the – fifty thousand! Will he send it off? Heavens above, supposing he doesn't send it off? I must tell them. They must force him to. For heaven's sake, what if everything has been in vain? But they can still rescue me. Paul! Cissy! Why can't you hear me? Don't you know I'm dying? And yet I can't feel anything. Just that I'm so tired. Paul! I'm so tired. Can't you hear me? I'm so tired, Paul. I can't open my lips, I can't move my tongue, but I'm not dead yet. That's the Veronal. Where are you all? I shall soon fall fast asleep. Then it will be too late! I can't hear them talking. They're talking but I can't make out what they're saying. Their voices seem to boom. Do help me, Paul! My tongue feels so very heavy. – *'I think she'll soon be waking, Cissy. It's as though she's already trying to open her eyes. Cissy, what are you doing?'* – *'Embracing you, that's all. Why shouldn't I? She was not embarrassed either!'* – No, I was not embarrassed. I stood in front of everybody naked. If I could only speak you would all understand why. Paul! Paul! I want you both to listen. I have taken Veronal, Paul, ten, maybe a hundred tablets. I did not want to do it. I was mad. I don't want to die. You have to save me, Paul. You're a doctor. Save me! – *'She now seems to have quietened down again. Let's see – her pulse seems to be quite regular.'* – Save me Paul, I beseech you. Don't let me die. You still have time. But soon I'll fall asleep and then you won't realise. I don't want to die. So save me, please. It was only for Papa. Dorsday demanded it. Paul! Paul! – *'Take a look here, Cissy, don't you get the impression that she's smiling?'* – *'How could she help smiling, Paul, when you continue to hold her hand so tenderly?'* – Cissy, Cissy, what have I ever done to you for you to behave so wickedly towards me. Keep your Paul, but don't let me die. I'm still so young. Mama will be distraught. I want to climb many more mountains. I want to go dancing again. I want to get married one day. I want to travel more. Tomorrow we'll make up a party to climb the Cimone. Tomorrow is going to be a glorious day. The young rogue must join us. I cordially invite him. Run after him, Paul, he's following such a dizzy path. He's going to meet Papa. Address remains Fiala, don't forget. It's only a matter of fifty thousand guilders, then everything will be fine. There they all go, marching in their convict uniforms and singing. Open the door, Herr Matador! But that's all just a dream. And there goes Fred and the Fräulein with the husky voice, and the piano is outside in the open air. The piano tuner lives in the Bartensteinstrasse, Mama! Why didn't you write to him, child? You're so forgetful. You should practise your scales more often, Else. At thirteen a little girl should be more diligent. – Rudi went to a masked ball and didn't come home till eight o'clock in the morning. What have you brought for me, Papa? Thirty thousand dolls. I'll need a special house for them. Though they can go for walks out in the garden. Or to the masked ball with Rudi. Good day to you, Else. Ah, Bertha, so you're back again from Naples? Yes, from Sicily. Allow me to introduce my husband, Else. Enchantée, Monsieur. – *'Else, can you hear me, Else? It's me, Paul.'* – Haha, Paul. What are you doing sitting on that giraffe on the merry-go-round? – *'Else, Else!'* – Well, don't ride away. You can't possibly hear me if you ride off down the Hauptallee so fast. You are supposed to save me. I have taken Veronal. I can feel it creeping up my legs like ants, both the right one and the left. Yes, make sure you catch that Herr von Dorsday. There he goes. Can't you see him? He's jumping across the pond. He has murdered Papa, hasn't he? So then run after him. I'll run with you. They have fastened the stretcher onto my back, but I'll run with you. My breasts are shivering so. But I'll run with you. Where are you, Paul? Fred, where are you? Mama, where are you? Why are you all leaving me to run on through the desert by myself? I'm so afraid, alone like this. I'd rather fly. I knew that I could fly.

'Else!' . . .

'Else!' . . .

Where are you all? I can hear you but I can't see you.

'Else!' . . .

'Else!' . . .

'Else!' . . .

What can this be? An entire choir. And an organ too? I'm singing with them. What kind of a song is it? Everyone is joining in. And the forests, and the mountains and the stars. I've never heard anything so beautiful. I've never seen such a bright night. Give me your hand, Papa. We're flying together. The world is so beautiful when you can fly. Don't kiss my hand Papa, I am your child.

'Else! Else!'

They're calling from so far away! What is it you want? Don't wake me. I'm having such a pleasant sleep. Tomorrow morning. I'm dreaming and flying. I'm flying . . . flying . . . flying . . . sleeping and dreaming . . . and flying . . . don't wake me . . . tomorrow morning . . .

'El . . .'

I'm flying . . . dreaming . . . I'm sleeping . . . I'm drea . . . drea . . . I'm fly . . .

The Duellist's Second

I was twenty-three years old at the time, and it was my seventh duel – not strictly mine, you understand, but the seventh I took part in as a second. Smile if you like. I know that it has become the fashion nowadays to make fun of such proceedings. Mistakenly in my opinion, and I can assure you that in those days life was better, or at least had a nobler air – among other things, no doubt, because one sometimes had to wager it for something which in a higher, or at least different sense, perhaps did not exist, or at any rate when measured by today's standards was not really worth the candle, like honour for example, or the virtue of a woman one loves, or the reputation of a sister and other such trifling matters. Nevertheless it is worth remembering that in earlier decades one was often obliged to sacrifice one's life quite pointlessly at the command or wish of other people over far slighter things. It is true that in duelling personal inclination always had some say, even in cases where compulsion or convention or snobbery was apparently entailed. But the fact that one had to reckon with the possibility or even the inevitability of a duel, at least in certain circles – that alone, believe me, gave social life a certain dignity, or at all events a certain style. And it gave the people in these circles, even the most ridiculous or ineffectual among them, a certain bearing, the appearance even of an ever-present readiness to die – even though such words might well seem inflated to you in such a context.

But I am digressing before I have begun. I was going to tell you the story of my seventh duel, and I see you smile once more because I again refer to it as my duel, even though, as on previous occasions, in this case too I was only the witness, not the duellist. I was only eighteen and a cavalry volunteer at the time of my inaugural engagement as a second in an affair of honour between a comrade and an attaché at the French Legation. Not long after that, the well-known amateur equestrian Vulkovicz chose me as his second in a duel with Prince Luginsfeld, and from then on, although I was neither a nobleman nor a career officer, and even of Jewish origin, whenever a second was needed, especially in more difficult cases, people turned with particular partiality to me. I will not deny that at times I rather regretted participating in these affairs only, as one might say, peripherally. I should have been only too glad to confront a dangerous opponent, and am not even sure which at bottom I should have preferred – to triumph or to perish. But it never came to that, although there was frankly no shortage of opportunities, and as you can imagine no one ever doubted my readiness to fight. Perhaps, moreover, that was part of the reason why I was never challenged, and why in the cases where I felt myself obliged to demand satisfaction, matters were always settled in a gentlemanly manner. At all events, I was heart and soul a second. To me the consciousness of being at the centre, or rather the periphery of another person's destiny, has always had something moving, exhilarating and glorious about it.

This seventh duel which I want to tell you about today, however, differed from all my earlier and subsequent adventures in that I moved from the periphery to the centre, as it were, in that I turned from an incidental character into a leading player, and in that until today not a soul has heard anything about this strange affair. I would not even have told you, with your perpetual smile – but since in reality you don't exist, I will pay you the compliment, young man, of talking to you as someone who at least has enough tact to remain silent.

It really makes very little difference where and how I start. So I shall tell the story as it occurs to me, and begin at the point that first comes to mind, the moment when I boarded the train in the company of Dr Mülling. You see, in order not to arouse the least suspicion, particularly in Eduard's young wife, we had already left the residential district by the lake on Monday morning, carrying precautions so far as to purchase tickets all the way to Vienna at the booking office, although of course we got out at the station of the little town where the duel was to take place the following morning.

Dr Mülling was a long-standing friend of Loiberger's, about thirty-five and so roughly the same age as him. As for me, apart from my general suitability alluded to already, I owed the honour of being selected as the second witness to the fact that I was spending my vacation in the same summer resort as Loiberger, and was quite frequently a guest at his villa. I never particularly liked him, but the house was very sociable, many agreeable people came and went, there was plenty of music and tennis, outings and rowing trips were organised, and after all, I was only twenty-three. The reason for the duel I was given was that words had been exchanged between Eduard Loiberger and his opponent Urpadinsky, a captain in the Uhlan regiment whom I hardly knew. On Sunday he had come on a

visit to the lake on leave from his garrison, evidently for the sole purpose of this verbal altercation which was to serve as a pretext for the
duel, but the year before he had spent the whole summer there with
his wife.

Both gentlemen were clearly in a hurry to settle the affair. The
preliminary discussion between the seconds had already taken place
in Bad Ischl on the Sunday evening, a few hours after the exchange
of words. Mülling and I were instructed by Loiberger to accept the
conditions of the opposing seconds without argument; they were
onerous.

And so on Monday Mülling and I arrived in the little town.

We first of all went over the ground that had been designated as
the venue for the rendez-vous the following day. During the short
drive that followed, Mülling talked about his travels, his university
studies long ago, student fencing-matches, professors, examinations,
villas he had designed, rowing championships and various chance
common acquaintances. I was about to take my final state examinations at the time. Mülling was already quite a well-known lawyer. As
if by agreement, we didn't say a word about what lay in store for us
the following day. No doubt Dr Mülling knew more about the reasons for the duel than he thought it prudent to confide in me.

In the evening Eduard Loiberger arrived. He had interrupted his
summer residence on the pretext of joining a prearranged climbing
tour in the Dolomites, and the marvellous August weather at the
time certainly made this sound a very plausible excuse. We too
greeted him innocently enough and conducted him to the celebrated
guesthouse on the market square, where we had reserved the best
room for him. We had our evening meal together in the dining-
room, chatted animatedly, drank, smoked and avoided making ourselves conspicuous, even to the two officers sitting at the table in the
corner opposite. Dr Mülling gave a factual report on the location
where the duel was to take place next day. It was the usual forest
clearing, of the kind that seems set aside by fate for these occasions –
and a small tavern lay close by, where, as Mülling cheerfully
observed, many a breakfast of reconciliation had already taken
place. This however was the only allusion to the reason for our presence; otherwise we talked about the sailing regatta arranged for that
coming Sunday, in which Loiberger too, the victor of the previous
year, was to take part – about a planned extension to his villa, for
which he, a manufacturer by profession but an amateur enthusiast in
all sorts of other fields, had drawn up the plans – about a cable railway up a nearby peak nearing completion, the layout of which

Loiberger found fault with – about a court action Dr Mülling was to conduct for him, in which considerable sums of money were apparently at stake – and about various other matters, until towards eleven Dr Mülling remarked with a thoughtful smile: 'Perhaps it's time to go to bed, it never hurts to have a good night's rest on such occasions, even for the seconds.' We took our leave of Loiberger who went off to bed, but the two of us strolled about the little town in the beautiful warm summer night for an hour or so longer. I can remember little about that nocturnal walk except the heavy black shadow cast by the houses in the main square upon the moonlit paving, and nothing about our conversation. What I do know is that we did not discuss the impending duel.

I can clearly recall the carriage ride on the following morning, however, indeed I can still hear the resounding clatter of the horses' hooves as they carried us along the dusty road towards the forest clearing. Loiberger talked with exaggerated earnestness about a species of Japanese shrub recently introduced to Central Europe, which he too intended to plant in his garden, and leaped out of the carriage with that elasticity which press notices at the time invariably mentioned as the special attribute of ruling princes. This crossed my mind and I smiled involuntarily. At that same moment Loiberger looked at me, and I felt a little ashamed.

The duel itself has lodged in my memory as almost like a puppet show: Eduard Loiberger lay there just like a marionette after his opponent's bullet struck him down, and the regimental doctor too who certified his death seemed puppet-like too, a gaunt elderly man with a Polish moustache. The sky above us was cloudless but of a curiously sombre blue. I looked at my watch – it was ten to eight. The written report and other customary formalities were soon completed. And indeed, I was glad that we should still be in time to catch the express train at nine o'clock, since to have been obliged to remain in that unhappy town even an hour longer would have been quite intolerable.

We walked up and down the platform unnoticed and in silence – two elegant tourists on a summer journey; then, as I drank a coffee, Mülling read out from his newspaper that the King of England and his Prime Minister were expected in Bad Ischl in the next few days on a visit to the Emperor. We launched into a political discussion – actually, it was more of a lecture by Dr Mülling, which I interrupted rather pointlessly with uninformed remarks. When the Vienna train pulled in, I breathed a sigh of relief, almost as if everything that had happened could be undone and Loiberger restored to life. We were alone in our compartment; after a long silence Dr Mülling remarked, as if by way of apology that he had not spoken earlier: 'One doesn't grasp it at once, however well prepared one may have been.' Then we both talked about all the other duels we had participated in as seconds, harmless ones and others less felicitous – neither of us had been involved in a fatal duel before. We talked about today's duel and its tragic outcome without sentimentality, indeed more from an aesthetic and sporting point of view. Loiberger, as was to have been expected, had conducted himself splendidly, while the captain had been less calm and much paler, indeed it had not escaped our notice that before the first exchange of fire his hand had been trembling. Both fired at once, and neither bullet found its mark; with the second exchange the captain's bullet had grazed Loiberger's temple and Loiberger had involuntarily put his hand up to the spot, and then smiled. With the third exchange, however, immediately after the command, he had sunk to the ground before he had fired himself.

And only now, as though he had been released from a pledge, did Dr Mülling observe: 'To tell the truth, I saw it coming; indeed I already expected it last year. Both of them, our friend Loiberger as much as Frau von Urpadinsky – you never met the captain's wife of course: a pity – could not have behaved more incautiously. The whole resort knew of the affair, only the captain himself had no idea, even though he frequently came down from his garrison on visits to St Gilgen. It was not until the following winter that he allegedly began receiving anonymous letters; whereupon he took the matter up, and eventually, under the relentless pressure of his questioning apparently, his wife seems to have confessed. After that the rest was a foregone conclusion.'

'Incomprehensible,' I said.

'In what way incomprehensible?' asked Mülling.

'When one has a wife like Loiberger's – I always thought it was the happiest of marriages.' In my mind's eye I saw Frau Agathe, looking like a young girl, like a bride: and indeed, when one saw the two of them, Eduard and Agathe, together, one would have taken them for a pair of lovers rather than a married couple – even after four or five years of marriage. On the excursion up the Eichberg fourteen days earlier, for instance, when we had halted in the sun at noon – there were seven or eight of us as I recall – to tell the truth I hate these mass excursions, and for my part had only joined them for the sake of Mademoiselle Coulin – I recalled how Agathe appeared to have fallen asleep, or perhaps had only closed her eyes because the sun was dazzling her, and how he had stroked her hair and brow, and they had smiled and whispered like a couple of young lovers.

'And do you think,' I said to Mülling, 'that Frau Agathe suspected anything?'

Mülling shrugged his shoulders. 'I don't think so. At all events, she had no idea about the impending duel, and to this hour she still doesn't know that her husband is dead.'

Only now did I realise with something like alarm that the train was bringing us nearer and nearer to the unhappy woman. 'Who is going to tell her?' I asked.

'There would seem no alternative but for the two of us . . .'

We can't possibly appear together, I thought, like two committee members delivering an invitation to a ball.

'We should have telegraphed from out there at once,' I said aloud.

'The telegram,' said Mülling, 'could only have been a kind of advance notice. We really can't get round reporting personally.'

'I will take it on,' I said.

There then followed a lengthy discussion which had still not finished when our train pulled in at Bad Ischl station. It was a glorious summer's day, and the platform was crowded with new arrivals, excursionists and people waiting – and as there were various acquaintances among them, it was not altogether easy making our way unimpeded from the station building out into the street; but at last we found ourselves seated in the coach, without having been accosted by anyone, and were driven away. The dust whirled up behind us, the sun blazed fiercely, and we were relieved when the resort lay well to the rear and we were on the open road and soon turning into the wood.

Even before we could see the first peasant houses of the village around the final bend in the road, Dr Mülling had agreed that I, as the one least involved, should bring Frau Agathe the mournful news.

The lake lay there glittering with a thousand tiny shards of sunlight. From the opposite bank which lay veiled in a haze of excessive brightness, the spruce little steamer drew closer like a toy, while youthful bathers swam delightedly towards the heaving wake it left behind. Soon we drew up before the inn, which on scarcely sufficient grounds was called the 'Grand Hotel'. I got out, and Dr Mülling ordered the coachman to drive him on to the villa where he had rented a room, shook my hand and intimated that he would call for me at four o'clock that afternoon.

I changed out of my travelling clothes, which didn't seem to me quite appropriate to my mission, into a dark grey suit and black striped tie. After all, I had to rely on my own intuition and good taste, since there was of course no universally accepted protocol for the kind of visit I was about to make. I set out with a heavy heart.

Off to one side behind the inn a short cut with intermittent views of the lake led past a number of smaller rustic houses to the white – and to my taste inordinately resplendent – villa Loiberger had built for himself, naturally according to his own specifications. I deliberately walked slowly, to avoid betraying myself at once by arriving out of breath; yet on the whole I felt fairly calm, or at least in control. I told myself that it was simply a matter of fulfilling a duty – and I wanted to carry it out with as much decorum as possible; I must let no more of my inner involvement be noticed than good form permitted.

The garden gate stood open, the artistically laid-out flower-beds were a blaze of colour, to left and right sunlight fell on the white benches, a red and white awning extended over the wide verandah with its bright red basket-chairs, above it the first floor windows stood wide open, and the sun caught the balcony in front of the little attic window at an angle. There was no-one in sight. All about everything was quiet, and only the crunch of the gravel underfoot seemed to me unusually loud. It was nearly lunch time, so perhaps they were already at table, or Agathe on her own at least, since Eduard was away on his tour of the Dolomites. Yes, this was my first thought, before I realised with a start that at that moment he was laid out in the mortuary of a little garrison town. And suddenly I felt that what I had to face in the next few minutes was so grotesque, so intolerable, so impossible to go through with, that I was seriously tempted to turn round before anyone saw me and simply run off to explain to Dr Mülling that I was incapable of conveying the gruesome news to Frau Agathe alone. Just then a servant stepped out from the darkness of the inner room onto the verandah and greeted me. Clearly he had become aware of my approach. He was a young fair-haired man in a blue-and-white striped linen jacket, and coming down a few steps towards me he said:

'No-one is at home, sir. The Master left yesterday and Mistress is still down by the lake.' As I made no sign of leaving, he added: 'But if Herr von Eissler wouldn't mind waiting, Mistress should be back at any moment.'

'I will wait.'

The servant seemed a little surprised, struck perhaps by the tenseness, the inexplicable earnestness of my expression, so that with a hastily assumed airiness I looked at my watch and remarked: 'I just have something to inform your mistress of,' and repeated: 'I will wait.'

The servant nodded, went on ahead, moved aside a chair which was blocking the middle door into the drawing-room, let me pass, motioned vaguely toward the various seating arrangements all about, disappeared into the adjacent room where I could see the table immaculately laid for two, closed the door and left me.

I stood there in the summery yet cool, shadowy room like a man under arrest and awaiting close interrogation. Dominating the room was the black ebony piano, which awakened memories of the last musical evening I had spent there recently. Agathe had accompanied her friend Aline in a Schubert song. I could see her slender fingers hovering over the keys, indeed I almost thought I could hear Aline's voice intoning: 'Then to Silvia . . . let us garlands bring.' Later, while the rest of the company had remained in the drawing-room, I had sat in the garden alone, made slightly drowsy, even happy, by the warm night air, the music and no doubt also by the champagne, which at parties in the Loiberger's residence was seldom absent. Perhaps I even fell asleep, and as in a dream Agathe walked past me with some gentleman or other. I was sitting in darkness, so that at first they did not notice me. But then suddenly Agathe became aware of me, and as she went past she raked her fingers through my hair, ruffling it playfully, and then was gone. I did not think any more about it. For she would sometimes behave in this way. Quite unconstrainedly, yet always with a marvellous grace – as for instance in the way she would seldom address her friends by name or title, but instead find some pet name for them which, far from always suiting their character or manner, often expressed the opposite, or then again sometimes nothing in particular. She referred to me, for instance, as 'the Child' – and admittedly this made some sense, since in those days at twenty-three I looked even younger than I was. I continued sitting quietly on my bench in the dark and waited for the two of them to come past again, which happened sooner than I had actually expected. And this time Agathe nodded to me, even though she was not in a position to re-cognise my features clearly. She often did this: nodding several times in quick succession by way of greeting. I had seen her greet people like this when leaning against the railing at the swimming-baths; also on walks when she encountered an acquaintance; but she would also nod like this to flowers she plucked, or salute a mountain lodge in the same way before going in; it seemed to be innate in her, and not merely a matter of habit, to greet everyone and everything as if to make their personal acquaintance, however fleeting the relationship.

Only now for the first time did I become clearly conscious of this idiosyncrasy of hers, as I awaited her arrival in the summery shade of the drawing-room, and my fingers played aimlessly with the fringe of the Indian shawl that served as a piano-cover.

Suddenly I heard women's voices and footsteps on the gravel drawing nearer, then a woman's laughter, then feet coming up the steps – and my heart stood still.

'Who's that?' cried Agathe, a little startled. But when she recognised me she at once added gaily: 'Ah, the Child', and held out her hand. I bowed more deeply than was normally my way, and kissed her hand. She turned at once to Aline, who was standing a little behind us, and said: 'Well, now you can both stay to lunch.' And addressing me again: 'You see, I am alone. Eduard has been away on a mountain tour since yesterday.' And with a not altogether cheerful laugh: 'If you can believe him!'

Meanwhile I had also kissed Aline's hand, and when I raised my head I caught her eye twinkling merrily at me with an unwelcome look of understanding. There the two of them stood in their summer dresses, the dark Aline in bright yellow, the fair Agathe in soft, pale blue, the two of them for all the contrast looking almost like two sisters. Both were wearing the broad-brimmed Florentine hats that were then in fashion, and Agathe took hers off and laid it on the piano.

'No, dearest,' said Aline, 'I'm afraid I can't stay. I'm expected at home for lunch.'

Agathe pressed her a little, but she did not sound very convincing. And while she spoke to her friend she glanced at me with a look so questioning, so full of promise, so enticing that I became almost giddy. And suddenly I realised that it was not the first look of this kind that she had given me. Aline took her leave. 'Good-bye, dear Lady,' I said and became aware that it was the first word I had uttered, so that it seemed to me unduly loud, as if shattering the silence in the room. Agathe accompanied her friend across the verandah and down the steps into the garden.

Why had I not spoken out while Aline was still there, I thought. Would it not have been a thousand times easier? The next minute Agathe was again before me. 'Dear Lady,' I began, 'I have some sad news for you.' – No, I failed to articulate the words. To anyone with a propensity for mind-reading they would have been easy to discern, yet not a sound had crossed my lips. Agathe stood before me, her light blue dress softly illuminating the deep shadows of the room, but she did not smile, indeed it seemed to me that I had never seen her face so serious. Now, since she was alone with me, I was well aware that anything suggesting triviality, flirtatiousness or purely social intercourse ought to be excluded.

'I'm so glad you are here,' she said.

I said nothing in reply, as no words would have been adequate. All sorts of dimly apprehended incidents over the last few days were suddenly beginning to make sense. I was again struck by the way she had clung to my arm on that excursion recently and run down the forest path with me; then again I remembered how that night in the garden she had ruffled my hair with her slender fingers; and that word of greeting struck a tender chord within me: 'Child.' I had not understood any of this, not dared to understand it. Remember how young I was! It was the first time that a beautiful woman, a woman I took to be a loving and beloved wife, seemed to be offering me her heart. How should I have anticipated this? And if she expressed her pleasure at my coming so openly, this could mean that she thought me sufficiently impetuous and sufficiently in love to make calculated use of her husband's absence in making this bold and unexpected visit.

'Luncheon is served, Madam.'

Agathe made a slight gesture in acknowledgement. I turned round. We went into the adjacent room. It was Agathe's boudoir, the window stood open, white lace curtains screened us from outside, and the breeze and indistinct colours from the garden shimmered through.

Agathe and I sat opposite each other. The servant, now in a shiny dark blue jacket with gold buttons, came in and out serving us. Everything was laid out with exquisite taste. A simple meal, and to drink, only champagne. Our table conversation was completely innocent, as it had to be, yet at the same time wholly unconstrained, not only on her part but on mine. But as we talked about the everyday concerns and little incidents of country life, about past and planned excursions, about the forthcoming regatta on Sunday, and Loiberger's intended participation and chances of success – even though I did not for one moment forget that Eduard was dead, and that I had come here solely to report this to his wife – I experienced my presence here, this sitting face to face with Agathe, the gentle fluttering of the curtains, and the servant's silent comings and goings not in the least as like a dream, but rather as another lesser order of reality. It was from this other reality that the shrill whistle of the steamer reached us, in this reality that I was conscious of the lake lying before us in the midday glare; it was in this other reality too that Aline had departed, and there too that the man was lying whom I had seen sink

down dead at the edge of the wood that same morning. And more
real than all of this was what passed between Agathe and me – not
what she said but the tone of her voice, the desire in her gaze, our
mutual longing.

The meal was at an end, the servant did not return, we were alone.

Agathe rose from the table, came over to me, took my head in both
her hands and kissed me on the lips. It was not an ardent kiss, rather
it was gentle, there was more kindness in it than passion, it was sis-
terly and yet intoxicating, it was ceremonial and lascivious at one and
the same time.

And later, with her arms around me, I slipped into a thousand
dreams.

We are lying outstretched upon a sloping meadow; it is the one
where lately she lay with Eduard. I marvel at how calm she is,
untroubled by the slightest apprehension that something terrible has
happened – I myself do not know what and do not think about it, all
I know is that we must go as far away as possible. Now we are sitting
in a railway carriage; the window is open, the curtains are not fastened and flutter to and fro, fragmenting the images of a changing
landscape rushing past – woods, meadows, fences, rocks, churches,
isolated trees – all with incredible speed and without the least connection. Fast enough for no one to be able to pursue us, not even the
people travelling in the same train; this is hard to grasp but so it is.
Suddenly I hear her name being called outside, and I know it is a
telegraph boy looking for her. I become consumed with anxiety that
she might hear it. But her name is uttered more and more faintly
until finally it fades away completely, and the train careers on. On
and on we travel – we travel on for ever. Now we are in a casino – it
must be Monte Carlo. How can there be any doubt? Of course it's
Monte Carlo. Agathe is seated at the gaming table surrounded by
other people, she is beautiful, she is completely calm, she plays, she
loses, she wins, and I look about on all sides to see if anyone is there
who knows her, and could perhaps reveal the fact that her husband
is dead. But they are strangers every one – brown faces, yellow faces,
even an Indian with a huge red feather head-dress is seated at the
gaming table. There is Aline in the doorway. Why has she come after
us? Just so as to break the news to her? We must be off at once. I touch
Agathe on the shoulder and she turns to me with a look replete with
love. And again the train rushes on, with us on board. Someone
peers in through the open window – how can that be possible? He
must be clinging to the window-ledge outside. He is holding a piece
of paper in his hand: the telegram, without a doubt. I push the man

backwards, he reels and falls, where to I've no idea – I can't see him any longer. What a stroke of luck Agathe has not noticed anything. Of course she hasn't. She is holding a large English magazine . . . and leafing through it, looking at the pictures. How odd, there's a picture showing the casino earlier, and her and me among the players. How fast news travels! Supposing her husband gets to see this picture – what will happen to us? Will he kill me too, just as he has killed the captain?

And all at once I am back in the villa, in the room, on the divan where in point of fact I really am. It all seems real enough and at the same time, too, a dream. I am dreaming that I am awake, I am dreaming that my eyes are open, wide open and staring at the fluttering curtains. And I can hear footsteps, the slow footsteps of six or perhaps twelve men. I know that they are bearing in the bier with the corpse, and I flee. I am outside on the terrace. I must get down the steps. But where are the men, where is the bier? I cannot see them. All I know is that it is coming inexorably towards me and that there is no escape. Suddenly I am standing in the garden all alone, but it is not a real garden, it is like one out of a toy-box; it is exactly like one I received as a present years ago. I never realised before that one could go for walks in it. There are even little birds sitting in the trees. I've never noticed them before. And now they are all flying away, to punish me for having noticed them. The servant is standing by the garden gate and bowing very deeply. For Herr Loiberger himself is on the point of coming in. He has no idea he is dead, and yet he is wearing a white raincoat. I must accompany him into the house to see that no one else lets him know that he is dead; he would not survive it, I say to myself – and laugh at the same time. Already we are sitting down to lunch, and the servant is waiting on us; I am surprised that Eduard puts food on his plate – after all, he doesn't need it any more. Agathe is sitting opposite him and I am no longer present. But I am sitting on the window sill and every now and then the curtains billow and subside above my forehead. I long to see their expressions as they gaze at one another. Suddenly I hear his voice – oh God, if only I could see – and can hear him say quite clearly: 'So you are having breakfast with the man who shot me!' It doesn't surprise me in the least that he should say this, as I have indeed already done so. What I find strange is that he should make such an inept remark. He should surely know that it is quite usual to have breakfast together following a duel.

Again footsteps in the garden – the bier – how odd, first the corpse and then the bier – what a snob he is – and now funeral music. A military band? Well, of course, since he has shot a captain. And applause? Naturally – he won the regatta, didn't he? I jump swiftly out of the window and run as fast as I can down to the lake. Why are there so few people there – and no boats at all? Just one tiny skiff, and in it Agathe and I. Agathe is rowing. So, all of a sudden she knows how to row. Only recently she said she couldn't. And now she has even won the regatta. Then I suddenly feel a hand at my throat, Eduard's hand. The oars slip from Agathe's grasp. Our skiff is drifting aimlessly. She folds her arms. She is very curious to see whether Eduard will manage to throw me into the water. We each attempt to hold the other under. Agathe is no longer in the least curious. She moves off in the skiff. Of course, I think to myself, it must be a motorboat. I am plunging deeper and deeper. Why, why, I ask myself, and I want to say to Loiberger: it's really not worth our killing each other for the sake of a woman like that. But I do not say so because in the end he would only think I was afraid. And I surface again. The sky is infinitely vast, I have never see it so vast before. And again I plunge, even deeper than before. But I should not have to do so, I am alone after all and the whole lake belongs to me. The sky as well. And again I rise from the flood and death and dream. Indeed the deeper I plunge, the more inexorably I seem to surface again, and suddenly I am awake – utterly awake, more awake than ever. Agathe however was asleep, or at least she was lying there with her eyes closed. The curtains were moving with greater animation in the summer breeze that always tended to blow in across the lake at about this time in the afternoon. It could not be at all late yet. Judging from the position of the sun, scarcely more than four o'clock, the hour, that is, that Mülling was to call for me at the hotel. Was this something I was dreaming too? Was everything perhaps a dream? Even the duel? And Loiberger's death? Was it perhaps tomorrow already and was I asleep – in my hotel room? This seemed to be my last attempt at evasion. There was no doubting that I was awake, and that there Agathe lay sleeping and knew nothing. Now I was left with the stark choice, either of fleeing that same instant – or of speaking out, without a moment's hesitation, of waking Agathe and telling her. The news might arrive at any moment. Could I not hear footsteps in the garden? Was it not a miracle that we had not yet been disturbed? And in any case, even if no one yet knew anything about it in this house, in this resort, was it not unthinkable folly to linger here in this room, accessible as it was from every side, now that the usual afternoon siesta time was over? I had already risen to my feet – and now, as I was on the point of touching Agathe's shoulder, she blinked, as if my gaze had wakened her, and raised her hand to her hair and forehead, looking like a little girl rubbing the sleep out of her eyes; and no doubt she perceived me as no more than a vanishing image in a dream. But then she recognised my voice, for involuntarily I had whispered her name, and her face clouded over, she leaped up, smoothed down her dress, plumped up the cushions and put them rapidly in order. Then she hastily turned towards me and all she said was 'Go!' But I stood there as if rooted to the spot, completely incapable of saying what I had to say to her, indeed incapable of uttering a single word. What a coward I was! I would have to kill myself, there was nothing left for it. But I could not so much as move a step. All I could do was repeat her name, louder and more pleadingly than before. She gently took my hand and said: 'I love you very much, I had not realised how much I loved you. You don't have to believe me. But why should I tell you if it were not true? I want you to know this before you go.'

'When shall I see you again?' I asked. I didn't say: Eduard is dead. I didn't say: Forgive me. I didn't say: I was too cowardly to tell you straight away. No, I asked: 'When shall I see you again?' as though there were now no other questions that needed to be answered, as though there were nothing more to be said.

'You will never see me again,' she said. 'If you love me, you will, like me, be grateful for this hour together. If you don't want this hour, a wonderful and unforgettable dream, to turn into a bleak reality, a lie, a hundred lies, a chain of deceit and ugliness, then go, go at once, pack your bags and don't ever try to see me again.'

Inside me a voice kept murmuring: Eduard is dead – your husband is dead, everything you say is utter nonsense and you don't suspect it. There are no lies now, no deception, no ugliness, you are free. But I did not say any of this aloud, and everything suddenly became clear to me in a way I should not have imagined possible even a moment ago. And I said: 'It is not a deception, not a lie. It would only be a deception and a lie if, after this hour together, you stayed on here in this house and belonged to someone else again.' It was as though my earlier dream of travelling had assumed power over me, or as though I had assumed power over the dream.

Agathe went pale. She looked at me and I felt my face become completely tense. Then she put her hand on my arm as if to soothe me: 'We must be sensible,' she said. 'Or rather, we must start being sensible again. I do love you, but I don't belong to you, any more than you belong to me. And we both know it. It was just a dream, a miracle, a moment of happiness, unforgettable indeed, but over.'

I shook my head emphatically: 'Everything that happened *before* this hour is over, but our hour together has changed all that. You can never belong to him again, you belong to me and me alone.'

She did not remove her hand from my arm, but now grasped it and held it tightly. She even swung it gently to and fro, as though by doing this she hoped to wake me from some mad, inexplicable delusion. But my eyes were still staring fixedly and I knew they were scarcely filled with love, only wilfulness, and even menace. Her fear, I noticed, was increasing and so she tried again in a more bantering tone: 'Child,' she said, 'am I not right? I always knew why it was I nicknamed you the Child. Must I then be sensible for both of us? It isn't easy. Even for myself. But we must, we must be sensible.'

'Why must we?' I asked obstinately, hating myself at the same time.

'Indeed we must,' she said, and in her mounting anxiety was at once ready with the strongest, the most unanswerable argument: 'We must be sensible and not betray ourselves because you would be lost if he had any inkling . . .'

I smiled. I couldn't help it. For her rejoinder, her warning, the attempt to instil fear of the dead man into me, struck me as not only gruesome but unfathomably comical. At that moment I was within an ace of making some diabolical reply, and putting an end to this frightful conversation with a word of simultaneous annihilation and release. But I did not do so. It was at that very moment that I felt my powerlessness, felt that the dead man was stronger than I, and the only answer I could contrive to formulate, as if in desperate self-defence, was the foolish: 'And what if fate should decide in my favour in the end?'

She gripped me by the shoulder. There was fear in her eyes. 'What are you saying? You are out of your mind. We are both out of our minds.'

At that moment I felt that she was sorry for him – for him and not in the least for me – that he was everything to her and I was nothing . . . And at that same moment we heard footsteps on the gravel in the garden. I had only a few seconds more. It was not possible in those few seconds to tell her what had happened, and in addition to justify myself for having remained silent up to now. Until a few moments ago she might have understood, might have perhaps forgiven me. I might even have carried off a true and lasting victory over the dead man. But now I was the one who had died, who had been vanquished, indeed for an instant I myself felt as though I were a ghost, and the footsteps outside in the garden – although I knew that he was the last person who could walk into the room at any moment – announced the uncanny approach of Loiberger himself; just as he had done in my dream, he was striding through the garden, up the steps, onto the terrace. But whoever it might be, it was impossible in the few seconds I had left to tell Agathe what had happened, and in addition to justify myself for having remained silent. Even more unthinkable to leave her totally unprepared for what was about to occur, whatever it might be. Yet the only words that passed my lips were: 'Don't be afraid.' And as I uttered them I was really convinced that the very next moment her dead husband would enter the room. At first she looked at me with an uncertain smile, as though she wanted to let me know that I had no need to worry, and that no one would ever have the least suspicion of what had occurred between us over the past hour or so. But evidently she at once intuited from my look of desperate earnestness that my warning must have signified more than mere petty concern that she might betray herself. She still had just time enough to ask: 'What's happened?' But I no longer had the opportunity to answer.

The steps were already echoing in the next room. Without once looking back at me, Agathe went into the drawing-room, and there I followed her. Aline was standing in the doorway between the draw-ing-room and the terrace: she glanced at me with a look of perplexed astonishment, grasped the hands of her friend, whose face was now drained of colour, and, bursting into tears, folded her in her arms. Agathe's eyes however stared past Aline into mine with a relentlessly questioning expression, as if she were trying to suck the answer from my brow; I raised a finger to my mouth involuntarily, intending this miserable gesture as a plea to Agathe to betray me rather than her-self. Agathe's look, however, expressed more than I have ever seen another human look express: dawning recognition, even compre-hension, but also outrage, understanding, forgiveness, and yes, per-haps too something resembling gratitude.

By now Mülling too was standing in the door between the draw-ing-room and the terrace, between shadow and light. He looked at me enquiringly. No doubt he immediately understood my presence as an indication that I had been unable to bring myself to leave the unfortunate woman alone after I had delivered the sad news. He went up to her and pressed her hand without saying a word. Again, looking past Mülling, she sought my eye. No one spoke, neither she nor Aline nor Mülling, but it seemed to me that I was somehow more deeply enveloped in silence than the others. The summer stillness of the garden was distinctly audible. At last Agathe said – and my heart stood still as she opened her lips : 'Well, I would now like to hear the whole truth' – and as she became conscious of amazement on the faces of the others, and on mine perhaps a look of fear, she turned to me and added with admirable steadiness: 'I am sure you did not intend to withhold anything from me, but perhaps you naturally tried to spare me. I am grateful. But believe me, I am now sufficiently composed to hear everything. Give me your account, Dr Mülling, from beginning to end. I will not ask questions, nor will I interrupt you', and with a faltering voice she added: 'Tell me everything!'

She leaned against the piano, her fingers playing with the fringe of the shawl, and did not betray either herself or me by so much as a twitch of her lips as Mülling told the story. Aline had sunk down on the chair by the piano, her head propped in her hands. In all his inner perturbation, Mülling's professional habit of measured public speaking stood him in good stead. He related the course of events from the point when the two of us, he and I, had awaited Eduard at the station of the little town, to the moment when Eduard had fallen dead at the forest edge, and it was evident to me that he had given his account more than once to good effect already since we had parted outside his hotel. He spoke, moreover, as if he were making a plea for someone who had atoned all too severely for some long-settled, forgotten and in itself not very significant offence, and whose memory must be absolved from any blame. Agathe, true to her word, did not interrupt him with so much as a syllable. And only when Mülling had ended did she turn to him and ask whether any arrangements had been made on the spot. And when Mülling replied that the body would be released by the authorities at the latest by the following morning, she said: 'I will go to him this evening.' Mülling tried to dissuade her, saying that that day's evening train did not arrive in the little garrison town until after midnight, but she simply said: 'I want to see him tonight', and it was clear to all of us that she would try to gain access to the morgue that same night. Then Mülling offered to accompany her, as there were all sorts of things to see to which Agathe could not possibly carry out alone. She declined with a decisiveness that precluded any objections. 'All that is my responsibility,' she said. 'When everything is over, Dr Mülling, we will talk again.' I was filled with admiration and at the same time with horror. She did not address a word to me. She now wanted to be alone, and only Aline was to return later to help with preparations for her journey and receive instructions for the duration of her absence.

She shook hands with everybody, treating me no differently from Aline and Mülling. She did not even evade my gaze as we parted.

She really did make the journey that same evening – alone –- and brought her husband's body back to Vienna the next morning. The following day the funeral took place, which naturally I too attended. That day Agathe refused to see anyone. She never again returned to the lake.

Many years later we met again in company. In the meantime she had remarried. No one who saw us talking to one another could have suspected that a deep and strange common experience united us. But did it really unite us? I myself at least could have taken that uncanny and yet so happy hour in the summer stillness for a dream that only I had dreamed; so clear-eyed, so unremembering, so full of innocence was the gaze with which she met mine.

Notes

His Royal Highness is in the House

Page 20: *His Highness is pleased to enquire.* The aura of remoteness surrounding royalty is suggested by the Emperor Franz Joseph's titles, which included King of Hungary and Bohemia, Lord of Dalmatia, Croatia, Illyria, Galicia and Lodomeria, Grand Duke of Cracow, Duke of Krain and Bukovina, Margrave of Moravia, Duke of Silesia, Ragusa (Dubrovnik) and Zara, Prince of Trient and Brixen, and Lord Trieste and Cattaro. (See Franz Hubmann, *K. u. K. Familienalbum*, p. 11.)

Dead Men Tell No Tales

Pages 44/46: *Praterstrasse/Prater.* Originally a royal preserve, the Prater parkland stretching between the Danube Canal which hugs the medieval Inner City of Vienna and the Danube itself further to the east, was made over to the public by Joseph II in 1766 as a recreation area, linked to the city by the fashionable Praterstrasse. The fairground or Wurstelprater at the northern end, with its puppet shows and freak displays, steadily expanded and by 1895 included such spectacular attractions as 'Venice in Vienna', and by 1897 the familiar giant ferris-wheel. The chestnut-lined Praterallee which by 1890 already boasted three prosperous coffee-houses, running south-east to the more formal Lusthaus, became a regular venue for parades and spring festivities, as well as horse-riding and bicycling.

Page 44: *Carltheater.* Founded in 1781 as the Leopoldstädter Theater, and enlarged and renamed after the director Karl Carl in 1847, the Carltheater on the Praterstrasse was associated particularly with the dialect plays of Raimund and Nestroy and the operettas of Offenbach, Suppé, Lehár and Strauss. Schnitzler's maternal grandparents lived in the same building in the 1860s, and it was the Carltheater that afforded him his first glimpses of the theatre world. It was bombed in 1944 and later demolished.

Page 45: *Tegetthoff Monument.* Named after Admiral Wilhelm von Tegetthoff, who distinguished himself at the battle of Heligoland in the Schleswig-Holstein war against the Danes in 1864, this monument was situated at the northern end of the Praterallee, where it joins the Praterstrasse and five other roads, forming the Praterstern, where 'all the roads meet.'

Page 46: *Reichsbrücke.* Built when the course of the Danube was altered between 1870 and 1875 to prevent flooding in the city, and originally known as the Crown Prince Rudolf Bridge, the Reichsbrücke led from the continuation of the Praterstrasse out into open country.

Page 51: *Franz Josefsland*. New guest-houses sprang up in this hamlet near the old arm of the Danube, and it quickly developed into a resort for boating.

Page 56: *Ringstrasse*. Built along the flood-prone glacis round the medieval ramparts, which Franz Joseph had had demolished in 1857, the Ringstrasse with its Classical, Italianate and Gothic public buildings functions in Schnitzler as a sort of point of orientation, like the Liffey in Joyce's Dublin.

Lieutenant Gustl

Page 60: *Herr Doktor*. Here a legal title.

I'll slice off the tip of your nose. 'In an 1893 Viennese saber duel, a first lieutenant of the Hussars' fighting 'a reserve officer of the Dragoons . . . hack[ed] off his nose, which for the balance of the combat was stuck up on the wall by an attentive second. The Hussar was compelled to continue the bout *ohne Nase*. It was stitched back on afterward.' (Kevin McAleer, *Dueling*, p. 63.)

Page 61: *Horticultural Society*. Opened in 1864, the Society's Italianate exhibition building and fashionable garden complex on the Parkring also provided a venue for various choral groups and later for masked balls.

an organ. Perhaps, as a stage is also mentioned, the Musikvereinsaal in the Musikvereinsgebäude, designed by Theophil Hansen and built 1867-69 – but several other concert halls had organs.

Page 62: *Madame Sans-Gêne*. Overtones of brazen Parisian naughtiness are invoked by this allusion to Victorien Sardou's 1893 play of the same name, with its vulgar, outspoken, warm-hearted heroine – a role made popular by Sarah Bernhardt's lesser rival Madame Réjane.

amateurish fencers who can be the most dangerous. This may have been because 'in most saber duels thrusting was expressly proscribed, or the point might be ground down . . . depriv[ing] skilled fencers of half their technical arsenal.' (McAleer, p. 62.)

Page 63: *Sure to be a Socialist*. Schnitzler introduces the liberal-minded lawyer, of course, as a foil to Gustl's conservative military mind-set. Socialists were against duelling, rightly seeing it as a reflection of and means of reinforcing caste solidarity.

not all your comrades . . . to defend the Empire. This was the insinuation which particularly rankled with the military and led them to strip Schnitzler of his commission as a reserve army doctor. Insults which might warrant a duel were rated according to a scale of severity, from impoliteness through active cursing to an actual slap in the face with hand or glove. 'At the first level, the offended had the choice of weapons; at the second level, a choice of weaponry and style of combat; and in cases of third-level injury, the choice of arms, style and distance. (German-language codes recommended that all third-level insults be settled with pistols.)' (McAleer, pp. 47-48.)

Page 65: *Leidinger's.* Like the Café Griensteidl and the Café Central, Leidinger's on the Kärntnerstrasse was among the fashionable coffee-houses Schnitzler frequented with other members of the Young Vienna literary circle.

Page 68: *I am no longer fit to render satisfaction.* Because he has been insulted by a social inferior who could not be challenged, yet failed to punish him at once with the flat of his sword. 'According to contemporary reckoning, only about 5 percent of German society was *satisfaktionsfähig* . . . composed mostly of well-to-do professionals', such as the lawyer whom Gustl has challenged but now feels unworthy of combating. '*Satisfaktionsfähigkeit* rested not on an inward feeling of personal worth but on a highly cultivated sensibility of caste' (McAleer, p. 110) – hence Gustl's fear of scandal and thoughts of suicide. Schnitzler, whose father had ensured that he take fencing lessons, was opposed to a system in which civilians, who ostensibly shared the officers' sense of honour, could be obliged to render satisfaction or face social ostracism. The so-called Waidhofener Beschluss of 1896 declared Jews unfit to give satisfaction. (See Bruce Thompson, *Schnitzler's Vienna*, p. 136.)

Court of Honour. Set up after the Napoleonic wars as a confidence-restoring measure, Courts of Honour attached to individual regiments were intended both to safeguard the collective honour of the military and to adjudicate in matters of dishonourable behaviour between individuals, with the power to decide whether a duel should be fought and to strip an officer of his commission. Ostensibly there to smooth things over, they were often 'as influential in stimulating as in quashing many duels,' sometimes forcing officers to fight who would rather have apologised, and officiating according to a fixed protocol. Most duelling cases that came before the Courts of Honour were between lieutenants – hence Schnitzler's choice of hero. (McAleer, pp. 101, 86-107.)

Page 71: *Przemysl.* Strategically imporant in Austro-Hungary's eastern line of defence, this garrison town in eastern Galicia was to fall temporarily into Russian hands in 1915. The fact that officers were required to learn basic words of command in a dozen languages is a reminder of the extent and cultural diversity of the Danube Empire.

Page 74: *I've repaid everything.* Failure to pay one's gambling and other debts also constituted a violation of the code of honour and could lead to loss of one's commission. In Schnitzler's novella *Spiel im Morgengrauen* (1926), Lieutenant Willi Kasda commits suicide when a former sweetheart does not immediately help him out after a gambling spree.

Page 76: *Fischamend.* Town on the Danube south-east of Vienna, half-way to Heinburg.

Page 80: *Through Night and Ice.* Probably Fridtjof Nansen's *In Nacht und Eis* (Leipzig: Brockhaus, 1897), an account by the Norwegian scientist, explorer and later Nobel Peace Prize winner of his arctic expeditions between 1893 and 1896.

Page 81: *The Bosniacs.* Recruited from the mountain people of predominantly Muslim Bosnia, this regiment had its own distinctive uniform: collarless tunics, knickerbockers, ankle-boots, backpacks and a tassled fez. (See Hubmann, p. 93.)

Page 82: *Volksgarten.* The Volksgarten along the Ring boasted a semi-circular café where Johann Strauss the elder and military bands were accustomed to perform.

An Eccentric

Page 104: *Mitterwurzer.* Friedrich Mitterwurzer (1844-97), a grandiloquent Burgtheater actor, famous for his Faust, Mephistopheles and other tragic and demonic parts. He played the lead role in the première of Schnitzler's *Game of Love* (*Liebelei*).

Page 105: *eccentric singer.* At the more popular end of the *fin-de-siècle* entertainment spectrum, performers who cultivated various eccentricities were common. An example given by Rearick was the Parisian 'Jeanne Bloch (1858-1916), one of the most popular of many *excentrique* singers, [who] was both a singer and a natural comic. She often wore a colonel's cap for songs about the army, but her essential stand-by for comedy was her formidable girth. In a performance at the "Cigale" music hall, her partner tried to but could not fully embrace her. A spectator cried out, "Make two trips," and Bloch as well as the audience broke into hearty laughter.' (Charles Rearick, *Pleasures of the Belle Epoque*, p. 102.)

Page 105: *Lewinsky.* Josef Lewinsky was a famous actor at the Burgtheater, which is today located on the Ring in a building dating from 1874.

Page 111: *Good morning, Sir.* In English in the original.

The Grecian Dancer

Page 113: *In Japanese or Chinese costume.* European interest in Far Eastern art was at its height in the late nineteenth and early twentieth centuries, Japanese prints influencing artists as diverse as Whistler, Monet, Van Gogh, Klimt and Beardsley. The importing of a Japanese shrub is mentioned in *The Duellist's Second* (page 195).

Secession. Representative of the dominant aesthetic of the Academy, from which Gustav Klimt, the architect Otto Wagner and their followers 'seceded' in 1897 in the name of greater functionalism in art, were the vast mythological paintings and opulently cluttered interiors designed by Hans Makart in the Burgtheater and in many of the *palais* along the Ring. The Secession exhibition building was designed by Wagner's pupil, Josef-Maria Olbrich.

Page 116: *Café Athénés.* While the Chat Noir gained a reputation for its shadow plays, and the Moulin Rouge for the can-can routines immortalised by Toulouse-Lautrec and Seurat, the Café Athénés was associated with the American dancer Lois Fuller, who explored the effects of electric lights on flowing drapery. As Georges Montorgueil recalls, 'she entered lightly, floatingly, giving the impression of a spirit which flies rather than walks. Her robe was so long that she found herself treading upon it. She held it in her two hands and raised her arms in the air. The audience cried "A butterfly! A butterfly!" She pirouetted faster and faster. There was a fairy-like image of a flower, and the audience cried "An orchid! An orchid!"' (Sisley Huddleston, *Paris Salons, Cafés, Studios*, p. 258.)

Page 117: *Legay, Montoya.* Gavriel de Montoya and Marcel Legay were *chanson* singers associated especially with the Chat Noir, Montoya publishing his *Roman Comique du Chat Noir* with Flammarion in 1897. Zelenski of the Cracow cabaret The Green Balloon remembered hearing Montoya at a Montmartre nightclub called Le Grillon as a boy, and how 'every evening, for many years, [he] used to coo his pleasant *Chanson d'antan* ("Song of Yesteryear") in his falsetto voice, like some huge bird desperately calling his mate.' (Harold B. Segel, *Turn of the Century Cabaret*, p. 238.)

The Prophecy

Page 122: *Bozen.* Now Bolzano, this once predominantly German-speaking town in South Tirol, between Innsbruck and the Dolomites, became part of Italy after the First World War. Meran, or Merano, is twenty miles northwest of the town.

Page 128: *mesmerism.* In 1889 Schnitzler published a paper 'On functional aphonia and its treatment by hypnosis and suggestion' in the *International Clinical Review.*

Page 129: *if anyone had heard us.* This, and the later mild impoliteness over which Herr von Umprecht remembers nearly fighting a duel, illustrates the sensitivity to slight engendered by the code of honour.

Pages 131/32: *A duel . . . which could leave me with a scar.* Scars, most commonly acquired at duelling fraternities, were a mark of distinction. 'The tantalizing combination of virility and breeding that the *Schmiss* delineated was catnip for young ladies of the era who by all reports would go limp with desire upon sighting one.' A fellow medical student tried to enlist Schnitzler into a fraternity 'with the adroit reasoning that "he thought a duelling scar would look well on me!"' (McAleer, pp. 146, 149.)

Fräulein Else

Page 141: *Mount Cimone*. Mount Cimone della Pala in the Dolomites of South Tirol.

Page 142: *Coriolanus*. Probably a Burgtheater production of Shakespeare's play.

the Abbé Des Grieux. The title figure of Prévost's novel *L'Histoire du chevalier Des Grieux et de Manon Lescaut* (1756) and the tenor lead in Massenet's *Manon* (1884).

Madame Renard. Marie Renard, the stage name of Marie Pöltzl (1864-1937), a mezzo-soprano well known for her roles in *Carmen* and *Manon*.

Page 143: *Marienlyst*. A Danish resort that Schnitzler was fond of.

Page 144: "*dîner*". The affectation is in English in the original.

Page 152: *Notre Coeur*. A novel by Guy de Maupassant published in 1890.

Page 164: *A novel by Temme*. Jodocus Donatus Hubertus Temme (1798-1881), a lawyer and member of the first German parliament set up after the revolution of 1848, also wrote popular crime fiction.

Page 167: *Herr Matador*. For northern Europeans Spain, like Italy, represented the sensual and exotic south (as it still does), as reflected in, for instance, Bizet's *Carmen* and Wolf's *Spanisches Liederbuch*. The matador, who traditionally received the bull's testicles and scrotum as a trophy, is clearly associated with both potency and death. Earlier (page 141) Else reflects that Paul is no matador on court; and Dorsday is associated with love and death.

Vicomte d'Eperies. Eperjes is the Hungarian name for Prešov or Preschau, a provincial capital in East Slovakia which until 1919 was part of Austro-Hungary.

Page 182: *Schumann . . . Carnaval*. In 1908 the 'Valse Noble' from this piece was among the dance interpretations offered by the Wiesenthal sisters at the Fledermaus (Segel, p. 214.)

The Duellist's Second

Page 192: *the virtue of a woman one loves*. 'The duel was . . . viewed as a sort of chastity belt engirdling society.' When a lady's honour was at stake, 'in lieu of virile husbands, brothers (followed by fathers, nephews, uncles, and fathers-in-law) might do in a bind.' And 'the dueling codes warned men of honor against wrangles spawned by "lascivious women or ladies of dubious reputation.' (McAleer, pp. 169-70, 175.)

neither a nobleman nor a career officer. A second, to be acceptable, had himself to be a man of honour capable of rendering satisfaction, as well as familiar with the protocol of duelling. He also had ideally to be mature and level-headed and able to resolve disputes amicably without loss of face. That Schnitzler's second is only twenty-three, and yet officiating at his seventh duel, is ironic testimony to his allegiance to the code of honour – to the fact that he is indeed 'heart and soul a second.' (See McAleer, p. 49.)

Page 194: *The preliminary discussion between the seconds.* This would involve arranging the site, type of weapon and terms, which in the case of a pistol duel in response to a third-level injury such as adultery could entail several exchanges at a range of as little as five paces, and all to be conducted, as Schnitzler's story indicates, within a tight time-frame. 'After the provocation, one had just twenty-four hours to challenge, and the actual duel was to take place within forty-eight hours of that. This may have been a way for procrastinators to get a wiggle on, and an implicit effort at reducing potential practice time. The underlying idea was that an insult could hardly be considered aggravated if patiently endured for any longer period. If a challenge was forwarded after the twenty-four-hour expiration, there was no obligation to accept it. The only exception to this rule involved seduction, where many months or even years might elapse before irrefragable evidence could come to light permitting the matter to be taken out of mothballs.' (McAleer, pp. 50-51.) Later we learn that Urpadinsky had exacted a confession from his wife.

Bad Ischl. This resort on the Traunsee in the Salzkammergut was the regular summer residence of Franz Joseph and Elizabeth, who received the Kaiservilla as a wedding gift, and consequently became one of the centres of fashionable society. It was here that the imperial couple first met the actress Katerina Schratt, who was to become one of their intimate circle and later the Emperor's mistress.

the usual forest clearing. Like the carriage ride from Bad Ischl and the studied *sang-froid* of the participants, the secret and secluded meeting was part of the ritual scenario, but it is also a reminder that duelling was illegal. By having the regimental doctor officiate and write a report for the regiment's Court of Honour, Schnitzler ironically draws attention to the army's connivance in the practice.

Page 196: *With the third exchange.* If the terms were particularly onerous, the exchanges might continue until one or both combatants was or were no longer functional.

Page 199: *'Then to Silvia . . . let us garlands bring'.* Schubert's setting of Shakespeare's 'Who is Silvia?' from *The Two Gentlemen of Verona*, IV.ii.40-54.

Further Reading

Crankshaw, Edward, *The Fall of the House of Habsburg* (London: Longman, 1963)

Francis, Mark, ed., *The Viennese Enlightenment* (London: Croom Helm, 1985)

Gay, Peter, *Freud, Jews and other Germans* (New York: Oxford University Press, 1978)

Hubmann, Franz, *K. v K. Familienalbum: Die Welt von gestern in alten Photographien* (Vienna: Verlag Fritz Molden, 1971)

Huddleston, Sisley, *Paris Salons, Cafés, Studios* (Philadelphia: Lippincott, 1928)

Janik, Allan and Stephen Toulmin, *Wittgenstein's Vienna* (London: Weidenfeld & Nicolson, 1973)

McAleer, Kevin, *Dueling: The cult of Honour in fin de-siècle Germany* (Princeton: Princeton University Press, 1985)

Rearick, Charles, *Pleasures of the Belle Epoque* (New Haven: Yale University Press, 1985)

Roberts, Adrian Clive, *Arthur Schnitzler and Politics* (Riverside: Ariadne Press, 1989)

Roth, Joseph, *The Radetzky March*, trans. Joachim Neugroschel (London: Penguin, 1995)

Schnitzler, Arthur, *My Youth in Vienna*, trans. Catherine Hutter (New York: Holt, Rinehart & Winston, 1970)

Schorske, Carl E., *Fin-de-Siècle* (Cambridge: Harvard University Press, 1986)

Segel, Harold B., *Turn of the Century Cabaret* (New York: Columbia University Press, 1987)

Swales, Martin, *Arthur Schnitzler: A Critical Study* (Oxford: Clarendon Press, 1971)

Thompson, Bruce, *Schnitzler's Vienna* (London: Routledge, 1890)

Weber, Eugen, *France Fin de Siècle* (Cambridge University Press, 1986)

Yates, W. E., *Schnitzler, Hofmannsthal, and the Austrian Theatre* (New Haven: Yale University Press, 1992)

Zweig, Stefan, *The World of Yesterday* (Sydney: Cassell, 1945)

ANGEL BOOKS

Angel Books publishes classic and modern European literature in new translations which, in capturing the distinctive
impact and flavour of their originals, are literary per-
formances in English. Critical introductions and any
necessary annotation are provided.

Angel Books' programme focuses on authors and works
not currently or adequately available in English.

For a complete list please write to Angel Books, 3 Kelross Rd,
London N5 2QS

Other translations published by Angel Books

Fiction

Theodor Fontane
Effi Briest
Translated by Hugh Rorrison and Helen Chambers
0 946162 44 1 (paperback)

A new translation (shortlisted for the Weidenfeld Translation Prize 1996) of Fontane's celebrated story of adultery in Bismarck's Prussia.

'Accurate as no previous translation has been . . . you can hear Fontane himself in it and understand for the first time, if you have no German, why this is a novel to draw tears.'
David Sexton, *The Guardian*

'The reputation of a book not read in the original can be changed - in this case much for the better - by a good new translation. The Rorrison/Chambers version brings *Effi Briest* vividly to life in a way that previous translations have not.'
Hermione Lee, *Sunday Times*

'Atmosphere and nuance are easily lost in translation. In this new translation, however, they are well captured . . . It stays faithful to the original without sacrificing naturalness, and its informal tone is often close to Fontane's own. This tone is so important in Fontane's work that it can be said that only now is the English-speaking reader in a position to enjoy the novel as it really is.'
Alan Bance, *Times Literary Supplement*

Theodore Fontane
Cécile
Translated by Stanley Radcliffe
0 946162 42 5 (cased)   0 946162 43 3 (paperback)

The first English translation of the second of Fontane's 'Berlin' novels. At a fashionable spa in the Harz Mountains an affair develops between an itinerant civil engineer and the delicate, mysterious wife of a retired army officer. The dénouement is set in the bustling capital of a newly unified Germany.

'*Cécile* is written with wit and a controlled fury and Radcliffe's elegant translation does it superb justice.'
Michael Ratcliffe, *The Observer*

VSEVELOD GARSHIN
From the Reminiscences of Private Ivanov *and other stories*
Translated by Peter Henry, Liv Tudge and others
0 946162 08 5 (cased)   0 946162 09 3 (paperback)

Garshin was Russia's outstanding new writer of fiction between Dostoyevsky and the mature Chekhov, a 'Hamlet of his time' who gave voice to the disturbed conscience of an era that knew the horrors of modern war, the squalors of rapid industrialisation, and a politically explosive situation culminating in the assassination of Alexander II. This major selection includes almost all his published novellas and short stories – including some of the best Russian war stories and densely semiotic narratives like *The Red Flower* and *The Signal*.

'Garshin's supreme gift is an acute moral intelligence steadied by the economy of his style . . . he anticipates Babel; and it is legitimate to hear in the spare articulation of his prose the rhythm of Pushkin.'
Henry Gifford, *Times Literary Supplement*

Six German Romantic Tales
Translated by Ronald Taylor
0 946162 17 4 (paperback)

Heinrich von Kleist: *The Earthquake in Chile* and *The Betrothal on Santo Domingo*; Ludwig Tieck: *Eckbert the Fair* and *The Runenberg*; E. T. A. Hoffmann: *Don Giovanni* and *The Jesuit Chapel in G.*

'All the varieties of the German Romantic movement are here: magical, musical, political and aesthetic . . . Excellent translations.'
Stephen Plaice, *Times Literary Supplement*

HENRYK SIENKIEWICZ
Charcoal Sketches *and other tales*
Translated by Adam Zamoyski (author of *The Polish Way*)
0 946162 31 X (cased)   0 946162 32 8 (paperback)

The best of Sienkiewicz's short fiction – three novellas with contemporary nineteenth-century backgrounds. The title-story is a headlong satire on Polish provincial life under Tsarist rule. In *Bartek the Conqueror* a Polish hero of the Franco-Prussian War finds he is no match for the Germans in the postwar peace. *On the Bright Shore* is a deliciously observed study of manners and morals among the expatriate Polish gentry on the French Riviera in the 1890s.

'Zamoyski's sprightly new translations demonstrate that the passage of a century cannot disguise the wit or lessen the bite of these three novellas.'
Publishers Weekly

THEODOR STORM
The Dykemaster (*Der Schimmelreiter*)
Translated by Denis Jackson
0 946162 54 9 (paperback)

A miniature epic of the eerie west coast of Schleswig-Holstein, with its hallucinatory tidal flats, hushed polders, and terrifying North Sea.

'Translations of the high standard achieved in this fine edition are more than ever in demand.'
Mary Garland, editor of *The Oxford Companion to German Literature*

Verse

PIERRE CORNEILLE
Horace
Translated by Alan Brownjohn
0 946162 57 3 (paperback)

This powerful drama, a work that helped launch French classical tragedy, lays bare the sinister nature of patriotism.

'Corneille's rhyming alexandrines have been superbly translated into a flexible blank verse which captures the nuances of meaning . . .'
Maya Slater, *Times Literary Supplement*

HEINRICH HEINE
Deutschland
Translated by T. J. Reed; bilingual edition
0 946162 58 1 (paperback)

The wittiest work of Europe's wittiest poet.

'a fine example of superior political poetry. This translation triumphantly conveys the satirical power, ironic tone and humorous accessibility.'
Anita Bunyan, *Jewish Chronicle*

FERNANDO PESSOA
The Surprise of Being
Translated by James Greene and Clara de Azevedo Mafra; bilingual edition
0 946162 24 7 (paperback)

Twenty-five of the haunting poems written by Portugal's greatest modern poet in his own name - the most confounding of his personae.

'Indispensable.'
J. Pilling, *P.N Review*